WILD HEART

Bob locked the door. Then Clea perched on the edge of his desk as he sprawled in a big tan leather chair, admiring her.

"Thank you for helping out, Wild Heart."

"Anytime. We're friends now and that's valuable to me. I'll always be there for you."

"And you know you've got the same from me."

Bob's glance roved over her lazily. The earth-brown hair was tinted to a dark reddish cast and layered in a shoulder-length cut. She wore little makeup except for bronze blusher on her dark skin, and her eyes were expertly done with kohl. Wide metal hoops were fastened in her ears and the gold gleamed against her skin.

"Come here," he said softly.

It seemed to Clea that she moved not of her own volition. When she reached him, he said, "Sit down."

He patted his knee. She pretended to ignore him.

"I don't see but one chair here. Am I missing something?"

He patted his knee again. "All in friendship. You're safe."

Smiling, she sat on his knees, driven by habit and need. "For just a minute." She crossed her legs.

"No. Don't cross your legs."

Startled, she asked, "But why not?"

He grinned wickedly with half-closed eyes, teasing her. "Because I intend to get between them."

BOOK YOUR PLACE ON OUR WEBSITE AND MAKE THE ARABESQUE ROMANCE CONNECTION!

We've created a customized website just for our very special Arabesque readers, where you can get the inside scoop on everything that's going on with Arabesque romance novels.

When you come online, you'll have the exciting opportunity to:

- View covers of upcoming books

- Learn about our future publishing schedule (listed by publication month and author)

- Find out when your favorite authors will be visiting a city near you

- Search for and order backlist books

- Check out author bios and background information

- Send e-mail to your favorite authors

- Join us in weekly chats with authors, readers and other guests

- Get writing guidelines

- AND MUCH MORE!

Visit our website at
http://www.arabesquebooks.com

Wild Heart

FRANCINE CRAFT

BET Publications, LLC
http://www.bet.com
http://www.arabesquebooks.com

ARABESQUE BOOKS are published by

BET Publications, LLC
c/o BET Books
One BET Plaza
1900 W Place NE
Washington, DC 20018-1211

Copyright © 2004 by Francine Craft

All rights reserved. No part of this book may be reproduced, stored in a retrieval system, or transmitted in any form or by any means without the prior written consent of the Publisher.

If you purchased this book without a cover, you should be aware that this book is stolen property. It was reported as "unsold and destroyed" to the Publisher and neither the Author nor the Publisher has received any payment for this "stripped book."

All Kensington Titles, Imprints, and Distributed Lines are available at special quantity discounts for bulk purchases for sales promotions, premiums, fund-raising, and educational or institutional use. For details, write or phone the office of the Kensington special sales manager: Kensington Publishing Corp., 850 Third Avenue, New York, NY 10022, attn: Special Sales Department, Phone: 1-800-221-2647.

BET Books is a trademark of Black Entertainment Television, Inc. ARABESQUE, the ARABESQUE logo, and the BET BOOKS logo are trademarks and registered trademarks.

First Printing: October 2004
10 9 8 7 6 5 4 3 2 1

Printed in the United States of America

*To Myles Edwards Jones—in memoriam.
I will always love you, miss you.
"Good night, sweet prince: And flights of
angels sing thee to thy rest."*
　　　　　—Hamlet, William Shakespeare

*To Vivian and Carlos—sweethearts after my
own heart.*

*To Delores Sumbler, a superior, warm, and
really together person.*

ACKNOWLEDGMENTS

My heartfelt thanks to Charlie Kanno,
who is tops in everything he undertakes.

Chapter 1

"You will know joy and happiness beyond your fondest dreams, but first will come pain and deepest sorrow."

Clea Wilde stood in front of the blind end of the long, curved bar of her famous nightclub, Wilde's Wonderland, taking in the neatly lined bottles of liquor, the polished glasses, and the blenders. She mused over her shaman grandfather Papa Curtis's warning to her. His eyes had been sad on her last visit.

"The very stance of your body tells me you miss him badly," he'd said. "You've got to find a way to get back to him."

Clea shook her head. No, there was no way to get back to Dr. Bob Redding. That part of her life was over.

It was noon in early May and her employees moved about, beginning to ready the club for a big night. Someone's throat cleared behind her, but she didn't turn around.

"Hello, Wild Heart." The baritone voice was soft and caressing and she stood still, her heart racing. She couldn't face the wall forever.

Turning slowly, she heard her voice shaking as she returned his greeting. "Hello, Bob." The tears that stood in her eyes angered her. It had been three years and she should be over him.

"How are you?" he asked her.

"I'm fine. And you?"

She forced herself to look at him then, drinking him in

the way someone marooned in a desert drinks desperately needed water. He hadn't changed. He was thirty-eight now, walnut-brown with a few sprinkles of gray threading his soot-black, curly hair. He was a beautiful man, not a pretty boy, but rugged, masculine, with a six-foot-two-inch, well-toned body of rippling abs, pecs, and biceps. The slow heat she'd always known with him began in her brain and spread the length of her body. Tender, hot, and passionate at once, his caring face had always mesmerized her. His forehead was high and squared. He had a prominent nose, a wide, sensual mouth, heavy, silken black eyebrows, and a mustache over a squared chin. His startling eyes had always moved her. They were light brown with large sea-green flecks and they missed nothing. How often had she gotten lost in them?

"We need to talk," he said, his voice still soft.

She licked dry lips and hesitated. She couldn't be close to him again.

"Please." His eyes narrowed.

"Hey, Doc!" Sid, Clea's head bartender, greeted Bob as he came up. "Welcome back. Is this for good?"

"Yeah, I'd guess it is," Bob said as the two men hugged. Sid's florid face lit up. He and Bob had been good friends. "I'm reopening the clinic, so I'll be around."

"Hey, you've been missed and the community needs you. We all need you." He shot a quick glance at Clea as her legs shook.

Sid patted Bob's back. "You come around often now," he said. "You were a better bartender than most anybody. I'll leave you two alone."

Bob turned to her. "Let's talk, Wild Heart. I've got a lot to tell you."

Clea expelled a long breath. "Okay. We'll go to my office."

She came from behind the bar and walked beside him to the stairs. On the steps he smiled at her wide-hipped, narrow-waisted body moving gracefully. He watched her great, long legs in her short skirt and the flared calves and trim ankles. His mouth watered with the memory of what they'd known together. At her office door, she paused, opened it, and he took the knob and pushed it farther in, his hand brushing hers. That slight touch made her tingle.

He closed the door and caught her in his arms, pressed her against the wall by the door, and spread his hands on either side of her face. Imprisoned, she couldn't get her breath before his mouth savaged hers. His tongue fiercely entangled with hers as she fought to steady herself, to hold back.

She was drowning then in ecstasy as his hard body fed on her softness. Her breasts against his hard chest were live things, hungry for his hands, his mouth. She gasped and forced her face away with superhuman effort. "This isn't fair," she whispered.

His eyes were haunted then as he told her the old adage "All's fair in love and war."

"You said you wanted to talk. We're not talking."

"We *are* talking, Wild Heart, the way we've always talked: with our bodies and from our souls."

Whimpering then, she closed her eyes as his mouth found hers again and the hard bulge of his shaft against her threatened to undo her very sanity. He was slower then, a little less savage, and she was more relaxed. Their hearts were drumbeats, with a drum's mesmerizing cadence. Memory swept her so sharply she hurt as she pressed closer. Their love affair had ended, she thought; then amended that to *their love affair would never end.*

It was a long time before they shakily pulled apart and he splayed one of his hands against the wall and studied her face. Dear God, he thought, no woman ought to be this beautiful. Her beauty wasn't nearly just physical. She had warmth and love and caring, a bone-marrow-deep sensuality and sexuality.

She'd always worn her soft dark brown mass of hair in many styles. Now it was chemically relaxed and simply styled to flip up at the ends. Her clove-brown, oval face with its high cheekbones and almond eyes under straight eyebrows, her straight nose and lush lips atop a long, slender, delicate neck never failed to make him think of goddesses. The small, flat brown mole beside her mouth he'd licked so often made him smile sadly. He didn't want to let her go. With Clea he always paraphrased the words in the biblical Song of Solomon. No, not the actual quote, he thought, "I am black, *but* comely, O ye daughters of Jerusalem," but "I am black *and* beautiful."

"Let's talk," she murmured. "You wanted to talk."

With half-closed eyes, he studied her, loving what he saw. "Still running with the wolves?"

She laughed a little. "Always have. Always will. I'm glad I was born into a family that encouraged it."

"I always encouraged it, too. That part of you fascinates me. *You* fascinate me."

Clea smiled then. "I know and thank you. I treasure that special, leather-bound copy of *Women Who Run With the Wolves* you had made for me. I'll always remember the time we spent reading it together, poring over it. Not many men would be that interested."

He took her hand, squeezed it. "When I saw the title in a D.C. bookstore, picked it up, and leafed through it, I knew it was you. We could do it all over. We don't have to live on memories. I'm back for good. Let's try again, Wild Heart. You're in my blood. . . ."

He was going to kiss her again and she had to stop him. "We didn't marry," she said evenly, "because your mother hates me."

His sensual mouth was set in a grim line. "You were never marrying my mother, just me. I would cut loose from the whole damned world for you, Clea."

Hot tears stood in her eyes. "I know and I love you for it, but we both wanted children, Bob. I grew up in a happy family and I want my children to be happy. It would tear me up for Reba to be at my throat, hating me the way she does, arguing, feeling that I'm not good enough for you. Our children would suffer. You come from a proud, old family and her roots go back to the Mayflower. Your father was a renowned heart surgeon. My family is loving, wonderful, but quite ordinary."

Bob stroked her wrist. "I came to love your family more than I love my own, except for my father; we had a precious bond. And he approved of you, wanted us to marry."

"I know and I'm grateful. I'm so sorry he died, but even when he lived, Reba fought me. Your mother is a powerful adversary."

"She only has the power we let her have over us."

He reached out and smoothed her eyebrows in a remembered touch, and her breath caught. "We could move away," he said. "I have friends all over, even on Diamond Point."

Clea shook her head slowly. "No. My family is here in the U.S. and I need to be close to them. Jack's legacy to me, Wilde's Wonderland, is here. I can't move away."

"Maybe Papa Curtis and Mama Maxa would like to be with us on Diamond Point. You could start a new night club. I'm a good bartender."

Clea smiled. "You're one of the best, but no. My grandparents are rooted on their little farm. They'd never leave." She paused a long moment before she said, "After all this time, I want to know more about Laura's death. I've been having dreams about Jack and he asks me to help find her killer, or try to. She was your wife, Bob. Don't you want to know who killed her?"

Without hesitation he answered, "You know I do and I'll help in any way I can, but I've kept in touch with the police here and nothing new was ever uncovered."

"I know. It's been three years, but the people at the police department say they never give up. My father died of a broken heart because of this. He loved Laura, wanted to marry her. People say he killed her because she was going back to you and he couldn't take it. I knew my father too well and he'd never kill."

"And you know I loved Jack like a second father. I don't think he'd kill either. You know I'll do whatever I can to help."

"Thank you."

He drew a deep, ragged breath. "I love you, Wild Heart. I'm back and I'm going to crowd you, press you hard. The way I just kissed you was a beginning. I've tried it without you and I can't make it. My life's too empty and no one else fills it the way you did. What we have is too precious not to last."

"What we *had*," she said gently. With an edge of desperation, she told him, "You're not listening to me and you've got to listen...."

"I *am* listening," he said softly, "to both our hearts."

That afternoon, Clea stood in her office and touched her lips, looked at the smooth cream wall that Bob had pressed her against, and her knees felt weak again. She had to stop this. She glanced around her at the spacious cream-colored room with its pale yellow leather sofas, her massive curved oak desk, and her stunning collection of floral paintings. She had been happy here.

She crossed the room and looked through the very large window that let her see the entire club floor, but did not let others see in. Wilde's Wonderland was beautiful by any standard. The highly polished hardwood floors glittered, were perfect for dancing. And the ambiance of the place was cozily romantic. There was a big revolving stage, modern crystal chandeliers, and excellent lighting. Everything was state-of-the-art.

Clea booked the best small bands in the country and used local talent as much as she could. Now she was excited that Rhapsody and its charismatic leader, Nick Redmond, would perform in a few weeks and she would sing her new songs with them.

Going back to stand at her desk, she found she kept looking at that wall by the door, kept thinking about

Bob. Passion rose in her then and she fought to keep it down. She knew what she knew, that they had no future. Reba had seen to that.

She paused at a soft knock and Alina, her assistant manager, came in.

"You're shining," Alina said. "He always does that to you."

"I'm going out of my mind," Clea fretted. "Why can't he let it go?"

Alina smiled sadly. "Because in your heart you don't want him to."

Alina's lovely pale beige face was warm with sympathy. "I've got a wonderful husband, four kids, a great job with you, and I'm happy. As your best friend, I want the same for you." She came to Clea, hugged her. "Give it a chance. Take a chance. It's better than living with hurt the rest of your life."

Clea bit her bottom lip. "Carlton's getting serious. He loves me and I like him a lot."

"He's not Bob and you don't love him. You never will."

Clea shook her head. "Love isn't everything. In some countries people seem to live happily with arranged marriages where love isn't even considered. In romance novels people sometimes marry and fall madly in love later on."

"This isn't a romance novel, sweetie. Carlton's not for you."

Clea laughed a little. "I'm going to the bathroom, then let's get out of here. This is Thursday and we've got a big night ahead with all the in-search-of singles."

In her big bathroom, Clea washed her hands, dried them under the dryer, and smoothed on lotion. She glanced in the mirror. Her eyes were lit up and she closed them. Why did he still affect her so? Now it was as if he stood behind her, his big body pressed into hers. He kissed her neck in fantasy, and something in her belly fluttered . . . *Stop it!* she commanded herself. *It isn't going to happen.* And his words came back to her: "*I'm going to crowd you, press you hard.*"

"You're not, you know," she whispered to herself, "because I'm not going to let you."

Clea sighed as she started out of the bathroom. The door stuck and she tugged at it, mild panic rising. She'd had claustrophobia all her life. She pulled hard again and still it stuck. This wasn't the first time. Why hadn't she or Alina gotten it fixed? She pushed the door hard, then knocked; in a moment, Alina pushed it open.

"Sorry, sweetie. I know how you are about getting trapped in closed spaces. The man was supposed to come in yesterday. I'll make sure he gets here today."

Clea's cell phone rang and she retrieved it from the big pocket of her blue chambray tunic to hear a worker tell her that the repairman was there to fix a door.

Clea smiled with relief. "Send him right along."

Chapter 2

Later in the same month, Dr. Robert Redding walked up the short corridor of the Crystal Lake Community Clinic his father had founded and Bob now headed. It was nine o'clock in the morning and more patients were coming in. He was happy to see parents bringing in children to be examined and given good health advice. Running a hand over his curly black hair, he thought he should have been a pediatrician the way he loved children.

His chief nurse, Gloria Edmonds, came out of one of the examining rooms into the hall.

"We're getting it today," she said happily. "We've been open three weeks and already we're doing a rushing business. It's like old times, Doc."

Bob looked at his chief nurse's stocky figure, her rounded dark brown frame, and her cheerful, attractive face. Gloria had six children with a good husband and she was one of the best mothers he had ever known.

"We could use another hand," she said. "Janice is out with a miserable cold." She looked at him obliquely. "Think Clea would like to help? This is Monday, one of her days off. But then maybe she had catch-up work to do. They're always so busy."

Bob flexed his shoulders. "It's worth a try. I'll call her."

Gloria smiled approvingly at her broad-shouldered boss in his white medical jacket, then she grinned. Handsome city. "You do that." Gloria had been sorry to see the couple break up three years ago. She had thought them the perfect pair and so vividly in love.

Bob cleared his throat. "I'm glad to see Artie Webb is coming in for a checkup. I worry about that kid. Talk about the wrong choice of parents."

Gloria nodded. "Yeah. Marian said she and Cade were coming in with him. I said you wanted to talk with them."

"You bet I want to talk with them. Artie's running fifteen pounds underweight. His little ribs were pushing through when I went to their house a couple of weeks back. Something's eating Marian. Both she and the boy need a checkup."

Gloria shrugged. "Well, as you saw from the schedule, she's not having a checkup. Just Artie. Lord, I love that kid. He's so bright. His little spirit just comes at you. He's one of God's gifts to this world."

Bob drew a deep breath, said huskily, "I love Artie as my own kid. In my years of practice, I don't think any patient has affected me the way he does. In the best of worlds, he'd be mine."

Gloria's eyes on him were warm, sympathetic. "Yours and Clea's," she said softly.

He didn't comment on her statement but his heart expanded, beat faster.

"Well, I've got 'em waiting in the wings," Gloria said. "Back to the trenches." She went in the door of another examining room.

Bob went into his fairly large, plainly furnished office and closed the door. He meant to do big things with his clinic this time. His renowned father, Madison Redding, a heart surgeon, had first founded it over the objections of his wife.

"You're such a great man," she'd cajoled him. "So many highly placed friends. Wonderful connections. We go to the White House for social functions. My dear, *why* do you want to be involved with the community riffraff?"

As a teenager, Bob had come in on this conversation

and had listened to his father's angry words, watched his face. "Don't ever call people riffraff, Reba. We were all created by God and I, anyway, know that only by the Grace of God do I fill the shoes I fill. My parents were poor. Have you forgotten that?"

His mother was so beautiful, Bob had thought then, and so cold. "Your parents were strivers, dear. They fought to give you every advantage. Your father didn't drink and lie around with other women, gamble his money away. They were poor aristocracy."

His father had shaken his head. "Don't deify them. Mother and Dad liked beer and occasional good times. They had fun together. *We* once had fun together." He'd shaken his head. "The way you and I don't seem to have fun together anymore."

His mother hadn't answered that. She was a very busy woman, much sought after for her social skills and the beauty and expertise she lent to any gathering.

Bob sighed now. This clinic was his heritage. He had made a difference as a new doctor. Then he had left after the death of his father and the breakup of his engagement to Clea. He intended to make a far greater difference now. He rubbed his chin and sighed. These were his roots, but if he could get Clea back and they had to go away to find their happiness, he'd have to leave again. Did she still love him as she *had* loved him? As they'd loved each other.

The way she'd let him into her warmth on the day he'd kissed her, his first day back, made him think she did. But his brother, Ruel, had told him about Clea dating another man, some dude named Carlton Kelly, a wealthy West Coast record mogul who was interested in the songs she wrote and even more interested in her.

Bob's heart constricted with jealousy. She was *his*, damn it, he thought, and he didn't share. Smiling at himself, he picked up his phone and dialed Clea's cell phone number. She answered on the first ring and he asked if she could come over. After a minute's hesitation, she said she could.

"Give me an hour," she said. "How're you guys fixed for food?"

"We're always starved here, especially for your delicious fare."

She laughed. "Flattery will get you everything. I've got a big crock of beef stew with wine. I'll bring it with a lot of other stuff."

"Thanks, Clea, for still being there for me."

A lump came into her throat. "Don't thank me, and you're welcome. We're still friends, aren't we?"

"I want a hell of a lot more than that, Wild Heart."

Clea was glad he couldn't see her body arch, feel her heart racing. "I'll be there shortly."

Clea was as good as her word. She pulled into the parking lot of the big white-painted brick clinic. Gloria saw her get out and open her car trunk. "I'm loaded," Clea called to her. "Gotta have help."

"You hang on," Gloria said. "I'll get you our finest."

In a few minutes she came back out with Bob and a cart and the three of them began to unload the many packages and utensils of food.

Inside, things became hectic. Clea stored the food and went out to help with patients. "I want you to sit in with me while I talk with Artie Webb's parents," Bob told her. "I'm afraid I may have to read them the riot act. I'm examining him in a couple of minutes. Wish me luck, because I'm scared of what I'm going to find."

Clea nodded. She knew little Artie Webb well. In season, Marian, his mother, sold her tomatoes for use at Wilde's Wonderland; Clea paid the best possible price. Artie always came with his mother, and Clea had come to love the little boy who was so talented as an artist and so charming. Even in the off-season, Marian came by just to visit and admire the club. For a brief while Marian had done salads for them. Then she'd told Clea, "Cade doesn't want me to work. Doesn't trust me to be away too long. Who'd want me now?"

Gorge had risen in Clea's independent chest. "You're an attractive woman, Marian. Don't let yourself go down. You're so young. Fight to keep it together."

Marian had seemed to take heart then and had looked better the next time Clea had seen her. Then she'd stopped coming by.

In the examining room, Bob looked at Artie Webb's naked, frail body and tears of rage stood in his eyes. The spindly arms that had been covered by a long-sleeved old blue polo shirt too hot for the day were full of fresh deep bruises. There was a bandaged gash on one of his thighs. Yellowish fading bruises were all over his calves.

Bob hugged the boy fiercely. "What happened, Artie?" he asked quietly.

The boy emotionally fled him, landed on safer ground. "Hey, Doc, I'm so glad you're back. My mom got me a Harry Potter book and I've been reading it. Great stuff. I missed you." The little boy's lips quivered and he laughed and cried at once.

Bob put his arm around Artie's shoulder. "As a matter of fact, I've got a Harry Potter book just for you, the latest, and I put your name in it. But you know something, Artie, I've got a friend in London and he's going to get the author to autograph a copy for you—just for you."

"Autograph?" Artie asked, his voice still quavering.

"Yeah, sign her name. And your own name'll be there. Like that?"

"Hey, neat!"

"What happened to your arms and legs, Artie?"

"Nothing," he answered too quickly.

"Did someone hit you? Beat you? Rough you up? Do you play too roughly with the other kids?"

Artie scratched his ear. "Dad doesn't let me play with the other kids much."

"Did your dad do this?"

Artie began to shake his head and big crystal tears slid down his cheeks. He wiped his face on his sleeve as Bob got up and handed him a big box of Kleenex. "I'm bad," the little boy said. "I knocked over a glass of milk at the table last night. I'm always doing something wrong. Dad says he's going to make me grow up right. He shakes me till I can't breath." The little boy stopped, alarmed at what he'd just confided. He looked at Bob from frightened eyes and asked breathlessly, "You won't tell him I told you? He gets mad at me and it scares me. Did your dad punish you for being bad, Doc?"

"No, love," Bob said sadly. "He never did punish me the way your dad punishes you. He talked with me, told me what he expected. Artie, I'm going to start coming out to see you more. Are you still taking the cod liver oil?"

"Yeah. Mom gives it to me. Ugh." He made a face. "Dad says it's a bunch of shit." Bob flinched at the vulgar word coming from so small a boy, but he knew where he'd gotten it from.

"Dad says *he* never took cod liver oil and he's a fine specimen."

Bob smiled at Artie's correct enunciation and aplomb at using that description.

Taking his time, Bob continued to examine Artie. Before he had left Crystal Lake a few years back, he'd found Artie developing rickets at a little over four years old and he'd told his mother to give him cod liver oil and plenty of fresh fruits and vegetables. She had done that until they'd moved away to D.C. for a year or so. They'd come back and the disease was pronounced. Marian pleaded that they just didn't have the money to spend on *unnecessaries* like cod liver oil. Food was hard enough to come by.

"Damn it, Marian!" Bob had exploded. "*This* is a necessity." He had explained about brittle bones that couldn't hold the child up. "I'll send you a case of cod liver oil and when that's out, another case, but I want him to have it."

She'd agreed and the boy's medical exams had greatly improved. He still needed more fruits and vegetables, but the cod liver oil helped. When Bob left, he had called and asked Clea to continue taking them the oil and she had. Now Artie was greatly improved bonewise, but his muscles, skin, and spirit were being abused and that sickened Bob.

Finally finishing his exam, Bob patted Artie's fragile back and smiled as the boy looked up at him with adoring big, brown eyes.

Bob shook his head. "Love you, kid," he said. "You're the greatest. I wish you were mine."

Artie looked at him fearfully. "I'd like that, being your kid, Doc," he said in a near whisper, as if he were afraid to voice the words.

Fifteen minutes later, with Artie reading his new Harry Potter book and being looked after by a clinic worker, Bob sat across the desk from Arties' parents, Cade and Marian Webb. Clea sat in for support and in case Cade wanted to start something that led to legal trouble.

Bob cleared his throat and took his recorder out of the desk drawer. "With your permission, I'd like to record this session." He nodded at Cade.

"Why?" Cade asked. A good-looking, cocoa-brown man with a thatch of wavy black hair, Cade was a woman's man and didn't get along particularly well with his own gender. He kept glancing at Clea, his eyes raking her body as if his wife were not in the room.

"A formality," Bob told him. "There will be harsh things said in a few minutes. I need to keep the record straight."

"It's all right, Doc," Marian said, then to her husband, "honey, please."

"Hell, anything the doc does is all right with you, Marian," Cade snorted. "Well, go ahead. I guess it's all right." He gestured expansively toward Clea, jerked his head, asking, "Why's she here, except to glamorize the room?" His eyes on Clea were openly lustful.

"She's here as an interested witness. A social worker wasn't available."

"What the hell're you planning to say?" Cade asked belligerently.

"Honey," Marian cautioned him. A small, defeated woman who could have been pretty with her tea-colored, smooth skin and brown hair, Marian stood as a buffer between her husband and the world, including her son.

Cade settled back. "Let's get on with it. How'd my boy check out today?"

"He's full of bruises," Bob said tightly. "Would you know why?"

"Hell, kids get bruises," Cade said easily. "It's called growing up and learning to be a man. I roughhouse with Artie. Other kids beat him up, even girls. He's such a sissy. I'm not going to have that, even if I have to skin his hide."

"Do you beat Artie?" Bob asked bluntly.

"I cuff him about sometimes—the way my father did me. Like I said, the boy's a sissy, with his nose always in some damned book. His mother encourages that kind of thing. I don't." His voice went low. "I tell you, Doc, pure and honest, I'll raise him to be a *man*, or I swear I'll kill him."

Anger rose in Bob's throat the way he had seldom known it before. "What you're doing is called child abuse, Mr. Webb," he said coldly, "and Artie is far too valuable a child to have to endure it. Any child is too precious to be abused, but Artie is special, gifted. Don't you realize that?"

"*I* do," Marian said. "He's really bright."

"A damned sissy," Cade began. "No son of mine—"

"Don't call the boy names," Bob said savagely. "Can't you see what you're doing to him? He'll soon be fulfilling prophecy. I want you to stop manhandling him, Mr. Webb, and I'm going to have to report his bruises to authorities."

Cade Webb's mouth opened and for a moment or two no words came. Then he got his wind. "What I do with my kid is none a' your damned business, Doc. I run my house and you run yours. I raise my son and I reckon you got none to raise is the reason you're meddling in *my* business. Now you go ahead and report to whatever the hell authorities you want to. I ain't changing my methods of raising my son."

Bob's every nerve frayed then. "You're running the risk of losing him. Do you love your son, Mr. Webb?"

Cade laughed harshly. "What kinda damned fool question is that? He's mine. I'll tell you about love, Dr. Redding; it's a word I don't use. I'm a strong man and strong men don't spend time thinking about love. It's something women and fools use to get by. Artie's my son and I take care of him. Feed him. Clothe him. Keep a roof over his and my wife's head. Don't talk to me about love. It's messed up more people than I can tell you about."

Bob rocked as he listened intently with sorrow in his heart. Artie deserved so much more. "Children need love to grow," he said softly, more to Marian than to Cade. But then, he thought, Marian already understood.

Cade pounded one fist in the palm of his other hand. "Children need *discipline*," he railed. "This is a hard world, Doc, maybe not for your kind, but for mine, for Artie's kind, because he's *my* son, not yours. Like I said, you got no kids, so maybe that's why you don't know. Like I said, I'm raising Artie and he's mine to raise or kill trying." Cade's smile was twisted, malevolent, his voice a growl. "So butt out, Doc. You get too close, I moved to D.C. once and maybe I'll move there again."

Something squeezed dry in Bob then at the thought of not being able to help Artie the way he wanted to.

He glanced at Clea, who frowned, looking stricken and angry.

Cade pushed his chair back. "You got anything else to say? Because I'm gearing up to leave. I've let him take the damned cod liver oil like you recommended. I've bought more fruit, even planted a little garden mostly for him. But I'll keep on tussling with him, Doc, hard, manlike, because he's got to toughen up to fit into his world—and mine. Do you understand?"

"I understand where you're coming from, even if I don't agree, but I want you to think about what I've said. Some children are born more fragile than others. Your son is one of them. He's brilliant, Mr. Webb. Do you know that?"

"Hell yes, I know that. Artie's got a better vocabulary at seven than I had at fifteen." His laugh was scathing. "What's it gonna get him in my world? A broken head? A heart full of stab wounds? Bullet holes in his chest?"

"He doesn't have to live in that world. God has given him the brains, the talent, to get out, live in whatever world he chooses."

Cade grunted. "*I* sure have lived without many choices. I don't reckon it'll kill Artie to do the same. Come on, Marian, go get the boy and we'll be leaving." He coolly glanced at Bob, then ogled Clea again. "I'd thank you, but I don't think I've got anything to thank you for."

Bob picked up a tube of ointment from his desk and handed it to Marian. "Use this on Artie's sore," he said, "and I'd like to see him in two weeks."

"Okay," Marian said tiredly.

As Marian timidly accepted the ointment and put it in her purse, Cade looked from his wife to Bob, then back at Clea, thinking he sure would like to get next to that. A glint of hostile fire struck him as Bob looked at him. Cade looked down. He was one tough hombre until he was face-to-face with another man's toughness, then something quailed inside him and he backed down.

* * *

Things had quieted about two-thirty that same afternoon. The clinic staff had enjoyed the food Clea brought. Clea and Bob were in his office. "Make Doc relax a bit," Gloria had said to Clea. "Stay on and keep him company. I'll hold down the fort, and I'll have his calls held."

Bob locked the door. Then Clea perched on the edge of his desk as he sprawled in a big tan leather chair admiring her.

"Thank you for helping out, Wild Heart."

"Anytime. We're friends now and that's valuable to me. I'll always be there for you."

"And you know you've got the same from me."

Bob's glance roved over her lazily. The earth-brown hair was tinted to a dark reddish cast and layered in a shoulder-length cut. She wore little makeup except for bronze blusher on her dark skin, and her eyes were expertly done with kohl. Wide gold hoops were fastened in her ears and the gold gleamed against her skin.

For moments he deliberately lingered on her face, saving the deeply curved body that always unsettled him. Her hips flattened against the desk were wider still and her high breasts called to him. She wore a plain, scarlet silk, low-cut blouse above a short, black silk broadcloth short skirt with a split on one side. As his glance got to her legs and the fabulous, bare calves with the slender ankles, he sighed and swallowed hard. He patted his thigh, his crotch tightening.

"Come here," he said softly.

It seemed to Clea that she moved not of her own volition. When she reached him, he said, "Sit down."

He patted his knee. She pretended to ignore him.

"I don't see but one chair here. Am I missing something?"

He patted his knee again. "All in friendship. You're safe."

Smiling, she sat on his knees, driven by habit and need. "For just a minute." She crossed her legs.

"No. Don't cross your legs."

Startled, she asked, "But why not?"

He grinned wickedly with half-closed eyes, teasing her. "Because I intend to get between them."

Clea found her breath shutting off with intense desire, but she told him, "And the road to hell is . . ."

He threw back his head, laughing, then finished her sentence, "paved with good intentions. At least you know it's good. Just teasing, baby. Reliving old times with a vengeance."

His arms went around her waist and he squeezed her quickly, then relaxed his hold. She groaned in the back of her throat. His big hands on her felt so good. His hands nearly encircled her waist as he pushed her up. "I've got a present for you in my closet."

She got up and sat on the desk again, thinking. They had always given each other frequent presents. He came back from the closet with a large and beautiful basket of luscious, huge white peaches wrapped in plastic and tied with a big red bow. He carried a small Zip-Loc bag with a halved red-centered peach with the stone removed.

"They're special," he explained. "Someone at the Fruit Center called me about them and I knew I had to get a supply for you. They're of Asian origin, only lately grown in this country." He held up the Zip-Loc bag. "You can see from this one what they look like inside."

"They're gorgeous," she said happily. "Thank you so much. Talk about your exquisite taste."

He laughed huskily. "I picked you, didn't I?"

"Silver-tongued devil."

He unzipped the bag holding the peach half and took it out. "Put both hands behind you," he commanded her.

"Why?"

"Don't ask so many questions. I'm the dominant one, remember?"

She did as he asked, wondering. With one big hand he held both her slender hands in one of his, then as she sat, incredulous, he took the ripe peach half and rubbed it across her mouth, her cheeks near her mouth, then her chin. She tasted the wonderfully sweet juice and jumped.

"My blouse," she shrieked. "You're going to ruin it!"

"I'm sorry about your blouse, sweetheart, but I'll buy you a couple more. I have to do this. You've got me in thrall."

His mouth came down hard on hers then and her open mouth received him avidly. The peach nectar was so sweet on both their tongues. Flames shot from her brain and scalp to the tips of her toes. Dear Lord, she thought, she was burning up for him. For a few minutes, their tongues intertwined in a mad dance of desire. Gently he sucked her bottom lip, put a knee between her knees, and continued to hold her tightly.

He let her hands go then and she wrapped her arms around his neck, held him in a frantic embrace, moaning softly, mindful of where they were.

She knew then why he'd spread the peach juice on her face. He licked the juice from above her mouth slowly, with tantalizing precision, then moved to her left cheek and licked harder as her nipples hardened and fought for his mouth on them.

She tasted, he thought, like nothing he had ever tasted before except her. His shaft rose as he continued the slow, inexorable licking across her cheek, chin, and other cheek. It was a long time before he had licked all the peach juice off and he tongued her face with more small, darting kisses. Dear Lord, he thought, this was satisfaction with a capital S.

When he pulled away a little, she pulled him back, and this time her mouth fastened on his, kissing him with ravening hunger, lust, and passion burning for him in her every cell.

Then fear struck her and she thought, *No, this has to stop!* Breathing raggedly, she pushed him away. "So much for friendship," she said softly.

He spread his hands as if in apology. "Sometimes I lie, but my heart never does. Not where you're concerned."

"I've got to go," she said suddenly. "Thanks so much for the peaches." She glanced at him slyly. "I've only tasted the juice. I'm sure I'll enjoy them."

"I'm going to keep the other half, eat it, and remember you. Don't go, Wild Heart. Not yet. I need your company."

She stayed an hour longer. They kept looking at each other, but they talked about Artie and his family and did not kiss again.

"You're going to report Cade then?"

"You bet I am, first thing tomorrow. I've got to save him, Clea. Cade could kill Artie trying to make him into his idea of a man. And Marian isn't strong enough to protect her son."

Clea's heart hurt for them both. He looked sadder than she had known him to look since they'd broken up over three years ago.

Chapter 3

The following Wednesday morning Clea came awake feeling blue and uncomfortable. Her big bedroom, done in shades of dark rose and ecru, was cool and a breeze drifted in from the open window. It had rained the night before and moistness lingered in the air. She glanced at the luminous clock dial on her night table. Five o'clock. She didn't usually rise until five-thirty.

Sitting up, drawing her knees up beneath her chin, she suddenly remembered what brought this depression on and she said it aloud. "July eighteenth. Bob asked me to marry him four years ago this night." Now she thought, *He took me dancing. I said I had plans for expanding Wilde's Wonderland and he grinned.*

"With you being my wife," he had said, "I'm not sure you're going to have time for a larger place."

She drew a deep, sharp breath that hurt. He had brought her a white, yellow-throated catalya orchid and he had been so sweet, kissing her by surprise. She had not expected it so soon. They had dated only two months.

The memory was wired to her brain. He had said, "Well, Wild Heart, do you accept my proposal?"

And without hesitation she had answered, "I would marry you this minute. I love you so much."

She had been afraid he wouldn't ask; they were so different. She had met his family formally only once as they courted. Then after Bob had placed the five-carat emerald-cut engagement ring on her finger, he had taken her again to talk to his mother. Ruel, his brother, had been there, had been cordial.

Reba Redding, Bob's mother, had been downright cold. A pale-skinned woman with dark auburn, superbly coiffed hair and sea-green eyes, she'd held her exquisite beauty into her late fifties. "I see," she'd said, then she hadn't bitten her tongue. "I had hoped Bob and Colette would marry. She's the daughter of my dearest friend who died last year. You know Colette Waring, the Virginia state senator's daughter, don't you? She's beautiful. Brilliant. She and Bob would have been a perfect match."

"Mother, really . . ." Bob had sputtered. "Marriage is a matter of choice. My choice. Colette and I never became close. We were never more than friends."

They hadn't stayed long and Reba Redding had never warmed to Clea or invited her back. She hadn't even looked at the engagement ring.

Clea rolled her head around on her shoulders, loosening up. Sensual dreams of Bob and her had shaken her very bones the night before, and a slow smile curved her lips. She got up and closed the window, drew on a jade-green silk kimono. Going to the kitchen, she drank a glass of orange juice she'd squeezed and left in the fridge the night before.

In her fitness room she took running gear out of the closet and put it aside. She wanted to read the paper before she ran.

Opening her front door to get the morning news, she jumped as a rangy form came onto the porch, then breathed a sigh of relief.

"Morning, Clea. How's things?"

"Hello, Dunk. You're very early."

The chocolate-brown nineteen-year-old grinned. "Getting a head start." He held up a plastic bag. "Got your special belt finished. Thought I'd bring it over so you could try it on, admire it, get used to it. I was going to leave it in your screen door it's so early, but I know you get up early. Hey, I'm doing great stuff with metal."

"I know I'll like it. You're so good." She took the bag from him. "Would you like coffee, orange juice, some breakfast?"

He shook his head. "No time. I've got a couple of orders to fill, then I'm coming back and do your grocery shopping. I've located some gigantic shrimp at a good price I think you'll like. I'll be back here around one and I'll be over to Wonderland around three. Anything special you'd like me to do here?"

Clea shook her head. She could think of nothing. "No. See you later."

"Then I'll be off." The youth lifted his hand in salute. "That's a great kimono you're wearing. Suits you to a T."

"Thank you."

His late father had been an expert leather craftsman. Merchants in Crystal Lake and D.C. had become interested in his wares. Dunk's name was Duncan Hill, but everyone called him "Dunk" because he was a whiz at putting a basketball through the hoop. But Dunk had no interest in the sport beyond making the basket again and again. He intended to be a stellar businessman. "I'll have me a chain of leather stores by the time I'm thirty-five," he said often.

She watched him go down the walk. Dunk's schizophrenic mother had died the year before, and he lived alone. He had graduated from high school the past year and had not registered for college so he could grieve. He was Clea's all-around helper and he'd been close to her since he was a boy of eleven or so. Dunk made and sold leather goods, mostly fabulous belts and wallets. Now he was branching out into metal belts and jewelry.

And Dunk loved computers. He had three. Clea smiled and shook her head. Where did he get all his energy? But it bothered her that he had few friends. He liked girls, was extremely courtly to Clea and others, took an occasional date to the movies, but there was no one girl he favored.

Clea had eaten a light breakfast and done a few sit-ups

when her door chimes sounded. As she opened the door, a smile blossomed on her face.

"Bob! I thought you'd be turning over for a second snooze about now."

He held out a white florist's box. "Like you, I get up early, but you already know that. This is for you. Open it and invite me in."

He wore a white short-sleeved polo shirt over rippling biceps and pecs and she felt her breath catch. She wanted so badly to stroke his heavy eyebrows and silken black mustache.

He looked at her in her green kimono and whistled. "Looking good, Mama." He grinned. "Your hair looks like I've just rumpled it.

"You're so fresh," she said, laughing. "Would you like some breakfast, or anything else?"

His mouth curved in a droll smile. "I'd love some anything else."

"The anything else is orange or some other juice, or coffee, tea, whatever you wish."

"You're not listening to what I wish. I'm not due at the clinic until nine. We've got a lot of time."

His narrowed glance was on her mouth. She thought about him licking the peach juice from her face and her body got hot. She could feel moisture start in her nether parts. "I've been eating your peaches. They're *so* sweet and juicy. Fat city. Would you like one—or two?"

"They're for you. Sweet and juicy, like you. I had waffles and maple syrup for breakfast. I only want a cup of the strongest coffee you can make me—and the best."

He sat at the table, glancing at the newspaper headlines.

"You're in luck. I ground fresh coffee beans for my coffee and I made it strong. I'm using double-strength powdered milk these days to fight cholesterol, also a great natural sugar, Splenda. Have you heard of it?"

"I use it. You'll make a good doctor's wife."

Looking at him, she begged, "Don't. I want us to be

friends. We were the best of friends before we were lovers, engaged. I've told you what I can stand, and what I can't. You know it breaks my heart, but it's what is. What's real."

She poured the coffee, fixed it, and set a mug before him. He took a long sip. "My mug," he said. "Thanks, love. I'd like to use it every morning." His voice went husky.

She fixed herself a second cup of coffee and sat opposite him. She opened the white box and tears stood in her eyes with the memory of another white orchid and a far more blissful time. "Thank you," she said. "It's beautiful, like everything you've ever given me."

"You're very welcome. I try for things that're like you, beautiful all the way through."

"You flatter me."

"I could never do you justice."

He sipped his brew. "This is really great coffee. You've been in training all your life to be my wife."

"You know," she said softly, "in many ways I can see where your mother's coming from. Her great-grandfather was one of the landed gentry in southern Virginia. He was white, yes, and like so many white men of that era, he fathered black children, but he was different. He had only one black woman and he built her a nice house, educated their children in France, left her land and money because his wife was an invalid.

"That was your mother's heritage; she married well—a prominent heart specialist—one of the country's best. You're a really first-rate doctor with a great heart. Ruel is a successful lawyer who practices with his wife. Your mother doesn't know anything but the best and it's what she wants for you."

Bob drank the last of his coffee, set the cup in the saucer, and looked at her thoughtfully.

"And you, Wild Heart? You're *my* kind of first class. Your father, Jack, was my friend, and I revere him. He was a gambler, one of the best. He built Wilde's Wonderland from scratch and he roamed the country and parts of Europe, studying the field. You loved him, wanted to follow in his footsteps. You finished in business administration at Howard, went into business with him as you'd been all your life. Then you got an MBA at the University of Maryland. . . ."

"It's not Mayflower heritage blood."

"And it damned well doesn't need to be." He reached over and covered her hand with his. "Clea, you're passionate, loving, empathic, caring. In my book, you're a queen among women. You grace this earth like any angel and I wouldn't swap all the gold in Fort Knox for what I've known with you. I'd take you in place of heaven. Song of Solomon comes to my mind whenever I think of you. We used to read it to each other and I'm hoping we will again."

His eyes pleaded with her and her breathing shallowed.

He looked at the flower. "I brought you that orchid because I want you to remember the night I first told you I loved you and you said you loved me too. I asked you to marry me and you said yes, the way I'm hoping you'll say it again. I wanted to send you orchids when I was away, but I was hurting and angry, selfish. I couldn't even *try* to understand. I drank way too much to kill the pain, but it dulled my memory. You're not one tenth as sorry as I am."

She pulled her hand from beneath his and put it on top of his, hating to break the deep connection. "I need to get to running," she said softly. "Why don't you run with me?"

"I'd like to, but I wouldn't be comfortable in this. I guess I could go back home and change."

"No. You left a set of sweats. They're still in the closet."

"Then what are we waiting for?"

In the ten-acre stretch behind her white stucco, blue-tile-roofed Spanish-style house, there was a two-and-a-half-mile running track that doubled back, giving a five-mile run. Bob and Clea ran easily at first in their gray sweat gear, gray headbands in place, running shoes and pedometers on their bodies. The air was so crisp, so full of spring. Newly sprouted trees lay just beyond them and azaleas bloomed around the large toolshed they ran by. Last night's rain had washed the atmosphere to a pristine clarity.

"This is like old times," Bob said.

"Yes."

"I was really fit then. You still are and I will be again. Let's start running together often."

She hesitated, then, "That would be nice."

"Wild Heart, you don't know how I've missed you."

"No more than I've missed you," she murmured.

A cardinal sang a lusty song on a tree branch and Clea's heart soared. After a very little while as she ran with Bob's big form beside her, she began to get a runner's high more pronounced than usual. She was feeling old joy, old passion. A runner's high was something she could never clearly define. It was a mixture of exhilaration, warmth racing through her body, oxygenated tissue, and *glad* blood flowing.

She turned to Bob. "I'm getting a runner's high. Are you?"

"Felt it a couple of minutes ago. I'd almost forgotten what it feels like. Next to you, it's been one of my best feelings."

"Then we *will* do it again."

They ran for the rest of the time as the sun climbed, then headed back to the house. It had been a very good time, Clea thought, and she didn't want it to end.

The went in the side door because Clea wanted to check her birdhouse. A new blue jay had joined two other birds, and on their perch all three watched her with guarded, bright eyes.

"I'll come in, change, and get going," Bob said. "I've got a busy day."

"And I've got a busy day preparing for Friday night. I'm introducing my new song. Will you be there?"

"I'll be there. Want to show me the song?"

As Clea started to answer, she opened the side door and a chill struck her.

"What is it?" Bob asked.

"I don't know," she answered slowly. "I've just got a strange feeling." She looked around, sensing another presence—alien, malignant.

Bob looked at her. "You're a shaman's granddaughter, Clea, and he's taught you a whole lot about that mystery. You've always divined things. Look around while I'm still here and I'll help you."

They went through the house and found nothing amiss, but the chill in her body persisted. She was so tense. Finally she said, "A little later I'm going to call Papa Curtis and Mama Maxa, see if they're all right. Sometimes when illness or some trouble strikes someone I know, I feel strange."

"Good idea." Bob's face was tender with concern.

The odd sensation left her body then and she relaxed, felt warm again.

"Would you like a cherry Danish?" she asked him. "I've got some of the best and the exercise has used up my breakfast."

"I'll take one with me."

"Fine. On second thought, I'll eat mine tomorrow. I'm eating far less these days."

He looked at her luscious, shapely body and smiled. "It's not like you need to lose weight. I like curves, some meat."

"I'm thirty," she said, "not far from thirty-one. I've been reading for a very long time that people live longer when they eat less. Scientists have done so many tests on lab animals—"

"We're not lab animals, sweetie. I'll opt to keep on enjoying my steaks and potatoes."

Clea hunched her shoulders a bit, laughed as she

moved about, bagging the cherry Danish. "I know from the year I've tried eating less I've lost some weight, my brain works better, and you know something, I think my libido's gone up. If I had one, my sex life would probably be better."

Bob put a finger alongside his cheek. "Hmm, in that case, maybe I'll give up eating altogether."

They both laughed and he got serious. "I'm glad to know you don't have a sex life, Wild Heart. I thought you might have something going with this Kelly guy. Good to know I don't have to find an excuse to punch his lights out."

She made a face at him. "Stop playing caveman. I meant to keep you guessing. That statement just slipped out." Her face got serious then. "But Carlton and I are getting closer. He likes my new song I'm performing Friday night. Nick Redmond and I are going to record it and he's set to promote it all the way. You'll meet him Friday. He's a great guy."

Jealousy struck sharply through Bob's body and his brain. Just because she wasn't sleeping with this Kelly guy didn't mean she wouldn't be. He swallowed hard. The thought of her making love to another man drove him crazy. She belonged to him, as he belonged to her.

They went into the living room and Clea picked up the remote to turn on the TV, then decided on the CD player. Stevie Wonder's old hit, "I Just Called to Say I Love You" soared.

"Dedicated to me?" Bob grinned.

"You're all wet," she told him. Peace spread through her now, along with the excitement Bob's presence always brought. They sat on the sofa close together and he ran a hand over the back of her hair, squeezed her shoulder.

"I'm going to shower and go, honey," he said, stretching.

"You've got time. You said you didn't have to be at the clinic until nine."

His eyes got dreamy. "I romantically saved you day before yesterday, didn't I?"

His eyes were on her face, remembering the long, long kiss, the taste of the peach juice, and her own special sweet skin flavor.

"I forgive you, this time," she said, "for kissing me like that, but—"

He held up a hand, shushing her. "I paid a price for that kiss, Wild Heart. Listen, that night I woke up with an erection I couldn't tame. I wanted you so bad I was dying with it. Several times I started to get in my car and come over. I even lifted the receiver to call you. Talk about hell. Talk about torment. I hope you'll let me kiss you again and often, but not like that until I can convince you to come back to my arms for good again."

Clea touched her tongue to her lips. "Thank you. That seems like a good idea," she said softly. But she felt sad. That kiss had thrilled her to her bone marrow, and every cell of her wanted more of the same.

She kept on her sweats while he showered. Picking up the phone, she dialed a number and Mama Maxa answered.

"Is everything all right with you two?" Clea asked quickly.

"We're fine," her grandmother said, "and you, love? You sound a bit tense."

"I'm okay. Bob's here. We just ran together."

"Aha. Does this mean—"

"No, we're not back together. That's over and I've moved on. He's opened the clinic again. I help from time to time. He's always coming by and you know he used to bartend at Wonderland for kicks."

"I remember. Does *he* say it's still over?"

"No," she said shortly. "How's Papa Curtis?"

"Off hunting, fishing with a bunch of cronies. Last time, they brought back perch you wouldn't believe. We still have great venison in the freezer. Listen, love, I want

WILD HEART   41

to invite you down Monday a week from this Monday. Can you make it?"

"I'm sure I can. What's the occasion?"

"Nothing special. We just want to see you. I'm going to call Bob and invite him. Please give me his number, honey."

Clea gave her the number. "He might be too busy to come. I'd enjoy a loner's trip down. It would give me time to think."

"Bob's good company. Oh, Clea, you don't know how my heart hurt when you two broke up. Papa Curtis and I had visions of our grandkids from birth to grown-up. It's been so long since I've held a family baby in my arms. Bob loves you with a love few women ever know and he's a superb man. Couldn't you just learn to live with Reba Redding's hostility?"

"No, Mama Maxa, I can't," Clea answered. "I had Jack and you and Papa Curtis. So much love has gone through my life all my life and I want my children to know the same."

"They'd have you and Bob—and us."

"And Reba would always be a thorn in their side. They'd be *my* children and she thinks I'm not good enough for her son."

"He's always told me you're the best thing that ever happened to him. Is he still there?"

"Yes, but he's showering now. Call him at the clinic around one if you must, but I wish you wouldn't."

"Forgive me, love, but Bob is like a son to us, the son we haven't had since Jack died. Bear with us on this."

"Okay. Then I'll see you Monday. I'm sure we'll talk several times before then, but I'll be starting before daybreak so we'll—or I'll—get there pretty early."

"Fine. I'm preparing a Native American feast. Pure Cherokee. I've woven some new baskets for you, and Papa's framed the most beautiful wolf photo you'll ever see."

"Wonderful." Wolves, Clea thought, her Cherokee

grandfather's guardian spirit. His Indian name was Gray Wolf. Mama Maxa's was White Cloud and Clea's was Brown Dove. Clea's mother had died when she was ten and her grandparents had raised her with love and warmth. Her children would have that same thing, she vowed.

Bob came out of the shower with his curly hair wet and his eyes shining. Clea bit her bottom lip. How many times after showering had they made passionate love? She felt sick with frustration.

"Feeling better now?" he asked.

She nodded. "A lot better. But I've had these feelings before. I had them before Jack had the heart attack and died, before they told your father he would die of his cancer."

"I surely remember," he said quietly.

She told him about her grandmother's invitation, asking, "Are you free to go?" Some part of her hoped he wasn't.

"I'm always free to visit those two. Next to you, they're my favorite people."

"I'll be leaving very early."

"*We'll* be leaving early. Do *you* really want me to go, Wild Heart?"

"They're dying to see you. They're so happy you're back."

"You didn't answer my question. From your heart?"

She looked at him with half-stricken eyes. "From my heart," she said slowly, "I want you to go."

He hugged her then, not pressing hard against her, and she was grateful. She wondered then how she was going to live with his presence and not being a center of his life, not feeling his kisses, not thrilling with the savage passion of him inside her. Could she give up Wonderland, settle somewhere else? She couldn't and she knew that now.

***

After Bob had gone, some of the discomfort she'd felt when they came into the house from running came back. She took the belt Dunk had made from the plastic bag and held it. Fashioned of medium-size heavy gold chain, it had one strand that fastened around her slender waist, then three scalloped rows caught with small bars that fell beneath the first chain. Going into her bedroom, she removed her sweats and slipped the belt around her waist on top of her cotton panties.

This was going to be a sensation with the dress she planned to wear Friday night, she thought. Carlton was a man who loved fashion. He was helping Dunk get a toehold in the industry, and he would love this. With him, her children would have love *and* peace. His mother adored Clea, fully approved of her. Why was her heart so still when she thought of Carlton?

Moving about, Clea thought there was one thing she needed to do, get her week's worn undies together and wash them. She got the big mesh bag from the linen closet, went to the small hamper in the bathroom, and opened the lid. The hamper was empty.

She guessed then that Dunk in his zeal to help her had simply thought this was part of the laundry and put it in the washer. Would he have thought to put the machine on the gentle cycle?

In the laundry room, the washer and dryer were empty. Then what? She had an excellent memory and she had not put the undergarments anywhere else. She went to her kitchen phone and dialed Dunk's cell phone.

"Yo," he answered.

"Did you wash for me yesterday?"

"Nope. Didn't see anything to wash except a hamper of underwear. Why d' you ask?"

"Ah," she began and thought better of it. What in the hell was going on?

"Okay," was all she said.

"Hey, you sound breathless. I'll be there with the groceries before you leave. Any changes?"

"No. Oh yes, please get me a couple of liters of ginger ale."

"You bet."

Not until that night when she checked her e-mail did she see it. In her in-box was a message, sent from someone calling himself *Your Worst Nightmare*. There was an ID line and the subject *Plans for Wild Heart*. There was a brief message.

> I have pressed your soft, soft undies against my face, rubbed them against my face, stroked them. Dreamed with lust. You will never guess what happens next.
>
> Your Worst Nightmare

Sitting before her computer, Clea felt waves of fear go through her. She picked up the receiver to call Bob and decided against it. Some fool. Some prank. Personal computers had unleashed their own kind of insanity. It didn't have to mean anything special.

But her underwear was gone. Someone had taken it while she and Bob ran. Her side door was usually unlocked. One murder had happened in Crystal Lake in ten years. Some kids were beginning to go bad. It was likely a juvenile prank.

She pursed her lips, made herself relax. If the perpetrator made further contact, she would talk with Detective Mitchell Tree at Crystal Lake's police department. Bob was his family doctor. She considered him a friend.

The hairs on the back of her neck rose a bit. She put the phone back in the cradle. It had begun to signal a "please hang up" sound as she leaned against the chair back. This sounded like something an out-of-control teenager would do. Dunk was the only teenager she knew well, and he was focused, centered. He had no time for this kind of foolishness.

She thought then of someone else. Pantell Hood. Pantell had often helped her before she fired him for sadistically assaulting her customers as head bouncer. He was a man-child and he came into Wonderland often arguing for his job back.

Pantell had a mean streak a mile wide and she wished she'd fired him long ago. She thought now she'd wait and see what happened next.

In bed, again she started to call Bob and again decided against it. For the first time since she'd lived in this house, it seemed too big, too empty. But to her surprise she slept and gray wolves loped and circled back around her, protecting her, chasing her enemies, keeping them at bay.

Chapter 4

Friday nights were always special at Wilde's Wonderland, but tonight was even more so. Festive balloons and streamers decorated the club. The air was heady with the perfume of dozens of full-bloom gardenia plants set about in ceramic tubs. Floors and glassware glittered, the lighting was a pale soft rose, and the band played a series of seductive songs. Clea and Alina were both in high spirits with the promise of a big night ahead. At eight P.M. customers were already beginning to come in large numbers.

Dressed in a silk, off-the-shoulder vanilla dress with a short split and backless natural-colored leather sandals, Clea greeted people, never stopped smiling. Alina wore black, outlining her superb heavy figure. Tonight Clea would introduce her new song and sing it with Nick Redmond's combo, Rhapsody. She moved to the bandstand and got a big grin from Nick.

"Looking go-o-o-d, Mama," he complimented. "I'm really proud to be backing you on this one."

Clea smiled. "I feel the same way. Is Janet coming?" Janet was Nick's wife.

"You bet; she's coming later. Has Carlton gotten here?"

"Not yet."

Nick looked at her closely; they had become good friends. "Are you two becoming an item?"

Clea raised her eyebrows, shrugged. "Who knows? Maybe. I could do worse."

"He's a nice guy."

Clea agreed and frowned, realizing she kept looking around for Bob. When he had lived here before, he'd been at every major happening she'd had.

She moved away to Alina, who said, "We're packing them in, baby." Then she grimaced, her beige skin reddening. "Pantell's here."

"He's here often lately." No sooner had she spoken than a tall dark brown man with coarse, close-cut black hair came up. It was obvious he'd been drinking.

"Well, boss lady," he said gruffly, "still not willing to take me back?"

Clea didn't smile. "I don't think so, Pantell. Haven't you found a job yet? I offered to give you any help I could."

He nodded. "Yeah, I know you did. Trouble is, this place has got in my blood."

"You were being too rough, too sadistic. I warned you again and again. You didn't listen."

He sighed. "Yeah. If you'd give me another chance—"

A commotion started near the door. There were six bouncers on nights like this and Clea started over. Alina and Pantell went with her. "What's the problem?" Clea asked one of the bouncers.

The biggest of the bouncers turned to her. "We're handling it. Couple of dudes high on marijuana tried to crash it, talking loud, being vulgar. We don't have that here."

One of the culprits, who looked no more than twenty, with bulging biceps got nasty then, spewed a string of invectives in a loud voice. Pantell fixed him with his meanest look, growling, "You knock it off or you're gonna lose some teeth." His adrenaline was coming back with memories of the job he'd lost. His furious eyes locked with the man's and the culprit backed down, shaken. There was a devil behind those eyes.

Clea placed a restraining hand on Pantell's arm. "Don't threaten," she said. "They're handing it." Four bouncers had closed in on the men, had called the police, and two security guards—policemen who moonlighted—were right there.

"Their asses would've been on the floor and their heads bashed in if it'd been *my* show," Pantell muttered.

Clea patted his arm. "One day you're going to have a heart attack taking on the world," she said gently. "Relax. Go and have fun."

"Aw, Clea, you really ought to hire me back. Four bouncers, two cop security guards to handle two high punks. Hell, I—"

"Pantell, cool it. This is an order. Go! Have fun."

For a moment he looked angry, crestfallen. Then he said, "Okay, okay. You singing tonight? You sure look good."

"Thank you and yes, I'm singing."

Pantell shook his head, glancing again at the doorway the miscreants had been taken through. "I can't wait to hear this."

A slight chill swept over her and light goose bumps dotted her arms. She had not thought about Wednesday night's computer message tonight, the message that had ended: *You will never guess what happens next.* What would anybody want with her underwear? She hated thinking about it.

She stood breathing deeply. Pantell used to help her, get her groceries, run errands. He had never washed for her, but he had picked up clothes from the cleaners and the laundry, including hand laundry. And Pantell was always on the computer. He was surprisingly good with the machines. He and Dunk had long conversations about them. Now she asked him, "Why don't you study computers while you're not working? You're crazy about them."

"Yeah," he answered quickly. "I am at that. Maybe. You care what I'm doing with my life? Mr. Jack hired me. You remember?"

Did his eyes really look shifty, or was she imagining it? "I remember," she said quietly. Jack had kept him on an even keel, something she hadn't been able to do.

"Dr. Bob's back in town," he said. "Maybe he's got something for me to do."

"I'd check it out if I were you. Pantell, don't start drinking. It got you in trouble before."

He laughed harshly. "Don't remind me." Pantell had gone to jail for stalking his longtime girlfriend when she broke up with him. He had struck her, threatened to do her further harm. She said he forced her to have sex with him, threatened to kill her. But he had sobered up, apologized abjectly, and promised not to bother her again and she had withdrawn the charges. He had been on good behavior since then, but had gotten more and more sadistic at the nightclub. Sadly, Clea had been forced to let him go four months earlier. She knew how it hurt him. He was married to the job.

Clea went to Dunk with his leather-covered board of exquisite belts, wallets, and jewelry. "How're you doing, honey?" she asked him.

"I'm at my best," he said, grinning. "Business is so good, I may retire a rich man on this one night. Clea, you look fab-u-lous. Phat-to-death. You singing?"

"How'd you know?"

"You usually are when you're lit up like that. If I were five years older . . ." He growled like a tiger as Clea laughed. But it unsettled her a bit that his eyes on her were narrowed, his expression that of a far older man. Dunk and computers. The message said he had held her underwear to his face. . . . He seemed to her the perfect teenager, like a younger brother. But Dunk was brilliant, with a late schizophrenic mother whose genes he carried. Was he getting ill, going bad? Another light chill struck her and she folded her arms over her chest.

"Hey, what's wrong? You look some kinda bothered." Dunk's face was tender with concern.

"It's nothing. I just hope everything goes well."

"I'm betting on it." He kept looking at the belt he'd fashioned on her waist. "I ain't said it, but that belt is da bomb."

"Thank you," she teased. "I picked it up from a thrift shop."

"Yeah, sure." He laughed. "I was inspired when I created that."

Someone called him to their table. Alina came to her. "I hope that was our quota of trouble for tonight."

"I sure hope so. We're lucky that we don't usually have much trouble. Most people come to have a good time." They usually had an upscale clientele. Later she'd tell Alina about the missing undergarments. Tonight she intended to tell Bob and wondered if she should. He'd worry and he had his hands full with the clinic. One little message didn't constitute danger. . . . And her mind filled it in for her: didn't constitute danger—*yet*.

Wilde's Wonderland hummed with activity. Extra bartenders had been put on. Waitpersons cheerfully moved about, the females in scarlet miniskirted dresses, the males in tuxedos. Nick Redmond always drew crowds, and tonight was no exception. His voice had never been so mellifluous and there was a long line outside clamoring to get in. People of every age were hugely enjoying themselves.

Someone came up behind her, murmured in her ear, "Who *is* this gorgeous woman?" It was not the voice she had expected. She turned. "Carlton, you flatter me so."

"Mountains at sunset are not more beautiful."

She put her head to one side, batting her eyelashes, and flirted. "You're looking handsome—as always."

"You think so? I did it all for you."

Carlton Kelly *was* a handsome man. Light-skinned, with reddish brown, flat-grained hair cut and styled by his personal barber, his cream-colored silk and wool suit from London's Savile Row. He wore a dark red and cream silk foulard tie. He looked rich. He was rich. His only jewelry was a very expensive Swiss watch.

"Dance with me," he murmured.

"I'd love that." They moved through the wide patio doors onto the dance pavilion with its enhanced sound system and he held her close. She could feel the steady beating of his heart as he put his cheek against hers.

"When do you sing?"

"In just a little while."

"Your song is going to be a winner. I love it. Clea, I'm leaning on you to record it. You've got a great voice. Why don't you let me take you places with it?"

"Thank you, but I like what I'm doing here."

"I think you're making a mistake. With you singing and Nick Redmond backing you, we'd be number one on all the charts."

She shook her head. "I'd have to be developed, all those radio and TV interviews, mass audiences, magazine and newspaper interviews. I'm a private person, Carlton. I could never sit still for the hype."

"You might find you like it. But you are going to record this one CD? I want you to write songs for an album. You've got a gift—use it. A gossip columnist said I'm your secret lover. I don't intend to keep being so secret." He held her a bit away and smiled at her, as his eyes went dreamy.

"You're not secret now. We're wonderful friends."

"But I'm not your lover and I want to be." He drew her close and breathed in the fragrance of her hair and skin. Nick Redmond played his signature song, "What I Want from You," and the crowd was loving it. As they danced, Nick's combo did two encores.

"He's giving us a long dance and I'm grateful," Carlton said. "Listen, this song you're going to do tonight, well, I wish it was for me. It could be if you'd give me the chance. I can give you everything you want."

"I have a lot of what I want."

"You haven't got a husband, a baby or babies, and I think you want them. I'd like to give you those things. Let me—"

"Carlton, I—" Her head jerked up then and she saw Bob sitting alone at a nearby table inside staring at them through the glass wall. Her breath caught in her throat and a feeling of deeper warmth spread through her. Carlton saw and didn't comment, but steered Clea farther back onto the pavilion.

Bob sat with his long fingers wrapped around a piña colada. He raised the glass to his lips and the cold liquid slid down his hot throat. *Don't hold her so close, damn it,* he thought. *I don't like the idea of another man claiming her the way I know you're doing. Wild Heart's mine. She'll always be mine, the way I'll always be hers.* God, he was dying inside wanting her. Aware of an ache in his groin, he leaned back, listening to the music. He was a catholic reader and leafed through good tabloids, so he'd seen Carlton Kelly's photos, recognized him.

He wondered then about Clea and Carlton, a debonair, handsome man. Bob and his brother had inherited six and a half million dollars each from their father, set up in trust funds that had become available when each was thirty. The family owned a rubber plantation in Liberia. His father had invested wisely since his college days and had hit several lucky streaks in the stock market. He'd come in on IBM, later Microsoft and other great high-tech stocks. And Bob had inherited his father's talent for investing. But he was no match for Carlton Kelly, who owned Sepia Gold Records and, he thought, might damned well be a billionaire before he died. The man was a musical and financial genius who had become a global figure.

He glanced at his Rolex watch, a gift from his father when he graduated from medical school. And he glanced at his gold nugget cuff links from Alaska, a gift from Clea. He collected cuff links and she had a penchant for getting him the ones he loved.

When was she going to sing? He drummed his fingers on the table and his thoughts were all of Clea. He was here to enjoy Rhapsody, one of his favorite groups, and see and listen to Wild Heart sing, not to look at her and some bastard cuddle on the dance floor. His eyes sought them out again and found them moving to a slow, sexy tune. *Don't press against her body too hard, buddy.* He growled deep in his throat. Unbidden memories crowded him then, visions of Clea and himself entangled on a big bed. Now his chest constricted. In the continuing vision, he was inside her and she was wrapped around him. Lord, he thought, clenching his teeth, he didn't need this grief.

Clea and Carlton came off the dance pavilion then. She saw Bob immediately, smiled, and led them over. She stood, glowing. "I'm so glad you came. Let me introduce you two."

Bob stood to acknowledge Clea's presence and remained standing until she was seated. The two men shook hands and smiled, narrowly appraising each other quickly, then their attention was on Clea. Her heart thumped so hard she wondered if the men could hear it. She breathed slowly, looking at Bob. He was drop-dead gorgeous, she reflected, in black Italian silk with a black turtleneck pullover. His eyes on her were smoldering and the large sea-green flecks in his light brown eyes flashed fire.

They had hardly been seated when he asked her, "Dance with me?"

She hesitated. "I'd love to, but I go on in a very little while and I need to go to my office to get something. After I sing?"

He nodded. She looked so damned beautiful, so lit up.

Carlton leaned back, tapping his fingers on the table. "I'm trying to get Clea to record an album with us. I could make her a household name."

"Is that what you want?" Bob asked her bluntly.

Clea shushed them both. "Let me concentrate on what I'm going to sing. Don't make me make choices now. Listen, you two, I've got to go. Get acquainted. Enjoy my song."

She rose and left them, her tall, graceful figure threading through the crowd on the way to her office. Both men watched her. Carlton began to say something, then fell silent.

"May I join you two guys?"

Bob got up and pulled out a chair for Alina. "You bet you can. How are you, Alina? You and all four kids and Miles?"

Alina smiled widely. "They're all super except that Miles and one of my creations has a light bug. You might be seeing us tomorrow, Bob."

"I'll be there."

"Carlton, how're you doing?"

Carlton grinned. "Couldn't be better. When Clea sings, all's right with my world." He thought a moment, beckoned a waitperson, gave her an order for a straight scotch on the rocks, and said thoughtfully to his companions, "As a matter of fact, whenever Clea's around me, I need nothing else."

Alina shot a quick glance at Bob, who had taken on a poker face, but a muscle twitched just above his right eyebrow. Keeping the peace, she began a desultory conversation about Wilde's Wonderland and the crowd that night.

With pastel spotlights on her, Clea talked to the audience about her latest song. She perched on a high stool, her Gibson guitar on her lap. Bob's heart leaped when he saw that she wore his white orchid pinned to her bodice. When she had spoken a few words, the audience grew hushed and against Nick Redmond's famous sensual cadence, Clea began to hum the tune.

Copies of the song lyrics had been passed out and people studied them. Clea seemed locked into her own world then and her face bore an unearthly radiance.

"She would be a world-class crowd pleaser," Carlton murmured. Bob didn't comment.

"Well, I intend to enjoy this," Alina said. "I've got an *assistant's* assistant manager helping me, so I'm free for the moment."

"Let me buy you a drink," Bob said.

"Thank you, but I've set the table up. I know your favorite drinks and I've ordered them. See, here they are. Enjoy!"

The drinks were set on the table, but Clea's song had begun, so they listened with rapt attention. Four hot guitars, including Clea's, moaned, and the instrumental sensuality relaxed the crowd as Clea began, her soft mezzo-soprano voice caressing them, as she stood and spoke the title of the song. "Just Can't Let You Go!"

"Yeah, baby!" a male fan called out. "Just can't let *you* go!"

Bob sat forward, his throat tight. Carlton turned his chair around to face the stage.

Clea breathed deeply and began:

You put your red-hot magic
On my body and my soul.
Now I've got a hunger for you
That's way out of my control,
And I JUST CAN'T LET YOU GO, babe!
I just can't let you go.

Clea began to rock, to sway. She threw back her head and took them with her as she continued.

After all your fevered lovin'
After what you laid on me,
I think I'm gonna lock you up,
And then throw away the key,
And I JUST CAN'T LET YOU GO, babe!
I just can't let you go!

Shrugging, hips lightly gyrating, she was a younger, modified Tina Turner.

You know we are great together,
Lovin' hearts that now beat as one,

As we rock in our wild passion,
And the joy has just begun!
And I JUST CAN'T LET YOU GO, babe!
I just can't let you go!

Her voice quieted then, became mournful, hushed, pleading with a lover.

Never, never talk of leaving.
I just can't get enough of you.
You hold me with your deep kisses,
And old thrills become the new.
And I JUST CAN'T LET YOU GO, babe!
I just can't let you go.

When she had sung the title lines twice more, Clea bowed and, enthralled, the fans surged forward calling, "Clea! Clea! Clea! Again! Again! Again!"

Smiling, she blew them kisses and launched into a repeat of the song.

In the audience, Carlton slammed his fist onto the table. "That music is gorgeous. Damn it, Clea is a genius at this. I've never heard a better song, a better voice. And she arranged it, with a little help from Nick." His eyes glowed with possessive pride and Bob sat thinking that in the past Clea would have told him this information; now he hadn't known and it hurt.

Carlton's chest seemed to expand a couple of inches and a bemused Alina sipped her drink and glanced from one man to the other.

A small angry fire began to burn in Bob's chest as he thought, *Back off, Kelly, Wild Heart was mine from the beginning. She will be mine until the end.*

Moving in different social circles, Clea had finished college and Bob was in medical school when they began dating. They met at a fraternity dance at his school. She was someone else's date. From the start, they were drawn, had clicked, bonded, become engaged. One year of incredible rapture and she decided she couldn't take his mother's hatred anymore.

"I've got to make her see it my way," Carlton said. He grinned happily at Alina and Bob. "Wish me luck, you two."

"It's up to Clea," Bob said shortly.

"I agree." Alina felt wonderful about her friend's success.

When the song was finally finished and the fans had wound down, Clea sang two more of her old favorites. She blew them good-bye kisses and told them Rhapsody would take over.

"Excuse me," Bob said briefly, as he rose and went to the bandstand while Rhapsody segued into a lush, slow rendition of an old Marvin Gaye tune.

At the bandstand, Bob held out his arms to Clea. "I believe I have this dance."

She laughed happily, her heart racing with triumph and anticipation as his big hands encircled her waist and drew her close for a brief moment. He knew Kelly's eyes would be on them. Would it make Wild Heart nervous? Did she care about this man? Carlton could give her the world, Bob thought, but he couldn't give her love like the love she had known with him. He was certain of that.

Out on the dance pavilion, he held her pressed against him and she was sick with desire at the pressure of his thundering heart against hers, his lower body throbbing against hers. Why did he have to be so damned beautiful? She could have cried with frustration.

"If I had sung that song," he said against her ear, "I'd have dedicated it to you. Did you write it for me?"

Clea expelled a harsh breath, and light tears gathered in her eyes. "Don't go there, Bob," she pleaded. "We've left that place in our lives."

"You and I," he told her firmly, "we *can* go home again. We've never lost it for each other. What you wrote in that song, we lived, baby. And we can live it again. Let it happen, Wild Heart."

She tried to pull back a little, but he drew her tighter. "I can't," she whispered, "and you know the reason why."

Bob held her through two dance sets before he took her back to their table where Alina and Carlton both congratulated her profusely.

Carlton stood up, walked around to her, lifted her hand, and kissed it. "My love, you—*we* have got a knock-'em-dead winner here. Let's get started on this project right away." He ignored Bob's steely gaze.

Later, a tired and happy Clea lingered at the club until most of the crowd was gone.

"The assistant and I will close the joint down" Alina offered. "You go home and sleep late. You were so great."

"I'll take you home," Carlton said evenly.

"No. *I'll* take you home," Bob countered.

They were two alpha male animals now, protecting disputed female turf. Clea threw up her hands, laughing.

"Gentlemen," she said. "I'm a little over a mile away and I drove over. I'm here most nights and I drive myself home. I'm gonna do the same now." She blew them both a kiss as she stood up and went to get her purse and tote from her office.

At home a tired Clea happily let herself in and checked around. She frowned as she felt the same chill she had felt when she and Bob came in Wednesday from running, and it bothered her. She wished then she had let Bob or Carlton bring her home. She could have walked to work in the morning, picked her car up from the nightclub parking lot. Oh well.

Going to the refrigerator, she unpinned the orchid, patted it, opened the fridge door, and put it back into its box. She always checked the patio before going to bed. Occasionally a neighbor's dog dug in under the iron fence and vandalized her flower beds. She and the neighbor were going to have some hard words about that. As she switched on the brilliant patio lights, she froze, her breath coming faster. There were pieces of cloth scattered near the gliding doors.

Without a thought for her safety, she opened the doors and stepped outside. Bending to find out what the pieces of cloth were, she saw with horror that they were slashed and cut up pieces of her tiger, zebra, leopard, black, and dark red bikini underwear sets. She stood stock-still with fear, icy fingers trailing down her spine as her legs went weak. It took only a second to recall the computer message about how much the perpetrator had enjoyed the feel of these undergarments against his face. Another second and the words came that were so deeply engraved on her brain: *You will never guess what happens next!*

Reality took over then and she summoned the strength to turn and go inside. Mindful that the perpetrator could be watching her from a nearby spot, she moved more swiftly then. Her purse lay on the kitchen table. She locked the door and took her cell phone from it and dialed Bob's number, told him what had happened.

He was there in a very short while, holding her, soothing her, fierce in protecting her. He swore softly, enraged at the threat against her, then he called the police, who said they'd send someone over in a hurry. It hit her then. Why hadn't *she* called the police before Bob came? She was independent, but she knew she was in denial. Things like this just didn't happen in Crystal Lake, and not to her.

Bob drew the blinds in the kitchen and they waited. He kept stroking her. "Sit down," he kept saying. "Your're shaking. Relax as best you can."

She shook her head. "I want to keep standing. God, I feel so violated."

"You were violated," he said grimly.

It didn't take long for the police to arrive. Mitch Tree, a detective who came to Wonderland frequently came in. Big, florid-skinned, and sandy-haired, he and another cop went with Clea and Bob onto the patio, surveyed the cut-up pieces of undergarments. Mitch shook his head. "Lord," he said, sighing. "I think we've got a psycho on the loose."

Chapter 5

Moving quickly, Mitch and the other policeman bagged the pieces of cloth and took the bag out to their cruiser. They came back looking grave.

All four people were remembering three years ago when Laura Redding had been murdered. Her killer had never been found. Clea wondered if that murder had begun like this.

Mitch walked around the house as the other policeman checked the yard.

Finally Mitch asked them to sit down in the living room. He smiled crookedly at Bob, who was physician to his family of a wife and four young girls. "How're you doing, Doc?"

Bob shook his head. "After this, not too well."

"We'll get to the bottom of it," Mitch said grimly. He looked thoughtful for a couple of minutes. "First off, I think you ought to know Rip Jacy's escaped from state prison. It hasn't been on the news yet." He looked at Clea. "You know I was out for a few months on disability when we arrested Jacy. Please give me a brief rundown of the details. He could be behind this. I understand he hates you."

Clea nodded. "You're right, he does." She cleared her throat. "Jacy used to hang around Wonderland. I offered him a job; his wife belongs to my church. He worked off and on at the box factory and is a roaring drunk sometimes. Six houses in this area were broken into and only computers were stolen. He managed to elude police until one day I walked home and found his pickup truck parked on that side road near this house. He came out the side door and loaded a second computer on a cart outside.

"I hid behind the big oak there and watched him wheel the computers, put them on the back of his truck to cover them. I called police on my cell phone and they picked him up at his house, unloading my computers."

Mitch stroked his chin. "You testified against him. He got six years."

Clea nodded as chills ran through her. "After the trial he passed me in the court hallway, shackled, with police escorts. He said he'd come for me when he got out. His words were 'I'll keep you guessing when.' That's the last I heard." She shuddered remembering his devil-furious face.

Mitch scratched his head. "Of course he could be very shortly in Iowa, San Francisco, anywhere a plane goes. I understand Jacy isn't dumb. He's got relatives in Detroit. That's likely where he'll wind up, but you can bet he's trying to outsmart us, keep one step ahead."

Bob sat forward, caught Clea's hand. "That happened after I left? I'm sorry, honey. I wish I could have been here for you."

"Jacy's a mean drunk," Mitch said thoughtfully. "His wife has had him arrested for beating her. I'm thinking he could be the perpetrator who killed your wife, Doc."

Bob's jaw clenched then. "I hope you're able to bring him in." He turned to Clea. "How long ago was this?"

Clea thought a moment. "A little over two years. Jacy struck Mr. Manley, who's seventy. He had a heart attack and he's still not over it. For a while doctors thought he wouldn't make it. That added to Jacy's troubles."

Clea glanced at the officers. "Could I get you coffee, something to drink or eat?"

The two men shook their heads. "Thanks," Mitch said, "but we're fine. We stopped at a Wendy's." He patted his flat stomach. "Any more and I'd burst."

"Same here." The other officer smiled.

Clea thought of the e-mail then and told Mitch about it. He asked to see it and when she brought the printout back, he studied it carefully for a few minutes. He closed his eyes, rocking.

"Do you know," Mitch asked her, "if Jacy has access to computers?"

Clea shrugged. "He and Pantell Hood used to talk. Pantell told me Jacy wasn't all that good with them. Pantell laughed, said he guessed Jacy was better at *stealing* computers than using them. I asked him to go to the police; he refused. I tipped them off, then a few days later found him stealing my computers."

"I don't like the tone of this e-mail," Mitch said. "We could have a sex maniac on our hands as well as a murderer. It's a dangerous combination. Doc, tell me about before your wife was murdered. Did she mention anything about anybody she might be having trouble with?" He looked at Clea. "I know your father was a suspect. I never felt he was guilty."

"Thank you," Clea said quietly. "I never thought so either. He loved Laura, wanted to marry her."

Bob took up the conversation. "Yeah, Laura was afraid of somebody. She wouldn't talk with me about it. We'd separated as incompatible, were going to get a divorce, and she was in love with Jack, but Laura was terrified of loving any man. Her father had deserted the family when she was six and it shattered her. She was crazy about her father and he had seemed to adore her.

"She came to me, said she wanted to come back because she was in trouble. I felt sorry for her and I let her come back, but we slept in separate bedrooms, were never man and wife again." He looked at Clea, picked her hand up, and stroked it.

She looked at him with surprise.

"What is it?" Bob asked.

She shrugged. "Nothing."

But Clea sat remembering how painfully jealous she'd

been when Bob and Laura had gone back together. She'd railed at herself: *You gave him up. He isn't yours anymore.* His marrying Laura Hillman had wounded her so deeply. It had only been six months after she'd told him she wouldn't marry him. He had begun to drink too much, drive too fast. He had dated Colette, his mother's choice for him, then to everyone's surprise and his mother's anger, he had married Laura.

"My father died of a heart attack after he became a serious suspect. He was devastated." Clea felt hot tears gather behind her eyelids.

Mitch still rocked, bit his lip. "But you were never a suspect, Doc, as I remember it."

"No. I was away in Canada at a medical convention when it happened."

Mitch got up, sighing, and he said to Clea, "I see you've got one of the best security systems. Be sure you activate it as soon as possible. I suggest tomorrow. And get someone to stay with you until you do." He held up the printout. "Could you make me a copy of this?"

After the policemen left, Bob came to her, pulled her up, and hugged her tightly. "I'm spending the night, Wild Heart," he said.

"Thank you."

Angry, Bob stood holding his love. He would die for this woman, he thought, *kill* for her. And no one was going to hurt her while he was around.

They sat on the sofa for a long while and a wired Clea glanced at her beloved house she had lived in since she was a child. The living room was done in a Spanish décor with vivid colors of orange, green, and red. Romare Bearden collages lined one wall, and in a lighted alcove a Burn seascape of a calm sunset stood in splendor. There was a group of photos of beautiful wolves, Cherokee gods, possessors of the Cherokee souls. Her grandfather's Cherokee blood flowed in her veins and he was afraid of nothing.

She smiled wanly then. Mama Maxa was nearly all African and she, too, was afraid of nothing.

Bob got up, selected a CD of Mahler's "Adagietto" from his *Fifth Symphony,* and set it to repeat.

He came back, sat beside her, took her hand, squeezed it gently. "One of our favorites. I'm going to fix you valerian tea so you can sleep. Steve will fill in for me for a while today, but I intend to see that your security system is in place before I leave you."

She nodded and smiled briefly at him. "I'm so glad you're back."

"So am I. Clea?"

"Yes, love."

"You've got too damned much on your plate. Tonight was a triumph for you until this debacle. I'm not going to press you until you have a chance to get it together. I'll be your best friend, the way we were before we became lovers." He paused for a long moment. "Once this is past, when they've caught the bastard who's doing this, I'll start again. You're the love of my life, Wild Heart. There has to be some way for me to make you change your mind."

He kissed her forehead as she sat benumbed. Getting up, he went into the kitchen to prepare the tea. After a few minutes, she got up and joined him.

All her life she had been brave, living here alone after Jack's death, living with happy memories he, her mother, and her grandparents had given her.

"I feel spooked," she said softly. "I don't seem to want to be alone." She paused before she said, "When we go down to Hampton next Monday, I'm going to ask Papa Curtis to call up the spirits and see if we can find out what's going on."

"Good idea."

The water boiled quickly and he set the valerian tea to steeping, then came back and pulled her up. He sat on the cushioned chair and pulled her onto his lap. Her soft body was getting to him as his muscular, hard body and his deep protectiveness of her had begun a lover's conflagration in her soul.

He smiled sadly as he kissed her cheek. "We have to be careful. We're an incendiary pair. Let's try to remember only the calmer moments."

She laughed a little, murmuring, "Were there ever calmer moments for us?"

Looking at her gravely, he stroked her slender arm. "Surely there must have been, but I admit, I have trouble remembering them."

The tea soothed her. She took a warm shower and Bob lay on the bed thinking of exciting showers they had taken together. Then he ruthlessly suppressed his vision. Right now she was adrift, undecided, in trouble, and she needed a friend. But he closed his eyes, praying that in some near future, they would be lovers again, then wonderfully well-suited mates.

Drawing a terry cloth robe around her, Clea came out of the shower and stepped into her study. Her pristine white computer was on; she decided to leave it. The thought of Rip Jacy unsettled her, made her angry. His wife had told her he hated her. She had not thought to tell Mitch, but she would tell him later. Licking dry lips, she saw an e-mail that emblazoned itself on her brain:

Greetings Wild Heart!!!!
You will never guess what happens next.

Nightmare!

On her study wall, and an incredible lighted Burn painting of a storm at sea mirrored her feelings. Tomorrow she would tell Bob about the new e-mail. Tomorrow she would call Mitch. She couldn't face it tonight.

When she went into her bedroom, Bob sat up. "I'm going to sleep in the bedroom next to this one."

"No," she said, "please sleep in here. The bed is king-sized. We won't get in each other's way." She closed her eyes. "I can stand it if you can."

He looked at her and his heart turned over with love. "This ain't gonna be easy," he said, "but I'll take a shower and come back. Sweet dreams, Wild Heart. Nobody's going to hurt you while I'm here."

"Bobby," she said, "you look gorgeous in that suit."

"You used to call me Bobby, and men aren't gorgeous. *You* are."

"No, *you* are."

He shook his head. "Don't make me kiss you. I won't be able to stop. But I really should massage your shoulders. You're so tense."

She looked at him, yawned, said drolly, "Then *I* couldn't let you go. Take your shower."

She had called him "Bobby" from time to time after she told him he was so laid-back he should have a pet name. "What can we do to fix that? Think of a pet name you'd like. Can you fix that?"

And he had growled, "I can fix anything you've got that needs fixing."

She had gone into his arms then and they had made wildly passionate love.

She sighed.

He left the room then. She got into bed in her gown and summer robe, another layer of protection between her aching desire and him. Bob was there, but he couldn't stop the poison burning on her brain: *You will never guess what happens next.*

Chapter 6

Clea and Bob arrived at her grandparents' forty-acre farm near Hampton, Virginia, around seven A.M. on Monday a week later. They had set out from Crystal Lake around three A.M. and traffic had been light. Bob's black Porsche purred like a big cat as they neared the turnoff point. He reached over and touched her thigh lightly.

"How're you feeling, Wild Heart? You slept a bit and I'm glad."

Clea roused sleepily, sat up straighter. "I'm okay. I meant to help you drive. Why didn't you wake me up?"

"You needed the sleep," he said gruffly. "I can handle it."

As they drove down the winding lane, Clea looked at the farmhouse, a large, white-frame structure with a wrap-around, banistered front porch and big, sparkling windows that reflected the early sun. As they drove up, the door opened and Mama Maxa and Papa Curtis came out on the porch, down the front steps, and to the car.

Getting out, Clea and Bob were enveloped in bear hugs from the two older people.

"Lord, I'm so glad to see you both," Mama Maxa said. She looked at Clea narrowly. "You all right, girl? You look a little peaked and it's early."

Clea smiled and hugged her grandmother again. "You worry too much. I'm all right."

Mama Maxa reached up and patted Clea's hennaed, springy corkscrew curls. "I always love your hair this way."

WILD HEART

"Thank you." She touched her grandmother's front hair, then the back braided bun. "Yours is classically beautiful."

Mama Maxa smiled, patted Clea's arm.

Papa Curtis threw his arms around Bob for the second time and held him, patted his shoulder, rubbed his back. He loved this man like a son.

"You don't know how happy I am to see you again," Papa Curtis said. "You're a sight for weary eyes. I've missed you."

"And I've missed you both," Bob said. He turned to Mama Maxa, grinned, hugged her, and touched her unlined cheek. "You're still beautiful, I see."

Mama Maxa laughed her throaty, deeply sensual laugh. "Silver-tongued young devil. No wonder my granddaughter loves you."

"You two back together again?" Papa Curtis asked and waited on the hoped-for answer. Bob looked at Clea, who shook her head slowly.

"We're very good friends now," she said evenly as she took Bob's hand. "Things work best this way."

The two older people looked sad then and Clea looked closely at the beloved grandparents who had kept her for a couple of years when she was eleven after her mother died. They were her father's parents. Mama Maxa was very dark chocolate with black African hair that hung to her waist. She had only one broad band of silver across the front. She parted her hair in the middle, braided it, and coiled the braids into a big bun that lay against the back of her neck. Her skin was still soft and supple, her body still slim and shapely. She was seventy-four to Papa Curtis's seventy-seven. Her black eyes sparkled with mischief and joy; she and her husband touched each other at every opportunity. They left no doubt that they were still lovers.

"Perhaps one day soon," the older woman said quietly, "you will see your way clear to regaining the glory you two had."

Bob looked at Clea, his face grave. "I'd surely like that," he said.

"Perhaps," Clea murmured. "Who can know the future?" They stood on a low hill and she looked in the near distance at the rolling Chesapeake Bay that was a little over a half mile away. Sunlight caught and held the rippling water in a prism.

"Exquisite," she said. "It's fit company for you two. Oh, I love you both."

Inside the big blue and white kitchen with its white electric range and cabinets, the four people sat at a big, round oak table covered with a gaily flowered tablecloth. The room shone and a long rack of black iron and stainless steel copper-bottom pots and skillets hung over the stove and some of the lower cabinets. Bob and Clea had brought pineapple and raspberry Danish and homemade pizza.

"You're really good with this," Mama Maxa said to Clea. "Maybe I'll get a pizza stone." She stroked Clea's forearm. "You're so quiet, love. Too quiet. Something's bothering you. What is it?"

Faint tears stood in Clea's eyes then as her grandfather's probing black shaman's eyes searched her face. The tall old man's silver hair hung in long braids wrapped in leather on each side of his face. The Cherokee-red, lined face reflected good health and special knowledge. He got up, came to Clea's chair, and placed a hand on each side of her shoulders.

"I am a shaman most of my life," he said. "Your grandmother is a shaman, and you might have been one, but you chose otherwise and that is all right. The gods wish us to do only those things we want most to do. Tell me, what is it, child?"

Clea finished the last of Mama Maxa's delicious coffee laced with cream and good brandy and set her cup down. "I have to get something from my tote bag to show you."

When she came back from the living room she carried copies of the two e-mails, handed them to Papa Curtis, and told them what had happened. His face was grave, angry as he passed the pages to Mama Maxa, who gasped.

"You have called the police?" Papa Curtis questioned.

"Oh yes. I also activated my security system, which I had hardly ever used because we have so little crime. They're giving us special watch services, but their budget is tight and . . ." She bit her bottom lip.

"May I keep these?" Papa Curtis asked.

"I brought them for you to keep."

Mama Maxa stroked Clea's slender hand and there were tears in her eyes. "Oh, my dear. What kind of devil writes things like this?" A slight chill took her.

Papa Curtis nodded his head, thinking before he said hoarsely, "I will take this to the god house now, and tonight the gods will give me the substance of this man. I think it surely is a man. If the gods see fit to be kinder than they sometimes are I will get a vision, but at any rate, they will give me his substance. On this, they have never failed us. I will go now."

He got up and went out the back door to the god house.

After the older man left, the three drank more coffee. Bob looked glum, protectively glancing at Clea. Mama Maxa cleared her throat.

"The gods will tell us much before the night is over," Mama Maxa said. "You know, love, when you were here in April, Papa and I spoke with the gods about you and your life, about Bob." She licked dry lips. "The chief wolf god told us that you will know joy and happiness, but before that you would know pain and deepest sorrow. My heart bleeds with these terrible e-mail messages."

"You both taught me to fight," Clea said staunchly. "Jack taught me to fight. I am arming myself well. Whoever is doing this will not take out a weak victim." She lifted her shoulders, forcing herself to smile. "Listen, Mama Maxa, we're here for a Cherokee Indian dinner, and they take a while to prepare. Let's listen to some gospel music, then get started."

Mama Maxa nodded as sadness lingered on her face. There was a scratching at the back door and the older woman got up and let her huge gray-and-black-striped cat in. The animal ran immediately to his milk and food bowls, lapped and ate hungrily.

"Ah, he roams," Mama Maxa said, smiling, "but he seems to find little food. None of his lady friends seem to feed him. They make love to him, but they starve him."

Bob threw back his head, chuckling at Mama Maxa's remark. The woman was so delightfully earthy; she was a favorite among all the women he had known. His eyes moved from her to Clea and as their glances locked he felt his heart lurch. He loved this woman so deeply it scared him sometimes; that kind of attachment left you raw and emotionally ragged if it ended.

Clea looked down quickly. Bob had spent several nights with her since her slashed underwear had been found on her patio. She had ached with desire at his nearness, although after the first night he had slept in another bedroom.

Papa Curtis came in with a big buff and tan collie behind him. The dog trotted around the table for a pat from each person, but he was Papa Curtis's dog all the way.

Bob rubbed the dog's neck fur. "Hey, Rascal," he said, petting him. "You're still friendly, still look like a show dog." He fed Rascal a morsel of pizza, which the dog quickly gulped, then went back to his master's side.

"Sometimes I think we have the world's hungriest pets," Mama Maxa said. "He ate a wolf's share at sunup this morning."

Papa Curtis sat down heavily. "I spoke briefly with the wolf god," he said, "and the raven. They want me to cast a spell, come to them at eight tonight, and they will tell us what we need to know."

He looked at Clea closely. "I knew something was

wrong before you came and I have a wolf god caged and my tame raven on a perch. You have known these gods before."

"Yes," Clea answered.

They spent over an hour listening to gospel music and reading the Sunday papers. Papa Curtis liked the *New York Times*, Mama Maxa devoured the local papers and the *Washington Post*.

At eleven o'clock they began to prepare the extensive Cherokee Indian meal. Remembering, both Clea and Bob felt their mouths water in anticipation. Mama Maxa divided the chores and they began. Papa Curtis would do the fried chicken by an old southern African-American recipe, Mama Maxa the wild greens and the candied sweet potatoes. Bob liked preparing hominy from the already stripped-by-lye corn kernels and always did a superlative job. He also mixed the bean bread with fatback. Clea had done the garden salad and the blackberry cobbler from frozen or fresh blackberries since childhood.

Hymns played in the background as they worked. There was an air of gaiety, but a certain sadness underlay it all. Clea's trouble was on all their minds. When everything had been set to cook, Mama Maxa turned to Clea and Bob. "Why don't you two walk down to the bay? You used to have such fun there."

Outside, the two younger people followed the road down and soon stood looking out on the greenish blue calm water. They sat on a slatted steel bench and Bob turned to her.

He drew a deep breath. "I'm going down to Diamond Point for my birthday, Wild Heart," he said. I have to take you with me, keep you safe. I'm going to celebrate my birthday."

"July eighteenth."

"You remember."

"I don't forget anything about us."

"Will you come?"

She hesitated. "I don't think it would be wise, Bobby. Things happen when we're together."

"Good things."

"Yes, good things. Still . . ." She looked at him then, at the sharply etched love on his handsome face, at the light brown eyes with the big sea-green flecks that bespoke his love and his passion, his raging desire for her.

"I won't leave you alone," he said.

"I'll stay with Alina and her family. Her husband's nearly as big as you are, a construction supervisor who works out. Their house has a security system, so I'll be safe there. He used to be in security for Jordan Clymer."

"Not good enough. I'd worry. Help me celebrate my thirty-ninth birthday. I'm getting toward forty and I don't have a wife and a child or children, what I want more than anything. Look, sweetheart, I'll keep my grubby paws to myself while we're there. I just want your company. Separate bedrooms, hell, separate cottages if that's what you want."

To her surprise she told him, "I'll think about it, let you know soon."

He took her hand, pressed it to his lips as she thrilled to his touch. "Thank you," he told her.

"You proposed to me on your birthday—on Diamond Point. Do you remember?"

"Lordy, Wild Heart, how could I forget a time like that? I take out your ring from time to time, look at it, say a prayer that one day soon it'll go back on your finger. Clea, I love you so."

"We love each other," she said quietly. "That's why this is so sad."

Bob got up, found a small pebble, and tossed it into the water where they both watched the ripples spread.

They were silent watching the beautiful bay surge in the brisk wind that came up. An hour passed before Clea touched his face. "We'd better head back. Dinner should be almost ready."

Their steps were slower as they started back and Clea

studied the lovely, beautifully kept farm. Rolling meadows nurtured black angus cattle and sheep. Two sleek horses grazed—Mika and Kate. There was a big red barn and stable, a red smokehouse where hams and sausages hung in winter, and a potato house that carried white potatoes over the winter season.

Bob stopped at the old sugarcane mill where vats used to turn cane juice to rich, delicious syrup. "Antiquity," he said. "I love it all."

"It's what I want for my children," she told him.

He looked at her mostly flat belly in the navy knit slacks and sweater she wore and his eyes narrowed. He had a vision of her big with his child and for a moment he couldn't get his breath, so deep was his longing.

They sat down to dinner at six P.M. at a round table spread with fine ivory damask that was over seventy-five years old. Mama Maxa's treasured Limoges china, heavy Waterford crystal, and heavy plain silverware were all lighted by fat cream candles under glass and gave a festive air. The floral centerpiece was composed of pink and white gladiolas and maidenhair ferns.

"You've outdone yourself, lady," Bob complimented Mama Maxa.

The older woman's smile was broad. "This is in your honor," she said. "Lord, you just don't know how happy we are to see you again. I want you to come back as often as possible, and Clea doesn't visit enough."

"Yes, do that," Papa Curtis rumbled, patting Clea's hand. "You're right. Clea doesn't come often enough."

"Guilty." Clea's heart warmed with the shared love among the people around the table. In the candlelight, she looked at Bob's beloved countenance and the blood ran hot in her veins. He drew her, she thought, more deeply than a heavy magnet draws filings. Their glances met, held, and the older people looked on in fond approval.

"You have a standing invitation to visit me, you know," Clea told them, "but you're so in love with this place you can't tear yourself away."

Papa Curtis laughed heartily. "We're coming when you least expect it. Is the club still doing well?"

"It couldn't be better," Clea answered.

Leaning forward, Mama Maxa told her, "Jack would be so proud of you."

Clea could only nod. To think of Jack was to feel heartache. His presence was always with her. He had been hurt that Laura had married Bob, but he had taken it well. No matter. He would want her happiness. She thought now that she wasn't happy. She wanted this man, needed him. Reba's hatred wasn't everything. Bob loved her, wanted to marry her, wanted to put a baby or babies in her belly. For a moment she clenched her teeth; life couldn't get much sweeter than that.

"Sweetheart, you're not eating much," Mama Maxa chided her. "We've got all your favorites."

Clea forced a bright smile. "I know and thank you. I'm just settling in."

A heated look held between Bob and her, and she felt a deepened appetite for the delicious food. Biting into a piece of the succulent fried chicken, she complimented Papa Curtis, who chortled, "I have many gifts and this is one. Our gods are always pleased when I fry chicken. Make sure you take a crispy piece too. I made plenty so you and Bob can take some home."

"You're one precious man," Clea said, looking at him gravely.

Papa Curtis blushed red and he looked at his wife. "You think I'm precious, love?"

Mama Maxa's voice was husky with love. "My dear, I think you're everything that's wonderful."

Bob's bean bread was moist and delicious, filled with small chunks of prefried fatback and bacon. The candied yams were richly glazed, spiced, and lemon-flavored.

"You're going to get called on to make me bean bread at home," Clea told Bob.

He smiled at her roguishly. "I'll make you anything you want made, anytime."

"A gallant suitor after my own heart."

Bob and Mama Maxa smiled at each other.

The older people liked classical music, but preferred gospel and hymns. In honor of Bob and Clea they played Beethoven's Sixth Symphony throughout dinner. "His music is so beautiful," Mama Maxa said. "I close my eyes and I see our farm. It could have been written for us; no wonder it is called the pastoral symphony." Then she said fretfully, gazing out the window, "I've never liked daylight saving time."

"Oh?" Bob said. "You share my feelings. We don't have nearly enough darkness for me in spring and summer."

"Or me," Papa Curtis joined in. "God planned the world and nature set its rhythm. We interfere at our peril. I am forever sleepy during the false time."

The others nodded in assent before they fell companionably silent. After a while, Papa Curtis told Clea and Bob, "You both have a great heritage. Clea from mine and Jack's Cherokee heritage, and your grandmother from her mostly African heritage. Jack, of course, shared her heritage. Bob, you were blessed with a great father, a man I revered. And *you* are a great man . . ."

Bob looked up. "I thank you, but I'm not sure I deserve that compliment."

"Believe me, you do," Clea said quietly as their eyes locked again.

When the first part of the meal was finished, Papa Curtis leaned back in his chair, patting his stomach. "A sumptuous dinner," he said. "A sumptuous Cherokee dinner that we all shared in making. You know, I'm thinking now as never before of the Cherokee ways you were raised in, Clea. You were brought up to be equal to men in every way. Our way is the truest rendering of life as it should be.

"For us, women have always stood shoulder to shoulder with men. Children inherit through their mothers." He closed his eyes, grinning, then looked at Mama Maxa. "A couple of centuries ago, the British and the French called the Cherokee way of life 'petticoat government.' Well, I'm proud of those petticoats. A woman can only give herself to a man if she is his equal; she cannot be less than he is. And the whole culture gains. We have a life well worth living."

Bob nodded when Papa Curtis had finished. "What you've just said is a remarkable concept. I certainly feel this way of life is best."

Clea sat keenly aware of the psychic and sexual tension between Bob and her, the bone-deep yearning, and she groaned inside. Reba wasn't everything, she thought now. Should she change her mind, marry him? *Could* she? She was wracked with indecision.

Her blackberry cobbler was superb. Served in small portions with whipped country cream and brandy, the fat, black berries and the flaky dumplings and crust simply melted in the mouth. The others were as effusive in their praise of her as she had been of them.

When they had finally finished, they linked hands with cups of steaming black coffee set before them and said another prayer of thanks.

At ten minutes of eight they crossed the backyard to the twenty-five-by-twenty-five-foot cream stucco house to seek answers to the trouble that plagued Clea. The inside of the god house that sat in a far corner of the backyard was beautiful. Carpeted in shaggy dark green, the color of the meadow's oat grass, it was sparsely furnished with large, dark green cushions and a matching plastic-covered round oak dais in the middle of the room. Hanging fern and spider plants enhanced the setting. Polished brass lanterns gleamed softly.

A black raven sat on a wooden perch, its beady, black

eyes shining as it ruffled its feathers from time to time. A sleek gray wolf stood in a cage and looked out at them; intelligent, elegant, the animal seemed a part of the setting. He could not be free because wolves often turned dangerous around humans. Wolves' first law was protecting themselves.

Looking at the wolf, Bob smiled as he and Clea sat on the cushions. He took her hand and squeezed it, murmuring, "Women who run with the wolves."

"Always and forever," she murmured back.

Papa Curtis sat on the dais, loosened his shirt collar as Mama Maxa anointed his brow with eucalyptus oil and handed him a beaten silver cup filled with warm muscadine wine. He drank it slowly, steadily as she stood with her hand on his back. For a long time he sat there as the warm wine coursed through his veins.

"The gods are with us tonight," he told them softly. "I feel their spirit. They will help us."

And it seemed to Bob that the older man was right, there was an electricity in the air, a sense of something about to happen. An unexplainable sharp passion lay on the night air as they waited. It was eight o'clock and the raven left its perch and came to rest at Papa Curtis's feet.

"This is a very good sign," Papa Curtis said.

After a while Mama Maxa asked her husband, "Why do we wait?"

"You will see."

More minutes passed before the male wolf began to howl, almost as if singing. There was a moon outside and he was fulfilling his destiny. Finally he stopped.

"It is time," Papa Curtis said softly.

Drawing a deep breath, he tucked his legs under him, lotus fashion. He breathed deeply as he sought the special gods, selecting three of the many for tonight's magic seeking: the wolf, the bear, and the raven. Anticipation was palpable in the room as the old shaman sank into his trance. Yes, he thought, just as he went under, the gods were with him tonight. They would give him the answers he needed to know. Light perspiration filmed his face as he got up, crouched, and began to move about almost like a dancer.

After a few minutes he began to shout in hoarse, indecipherable language as he talked to the gods. Then he was quiet, listening. This interchange seemed to Clea to go on for eons of time as Bob gripped her hand tightly.

God and the Cherokee gods and all nature were all in her heart and soul. The universe demanded Bob as her mate to fill her body and her life. But she stubbornly held out. Her children would be happy as she had been happy, without strife and the virulent hatred Reba Redding held for her.

Papa Curtis was in tune with the gods now. The very word *shaman* meant "to know" and the gods were speaking to him. The wolf did not howl again. The raven sat quietly and the man held the absent bear god only in his vision. Then a mist seemed to fill the air in the lantern light and it was eerily still.

The pungent smell of pinecones and needles and the delightful perfume of catalpa bush branches soothed them as Papa Curtis danced feverishly. He stomped and kicked out his legs, incredibly limber for a man his age.

"Give me the one who does these evil deeds," Papa Curtis chanted suddenly. "Give me his *presence*. Give me his *spirit*. You have told me this is a violent man."

Agitated now, he hopped about around Clea and Bob. His breath was deep, ragged, and he moaned loudly again and again. Finally he gave a hoarse, triumphant cry.

"Tell us what you see, my love," Mama Maxa implored him, unsure that she could reach him now.

He breathed heavily and his voice was sepulchral, like a voice from the grave as he clasped his hands in front of him. "I thank the heavens that the gods are with me, because I smell the breath of evil so foul it sickens me to retching. I see the fierce light of fury so violent it nearly blinds me." He paused for a long moment before he continued in a hushed voice. "And there is cunning, devil cunning like the jackal and the coyote. Show me his face, I beg you. Give me his bodily presence. Let me *see* this man."

Sweat poured down Papa Curtis's face and body and he was alternately hot and cold. The gods were not always comfortable to be with, but he was grievously disappointed. The physical presence of the enemy did not come.

"Tell us what you see, love," Mama Maxa pleaded.

After a long moment he answered, "The gods are only with me *most* of the way," he began as he started to emerge from the trance. Sometimes in such trances he could not be reached at all, but sometimes Mama Maxa—herself a shaman—could reach him even in his trance. But tonight was special; she shared the gods with him without being in a trance.

He rested as he regained full reality and Mama Maxa mopped his face and neck with a big white towel, then removed his shirt and blotted the perspiration from his arms and shoulders. Bending, she kissed his brow.

Papa Curtis shook his head. "The gods would not give me a full sighting," he said. "I do not know why they hold back; I serve them well. But I will try again soon. I sensed our enemy's spirit, saw it so plainly. Did I tell you his spirit?"

"Yes," Mama Maxa said. "It is a truly terrible spirit."

"As wicked as I have ever known." He was grieved as he looked at Clea. "I will give you a silver and turquoise amulet that belonged to your great-grandfather, my father. Keep it close to you and it will protect you."

He pondered his next statement before he spoke from where he sat. "Bob's presence was very plain. He is your fierce protector even as we are. Stay close to him, my love. Let him back into your heart the way he was before. You will need him and he will be there. Walk with care. As I have told you, there is pain ahead for you and deepest sorrow, but remember that the gods also have told me that you will know joy and happiness."

He got up and staggered to Bob and Clea. Placing a loving hand on Clea's shoulder and the other on Bob's, he told them, "I must rest now. Sleep. The gods have worked my spirit hard. Be as one the way you were."

It was a blessing and a benediction and Clea felt it surround her, fill her heart and soul. Later, when they left for home with the silver and turquoise amulet in her purse, the older man was sleeping and she wondered if the gods filled his dreams.

Chapter 7

Out on the highway Bob drove as Clea mused on the day they'd just spent. Bob looked at her closely. "You okay?"

"Yeah, I am." Then as a slight chill coursed through her, she amended that. "Bob?"

"Yes love."

She began hesitantly, "When Papa Curtis was in that trance, after a few minutes I felt the presence of whoever is doing this. It was evil the way I've never known it before and it scared me. The god house smells good, but I smelled the odor of death too and that scared me . . . Did you smell anything?"

"No, but as you know I don't have the keenest sense of smell. I felt a whole lot there. It was eerie. There's a lot more to this world than what we see."

Bob drove expertly, listened intently before she continued. "But you know something, I'm glad he sought the gods, because I'm not afraid anymore. Whatever comes, I feel now I can deal with it."

Bob patted her hand on the seat between them. "Don't forget Papa Curtis cautioned you that I'm your protector. You're to lean on me, as much as a woman who runs with the wolves leans on anyone." He chuckled a bit.

"We lean, all right. Independence never meant needing no one. Thank you."

"For what?"

"For just being you. I want to drive after we've gone another seventy miles or so."

"Sure you want to?"

"Yes. You need a rest."

"I've rested all day. You're the one who was in on the vision. That must have made you at least a little tired."

"A little, but I'm feeling full of energy."

It had been on Bob's mind off and on ever since the night they had found the cut-up undergarments scattered on her patio near the side door, but he hadn't remembered to ask her. Now he said, "The other night when the police came and Mitch asked me about Laura and I said we didn't live together as man and wife when she came back . . ."

He hesitated a long moment before she asked, "And?"

"Well, you looked really startled. Surprised. Why?"

She was quiet then, wondering if she should tell him, because it was going to make him mad. "Reba told me you and Laura were planning to have a baby . . ."

Bob looked at her sharply, then jerked his attention back to the road. "Reba told you *what?*"

She repeated what she had said and he asked grimly, "And when did she tell you this?"

"A couple of months after you and Laura went back together."

"She came back. We didn't go back together."

"Okay. I ran into Reba downtown. She was all smiles when she told me and I wondered about it because I knew she didn't like Laura any more than she'd liked me."

"She knew Laura and I were just living under the same roof, nothing more. She wanted to hurt you, pure and simple." His hands clenched on the wheel. "God, I'm always amazed at the lengths my mother will go to when she wants to pull a dirty deed. And Dad loved her so much . . ."

"She's still a beautiful woman. She must have been a goddess when she was younger."

"It depends on what moves you. I guess she's hurt and manipulated me so much I long ago stopped resonating to her. You know something, Wild Heart. I miss stroking your engagement ring. I want to change this subject until I can cool down. Okay?"

She smiled then. "You're something else. Hold me away from you emotionally if you want the right answer as to my going with you to Diamond Point. You're more dangerous to me than any other threat."

"All right, I'll back off on that. I want the right answer. We could have fun."

"We always have fun." She paused for a very long moment. "I think you should know Carlton has asked me to marry him."

Bob felt his heart lurch and squeeze tight. "Why doesn't that surprise me? And what was your answer?"

"That I can't marry him while I'm still in love with you."

"You told him that?"

"I had to be honest. Carlton is a nice guy, one of the best, after you. And you know something? I was considering marrying him in spite of loving you. Even arranged marriages work very well sometimes and people become happy. People fall in love long after they're married. Love can be so many things."

"Don't marry him. Don't even think about it. Marry me."

"And give Reba a heart attack?"

"My mother's heart is a subject that enrages me. I've talked with her doctor many times since I became a doctor and I've checked her personally from time to time. There's nothing wrong with Mother's heart. Yes, her heartbeat accelerates sometimes, but there's no danger. She's used that ploy since Ruel and I were children.

"What did your father think about her heart? She suffered, took to her bed when we were engaged."

"She always did take to her bed when anything displeased her. She's a female Redd Fox in *Sanford and Sons*, except the situation isn't funny. It's lives she's playing with. Yours. My father's. Ruel's. And mine."

"You didn't say how your father reacted to what she did and we've never talked about it."

He laughed a little. "We were too busy, Wild Heart, too busy loving each other to talk about negative things. Dad loved her so he knuckled under. He used to tell us to be kind, that maybe she had a gut feeling about her heart that we couldn't know. He always said people had been known to have heart attacks and die when every test showed their hearts to be normal. Like I said, he loved her. There's no accounting for tastes . . ."

"I'm glad we had this conversation, Bobby. It explains a lot of things."

"I'm glad. If my mother ever tells you anything else, please come to me."

"I will."

The rest of the trip home was uneventful. With Clea driving, they ran into a soft, misting rain fifty miles from Crystal Lake. The mist reminded Clea of the fog that had seemed to be in the god house when Papa Curtis invoked the spirit of the gods. She thought about the amulet in her purse, decided she'd take it to a jeweler she knew and have it put on a chain, and she'd wear it around her neck at all times.

As she rounded the first bend on the way to her house at the edge of Crystal Lake, Bob had dozed off and Clea felt happy to be back. With a groan she thought of all the fresh and canned and frozen food they had to unload. Her grandparents had always been generous people as she was with them.

Clea hummed "Just Can't Let You Go" and felt happy. Another road bend and they'd be home. As she turned the bend, it hit her like a fist to her stomach. The lights from police cars flashed in front of her house. Three police cars. The clock on Bob's car dashboard registered one forty-five A.M. She called his name sharply.

"What the hell?" he exclaimed, coming wide-awake, sitting bolt upright.

A policeman stood by a police cruiser.

"Officer, what's going on?" Clea asked with alarm as she came to a halt.

"Ma'am," he said. "Are you the owner?"

"I am. Is Detective Tree here?"

"Go right in. He's here. He'll tell you. Nobody's been hurt or anything."

"Was there a break-in?" Bob asked.

"Go in," the young officer urged them. "Detective Tree will tell you all about it."

Three policemen were gathered on the patio at the side of the house. Bob and Clea rushed over, seeking answers. Clea gasped to see more slashed pieces of her undergarments. These were the lighter-colored panties and bras. Lacy. Some satin. Especially pretty. She felt nausea flood her bloodstream.

"My God," she whispered in the bright lights. "Is that blood on the pieces?"

"Sure looks like it," Detective Tree said shortly. "We'll find out in short order whether it's animal or human. Sometimes these clowns try to frighten you as much as possible."

This was no clown, but a snarling devil, she thought sadly. The gods had told them that.

"We got here only a little while ago," Mitch Tree said, "and we've been discussing just how to proceed. We're going to bag the evidence and we'll need to ask you some questions. The officers here will handle the yard, finish checking it out. Could we go inside?"

Clea, Bob, and Detective Tree checked the house. "We'll check the computer later," he said, as they checked her study. Then they sat in the living room as he questioned her. After a little while she asked if he'd like coffee for himself and the men. He grinned.

"I'm going to be a nuisance and say yes. This came

from out of the blue and I'd feel better if I were wider awake. We were going to stop on the way back."

The coffee didn't take long to make and Clea popped small pizzas in the microwave. The men in the yard came in, got their coffee in proper cups. They took a cup for the man stationed at the police cruiser in front.

When the food and coffee had been consumed, Detective Tree leaned back, a wide smile on his face. "Lady, thank you more than you know. Who's your pizza connection? I'll get there in a hurry."

Clea smiled back, pleased. "I make them and I'll give you two dozen frozen ones. Your wife and kids will love them."

"If they get to them before old Dad wolfs them down." Leaning forward, he got serious then as he finished the last of the questions. He began to get up. "Let's check your computer," he said. "As I told you, we're really beat for time and money, but I'm tracking this down. It takes time and we've got a wee budget these days, but I'm confident I will find out whose computer this garbage is coming from."

Clea felt anxious beyond the telling as she called up her messages. There were few and *Nightmare* was prominent. His message this time was more pointed, more threatening:

> Wild Heart, you always excite me, as I plan to surely excite you. This time the blood is someone else's. Next time soon, it will be *your* blood. Spilling blood is my passion. You'll never guess. . . .
>
>   Nightmare!

Reading the message, she felt dizzy and angry, helpless. But wolves, she thought fiercely, were the least helpless of creatures and wolves were her band, were the god-creatures she ran with.

Clea printed several copies, gave one to Mitch, then to

Bob, who swore softly and put his arms around her as her brain worked clearly.

She had raced the words through her mind again and again, studying them, winnowing what information she could gain. Finally she said, "The words don't sound like Jacy to me. Somehow they sound romantic, even mildly poetic. It's just a hunch. Someone more intelligent perhaps?"

Mitch grunted. "I've done a lot of research on Jacy, talked with his wife and friends. He's plenty intelligent when he wants to be, and I'm told he fancies himself a lover. He's had a year at community college with a major in English and his wife said he likes to try his hand at poetry. He's got a lot of options besides being a thug."

Clea's heart fell as she licked her dry bottom lip. She had hoped it wasn't Jacy, because she was afraid of him and he knew it. His hate-filled eyes and countenance still haunted her as he had made his threat that she would never guess when he would come at her.

Chapter 8

On Wednesday, following the visit to Mama Maxa and Papa Curtis, Clea walked over the polished main floor of Wonderland. Everything looked really good, she decided. Hardwood floors, brass fittings, and long racks of barware gleamed. There was the expensive, delightful fragrance of sandalwood and soft music from Muzak.

This was always a fairly slow night, with Thursday's tempo increasing a little. Friday and Saturday nights were crowded with glitzy people who looked and felt great and spent money as if it were going out of style.

A tall, slender, chocolate-skinned man walked in. "Yo, Clea," he greeted her. "I'm looking for my woman. Did she get to work?" He grinned impishly.

This was Alina's husband, Kemper, a science teacher at Crystal Lake High School. Clea had always thought he was one of the best-looking and most likable guys around.

"She's been here awhile," Clea said as Alina spotted her husband and came racing over.

The couple hugged as if they hadn't seen each other for a while and didn't have a passel of kids between them. "Is everything all right?" Alina asked anxiously. "Are the kids—"

Kemper placed a finger to her lips. "The kids're fine. I just got an urge to see you and I'm not too far away, so I drove over. Wanted to see your fine, brown frame and tell you in person how much I love you. And don't they say act and kiss like there's no tomorrow?"

Kemper kissed his wife then, long and thoroughly. They took no note of Clea, who stood nearly in delighted amusement. Her heart hurt with friendly envy and pained longing for a relationship like they had. Wonderland staff gazed at the couple, then began to smile broadly. Someone clapped a bit, but no one took it up. This was too personal.

Clea continued her rounds. Out in the kitchen, she inspected the big, shining steel equipment that helped handle the thousands of delicious sandwiches they made. She greeted the staff with a big smile. She never hired anyone who didn't have a better-than-average sense of respect and ebullience. Pantell Hood had been the one exception and Jack had hired him. Was it her imagination that Pantell hadn't been around as much as he had formerly been? She shrugged. Thinking about him brought thoughts of the threatening e-mails, and it pleased her that she was now much calmer. At least trouble wouldn't hit her unaware. She had been warned. Alina was going to handle things and she was going home early to meet Bob, who worried more about her than she worried about herself.

She sat in her office checking a ledger in preparation for her three-thirty appointment with her accountant. It was two o'clock and she hadn't eaten lunch. She thought it did wonders for the system to skip no meals but to eat less. She'd get someone to fix her soup, a small sandwich, and a salad before the accountant came, and she intended to do fried catfish for Bob at home tonight. Clea leaned back in her chair, pondering whether she would go to Diamond Point with Bob to celebrate his thirty-ninth birthday.

His face as he had said he wasn't married and had no children came up in fantasy. He'd looked so sad. Their birthdays were only two months apart. She'd be thirty-one and she, too, had no mate, no children. She ached with emptiness.

At a light knock she sat up straighter and Alina came

in, shut the door, leaned against it. "Brace yourself," she said. "You've got company you won't believe."

Clea didn't feel like company at that moment. "Has Kemper left?" she asked, yawning. "You two are something else."

Alina blushed. "He didn't stay long. He just wanted to emotionally ravish his wife. Don't you want to know who your company is?"

Clea shrugged. "If it's not Denzel Washington, I'm not interested."

Alina laughed and walked over to the desk. "Bob would kill him, and U.S. women would be on your neck." She hesitated. "Reba Redding is standing at annoyed attention waiting to be ushered unto you. I took my time getting up here. Let the glamorous old bat wait."

A frown creased Clea's forehead and her breath got suddenly short. "I wonder what the hell she wants."

"Your head on a stick probably. She was her usual charming, arrogant self. Lord, but she has on some gorgeous rags. I'm sure her clothes budget alone would run our household."

"You're happy," Clea said tiredly, "and I don't think she is. Bring her on." Clea's laugh was short, harsh. "Then maybe you'd better call the police."

Alina picked up her friend's hand and squeezed it. "You hang in there, tiger. It'll be the day when you can't win over the likes of her."

Seated on Clea's leather sofa, Reba Redding looked around her at Clea's office. She felt a sense of satisfaction she always felt when she knew she looked unusually well, and the leather lavender Armani outfit she wore made her look her best. Tan Ferragamo pumps made her legs shapely, young.

Soft, classical music played in the background. "What

can I get you to drink or eat?" Clea asked, noting that her voice sounded strained.

"Nothing, thank you. I won't be here too long. Do you like classical music?" And she continued without waiting for Clea to answer. "Somehow I didn't think you were the type. Ruel's told me you write rhythm and blues songs. I think he called them rhythm and blues. . . ."

"Yes. I'm very good with them."

Reba's mouth drew down in a droll smile. "My granddaughter and a niece of my daughter-in-law's listen to that music, although I don't pretend to understand or appreciate the music or lyrics." She lifted her shoulders, spread her hands. "Are your lyrics as raunchy as the ones I've heard these kids play?"

Clea drew a deep breath. "They're sexy. Some may call them raunchy. I guess it's a matter of taste. Being a teenager is a difficult time, Mrs. Redding. Hormones are exploding and they need an outlet. Songs are about as safe as anything can be. Songs help and mine are loving, tender, caring. I write country-western, pop, inspirational and gospel lyrics, and melodies too."

"Hmmm. Funny, Bob never told me that, but then you two weren't together too long. You're a bundle of apparent contradictions. Clea, I'm not going to beat about the bush. A few years back, you loved Bob enough to let him go. You must have realized you weren't suitable for him. . . ."

Clea drew and expelled a harsh breath. "I broke off with Bob because you hated me and I didn't intend to raise kids in an atmosphere of hatred. I've known too much love for that."

Reba's perfectly coiffed dark auburn-haired head came up and her sea-green eyes on Clea were cold, offering no hint of friendship. "You and Bob are so different, my dear. He was raised with every advantage. My roots go back to the Mayflower and his father was a world-famous heart surgeon. A U.S. president has visited our home. U.S. congressmen and women come to our house with fair frequency. While you . . . "

Clea was in her element now. She pitied the woman facing her with her arrogance and her hidden and denied pain.

"While I was raised with love so great it defies description," Clea told her. "My early years were beautiful, Mrs. Redding. I had love and affection, respect and caring I wouldn't swap for all the material and societal trappings in the world. I'm going to be less than humble and say I run a highly successful business. I have an MBA, great friends, a lot of self-esteem. And I'm happy much of the time. I think God has blessed me."

Reba swallowed hard. "And well you should be, in spite of your father's untimely death. I understand from Ruel that you have a close friend, a Mr. Carlton Kelly, who is a rhythm and blues record mogul, and that he wants to marry you."

"That's right."

Reba laughed shortly. "Why don't you marry him, be happy? Bob is my first born. I love him so much and I'm so proud of him, although I wanted him to follow in his father's footsteps. He changed courses after training as a heart surgeon." She sighed. "Such a disappointment. The clinic work isn't good enough for him."

"Even as I am not good enough for him."

"Oh, my dear," Reba said, her hands fluttering, "you choose not to understand."

"Perhaps I understand all too well."

"You're not making this any easier, Clea. Let Bob go! He would know then that he loves Colette, my goddaughter, if you let him go."

Clea's gaze probed the older woman's ruthlessly. "Bob knew Colette long before he knew me. His ring wasn't on her finger when I came along and we began."

Reba nodded. "In time I'm convinced they would have married if you hadn't come along. They enjoyed each other's company so much. They were together a lot. I think they were meant for each other. They've known each other all their lives. Colette is like my daughter."

"Perhaps they were too close for him to be romantically interested."

Reba's eyes got dreamy then. "No. I've walked in on them kissing and it was passionate. They would have beautiful children." Her voice sounded wistful then. "What do you intend to do? You and Bob are seeing each other again since he got back."

"You've noticed."

"I'm an active woman." She put an aristocratic hand to her bosom. "If it weren't for my heart, I'd be even more active." Clea was inwardly thinking of Bob's assessment of his mother's heart.

Reba leaned forward and her tone was accusatory. "I was returning from a friend's house before dawn Monday morning. There were several police cars around your house. We asked the policeman what the trouble was and he said he couldn't tell us. What *was* the trouble, Clea?"

Clea shook her head. "I can't tell you either. It was personal."

Reba's very fair skin reddened as she toyed with a ring of many carats on her finger. "Laura's murder left me on edge even if it did happen a few years ago. I wonder about every police car I see. A place like your club is bound to attract a rougher element. There is talk about mob connections, protection . . ." She shrugged.

"I run a clean shop," Clea said heatedly. "We do no gambling here. I have no mob connections and pay no protection."

"Then why can't you tell me about the other night?"

"Because I don't choose to. I don't think it's any of your business."

"My son is my business."

After a moment Clea told her, "Mrs. Redding, you should have cut the apron strings a long time ago. In spite of you, Bob is one of the world's finest humans, an exemplary man. You did your part, now why don't you let him go? Let him marry whoever he pleases? If that woman is Colette, I'll give them my blessing."

Reba began to get up. "You're a hard woman, Clea Wilde." Her voice carried rare bitterness. "I'm going to do whatever I can to dissuade Bob from marrying you if he still intends to. I see you're not wearing a ring and that's good. It means I still have a chance to make him change his mind. Thank you for talking with me and I will see you around, I'm sure."

Afterward, Clea watched handsome, sixty-two-year-old Reba Redding go down the steps and glide across the polished main floor. The woman looked around her, walked slowly as if she were studying the club as she had studied its owner.

Reba's fragrance had been expensive floral, not evil, but that was the public side of her. Clea knew the woman hated her and had just said she'd do whatever she could to get Bob away from her. Reba's eyes had been flat with old hatred.

Bob let himself into Clea's house around eight P.M. "Hey, sweet stuff," he called and she came out of the kitchen and looked with surprise at the very large, white cloth-covered object he carried, with long steel legs protruding.

"What on earth?" she began.

"Present for you," he explained.

She looked at the oddly shaped object. "A present on iron legs?"

He set it down and whipped off the cover. A forbidding-looking bird peered at her from his perch, silent for once.

Clea burst out laughing. "Thank you, I think, but this is going to take some getting used to."

"Where do you want the old boy?"

"Over here, I believe," she said, indicating a spot near a large rubber plant.

The parrot cocked his head to one side as if assessing Clea and his new surroundings.

"Am I right that this is an African Grey parrot, a big bird?" she asked.

"Right, and he's one of the best."

"They're expensive, Bob. I once started to buy one. That one set you back over two thousand dollars. How much over?"

"Never mind. Parrots like this make a better watchdog than a German Shepherd, and keep you better company."

"How much?" she demanded.

"It's a gift. You don't ask how much for a gift. You just accept it and be happy."

"How much?"

"Okay. Twenty-eight hundred and cheap at the price. Richard at the pet shop was his owner and the poor guy's getting allergies from his pet. This parrot has the world's best training, but I warn you, he's possessive." He spelled out the last word and Clea laughed.

"I'm not fond of possessive people or birds. How do I handle that trait?"

"You get company and he acts up, just throw this cloth over his cage—after you put him in his cage. I'm assuming you'll let him have the run of the house."

"If he behaves himself."

"Do you like him?" Bob looked a little anxious.

"I think I'm gonna love him. Does he have a name or do I get that honor?"

As if in answer to her support, the parrot ruffled his feathers and squawked, "Pretty girl! Pretty girl!" then whistled a deep, long wolf whistle that would make a sailor blush.

Clea laughed merrily as Bob said, "Wild Heart, meet Rufus, your protector and apparent suitor."

With Rufus settling in to his new surroundings, Bob

helped Clea serve dinner. They ate in the dining alcove on blue-flowered earthenware. The fried catfish came from the three-acre pond on Bob's place. The meal was simple, consisting only of that dish, scalloped potatoes with sour cream, and a big garden salad. It was one of Bob's favorite meals. Dessert was strawberry cheesecake she had made the day before.

Looking at Clea in pale blue silk pajamas with a surplice top, Bob leaned forward, "You look beautiful tonight, Wild Heart, and you seem more relaxed. Don't get too relaxed. Something tells me the devil after you means business."

Clea's blood cooled. "I mean business too. I own two guns and I'm a very good markswoman. He isn't going to find me easy prey."

He nodded. "I want you to be careful. Don't set yourself up for something you can't handle." Then he paused.

"My mother's got tunnel vision where I'm concerned," he continued. "She's never realized that my life belongs to me, not her. She's the same way about Ruel."

Later they stretched out in the living room and listened to Luther Vandross and his magic, then to Barry White. As Barry spun his magic, Bob grinned. "It's not hard to tell why he's called the make-out artist. That music is for making it in all its glory."

Clea nodded, smiling, remembering how they had once listened and what incredible things had happened. She sighed, causing Bob to look at her quizzically and ask, "How're you holding up, baby?"

"You mean about the e-mails, the messed-up lingerie?" she asked slowly.

"Yeah." His look was a fervent protective embrace.

She drew a deep breath. "You know I told you I'm just not running scared anymore. My security system is the best and we've been over this before, police and sheriff's cruisers patrol often. Papa Curtis's vision said this man is cunning, and a fool is not cunning. I say this to say he'd have to be a fool to blunder in with all this monitoring going on."

"I just hope you're right, Clea. Sometimes the smartest of us are fools. No more e-mails?"

"None, but I have a hunch that, give him time . . . Bob?"

"Yes honey."

Should she tell him? He had asked her to. "Reba was by to see me today."

He sat bolt upright. "What the hell did she want?"

"She wanted to talk about her son, you, and me, the big, bad female wolf."

Bob felt his chest constricting as Clea recounted the conversation, trying to fill him in with details. He listened intently and when she finished he looked at her levelly, saying, "So of course this knocks your going to Diamond Point with me to hell in a handbasket."

She smiled and got up, sat beside him, and he rose to a sitting position. "No," she said, "as a matter of fact it made me make up my mind to come with you. There's so much we need to discuss and both of us need a break. You're back so short a time, but things have been hectic and you need a rest." She hunched her shoulders. "I couldn't be more mixed up—"

"Hey, Wild Heart, it took a minute to sink in. You're coming with me!" He whooped and hugged her tightly as the parrot stirred and grumbled, "Graham cracker! Bring it on!"

Clea chuckled. "I think you've started something. Alina's going to have to keep him while we're away. I hope he likes children."

"He's adaptable; Richard told me that. I've had him a few days. Clea, you've made me a very happy man." He leaned forward and kissed the corner of her mouth.

Clea bit her lip. "You may not be so happy when I tell you this: I've been thinking a lot lately. Seeing Artie at the clinic has made me think about a lot of things. Reba's coming by today brought it down front—she's never going to stop hating me, trying to separate us, even from friendship."

"My mother's got her own life to live," he said firmly. "And she'd better start living it, because I sure as hell am going to live mine. What is it you want to tell me?"

She drew a deep breath. "Again I'm thinking seriously of saying yes to Carlton's proposal."

He caught her hand, held it too tightly. "Damn it, Wild Heart, you said just last Monday you wouldn't marry him because you love me. What changed your mind?"

She didn't hesitate. "Artie and Reba. Artie lives in a kind of hell and our children would know a little of that hell with a grandmother who hates their mother."

"We could move away," he said grimly. "Diamond Point. There're many other places."

Clea shook her head. "Not an option. I'm rooted here. You had to come back. You weren't happy away from here . . ."

"Because of you. I came back for you."

"And I'm glad you came. You add to my life what's been missing these past several years." She paused a long moment. "Bob, what about you and Colette? We never talked about her much."

"What about her? You and I were busy, Clea, busy being in love, making love like nothing I ever hope to know again with anyone else. Colette and I were childhood friends. In my teens I had rheumatic fever and she came and read to me every day for months. I took her to the junior and the senior proms. We kissed lightly, but never caught fire—at least I didn't. I went away to college and med school and that was that. Then I met you. Why do you ask?"

She disengaged her hand and stroked his. "I feel now that you might care more deeply for Colette than you know, but she's your mother's choice and you're in full rebellion against your mother. You couldn't love the Queen of Sheba if Reba approved of her. Is that my attraction for you perhaps—that she hates me?"

"No way. We were drawn to each other, Wild Heart, from the beginning, drawn to each other to the marrow of our bones. I'd give up my hope of heaven if that's what it takes to get you, and I know you feel that way too. Have the courage of your true feelings. Tomorrow we're going to visit Artie and his parents again. D'you know what Artie told me when he came to the clinic a couple of days ago?"

"If Artie said it, it was interesting," Clea murmured.

Bob smiled widely, looked pensive. "'Doc,' he told me, 'you oughta marry Miss Clea and have a little boy like me to love the way you love me.' Ah, Wild Heart, the wisdom of children."

Clea nodded in agreement as her body thrummed with wanting Bob, with needing him so badly it hurt. But she had to have clear vision now; her future was at stake.

Since the first wildly passionate kisses, Bob had kept his word. He was tender, concerned, and kept his blazing ardor in check. The trouble was, the more he held back, the more her heart and soul surged toward him, craving what they once had felt and dreamed.

Chapter 9

Bob and Clea sat on the front porch of Artie Webb's house on Saturday morning. Bob had finally been able to get a time when he and Clea and Artie's parents were free to sit down and talk about Artie. The yellow clapboard house was snug, attractive, and well-tended flowers bordered the large front yard. Looking around them, Bob was glad Artie at least had pleasant physical surroundings.

Cade seemed in a good mood this morning and Artie hung by his dad, but he had greeted Bob and Clea effusively. Now he moved from Cade's side to Bob's until he finally looked at Clea and smiled, saying to Bob, "You two gonna get married like I asked you?"

Bob threw back his head, laughing. "I'm trying, kid. Believe me, I'm trying."

"Artie!" his mother remonstrated, her eyes twinkling.

But Cade's dander came up suddenly. "You're too fresh, boy," Cade said angrily. "Haven't I told you about dipping into grown folks' business?"

Artie looked crestfallen, hurt, and Bob's and Clea's hearts went out to him. He had been so cute asking his question. Bob looked at Cade. "It's okay," he said. "I loved his asking. I wish I had him around all the time."

"And I certainly didn't mind," Clea said.

"No matter," Cade grumbled, "I don't tolerate fresh kids. He's got to learn. Artie, go in the house and play or do something."

"Aw, Dad," Artie whined.

Cade began to stand and his hand moved to his belt buckle. Artie's eyes were suddenly full of fear.

"Move!" Cade shouted and Artie scurried into the house.

Cade sat back down, full of good spirits again. "How's he doing, Doc?" he asked.

Marian was still with sad eyes. "Yes, how *is* Artie doing?" she asked quietly. "You ran tests when we were by earlier this week."

"He's not doing too badly," Bob told them, "but there are some things I'd like to see changed. Artie may be developing leukemia. He's got symptoms that bother me. I've called in Dr. Carl Heller, an eminent oncologist from D.C., and he's going to keep a close watch on him..."

Marian sat up straight. "But you'll still see him?" she asked anxiously.

"I'll never stop seeing Artie," Bob assured her. "He just needs more specialized help than I can give him."

"Leukemia," Cade said slowly. "Don't most people die with that?"

"Not anymore," Bob assured him. "We've come light-years from those days. Dr. Heller thinks Artie may have acute lymphocyte leukemia, but he has to run more tests. Now this is going to mean Artie's going into D.C. Dr. Heller is affiliated with Georgetown Hospital and has a large practice. He's one of the best oncologists in the country, so your son is in the best hands."

Cade sat musing. "What's this going to cost me?"

Bob looked at him levelly. "You've got good insurance." Cade was a sales rep at a large Crystal Lake rubber and tire sales company.

"The best," Cade said proudly. He loved his job and wished he loved his life as much. "However, there's always extras and specialists don't come cheap. Once or twice my insurance has turned me down."

Bob nodded, beginning to be angry that Cade seemed more concerned about money than about his son. "I think you may be pleasantly surprised. Dr. Heller knows you're not rich. We'll do what we can to hold expenses down." He fully intended to pay the extra charges out of his own pocket, make out an arrangement with his friend, Carl Heller.

Now Cade grumbled, "Boy's been more trouble than he's worth since he's been born. Now, me, I was always healthy as a horse. He's been no fit child for me. Doesn't care much for sports, whines when I roughhouse him, a regular sissy."

Bob felt his gorge rising and Clea frowned. Marian looked as if she were drowning in her own anger. Smiling wanly, she said to them, "Excuse me a minute. I'm going to check on Artie."

"Aw hell, woman, sit down," Cade said. "You're always hanging over the boy."

But for once his wife paid him no mind and went into the house.

When his wife had gone, Cade turned to Bob. "You're pretty crazy about my son, aren't you, Doc?"

"Yes, I am," Bob said.

"Well, don't get too used to him. Social worker called me yesterday, said she'd got some complaints about Artie's being bruised, asked me a few personal questions. Now I figure you just may have reported me."

"I did report you," Bob said evenly. "I told you I would. Artie should never, under any circumstances, be handled roughly, physically or emotionally."

"He's delicate, I reckon you'd say, like any little sissy." Cade's tone was scathing.

"He's *sensitive*," Bob said crisply, getting angry again. "So many gifted children are. I wish you appreciated him more."

"I could be mad as hell at you, Doc, but I'm not. Artie's *mine*. I'm his father and you're his wannabe." His gaze got distant then. "Just maybe God's got other plans for Artie. Like I said, I've always heard people with leukemia don't live out their time. I had a sister with it and she died at thirty-five, my age. Doctors couldn't or didn't help her. Now maybe God's got other plans for Artie."

"And maybe he intends to keep him here, blessing us all," Bob said shortly.

Marian came back holding two sheets of white paper. She had been standing quietly by the inner door and had heard the last part of the conversation. Now Bob said, "Artie will need to be driven in to D.C. twice weekly for appointments. Will you do this?"

Cade shrugged. "How long is this gonna go on?"

"Three months, four . . . for as long as it takes." Bob spread his hands.

"Well, I guess I'll *start* to take him," Cade said. "Who knows?"

Marian sat down heavily. "I'll see that he gets there," she said quietly as she and Clea exchanged warm glances.

"You know anything I can do to help, I will," Clea offered.

"Thank you," Marian said.

"I'm told," Cade said suddenly, "that a great-uncle in my family had leukemia. Died at thirty . . . "

Bob was determined to keep it on an even keel. "Thirty and thirty-five," he said. "Artie's only seven. By the time he reaches those ages we'll have cures that zap leukemia in a few weeks. We're already racing ahead. I'm full of hope for the kid."

"So am I," Marian said staunchly, her eyes on Bob warm with gratitude. She stood up, gave one of the white sheets she held to Clea, the other to Bob.

Cade laughed. "The kid would doodle all day if I let him."

A light shock went through Clea as she looked at the drawing. It was a wonderful likeness of her and it was far beyond Artie's seven years because it captured much of her generous spirit as well as her physical beauty. "This is really incredible." She looked from Cade to Marian, who looked so proud.

Bob stared at his drawing and his eyes misted. Why couldn't Artie have been his? This was talent to be reckoned with. These fluid, clean lines were magnificent with promise. Bob's strength and the kindness reflected in his eyes were captured on this sheet of white paper. He shook his head. He'd swear his soul was there. All this from a child of seven. A gifted child.

"He told me he liked to draw," Bob said. "He was going to show me some of his drawings. These are splendid. Does he have art instruction?"

Marian blushed. "I draw—some, but not like this. Yes, a teacher at his school is also an artist waiting to be assigned to a high school. She thinks Artie has a future as a wonderful artist."

Cade put his head down. "It ain't something I intend to encourage. Now, Marian here is a woman, so it's all right, I guess. She's pretty good too. Far as I'm concerned, painting pretty pictures is no undertaking fit for a man, and Artie's gonna be a man if I have to kill him to make him one."

Bob didn't want to hear anymore. He glanced at his watch. "We'll have to go," he said. "I'll be in touch Monday. Marian, you're home mornings?" She was a part-time nurses' aide at the local hospital.

"Yes."

"I'll just be calling to set up some schedules. Dr. Heller is to get back to me early. I think we'll be started by midweek. May we say good-bye to Artie?"

"I'll get him," Marian said without looking at her husband. Cade's face bore a surprised expression. Was Marian finally developing a spine to protect her son? Clea wondered.

A subdued Artie came out. At first he looked beaten down as he glanced fearfully at his father, but he came to Bob. "Good-bye, Dr. Bob," he said formally.

"You can do better than that," Bob said gruffly. "Give me a hug." He held out his arms. The boy hesitated.

"Go on, sweetheart, hug him," his mother urged.

Bob's heart beat hard as he hugged Artie firmly, held the thin body against him for a moment, wishing fervently for all that was best for him.

"Don't forget, I like hugs too," Clea said, smiling.

Bashfully Artie turned to her. "You're like my mom," he told her. "You're so pretty." Clea's arms went around him and he hugged her neck, breathing deeply so that her perfume enveloped him, thinking if his father hadn't been here, everything would be perfect.

"Artie," the drawings are magnificent," Bob told him. "You're our next Picasso, Romare Bearden, Jacob Lawrence all rolled into one."

"Hey," Artie said, "I know the first two. My teacher's got a big book she shows me. Who's the other guy?"

"He was a very good late African-Canadian artist," Clea said. "I've got beautiful postcards of his work and I'll leave some with Dr. Bob for you."

"Gee, thanks," Artie said. "You two really oughta . . ." he began, ebullience breaking through his spirit. His father fixed him with a laserlike look and the boy fell silent, thinking glumly that Dr. Bob and Miss Clea ought to get married and have a little boy like him.

At Wonderland that afternoon, Dunk came to Clea's office. He looked bothered. "What's eating you?" she asked him as he plopped down on a chair by her desk.

"Have you seen Pantell lately?" he asked.

"No, and I'm grateful for small favors."

"Well, I have and it seems to me he's going off the deep end. He keeps grousing about how you let him go, how unfair you were."

"I paid him a king's ransom in severance pay, offered to get him another job. He wasn't interested. Pantell was going to hurt somebody; he was beginning to get out of control. I don't feel like being sued for millions when I can avoid it."

"Yeah, I see where you're coming from. He's not

telling people how you've helped him, just how much you've hurt him. Do you want to talk to him? I don't mind him knowing I told you what he's been saying."

"Let it ride," Clea said. "I'll talk to a couple of people, figure out some way to handle him." She frowned. "Dunk, just how good is Pantell with computers?"

Dunk thought a moment. "Interested but only competent. We talked about this. He hasn't got the patience to really dig in. Why d'you ask?"

She shrugged. "Just wondered again. You know Rip Jacy, don't you?"

"Who doesn't? He is one mean *hombre*. I think he nursed on mean juice."

"Do you know if he's into computers?"

"Yeah, as a matter of fact he is. Now, Jacy could be really good if he applied himself. He really likes computers. I taught him for a lot of money . . ."

"When?"

Dunk thought a moment. "Just before he went up for stealing your computers. Why're you so hot on computers today?"

She didn't answer for a minute, rocking in her swivel chair. "Just thinking, wondering, curious."

"I heard on TV that Jacy's escaped. I hope to hell he's far away. I had come to really dislike the guy."

"Any special reason why?"

"Yeah. The way he talked about women was scandalous. And he's got a wife."

"Scandalous how?"

"Ah, what he'd like to do to them in graphic terms."

"Sexually?"

"Uh-huh, and the violent things he'd like to do too. It made me kinda sick."

"Can you be more explicit?"

Dunk sat up, expelling a harsh breath. "No, I can't, Clea. A nice woman like you has got no business hearing this crap. Just take it from me. You've met Jacy. He's been here and he's no one you'd want to meet on a dark night. And *you* ought not to want to meet him at high noon."

"Why?" she demanded.

He rocked his head back and forth. "Because he doesn't like you, thinks you're arrogant and full of yourself, was what he said. I jumped on him about that. I guess that's when I pulled away from him."

"I wish you'd told me."

"Why? He's not likely to come at you. I figure Jacy's a coward. So you turned him in, testified against him. What else could you do? He's stupid, not crazy. Listen, I gotta run. I've got all this new glitzy stuff I'm selling tonight. Wish me luck." Then he added, "Gonna go out in my backyard and dunk balls for an hour or so." He grinned. "Damn, I've gotten to be good."

Clea laughed. "You don't need luck anymore. You're the best."

Dunk got up, leaned over and kissed her cheek, and said good-bye. "With you and God in my corner, I surely need a lot less luck."

After Dunk had left, Clea felt compelled to go to her computer. She didn't go online as much as she had in the past. She admitted to herself that she was spooked. Now she rifled through some e-mail messages for five or ten minutes before an instant message flashed: *You will never guess.*

Just that and nothing else. She had not looked at her e-mail in her office since the vicious ones began, and this was the first instant message she'd gotten. She leaned back in her chair, her mouth suddenly dry. She was determined to be reasonably calm, keep her wits about her, but she couldn't stop seeing Rip Jacy's crazed face when he had threatened her and said he'd keep her guessing.

Chapter 10

Diamond Point
"*Bonbini!* Welcome!"

This was the heart's cry of the islanders on Diamond Point, the same greeting that enriched Aruba, just across the bay. Clea squeezed Bob's arm. It was late morning and they had just come from Aruba and to the excellent small shopping center on Diamond Point.

Clad in a white sports shirt and black summer trousers, Bob grinned happily and took Clea's hand. He bit his bottom lip hungrily as he looked at her gorgeous form in her blue linen dress that left her brown arms and a part of her shoulders exposed. She was quite breathtaking and she was getting her share of male attention.

They paused in front of a gift shop. "Let's stop here," he said. "I want to get Artie's presents first thing."

"Umm," she murmured. "We'd better call him this morning, too."

"I've got you covered." Bob shook his head. "Poor little guy. He's got my number with instructions to call at any time. Wild Heart, I'm really worried about him."

"I know you are and I am too. His mother's going through hell."

Bob sighed deeply. "I only wish his dad was different, but we have to work with what we have."

Inside the gift shop, they browsed for a short while before they selected a collection of exquisite shells, with several of the conches Artie favored. Clea could imagine

WILD HEART 111

Artie's delight as her heart filled with love for the little boy.

It took only a little while to reach their pale blue, large cottage by the Caribbean Sea. They stood on a broad white concrete balcony only a little distance from the water and both admired the rippling waves and the white foam caps. Their bags were in the living room.

A slender brown man of African and Asian blood came forward, extending his hand. "Ah, Dr. Redding, Ms. Wilde, it is so good to see you again. I have prepared your favorite seafood platters for lunch, my specialty, and a light dessert. I think you will be pleased. I have ordered everything you will need to make this a wonderful stay. And, sir, happy birthday tomorrow!"

Bob clapped the younger man's shoulder. "As always, Maxwell, you've done wonders."

The house was spotless, sparingly furnished with Kwiki wood and imports. The air smelled of the sea and varied flowers.

Maxwell beamed. "There is still so much to be done. This will be a very special occasion for you, sir."

"I expect it will. It isn't every day a man lives to be thirty-nine. I'm looking forward to it."

That afternoon, bags unpacked, Clea and Bob took a trek up to the long natural stone bridge fashioned by the sea and aeons of time. They had both seen it before, but its majesty still stirred them. The late afternoon sun caressed their skins as they walked, and a herd of mountain goats tripped along across from them. Kwiki trees were everywhere, giving the islanders shade and wood for furniture. Wild orchids grew in profusion and beautiful cacti, flowering and plain, graced the terrain.

Looking at Clea's dark, silken skin in the sunlight, Bob felt his heart nearly break with his need to hold her, be inside her. She saw and read his look and drew a sharp breath of regret and longing. She and this man were meant to be, she thought, and what was she going to do about it? He caught her hand, squeezed it.

Both smiled at lush Bushi bushes that held the erotically shaped fruit that tasted like strawberries. The elongated white rod seemed to press into the soft center. Bob cut off two fruits with his pocketknife and handed a half to her.

They walked on as they ate the delectable fruit and watched the setting sun.

"Let's go on to the cove," he suggested.

The cove had been a favorite spot when they were lovers, and had made them both delirious with happiness. Now they lay on the powdery white sand of this secluded spot that was fenced in against wandering goats. It was a spot for ardent lovers and Clea was sick with remembering.

"Let's come back tonight," she said shakily. "I used to fill my heart on this scene, and the memories lasted for ages."

"Let's do it," Bob told her and he raised his arm in an imaginary toast, saying "To old and wonderful pastimes!"

Back at the cove that night, they lazed on the sand and Clea took roast beef and chicken salad sandwiches out of a basket Maxwell had prepared for them in lieu of dinner. She put sugar cubes in an open bowl for Bob; she only took natural sugar. It was night and a full moon beamed. Trillions of blinking golden stars hung in the sky, blazing above them. A small, yellow-breasted brown bird set down on the white tablecloth and pecked at the sugar.

"A Barrica heel!" Clea exclaimed. "I didn't know they came out at night."

Bob shook his head. "They don't call them sugar thieves for nothing." They watched, bemused, as the bird pecked his full and flew off.

"Ah, Diamond Point and all its glory," Clea murmured as she took out of a bowl a few of the omnipresent cashew nuts that were one of the island's major exports.

Bob nodded at the small Bose music system he'd brought. "I thought we'd like to listen to Barry White," he said, "but the sounds around us are far more seductive."

"Are you trying to seduce me?"

He looked at her in the bright moonlight and she wanted to plainly see his light brown eyes with the large sea-green flecks, but she imagined the mischief that lay in their depths. "I always try to seduce you, Wild Heart. I've never been able to let a good thing go. And we were a truly good thing."

They took off their clothes and Clea's watermelon bikini bathing suit was getting to him. He hadn't seen her this nearly naked for so long a time. But hell, he grumbled to himself, he didn't need nakedness to send him flying where she was concerned; any old gunnysack would do.

"Want to go back to where the lifeguards are and swim?" he asked.

Clea shook her head. "No. I'm so content here. I'd like to bring some of those stars down from the sky and keep them."

"They'd burn you the way you're burning me."

"You say the sweetest things."

"That's the way you make me feel. Wild Heart, I'm never going to get over you, you know."

Clea felt a lump in her throat and her eyes stung. "That goes double for me." She shuddered as she asked him forlornly, "Bobby, what is going to become of us?"

He caught her to him then, his muscular, sinewy body crushed against hers, and his mouth on hers was passionate with wanting and with need. His tongue inside her mouth devoured hers greedily, then on her face, claimed the corners of her mouth, licking and darting small, fevered kisses until she felt she'd go mad with wanting him.

The past was prologue now and her blood was scalding. She felt tears of frustration dampen her eyes and she knew she would fight him no longer. "I love you," she said simply. "I will always love you."

His big hands swept her body before they lingered on the bikini bottom. She took one of his hands and placed it beneath the skimpy pants and her hand covered his.

He felt the silk of her flesh, the soft hairs, then the wetness like peach syrup that sent him reeling. "Sweetheart, please," he said, half drunk with pleasure.

"Yes," she breathed raggedly, wriggling out of her bikini pants and untying the bra of her swimsuit as he ripped off his swimming trunks and took a condom from the small packet. Hastily he smoothed it on.

There was no time for foreplay. Flames licked at their bodies as they fiercely sought each other. The tight muscles of her inner walls gripped him as he went inside her hungry body with hunger like her own. He had to steady himself, think of ice caps and snow-laden mountains, because it had been so long since he'd made love. She knew why he stopped and lay beneath him, half dreaming of culmination, present and remembered bliss mingled in her brain.

"Oh, my love," she murmured, "I love you so much."

He began to move inside her again, swollen greatly, hard and throbbing, his blood singing the way the blood of ecstasy sings. "I'm going to come too fast," he told her. "It's been too long."

"Go ahead. I'll be right with you," she told him and felt wildfire flash in her body, across her brain. She gasped with delight as he lifted her buns and clutched them, pulling out and sliding back with consummate grace, then going deep past her womb and thrilling endlessly as she gripped and held him. She cried out then and her sweet moans filled his ears as he exploded. She caught him to her feverishly and took his kisses with desire that shook her to her very soul. She felt the waves of ecstasy sweep her veins, melt her heart, and leave her body limp and relaxed.

"Damn it!" he said softly. "So much for lasting pleasure."

Clea smiled impishly with joy surging through her. "Encore! Encore!" she murmured throatily. "Give you a little time to rest, of course."

He hugged her tightly, his bloodstream still hot with passion as they lay on the powdery white sand, his head on her breasts.

"I could die now," he said groggily, "and count my life fulfilled."

"We're going to live a very long time and be happy."

He tensed. "Does this mean we're *on* again? I wish I'd brought your engagement ring. I was looking at it the other night."

"Give me a little more time to think."

"Okay, if you'll think with your heart and soul."

"I promise to, but those two sometimes have a mind of their own."

"Your *best* mind."

The night was very warm as silken trade winds fanned them. The big white-yellow moon urged them on but they fell asleep for a short while. He woke first and smiled at their swimsuits flung out from them. The scent of gardenia bushes wafted on the night air. He grew tumescent again and his shaft surged toward her. He stroked her face, then kissed the corners of her luscious mouth. She was dark in the moonlight, her clove-colored skin like China silk. *Dark and beautiful*, and the biblical quote from Song of Solomon came to him.

But Clea, he thought as he had thought so many times before, was black *and beautiful*, not just comely. He felt his breath catch in his throat as she came awake.

"I'd swear you drugged me," she murmured.

"Then what did I do to myself? I fell asleep too. It's our bodies' way of resting for the long haul."

"I'm thinking about the very long haul for us."

"What're you talking about, love?"

"Us and where we're going, but right now I want you inside me again. You just don't know how much I've missed you."

She encircled his shaft with her fingers, murmuring, "Rock city."

"You set me on fire," she told him. "You always did and I think you always will."

This time they went into extensive foreplay and he kissed her from her scalp to her toes, his tongue sweeping and nibbling along the way. He came back up to her physical center and lingered there, tasting the sweetness of her again, the soft hairs of her on his face once more. Then rising above her, he caught her buns and squeezed them, pressed her slowly and inexorably onto his shaft as she gasped with pleasure. She cried out and her soft moans went onto the night air. This was Diamond Point, she thought with rapture, and what they did here was heaven.

Deep inside her body, he was still for long moments, simply savoring the depths of his beloved. Her womb throbbed with wanting his child, and his shaft throbbed with swollen tenderness, wanting everything she had to give.

"We should play music," she said softly.

"We *are* the music. No symphony ever affected me like this. We're giving Barry White a run for his money."

The inner walls of her body clamored for him, demanding more and more and more. He began to move again, expertly, easily, as she clutched his buttocks, her hands feverishly pressing all of him into her. For a few minutes her legs were over his shoulders and the deeper entrance gave them glory. Her heart was full to bursting and she was filled with the present wonder of her life with him no less than the splendid world they moved in.

He stroked her breasts, then suckled them hungrily, laving them, feasting on the nipples. Finally, he raised himself up. "I've been afraid to do them justice," he said.

"Afraid to go inside you. Because when I do, I know I'll never be able to let you go again."

"I know," she whispered. "I feel the same way."

He wanted to plead his case then, make her accept that they must never be apart again, but he couldn't. What if she still wouldn't, *couldn't* come to him because of Reba? But, his mind amended, he had her in his arms now and she had never left his heart, his soul, his *life*.

"Bob?"

"Yes, baby."

"I love you."

"And I love you so much it scares me. You don't know the hell you've put me through."

"I didn't want to. I want us to be happy. I want to bring the children I'll have happiness. Is that so wrong?"

He shook his head. "No, but you're happy with me and—"

"I'm *only* happy with you. I know that now."

His arms around her then were relentless, wanting to make her stay with him, wanting to know often now what they had lost. He bit his bottom lip. He wanted her in all the positions they used to use and he was greedy for reliving their past times together. They had been endless in their inventiveness. Different positions. Different places. But this place was perfect.

She stirred now. "We made love in this cove when we were engaged," she said. "Remember?"

"There's nothing I don't remember. This time is even better, if that's possible. No, I guess not, because then we belonged to each other in every way." He sounded sad.

"I still belong to you."

"And I belong to you. Let's have it all again, Wild Heart." His voice went husky with desire and passion. Raw hunger hit him like a fist to his belly. He tensed, waiting for her response.

"We'll see," she said only, and he wondered why he felt hope beyond any she offered.

Clea wished at first the night would never end, but she

smiled thinking that tomorrow would be even better. And she had plans for Bob.

"Happy advance birthday," she told him.

He caught her to him. "Thank you, sweetheart. This is all the present, all the celebration I need."

"Aren't you forgetting something?"

"Maybe. What are you suggesting?"

"You want us to be together again. *We* want us to be together again. I wish I could give you the present we both want so badly."

His heart fell a little then. "You can, you know," he said. "Just make up your mind that we were meant for each other, that my mother's feelings about you and us don't matter. You've got the clearest mind I know. Make it work for us."

Her slender hands stroked his back, thrilling at the rippling muscles there, then his biceps, but her mind stayed on his inner being, his loving, caring spirit. He was inside her and she wanted to keep him there. Tears came to her eyes as she thought of the lines to her song "Just Can't Let You Go." Yes, he'd put his red-hot magic on her body and her soul, and she had a hunger for him that was way out of her control.

She murmured the title of that song and he asked what she said.

"Just something that is so frustrating," she answered, "and so *true*."

Rekindled to white-hot heat, he began to move deeply again, his loins on fire as he worked her with loving mercilessness, giving her everything that was within him to give. He waited patiently for her to reach her summit, and when she did on waves of frantic joy she cried his name. His tongue probed her mouth, tangled with hers as rockets went off in his body and his spirit soared and rejoiced.

Chapter 11

Clea glowed with happiness, yet she felt more nervous than she had in some time as she and Maxwell moved between the dining area and the kitchen. She had insisted that Bob be away from the cottage for several hours as she and Maxwell put the finishing touches on the private birthday dinner celebration. She glanced at the beautifully wrapped small, dark blue package that held Bob's birthday gift, and a smile tugged at her face. He was going to love this. She had phoned in the order from Aruba's best jeweler when she had decided to come here with him.

She breathed deeply. The house was fresh with the scent of carnations and roses; the rooms sparkled. She wore periwinkle silk harem pajamas with one of Dunk's gold chain belts and one of his wide gold bracelets.

She heard Bob whistling as he came up the walk and onto the porch where he knocked at the screen door. "Am I allowed back in now?" He carried a small gaily wrapped package.

"If you ask nicely," Clea said. He came in and she leaned into him as he caught her, held her. "Happy birthday, love." She led him into the dining room and went to the credenza, picked up and handed him the package, murmuring, "I see you've got a package, too. We're right back on schedule."

Clea knew when she said it that she had made up her mind about something, and it brought a flow of happiness to her.

"Yeah," he said. "We always gave each other gifts on both our birthdays." His voice got husky then. "I wish we could pick up everything where we left off."

Clea smiled at him, her glance lingering on his sensual mouth for a moment. She wouldn't kiss him now, wouldn't get caught up in the maelstrom she felt sweeping through her. "Let's open the presents," she said. "You first."

He loosened the wrappings and displayed a black leather jeweler's case. Snapping it open, he drew in a sharp breath and his eyes lit up. On a white satin bed, a gorgeous pair of platinum cuff links with intricate twenty-two-karat gold swirls shone up at him. His initials—RFR—were engraved in platinum. Robert Frank Redding. He drew her to him. "Sweetheart, these are the most beautiful ever. I love them."

He kissed the corner of her mouth, but she told him, "No, honey, no kisses just now. I couldn't take them. I keep wanting you again. Please wait to kiss me."

His heart expanded and he smiled, his eyes narrowed. "Only if you promise to make it up to me later tonight. Open your present."

Inside her jeweler's box lay a pendant consisting of a polished silver three-quarter moon and inside that moon a lovely, large turquoise stone. Six small diamonds flanked the turquoise oval.

"I love this," she told him. "It's meant to bless me, keep me, with God's help."

"You bet it is." He hugged her tightly. "Papa Curtis told you to stay close to me and I'm insisting on it."

"You don't have to insist. You know I will."

They moved into the living room and sat on a sofa close together. "Did you check your computer messages?" he asked her.

She nodded. "Nothing, thank heaven. Maybe I'll get a chance to breathe."

They had talked with Artie that morning, told him they were bringing him the shells and other presents.

WILD HEART

The little boy was ecstatic. Now Clea said, "I guess Artie's on your mind, too, the way he's on mine.'

"Yeah, but I think we made him a little happier today. I can't look at Cade Webb without wanting to do him plenty of damage."

She took his hand. "Let's just do everything *we* can, honey, and keep praying for the best."

They sat in silence listening to the sound of waves crashing onto the shore. The *ba-a-a* of mountain goats was in the distance and the soft breeze coming in the windows was air for lovers—soft and caressing.

Maxwell and Clea had outdone themselves for Bob's birthday dinner.

When they were seated, Maxwell opened a bottle of Dom Perigon and poured, and Clea toasted Bob: "May we do the best that is in us. May you have everything your heart desires!"

With a lump in his throat, Bob's glance caressed her and the heat of flaming desire swept through him. Clea smiled; she had her own vivid love to deal with.

Beginning with gazpacho, there was roast leg of lamb, wild rice, green peas almondine, asparagus, baby carrots, and mint jelly. The big garden salad was a meal in itself. This was Bob's favorite dinner and in the past Clea had made it for him.

At the festive table with its pink damask cloth and centerpiece of pink and white carnations and broadleaf fern, Bob took her hand. "You've outdone yourself, Wild Heart, and it's beautiful, but this is a vacation. You were supposed to rest."

"I'm resting when I do things for my man." Her eyes held his and a thrill went through him.

"Am I your man?"

"Don't you know by now?"

"I know you're my woman, my *only* woman. This food

is superb, but right now there are other things I'd rather be doing."

As his eyes made love to her, Clea blushed, murmuring, "Eat your dinner and if you're nice to me, it could lead to other things."

Bob laughed. "You're going to make me bolt my food to get to the 'other things.'"

Clea leaned back as his eyes devoured her. "You look happy. Are you?"

"Not completely. If I had you the way we were—no, if we were married or about to be, except for Artie, I'd be happy, and I expect my prayers to be answered about him."

"I certainly hope so; I'm praying too. Keep your fingers crossed about us. I've got a good feeling."

His heart leaped when she said it. "Believe me, I'll be waiting."

Full from the rich food, they decided to take their dessert of brandied strawberry cheesecake later. Throughout dinner Tchaikovsky's First String Quartet with its beautiful "Andante Cantabile" swirled around them. "I have the recording of a popular song from that music," Bob said. "It was about a couple in love who separated and they're pining to be together again. It's one of my favorites."

"I know. You played it for me when we were engaged."

"What do you have planned for us tonight?" he asked. He kept looking at her long, slender fingers, without his engagement ring. Picking up her hand, he kissed her ring finger, his tongue gliding over it.

Clea groaned in the back of her throat. They had to get outside, walk, be active. She was burning up with desire vividly reawakened the past night, riding high with love and what she had decided to do.

"What have you got going for us now?" he asked.

She didn't hesitate. "A long, long walk along the shore, then back here where the garden house is waiting."

"You're full of surprises."

"Oh, there's much more."

The music finished, the CD player shut off, and Clea smiled widely as Maxwell went through the room, gave them the A-OK sign, and stepped outside onto the patio. In a few minutes, there was the sound of violins playing the happy birthday song as Bob's face lit up. Then the group played the pop tune Bob had just spoken of. He caught her hand again, pushed his chair back, and pulled her up. "Good Lord, you're incredible," he said. "But you're making it hard for yourself because I'm never gonna let you go."

She was silent as his mouth moved over her face, loving her, rife with desire. Last night had been only a prelude; tonight they would play the symphony.

They sat on a blanket on the lawn for a couple of hours and Maxwell brought them generous portions of strawberry cheesecake with brandied whipped cream. Laughing, they fed each other under the full moon. "I think nature's doing her share to push us along," Clea told Bob. "Did you ever see anything so gorgeous?"

"Umm," he said, grinning. "I'm looking at you."

"You're prejudiced."

"A little."

The tide was calm and Clea's heart felt full as she watched the blazing galaxy of stars for the second night. Finishing the cheesecake, Bob smacked his lips. "Do I detect your presence in this cheesecake? My stomach thanks you."

She smiled. "Everything for your birthday is what I wanted and set out to do."

"Not quite everything," he said sadly. "Something major is still missing."

"Where there's life, there's always hope," Clea said lightly.

Her glance at him was arch in the moonlight and he

wished he could see deep into her eyes. "You look so beautiful tonight," he told her.

"And I'll look even more beautiful to you later in the garden house. Do I sound immodest?"

Bob drew a quick breath. He shook his head. "No. Is that where we wind up?"

"All night. Doesn't that music make you dream?" She spoke of the musicians who still played for them.

"They do, but I don't need them when I have you."

"Honey tongue."

"For a honeyed woman." He caught her hand, kissed her fingers one by one.

Maxwell came for their used dishes and said, "Sir, I hope this has proven to be a wonderful birthday for you."

"Beyond my dreams," Bob said, "and you two put it all together."

Maxwell bowed. "It was mostly Ms. Wilde who did it. I only helped."

Clea smiled at Maxwell. "Don't play down your part. We should all have such help."

They went into the garden house at ten-thirty with the musicians still playing soft love songs.

"Do they go on all night?" Bob asked.

Clea shook her head. "Only until eleven. They've almost finished. I'm glad you liked them."

In the soft light of the garden house, Bob felt his breath come fast and grow ragged with desire as he looked at Clea, forcing himself to go slow when he wanted to ravish her. He made himself look around him at the large bank of orchids along one wall, wild and cultivated, in every hue. A tall marble fountain stood in one corner, spilling sparkling crystal water from halfway up the walls, falling into a wide marble grotto below. One wall was all glass with doors that slid open, and the front of the garden house was enclosed in privet hedges and a wide wrought-iron gate. This was, like the cove, a lovers' haven, Clea thought.

Clea went about turning down the lights until there were only a few rose-colored bulbs shining. Bob stood with his legs apart; he felt he could howl like a wolf in search of a mate. Clea came back to him and he stood silent as she unbuttoned his shirt, then unfastened his belt buckle.

"Dunk would love it that you're wearing his belt, which I'll take off to make love to you."

"You always say make love *with* me. Why d'you change now?"

"Because I'm in my female wolf mode tonight and I mean to give you everything I have."

It was a statement of truth and it took his breath away. "I've got my own plans for you," he said. "I don't know if you can take it all."

"I'll do my best, and my best is usually a whole lot."

He reached out to begin disrobing her, but she stayed his hand. "I want to look at you naked, sculpt your body in my mind, this time not from memory the way it's been for too long. I love you even more now, and I finally realize how much I *need* you."

Her saying it brought wildfire coursing along his veins. Every memory they'd shared swept over him, and the memories of their lovemaking were the most vivid of all. When he was naked, she sat on the deep, natural-colored sofa, then got up and let out the bed, cautioning him not to help her.

"Statues don't move," she said, laughing as she sat on the edge of the rose-satin-sheeted sofa bed.

Bob posed for her, went into his Atlas mode as she admired his beautiful body—abs, pecs, biceps—the lean length of him that was developed just enough from the Pilates exercises he did. She decided then that she would begin the exercises when they returned to Crystal Lake.

After a while, Bob relaxed, came to her, sat beside her. "I'm an impatient man where you're concerned," he said. "I want you now. Don't make me ravish you."

She stroked his crisp, curly black hair and feathered kisses down the sides of his face. "I've missed you so much," she said. "Last night made me greedy. The music stops now and we're on our own. How'd you like some Barry White make-out music?"

"I'd love it. Brings back memories—great memories."

"We're going to have a present better than any memories."

"Bring it on," he said heatedly. "Don't make me wait."

She struggled away from his arms. "Just let me turn the music on. It's right here."

She turned on the small CD player and Barry White's velvet voice teased their emotions, enriched them both. Smiling, she turned back to him. "Strip me now, lover," she said huskily, and he did what she asked, hurriedly, but carefully.

"We've got a lifetime to do this in," she said. "Please don't hurry."

"What d'you mean?"

She was smiling so, her eyes alight, and her lovely body seemed to palpitate, thrum with pleasure. His mouth went hungrily to her breasts before she could answer.

"Do you still want to marry me?" she asked.

For a second or so he was so intent on her breasts he heard her belatedly. "Don't toy with me, Wild Heart," he growled. "I can't take that."

"I'm not toying, love. I'm going to marry you, if you still want to marry me."

He turned onto his side and caught her to him, hugging her fiercely, feeling the soft outlines of her luscious body, feeling her breasts splay against him, her breasts that seemed to have a life of their own. His heart was so full, he couldn't speak at first, then he found his voice as his big hands roved her body.

"I still want to marry you, more than ever. When?"

"Would tomorrow be soon enough? I don't want to withstand the pressure of being married in Crystal Lake. We have another day here. There's no waiting period."

"Hell, *tonight*, if you're willing."

She took his face in her hands, caressed it. "Tonight is for us to make special memories of our love, of you inside me, filling me the way only you can do. I want you now, love. Don't make me wait."

He pulled her to the edge of the bed and went on his knees before her as she closed her eyes and stroked his beloved face. Her female center pulsed with desire, drawing him as his tongue roved her with expert, seeking kisses.

"How can you be so sweet?" he asked her.

"That's because I love you so much. I turn to honey when I'm near you. I feel sweet with you."

After a while, he lay beside her, balled up his fist lightly, and tapped on her belly. She smiled, questioning him. "Do I ask who's there?"

"You know who's there."

She laughed delightedly. "Okay. Come in."

He spread her legs. "I thought you'd never invite me."

His finger worked the syrupy wetness of her center and she demanded the larger instrument she craved. Her fingers largely encircled the base of his shaft and guided it into her avidly seeking body. Taking a condom from an end table drawer, he smoothed it on and slid in slowly, taking loving care. She wrapped her legs around his back and her active muscles drew him in. Then he was rock hard, throbbing like wild heartbeat drums, and she cried out with almost painful need.

In a few minutes, he was swollen beyond belief and she moved her legs to his shoulders and cried out his name, then his pet name, cried out her love for him as the water splashed in the fountain, lit by moonlight in this lovers' room. The scent of roses and gardenias was everywhere. She had thought of everything to seal her love for this man.

"I always had to take care not to hurt you," he said. "You've got so much nectar now. Thank God for last night; at least I don't feel I have to gobble you up immediately. I can wait a bit."

"Don't wait. Now I'm greedy for us and more of the same. Bobby?"

"Yes, love."

"We're going to be Adam and Eve in the garden of Eden, but there will be snakes. . . ."

"I expect you're right, but we'll make it. We've got love and respect and passion on our side. A woman who runs with the wolves deserves it all, and I'm here to see that she gets it."

"You always were something special. We don't need condoms anymore. How many kids do you want?"

"A baker's dozen."

"Too many. Would six do?"

"Every one would have my heart, after you."

Her inner walls were gripping him, soothing and arousing him even more deeply. His breath came hard and he closed his eyes, her dark and beautiful face a cameo in his mind, as Barry White's magic tones and words surrounded them. Passion ruled and desire was king and queen.

A soft rain began, startling them because it hardly ever rained on Diamond Point or Aruba. "Nature sends us rain to make love by," Clea murmured. "She must know we've got a special something going on. Everything on earth is for us tonight. You feel so good inside me, but there's something I want to do."

"Okay."

Released, she began to slowly kiss him all over the way he had done with her. His crisp, curly black hair, scalp, face, shoulders, the rippling muscles of his chest and arms. Then she lingered on his nipples with circular tongue kisses and he groaned, pressing her head onto him, glorying in the rapture. Slowly she traversed his body as he lay physically almost inert, thrilling inside. Her love was a wolf woman's tonight, satisfying the mate she would have for life.

When he could take no more, he pulled her up, sat

her astride him, and entered her again. "Rain and pounding surf," she whispered. "Glorious."

The Barry White songs ended and an old Sinatra rendition of "You'd Be So Nice to Come Home To" spun out in silken cadences. "Something old for our coming marriage vows," she said.

"You're an amazing woman," he told her. "No wonder I love you so."

"And you're the love of my life."

His voice grew tense and he stopped moving for a little while. "Just don't ever leave me again, because I couldn't take it. You're sure about this, Wild Heart? I mean marrying me. I won't let you change your mind."

Her tongue went into one corner of his mouth, then the other. "More sure than I've ever been about anything or ever will be."

Astride Bob, Clea felt the masculine power of him as he rhythmically moved under her, his splendid body coupling with her own soft one. Leaning down, her long hair fanning his shoulders, she kissed him ardently, their tongues a tangle of wild desire.

Her soft moans of rapture filled his ears, gladdened his heart, and they went spinning out of control as he worked her slowly, with love so deep he hurt with it. She pressed his buttocks in to her, held him fast, and in a few minutes he spilled his seed into her waiting womb and shuddered as he felt her begin the multiple orgasms that moved him so. This was love, she thought, and this was ecstasy and this was one of the basic things life was all about.

They rested then, lying entwined in each other's arms. She got up and got a bottle of champagne from an ice bucket, brought it back to the bed, where he sat up and opened it. Two crystal flutes were on a table by the sofa. The whoosh of the popping cork made them both laugh as they poured a little of the liquid into their palms and spread it in each other's bodies. They drank the champagne out of the bottle, taking turns.

"College kids," she laughed.

He shook his head. "No, we'll be this way at ninety. I've got so many thrills in store for us." He caught her in a bear hug as he set the champagne bottle on the end table. "Wild Heart, I've been trying to digest it. I still can't believe you're really going to marry me. I've been through hell so long. What made you change your mind?"

She answered without hesitation. "Feeling my love for you again. Watching you with Artie and knowing what a wonderful husband and father you'll make. I was younger when I let you go. I know now the world is not a perfect place, and no one else makes me feel the way you do." She drew in a deep breath. "There'll be trouble with Reba, count on it. But I'm prepared to fight for you and our love."

"And I'll always be right by your side. Forever."

With champagne and love and desire bubbling in their blood, he stood up and pulled her to him. With her feet on top of his, he walked over to the waterfall, put his fingers into the falling water, and rubbed some of it onto her face and body. She shivered as the cool water touched her and her fingers stroked and dug into the hard flesh of him, seeking entrance to his very soul.

She paused, laughing softly, as he picked her up. "Bobby, this time tomorrow night, we'll be man and wife. Tell me I'm not dreaming," she breathed.

"You're not dreaming. *We're* not dreaming. This had better be for real."

Her blood was molten gold then, flooding her with satisfaction, and he groaned aloud at the ecstasy of her on top of him. He clutched her buns and drew her farther down onto him, and her womb gloried in his tender assault. Gasping for breath, they choreographed their passion for each other, and after a very long while she felt the faint ripples of complete satisfaction begin in her body, then grow stronger and stronger until she was drowning in ecstatic waves of feeling. Her body trembled wildly with orgasmic wonder and she cried out his name again and again.

And he felt the splendor of the woman above him, drew her still farther down onto his shaft as he swelled to his utmost size. When she cried out and the orgasms began to build in her wondrous body again, it brought a quick response and he lost himself in her body and her spirit. Fire and steam like that from a giant pressure cooker filled his loins and he exploded with satisfaction filling him like an ardent blessing. He and Wild Heart had a splendid past, he thought, and now they would know a glorious future beyond the telling.

Afterward, she lay beside him, both were spent and smiling. He lightly licked her breasts and tweaked them. "These will nurse my babies," he said. "Soon."

She laughed. "It usually takes nine months, impatient one."

"We've lost so much time."

She sighed. "Yes, but it's plain we're going to make up for it."

He caught her close, squeezed her for long minutes. "I'm going to wake Jason early so he can sell us a wedding ring. Later you'll get the one you want."

Jason Till was the best jeweler on the island.

"No. That one will be too precious. We'll make a good choice at first. Bobby?"

"Yes, love."

"I love you so."

Early the next morning they left the garden house arm in arm and Clea looked back. "I said we'd make memories to treasure all our lives and we did, didn't we?"

"We sure did. We'll go into eternity with last night, but there's so much more to come."

The morning air was fresh with the past night's light rain and both breathed deeply.

Clea lifted her arms, spread them to the heavens. "Two or three hours of sleep and I feel better rested than I can ever remember."

Bob looked at his love and grinned. "You hold up well, baby, and that's good because of what I'm going to put you through."

"Is that a promise or a threat?"

"Both. Just get ready for my total commitment to you."

"And mine to you."

They hugged each other with light moisture dampening them and went into the house.

"Let's shower, grab a quick bite, and wake Jason up. He can help us find a minister to marry us."

She hugged him then. "Oh Lord, I'm going to be married to a man who is everything I ever wanted."

"And I've got myself a woman who gives me everything I want and need."

Her eyes fell on the computer in the corner of the room. "I'll just check this," she said, "in case Artie or Alina sent another e-mail."

She booted up the computer and waited. Accessing her e-mail, she found a message from Artie:

> You guys have fun, you hear!
>   Artie

Another from Alina:

> Everything's under control.
> Stay longer if you want.

And a chill struck Clea before she'd seen the subject line and read the last message. No greeting, no complimentary close, just the hated message:

> Hurry home. I'm waiting for you!

Chapter 12

Back in Crystal Lake

"Wild Heart! Wild Heart! I love you!"

Bob laughed heartily. "The old devil. He was supposed to say that from the beginning." He turned to the parrot. "Rufus, it sure took you long enough."

Rufus turned his head to one side and peered at Clea intently. She, Bob, and Rufus were in the breakfast room just off the kitchen where Bob was cooking breakfast for them. He got a graham cracker from the cabinet, put it on a wide ledge near the parrot's perch. Rufus began to hungrily peck it up.

The sun was rising as Bob prepared to go in to the clinic early. "I'm pouring you some pomegranate juice," he said. "I'll take my old standby, orange juice. Just getting you prepped for pregnancy. Baby, you never know."

"You're rushing things," she said throatily. He had teased her about getting pregnant since Diamond Point, and every time he mentioned it her heart leaped with joy. Their very own baby. A slow sense of wonder filled her as she went to him, nestled in his arms. He patted her slightly rounded stomach.

"You've got a little bit of belly, which I personally love," he said. "It's going to be hard to tell when I get you with child."

"Early morning sickness?" she queried.

"Not always." He shrugged. "I figure we'll just know. The baby's mama started out to be a shaman."

A shadow crossed her face then as she remembered their session with the Cherokee gods, then the message that could only be from someone who hated her, wanted to hurt her.

After Bob left, Clea dressed and went outside to the front of the house. She stood for a long while, admiring the late beds of dark red dahlias and gladioli and the massive evergreens and oaks.

The large, beautiful redbrick house had been designed by a top D.C. architect. She and Bob had worked hard, with love and hope and dreams feeding them. Then she had thought she couldn't bear Reba's hatefulness and had brought the dream to an end.

Now she lived here after all with the man she so passionately loved. Children were going to be a dicey choice. Love didn't always conquer everything, she thought sadly.

But she knew her life had been slipping away from her. This was a game she intended to win. She thought then if Reba had known about her present trouble, she would smile and be pleased at how well this validated her opinion of Clea as a woman born to trouble.

Wonderland was lively later that afternoon. Alina hugged her. "Welcome back, honey chile. Everything went well." Her face got grave. "At least you got a rest and oh, you're a married woman now." Alina couldn't stay sad long. "You and Dr. Bob Redding; it's what I've prayed for for you."

"I think it's what I've silently prayed for too. I've never been so happy." Then she amended, "Except for . . ." Her voice trailed off again.

"Except for Nightmare—that devil. Clea, walk with God on this. You're one of the best people I've ever known and He's with you every nanosecond of your life."

"I always remember that. How do you like the black pearl bracelet?" Clea asked.

"It's what I'd expect from you. Gorgeous. Thank you again. I'll be wearing it so much you'll ask me to take it off."

"Diamond Point and Aruba have fabulous jewelry. I bought Dunk a hammered gold belt buckle. I think he's going to be tickled pink—well, brown." She grimaced. "We *do* get caught up in these color things."

Alina smiled. "Yes, we do, but life is darned good anyway. Dunk should be on shortly."

The women stood facing a wall of gleaming barware, and a male voice interrupted them. "Dunk's here! All stand and give honor."

Alina laughed. "I love the way you're so modest."

"I'd rather be king than modest," Dunk came back. He hugged Clea. "Alina and I talked a lot while you were gone." He took her hand. "Boy, that is *some* rock. And a wedding band to match. Congratulations! Can I be godfather to your first wee one?"

Clea drew a deep breath. "There's got to be a wee one first."

"It'll happen. I think I know my man Dr. Bob."

"I'm afraid a baby comes through me."

"With Dr. Bob's seed. Boy, it's going to be wonderful being a godfather at my age."

Clea laughed delightedly. "I haven't said yes yet."

"You will." He displayed crossed fingers. "I'm counting on you."

"Meanwhile, I've been carrying this little beauty in my smock pocket in case I run into you." She reached into her pocket and handed him the small red foil package, saying, "Open it now. I want to see your joy."

With the tip of his tongue between his lips, Dunk quickly undid the package and whooped, "Lordy Lord, you sure hit the jackpot. This is wonderful!" He hugged her tightly.

"Seminal?" she asked.

He was getting vocabulary training, was so smart. "What d'you mean?"

"Does it give you ideas of your own?"

"You better believe it. I saw a dozen spin-offs the minute I laid eyes on it."

Alina displayed her bracelet, saying to Dunk, "You've got nothing on me."

"They're both gorgeous," Dunk said. "Makes me feel loved. Look, I'm gonna hang around a bit today, more than usual. I'm at loose ends. What've you got that needs doing?"

Clea thought a minute. "One of the bathroom doors downstairs is a little warped. We've got the tools to shave it back a little and repaint the edges. I was locked in the one by my office, and I hate that. It scares me."

"That's right. You've got claustrophobia," Dunk said. "My mom had it."

"I've got it big time."

Only then did Clea become aware that Dunk looked anxious; his eyes were shadowed. She had noticed it when he spoke of his mom and she touched his arm, said quietly, "It's nearing the anniversary date of her death. How're you holding up, Dunk?"

He shrugged and his voice caught as he said, "Well enough. She suffered so much with her demons. She's in a better place. Look, I'm gonna get started. Think of other things you want me to do; I need to be busy. And, Clea"—he kissed her cheek—"thank you so much."

"Thank *you* for being around when I need you."

"I can't do less."

He left then and Clea looked around for Alina. She didn't see Carlton until he was almost at her side looking suave in a grayish tan Harris tweed jacket and pearl-gray trousers. He put his arms around her, hugged her tightly. "I'm coming on to you, but I can't help myself. I'm in town to talk with Nick Redmond and I had to come by."

"Carlton, what a nice surprise." She immediately thrust her left hand toward him. "Things have changed since I saw you last."

For long moments, Carlton couldn't get his breath, then his breath came hard. At first he tried to say it and couldn't, but he was a man of discipline and it came. "Congratulations, my love. Redding?"

"Yes. I would have called you. We just got back from Diamond Point."

"You were married there?"

"Yes."

"I don't wonder. That was for the best; too much interference here." He looked stricken as he said it and her heart went out to him. His heart hurt him; he loved this woman, wanted her for his own. "Mind if I say a few things?" he asked.

"No. Go ahead. I owe you that."

"I think you had it right when you refused to let yourself in for what Reba Redding has in store for you. I think you're going to regret changing your mind." He sighed and shook his head, stepped closer, and kissed her lightly on the lips. His voice and countenance were sad as he told her, "I'll always be there for you, Clea, no matter who else is in your life or mine. And we'll still be working together. Your latest song is gathering accolades; everybody thinks it's a winner. I know it is."

"You're right, of course," she said quietly. "We'll always be friends."

"And remember what I said, that I'll always be there for you."

Carlton faced and Clea had her back to the door when Bob came in, walked over to them, cleared his throat. "Good afternoon, Kelly," Bob finally said.

Turning to face Bob, Clea gasped as she realized with annoyance that Carlton would have seen him all along. *Men.* "I was telling Carlton about our marriage," she said as Carlton still stood too close to her.

For a moment Bob was shot through with fierce jealousy, but the love in Clea's eyes when she looked at him changed all that.

Carlton extended his hand as he moved a little away

from Clea. "Congratulations!" he said with grave urbanity. The two men shook hands, firmly, civilly as Carlton said, "You got the prize I wanted, but congratulations all the same."

Clea went to Bob, lifted her face for his kiss, and he intended to give her a light kiss, but she was ardent and it egged him on. His body tensed with passion for her and he thought about a time facing them tonight when they would be alone.

Carlton looked at them, his eyes shuttered. "Fail her in any way, Redding," he said, "and I'll be waiting to pick up the pieces."

Bob laughed shortly. "There aren't going to be any pieces. We're coming out whole all the way."

"We'll see," Carlton said evenly.

Carlton left then and Ruel came in as he infrequently did, saying that nightclubs simply were not his or his wife's style. Now Clea greeted Bob's brother, clapped him on the back. Ruel kissed Clea's cheek, said to her, "You're making my brother a happy man. And, Clea, don't worry about Mom. She'll come around in time. Anne and I will have you two and Mom over soon."

He was charming, more friendly than usual, and Clea breathed a sigh of relief.

"Clea's moving in with me, of course," Bob said, "so we'll also be having you two over soon." He smiled widely then. "And thanks, bro, for coming around. I can only hope that as you say, in time Mother will accept us as a happy, married couple."

Ruel smiled. "Oh, she will always accept *you;* you're her absolute favorite. It's Clea who'll have some trouble. Look, I've got to run. Three meetings today. My best wishes."

He left and it was only a little while before Bob reluctantly left without saying anything more about Reba or Carlton. There was a special new band in tonight and they were on the stage practicing. Clea thought they had great promise and already they drew enthusiastic crowds. Remembering a ledger she'd left in her car that she needed, she walked out to the parking lot where her burgundy Porsche sat in its special spot. The back tire on her side looked a little flatter and she kicked it, frowning, before she walked around to the other side and gasped as she found both tires flat. The slash marks, vicious and gaping, were quickly apparent. Whoever did it had meant business. Dread filled her, weighting down her chest.

Dunk came up from the street. "Howdy," he began to say when she pointed out the tires.

"My God!" he exclaimed. "Who could have done this? Did you see anyone?"

"No." She felt slightly dizzy. "Did you pass anyone on the way in?"

"Uh-uh. I went to pick up a can of spackling from the hardware store. I was there for a while chatting with a guy I know from school. I didn't look at your car as I passed."

He glanced at his own black Hyundai parked near her car, walked around it, finally saying, "I don't see anything wrong with the other cars."

"I'm calling the police."

"Yeah. That's good."

Taking her cell phone from her smock pocket, she dialed with stiff fingers. Mitch Tree was out on a call and she left a message for him to call her. Turning back to Dunk, she saw the anxious look ride high on his face. His hands were shaking.

"You look really bothered," she told him. "Mitch and his crew will get to the bottom of this. Think hard now, did you see anyone coming in or leaving as you walked away from the parking lot?"

He nodded. "I *am* thinking—hard—and I'm coming up with blanks, but I'm going to relax and think. I'm at my best then. Clea, let's go back inside."

Walking along, she thought of so many things: the cut underwear, then the cut and *bloody* underwear. Each and every computer message, all cryptic.

Chapter 13

In his office, Bob leaned back in his swivel chair as he looked at Artie and Marian.

"How'm I doing, Doc?" the small boy queried. He looked so wan today, but his strong spirit buoyed him.

"I'm going to be honest with you, Artie, because we're going to lick this thing. You're not doing quite as well as when I left. What's on your mind these days?"

Marian looked from her son to Bob, her eyes sick with fear.

"I missed you. You won't go away again until I get well?" Artie asked.

"You bet I won't. I'll be right here for you, but we talked when I was on Diamond Point. And I'm going to invite you and your parents to go back with Clea and me one day soon. Would you like that?"

The boy nodded dully as if he couldn't envision that far ahead.

"Another thing. Clea and I got married on Diamond Point."

The boy's eyes lit up and his frail body leaned forward. His eyes actually shone with joy. "Oh boy! You'll have a baby and I want to be the godfather."

"Sweetheart," Marian said gently, "parents ask whoever they want to be godparents. It isn't a volunteer situation."

"I trust *you've* got a godfather and a godmother," Bob said.

Artie shook his head. "I'm reading a book that tells all

about a little boy whose godfather saves him. I want to be a godfather to your baby and Miss Clea's."

Bob and Marian looked at each other. The three sat in chairs close to each other and Bob leaned over and smoothed Artie's hair. "Kid, you're going to be the best godfather a baby could have. If you want, Clea and I will even let you name our first baby."

"Hey, that's way cool!" Artie exclaimed. "I can't wait. Tell Miss Clea I love her."

"I sure will and know that she loves you too."

A clinic worker took Artie then and Bob faced Marian alone. "His doctor is hospitalizing him for a spell," Bob told her.

Marian's hands were clenched in her lap. "Tell it to me straight, Dr. Redding. Is Artie going to make it?"

"If Artie's spirit and Dr. Heller's expertise and what I know and feel can do it, he will." His voice got grim, strained. "How is the boy's relationship with Cade these days? That could be a major key."

Marian, brushing the black curls back from her face, said bitterly. "He holds the key all right, and he's throwing that key away. Artie is just another bother in my husband's life. He's had a hard life, I know, but he never seems to get it. I believe children need and deserve respect, and you and I try to give love and respect to my son. Cade doesn't see it that way. He keeps saying he got no respect, little love, and he made it, that Artie will do the same. The boy is so sensitive . . ."

Her eyes were dry but tears muffled her voice.

"He's going to have to be hospitalized in a day or so," Bob said gently. "Pray for him. I'm praying—"

"I pray for him all the time. I don't know what I'll do if he doesn't make it."

Bob patted her shoulder. "Leukemia is no longer a death sentence. There are remarkable cures. If we could just reach Cade, get him to change."

* * *

Exhausted, Bob went home early. He found Clea in their bedroom, sitting on the chaise longue, practicing the song she would feature at the clinic picnic. He bent and kissed her. "You look frazzled," she said. "Hard day?" It was one of her days off.

He told her about Artie then and she looked sad. Then Bob smiled. "He wants to be godfather to our first child."

Clea laughed merrily. "Dunk told me today he wants to be the godfather. No reason we can't have two. So much love for a kid who isn't even a blip on our radar."

He grinned. "I keep planting my seed. I can do it more often."

"Ummm," she said. "When would we have time for anything else? My soil had better be fertile. Give us time. Did you have a hard day?"

"Yeah. Lots of vaccinations, a couple of emergencies—and the pain of little Artie Webb. It could be so different. I'm afraid for Marian if anything happens to her son."

He fell on his back onto the bed. Clea got up, untied his shoelaces and unbuttoned his shirt. "Did you have lunch?"

"Half a cheeseburger. I kind of lost my appetite with Artie's troubles."

"You've got to take better care of yourself, honey." She bent and kissed his brow and his arms encircled her.

"I'll sleep a bit," he said, "and I need you before dinner. Clea?"

"Yes, love."

He stroked her back slowly. Lord, she looked beautiful in aquamarine lounging pajamas with a surplice top outlining her luscious breasts. Suddenly his expression was intense. "I need to be inside you when something hurts me, when I'm anxious or scared. You give me comfort, Wild Heart. You soothe my heart and my soul. And you don't need me the way I need you."

"Yes, I do," she said gently. "You do all those things for me when you go into my body. Oh Lord, how I regret the time we've wasted. You go to sleep now. I'm going over to my toolshed to get some plant fertilizer to transplant some dahlias to pots for the clinic picnic."

"Wait until I sleep a bit and I'll take you."

"No. Sleep a long while. I'll be okay. Dunk's doing some cleaning so I can rent out my house. I won't be alone. He'll go with me."

"Take your cell phone. Call me." He was already drifting off.

Clea got everything together swiftly and closed the bedroom door behind her. She found Violet and Albert, the couple who handled Bob's estate, in the kitchen. They greeted her warmly.

"You're what this place has always needed," Violet said, "what Doc's needed. You're a joy to have around, Miss Clea."

"Just Clea. I call you two by name. Grant me the same. I love the smooth way you run the place, and you've been with him since he built this house."

"Yes," Albert said. "He paid us the whole while he was away. We didn't want him to, but he insisted."

Looking at their late-fifties faces, she with smooth beige skin and he with dark chocolate skin, Clea basked at the warmth and the efficiency mirrored there, the love. She knew why Bob wanted to keep them.

Clea glanced at her watch; it was later than she'd thought. Other items were needed for the clinic picnic, so she should go into town. Was she forgetting something? No, it didn't seem so.

Driving, she was halfway there when her cell phone rang.

"Yo, Clea, bear with a change in plans."

"What change, Dunk?" she asked with a little irritation. He was a quintessential teenager when it came to scheduling.

"Well, a guy who can really help me wanted to talk with me and it's taking way longer than I expected. He's showing me some awesome wares. How about if I get started tomorrow for sure? I'll go like the wind."

She smiled a little then. When Dunk did perform, he was the best. "Sure," she said. "And good luck." With a trace of fear she considered turning around, but shrugged. She had to get started on transplanting those dahlias. The picnic was only two weeks away and there was so much to be done.

She jumped a bit at the figure flagging her when rounding the corner. Pantell Hood. She slowed and came to a stop beside him. He seemed twice as big as usual. "Boss lady!" He grinned as he leaned down into the car, his liquor breath so strong she flinched. She had never been afraid of him. *Don't start now,* she cautioned herself.

"What can I do for you?" she asked with a calmness she didn't feel.

"Listen, if I begged you, busted my butt to do everything just right, treated people with respect the way you asked me to do, would you reconsider? My mama lives fifteen blocks from your house and I make it my business to go by every day to keep an eye on your place. I'm really sick with missing my job and I've just about stopped drinking."

Clea shook her head. "Just about isn't good enough. I smell liquor on your breath."

"A few beers."

She drew a deep breath. "Pantell, I'm sorry I can't talk, I'm a bit rushed. You've got a lot of strengths and you can be a personable guy. There're lots of jobs out there. Be good to yourself and take one. I've got to go now."

He didn't press her further, but he looked so angry and disappointed. "I'm gonna make you see the light if it's the last thing I do," he muttered. He turned away then and went lumbering around the curve of the road. She drove on, parked in her driveway, got out, and walked back to the toolshed in the meadow.

Unlocking and entering the small brick building, she

always felt a sense of comfort. It was only a toolshed, but she had indulged a feeling for whimsy. *Peanuts* comic strips lined the walls. The sardonic *Garfield* comic strip was very much in evidence. She had planned to get a cat one day; her last one had died. But parrots and cats could be archenemies. Now, where had she put the plant fertilizer she had bought on sale?

Some of Dunk's jeweler's tools were stored here, and she thought about the lanky young man with affection. She tapped a vein of memory. Oh yes, behind those pottery vases in a large space. There was a series of *Mutts* comic strips she paused to admire. She turned on the small transistor radio she left in here and country music filled the air. She stopped to listen to the words of two songs.

Then her breath almost stopped as the door creaked shut and there was the sound of rasping in the lock. She felt in her pocket for the key; she had locked the padlock onto the door. It took every bit of strength she had to stay afloat. How long could she breathe in this windowless room? Panic surged throughout her system and she whimpered with fear. Pantell? Rip Jacy? Was some teenager teasing her? Few kids were vicious in Crystal Lake, but there were some.

She got her cell phone from her jacket pocket, pressed the on key. Nothing happened. She realized then that the phone had died. She'd forgotten to charge it.

Bravely, she went to the door, beat on it, cried out for a very long while, holding it together, fighting the claustrophobia that welled in sickening waves inside and around her. Why hadn't she turned back? Pantell had looked angry at her continuing refusal to hire him back. He had done odd jobs for her at home, used the toolshed. Would he hurt her? She had no doubt that Rip Jacy would. Mitch had said that Ella Jacy would talk with her. What would that story be?

Summoning all her wits about her, she began to jog in

place, then up and down the room that suddenly seemed much smaller—and it helped. She had spent too much time here today. Many people knew about her claustrophobia; certainly Pantell did. She glanced at her watch; almost an hour had passed. She had never been locked in like this before. Was someone still out there? She went to the door, picked up an old hammer, and beat mightily on the door. All she got was silence.

She kept jogging, praying, singing, laughing hysterically, anything to keep the beasts of craven fear at bay. She would never give in, she vowed, but her heart was thudding and her skin was damp with fear.

Suddenly she heard Bob's cry of "Clea!" and she wept with relief, jumped up, and met him at the open door. Nearly two hours had passed. He caught her to him fiercely. "What the hell!" he thundered. "There was a long piece of iron holding the door closed."

Stroking her back as she clung to him, he told her how he had come awake after a short spell of sleeping, called her, and got no answer. He had called Dunk and found he hadn't come to Clea's house that day. Alarmed, he had set out looking for her, come to the toolshed, and found her.

"Thank God you came," she said. "I don't know how much longer I could have held out."

He kissed her face that was wet with tears and held her as if he could never let her go.

"I saw Pantell on the way in," she told him. "He looked very angry when I said I couldn't take him back."

"You're going to have to be more careful. Take no more chances. Do you understand me?"

"Yes," she said meekly. "Thank you for always looking out for me, taking care of me."

He kissed her face, smoothed her Afro-aureoled hair, then growled, "Baby, you're my everything. I couldn't make it without you."

At home Mitch came late and talked with them.

"We've examined the toolshed, the premises of your house, and nothing's amiss. Pantell Hood is the kind of childish man who'd do a thing like this and I'd guess that to his mind he's got a real beef with you." He sighed. "Then there's Rip Jacy. We believe he's in the area. His wife said she'd come this afternoon or tonight to talk with you about Rip. She's really scared of him now. He's threatened you both.

"Still, I keep thinking Rip is smart enough to know that when he sent his wife the e-mail, he'd be the prime suspect *if* he sent the other computer messages."

Clea pressed a hand to her breast over the silver and turquoise amulet. She had been too afraid to think of it in the toolshed, but she had prayed and her prayers had been answered.

Ella Jacy came an hour or so before dinner. They invited her to stay, but she said she had to get home before too late. Shuddering, she told Clea and Bob, "He's out there somewhere, so you be careful the way I'll be careful." Then she thrust a copy of the e-mail at Clea. The title was *Guessing Game*, and it read:

My wife,

I'm using you as a conduit to Clea Wilde. I tell her as I tell you that revenge is sweeter than any dessert and I will have my revenge. She's going to pay for ruining my life.

Rip

Clea wondered at his use of a word like *conduit*. Mitch had said that Jacy was smart and liked to give the impression he was even smarter. He wouldn't know about her claustrophobia. Had he been watching, planning to come back and finish her off?

Clea checked her e-mail early that night, still fighting fear. She was a woman who ran with the wolves and she used her fear as a weapon against what she feared. Yet the message grated on her nerves like metal sharply rasping glass.

Wild Heart,

I'm back on target again. It is part of my revenge that it may be a day, it may be a month, a year before payback time. This is my longest message and a warning to you. Today should tell you I know where you are at all times. Clea, you are in my crosshairs now and you will pay, and pay dearly.

This time Nightmare locked you inside your tool house as he will lock you outside of life. YOU WILL NEVER GUESS WHAT HAPPENS NEXT!

Nightmare!

Chapter 14

She hadn't been careful; now she was paying the price. Clea had gone back to her house to pick up her last wolf photograph and move it to her new home with Bob. Dunk would be inside, she'd thought, but his car wasn't there. He hadn't called.

She stood near the corner of the side entrance on the patio and a vision came of her scattered underwear, all of it at once, a nightmarish blending of two times the monster had struck. Her mind also went to the toolshed in the near distance and being locked in there. She was still breathing shallowly, but turmoil filled her mind. Anger stiffened her spine at the fear she felt.

At a slight cough behind her, she began to turn, dreading what she would find, and she was not surprised. Rip Jacy stood close enough so she could feel his rank breath on her face.

"Well, Wild Heart," he began and his voice rasped with hatred. She was consumed with fear at his evil, but he didn't come closer. He glared at her, his eyes reddened, and he laughed a very low laugh that seemed to her to reverberate throughout the yard.

He stepped back and she saw the gun in his hand pointed at her heart. Would he kill her quickly? Or take his time? She thought of the amulet around her neck and focused on it. His voice was clear then, ringing as he said, "You will never *guess*," and the last word echoed, went onto the night air in multiples of *guess, guess, guess*. The gun fired and she waited to feel the pain, prepared to die....

"*Clea!*"

She came awake gasping for breath, sweat pouring down her body, as Bob turned on the bedside lamp and drew her close, cuddling, saying, "Baby, you were having a nightmare."

"Rip Jacy," she whimpered. "I saw him. He was at my house."

Bob rocked her slowly. "Calm down, honey. It was only a dream. Tell me about it."

At first she couldn't get her breath, then she told him the dream. He was quiet, steadily stroking her. For long moments they lay on the bed and gradually she quieted and sat up. He smoothed her soft, curly Afro and kissed her face.

"It's a little after five," he said, "so it's almost time for us to get up. Otherwise I'd give you a sedative. It was only a dream, sweetheart."

Clea shook her head. "My dreams are often prophetic. I had a series of really bad dreams about Laura before she was killed. I dreamed about Jack collapsing before he died of a heart attack, and he had shown no signs of heart trouble. I've taken the trouble with this madman in stride, but the dream scares me more than anything he's done so far."

Bob breathed deeply, thinking he was scared too. Clea's wolf nature led her to be brave, careful but brave.

"In the dream," Bob said, "do you know why you went to your house in the first place?"

"Yes. To get the last wolf picture I'd forgotten. It was in my bedroom and it was my favorite. I called it my guardian wolf because Papa Curtis gave it to me when I was born."

"Good enough reason. This will make you be very careful. You've got to promise me that, Wild Heart."

"I promise you *and* myself."

He stroked her abdomen and her breasts, long soothing strokes, not erotically, but for comfort. "I love you," she said softly. "How can I ever tell you how much I love you?"

"I think I know and I think you know how much I love you. We've got each other now, darling, and the best is yet to come."

"You're thinking of a baby."

"Yeah."

"And I really will be careful. Do you think they'll ever find Jacy? She shivered. "*If* it's Jacy. I saw something evil in Pantell when he stopped me on the road just before I was locked in the toolshed. I don't think I ever saw that in him. I know he can be mean. He beat up a friend in an argument, a woman he lived with. She refused to file charges against him. She told police he threatened to kill her. But I think Jacy's meaner because I think he's crazy. He expects to do his dirt and have you make no response."

Bob squeezed her shoulders. "Whoever intends to hurt you comes through me and *he'll* get hurt, badly."

Under his ministrations, Clea began to relax, to feel herself again, but she would remember the dream for a very long time and be spooked by it.

In their robes, they went downstairs to the kitchen. "I'll fix you breakfast," Bob said, "just tell me what you want."

"You're sweet," she said softly. "I'm hungry, so Canadian bacon, scrambled eggs with shrimp, waffles with honey. I'll do the orange juice; I want a really big glass. Grits with a lot of butter . . ."

Bob watched her and grinned. "Keep on. I'm delighted that you have an appetite."

She sat at the table, patted her stomach, and shot him a sensual glance. "We've done a lot of loving. Who knows if I'm eating for two already?"

Bob laughed and kissed the top of her head. "My seed is potent. It had better make good fruit." He began to get items from the refrigerator.

Albert and Violet came in. "Well, good morning," Violet said. "Do we have new hands on board? Let us finish whatever you've started."

Bob shook his head. "No. This is something I want to do. Go look at the sunrise when it comes up. Enjoy yourselves. That's an order."

Glancing at the younger couple affectionately, Violet and Albert left, but paused at the door. "Now if you need anything . . ." Albert said.

Laughter crinkled Bob's eyes. "I can handle it," he said. "This is a labor of love."

Back in their bedroom after a long, leisurely breakfast, Bob and Clea prepared to shower together when there was a knock on the door. Bob answered and Albert stood there, frowning.

"Cade Webb would like to speak with you, Dr. Bob. He says it will take only a few minutes and he looks very upset. I said I wasn't sure you could see him ."

Bob's face set in a hard line as he nodded. "I'll be right down. Offer him coffee, whatever else you wish. Seat him in my study."

They showered quickly before Bob dressed and went downstairs to find Cade Webb pacing the floor in Bob's large study.

"Good-morning, Cade." There was no warmth in his voice.

Words fairly tumbled from Cade's lips. "Thank you for seeing me. I had to come. I'm early because I have to get to work."

"Work's very important to you, isn't it?"

"I guess it is, but I don't want to talk about work." He paused a few moments and his voice broke as his words seemed to jam in his throat. "Artie's not going to make it, is he?"

Bob faced Cade like the adversary he was. "Do you give a damn, Webb? You haven't acted like it. You were the one who said God may see fit to take him and there's nothing anyone can do. Well, if there's anything *I* can do and his personal doctor can do and modern medicine, he *is* going to make it, no thanks to you."

Cade's breathing was ragged. "I know you don't think much of me and I don't blame you. I don't think much of myself right now. Maybe you'd understand if you knew I came up hard. My mama died when I was eight and my daddy beat us on schedule, because we kept living. He was a mean drunk the way I'm a mean drunk and he hated feelings, the way I hate feeling anything deep. To me, to feel is to hurt—bad, maybe to die. Oh hell, Doc."

Cade fought to hold back his tears and Bob's heart began to soften, but he held his ground.

"My wife tells me she never wants to see me again if Artie dies, and even before she said it I visited Artie in the hospital—took time off from work, which I never would have done before. He's fading, Doc, and I've never been able to admit how much I love him, never told him.

"I'm going back to the hospital and I've got to tell him I love him. I won't be able to live with myself if I don't. Talking with you helps. If you could be at the hospital when I go back, it'll help. I've just got to reach Artie, Doc."

Tears came down Cade's cheeks as he told Bob, "I cried last night for the first time since I was a little kid. At first I hated myself for feeling weak, but God put his hand on me and told me to keep on. Can you be there?"

Cade's eyes were pleading and his voice was raw with pain. "The last time I cried was when my mother died and it was the last time I prayed. I went on to become the hard man I am now. I don't know why Marian married me, why she's stayed with me. I had the world and I've thrown it all away."

Cade's despair filled the room and Bob was touched. He got up, placed his hand on the man's shoulder, and told him, "Let's be at the hospital for the first visiting hour. I want us to see Artie as soon as possible. Clea will want to go."

* * *

Little Artie Webb lay on his high, white hospital bed, wan and unsmiling, but his face lit up when the three grown-ups walked in.

"Dad," he cried, "you brought Dr. Bob and Miss Clea. Oh yeah, *Mrs.* Clea now."

They all hugged and kissed Artie, who looked surprised. "Dad, you don't like to kiss. You always say hugging and kissing is for sissies."

Cade sat on the bed by his son, put his hand on his shoulder. "I've said a lot of fool things in the past, but it's going to be different now. *I'm* going to be different. Artie?"

"Yes, Dad."

As Bob and Clea sat by the bed, Cade took his son's hand, kissed his brow. "*I love you, boy,*" Cade said with heartfelt tenderness, his voice breaking. "I haven't said it before, I don't think, and if I did I haven't said it often enough, but I *do* love you. Can you forgive me?"

Artie nodded, his face brightening. "But you always say 'forgive nothing, and get even for everything.'"

"I've been a fool and I'm asking you to help me change." He squeezed Artie's hand, patted it. "Can you forgive me?"

"Sure." He looked at his father, shy now from past encounters. "I love you a whole lot, but you never let me say it. You said it was for—"

"Yeah, I know, sissies, but I was so wrong. Listen, Artie, you get well and I'm going to let you teach me how to paint, well, draw anyway, if I've got any talent."

Artie's eyes lit up. "That'd be way cool. You never know until you try."

Bob smiled. That was one of Marian's favorite sayings. Still shaky, but already beginning to be secure in his father's new love, the boy looked now at Bob and Clea. "Gee, you sure look pretty, Mrs. Clea. My mom looks good in that color too."

Clea wore a pale yellow ruffled blouse and matching slacks. Artie's smile got a little wider. "Your Afro looks great. My art teacher tells me to notice everything about people, and I like noticing you."

Bob shook his head, smiling. "You know I think you're going to make a first-class ladies' man."

"Is that good?"

"You bet it is. It's what every male artist needs."

"Mom told me you've got some fabulous wolf photos and paintings at your house, Mrs. Clea. Could I see them sometime?"

"Any time you wish," Clea told him. "Just get well and out of here. I've got a wolf painting that has your name on it—oh yes, and an arrowhead you'd like that's over a hundred years old."

Artie whooped then, but fell back in a spell of coughing. His doctor came into the room, greeted them, and bent over Artie. "And how are we this morning, young man?" He glanced at Artie's chart. "I see your temperature's gone down from last night. How do you feel?"

"I feel a whole lot better, Doc," the boy said. "I've got a lot going on."

The doctor smiled. "You look much better, different from the sad little lad I left last night." Dr. Heller was grave when he said to Cade, "You mean everything to your son. He loves you. Treasure that love."

Cade sounded choked when he said, "Believe me, from now on I *do* and I *will.* I thank God for making me see the light before it's too late." His eyes pleaded with Artie's doctor to tell him it wasn't too late.

"Something seems to be perking him up," Dr. Heller said.

Clea, Bob, and Cade went to the anteroom to wait until the doctor finished his examination. It took a little while, but he was pleasantly surprised at the change he saw in Artie. He called Cade and Bob outside into the hall.

"Well," Dr. Heller said, "he certainly seems to be rallying, but we can't get too hopeful too soon. Dr. Redding, you know all too well what heartbreak can lie this way."

Bob nodded. "But he's much better in so short a time."

"Let's hope it's not just temporary."

"Give me any hope at all, Doc," Cade begged, "and I'll hold on to it. My kid's life is now my life, always has been. I just never knew it before."

The doctor patted Cade's shoulder. "Keep showing him all the love you know how to give. Visit him often. Be open with him. I don't have to tell you what love does. It has worked and will always work miracles. We're not the final answer; God is."

Cade's eyes filled with hot tears. "Thank you, God," he turned his head aside and prayed, "for giving me another chance. I won't blow it again this time."

Bob and Dr. Heller were silent before the sincerity and the feeling of Cade's short, fervent prayer.

"He will get well?" Cade asked anxiously.

"I don't know the answer to that, but if pulling out all the stops modern medicine has to offer and your love can do it, he will. Pray, Mr. Webb. Pray hard and pray often. Pray for a miracle. We so often get what we pray for."

Chapter 15

With Artie doing so much better and no further threatening computer messages from Nightmare or frightening incidents, Clea settled down to work on the annual clinic picnic. Twenty back acres had been set aside for what had in the past been large gatherings to celebrate the event. She and Bob were cochairpersons and she handle the enterainment. So many people had volunteered to help. The affair was catered, but people were free to bring any dish they especially liked. Dr. Steve Smith had cochaired the picnic while Bob was away. He left for further short training. Now he was coming back.

As the time approached, Clea felt the excitement more and more keenly. Lying on the king-sized bed in their master bedroom, she frowned because she felt a bit squeamish. It was twelve-thirty and today was Monday, one of her free days. Staying home, she had chosen to laze about. She had met Ruel downtown and he had pleaded a tight schedule, but had made a formal October date to invite them over.

"But then," Ruel had said, "since when did brothers and their wives need a formal invitation? Come by any time you feel like it. Take pot luck. In October, we just want to do something special."

Thinking about the encounter, Clea breathed a sigh of relief. It helped that Ruel and Anne were being kind, accepting her.

Bob had come home to pick up a bag of samples he

had left when a pharmaceutical rep came to his house. "How're you doing, baby?" he asked Clea. "Taking your daily nap?"

Clea smiled at him as she lay propped up on pillows. "That and I'm feeling a bit under." She looked somber. "It's been on my mind too that it was three years ago when they found Laura's body."

"Yeah. I always think about that too."

"Mitch came by just checking. We talked about Laura. He said they've got no new leads, but he feels that Rip Jacy could be the perpetrator. He's mean enough, wily enough. Bob, I can't shake that dream I had about Jacy." She shuddered thinking about it and Bob sat on the side of the bed, drew her to him, kissed her.

"Try to put it on the back burner of your mind. Remember, sure, but don't dwell on it. You look a little tired. Maybe you're overdoing it with the picnic planning? You know that affair was popular in my father's time; it was his baby. Everything will fall into place. Don't sweat it. What can I get you?"

"Nothing, sweetheart, but thank you. Massage my back a little."

"I'll massage anything you wish me to, love." He placed a hand on her brow. "You feel a little hot. I'm going to take your temperature."

"Let me go to the bathroom first."

He went to get his extra medical bag and in the bathroom Clea studied herself in the mirror. There were dark rings around her eyes, and placing a hand on her forehead, she decided she *was* a little feverish. As she opened the medicine cabinet, her glance fell on the early pregnancy testing kit and she drew in her breath, smiling. She lifted the kit and placed it on the sink.

She hadn't been sick mornings, but she had felt tired, sleepy midday for several days, for several hours in fact. There was a virus going around and Bob was busy. She hadn't wanted to bother him. She would check with her gynecologist tomorrow.

"Clea?" Bob called. "Are you all right?"

"Yes, I'm fine. Give me a few minutes. There's something I need to do."

Tense, she opened the kit, sat down on a terry-cloth-covered seat and urinated on the stick in the package. It only took moments to register positive. Joy flooded her, then she sobered. She would, of course, go in to be tested by her doctor, but this was one of the best tests, almost foolproof.

Placing the used kit in the trash container, she went back into the room where Bob sat on the bed waiting. She went to him, stood above him. He reached up and hugged her waist, throwing her body over his. "Are you going to like being a daddy?" she asked gently. "My pregnancy test is positive."

He exploded with laughter and stood up, crushing her in his bear embrace.

"Wild Heart," he whispered, "we've done it! How can I tell you what I'm feeling?"

"You don't have to," she answered, still thrilling to her new knowledge. "I know what *I'm* feeling. I'm still woozy, but at least we know why."

He kept hugging her, kissing her face, throat, arms. He made her lie back down. "I wish I could stay with you," he said sadly, "but more people are sick than usual. I've got to get back. I'm going to tell Violet to keep a weather eye out for you."

Clea laughed. "I'm pregnant, not sick, you goofball. How long will this last?"

Bob's eyes were merry. "The whole thing? Nine months."

"You're crazy and wonderful. I mean how long will my daily sickness last?"

He thought a moment. "Possibly throughout your first trimester, but I'm sure your doctor can give you something to counter it. You're going to have to slow down at Wonderland and maybe it would be a good idea to let someone else take over as cochairman of the picnic."

She raised her eyebrows. "And let some other woman work that closely with you? I'm going to be a jealous wife while I'm carrying your baby."

"Go ahead. You'll never have anything to be jealous of with me because I'm going to be a devoted husband and lover. They say lovemaking is fabulous during pregnancy."

"How would we ever know? We've got the ultimate. Superlative? Pile on all the adjectives."

She glanced at one of two wolf paintings on the wall in a lighted alcove. Her spirit ran with the wolves. Wolves were one of her Cherokee gods, but only God was her God. "Please keep the baby and us safe," she prayed silently.

Early that evening at home, Bob and Clea looked for the arrowhead they had promised Artie and couldn't find it. Clea had moved most of her paraphernalia from her house to Bob's—*their* house he kept proclaiming, "Because you were always supposed to be here."

Clea tapped the back of her hand to her forehead. "I gave you the box of arrowheads early on," she said, "because you wanted to have them appraised. Remember? You were temporarily living at home to be closer to your father when he was so sick."

"I remember. I put them on the back of a shelf in my closet. We'll have to go over and get them tonight. I'd like Artie to have that arrowhead tomorrow."

Clea looked at him and raised her eyebrows. "Why don't you go alone, sweetie? I'm not sure I feel up to it."

"Coward," he teased her. "This would be a good time to tell my mother about the baby."

Clea shook her head. "She hasn't acknowledged our marriage so far. No, not yet, sweetheart. I want to treasure this news and keep it just between us for a little while longer."

He looked at her quizzically. "How much longer? I want to shout it to the world. My wife's having my baby. As for not acknowledging our marriage, she's just being Reba. You weren't her choice, but you're sure as hell mine." They sat on the edge of the bed and he hugged her tightly.

"Not too much longer," she murmured. "We'll let the world know it soon."

"Go with me tonight. Be my anchor."

She laughed. "As if you need one. "You're the strongest man I know. I'll go with you, but you're your mother's favorite son and I'm sure she'd like to see you alone sometime."

"She forfeited her right to that," he said brusquely, "when she rejected you." He kissed her long and ardently. "When we come back, there are things I intend to do to and for you."

"Umm," she responded. "I've got a few things in store for you too."

Reba's housekeeper, Eunice, greeted Bob and Clea at the door, hugging both.

"Well, this certainly makes my month," the attractive early-sixties woman said. She smelled of lavender and Clea plainly saw her faded beauty. She had been the children's nurse and stayed on as a housekeeper. Reba leaned on her, but Eunice brooked no foolishness from Reba. Now Eunice called out, "Company, folks. Company to warm my heart—and yours."

Eunice led them to the parlor, just off from the living room, where they found Reba, Ruel, his wife, Anne, and Colette. Reba came to Bob, hugged and held him for a few minutes, and coolly greeted Clea.

"Doesn't Clea look smashing?" Eunice asked.

Reba looked at Clea, raised her eyebrows, shrugged as Colette spoke warmly and Ruel and Anne got up and came forward with hugs and pleasantries.

"Clea's a beautiful woman," Anne said.

"Amen to that." Eunice's eyes on Clea and Bob were doting. Clea was glad she had taken time to dress in coral handkerchief linen and coordinating seashell jewelry. At the moment, she didn't realize it, but Bob did. Her pregnancy lent a radiance to her dark complexion, made her eyes sparkle.

Reba stepped back. "Speaking of beauty, this is my idea of what it is. Stand up, darling." A surprised Colette stood, garbed in ice-blue silk with gold and pearl jewelry.

Colette laughed. "Reba, really, you can't take away the fact that Clea is beautiful." She turned her attention more closely to Clea. "And you're glowing. Marriage agrees with you." She was so languid with her very fair skin and midnight hair that fell in waves around her shoulder. "And you, Bob, happiness is rubbing off on you. I haven't had a chance to congratulate you. My best congratulations."

Colette's voice caught a little on her last words as Bob and Clea accepted her compliments.

With his arm around Clea's shoulder, Bob said gallantly, "I'm glad someone else knows what beauty is." He smiled affectionately at Colette. "You're both beautiful women, but I have to admit that Clea's beauty is above them all."

"Oh yes," Reba commented dryly, "'Behold, I am black, but comely, O ye daughters of Jerusalem.' We all have our preferences. When he was a child, my son—my firstborn—and I thought a lot alike. We still did when he grew up, but he changed when he met you, Clea. I never dreamed you two would go this far." She still didn't mention their marriage.

Eunice focused sharp eyes on Reba; the other woman needed her far more than she needed Reba, and tonight she didn't intend to let her get out of hand. Now Reba turned to her. "Remember, Eunice, what a precious child Bob was? Smart, handsome, intelligent. He's always been the love of my life. He's still all the things I've said he was, but we're not close anymore."

Reba looked at Clea accusingly. "We haven't been close since *you* came along."

"Mrs. Redding," Eunice said sharply. "You have two sons and they're both here. Remember that."

Ruel laughed easily, his beige skin flushing. "Never mind, Eunice, I'm accustomed to coming in second. I used to dream about being first, but I've got my own brood now and I'm happy." His wife hugged his arm, smiled at him.

They all sat down and Eunice served them pineapple punch, small pizzas, and fresh baked chocolate chip cookies.

"As usual," Bob complimented Eunice, "you put out a mean minifeast, but we can only sample. We had an early dinner."

"Do the best you can," Eunice said, delighting in the palpable warmth that moved between Bob and Clea. She knew very well that Reba Redding despised Clea, had always despised her, but Eunice liked her spirit, her drive, was happy that she made Bob happy. A childless widow, she thought of Bob and Ruel as her own children, and both men loved her devotedly, remembered each special holiday with a gift along with flowers and candy. Bob and Ruel had always been delighted to have two mothers, and Reba didn't mind. Colette was the only friend she had other than Reba.

Once they had finished eating, Bob told his mother why they were there.

Reba thought a minute. "Oh yes," she said finally. "I straightened up your room. I found the arrowheads and wondered about them. I just assumed they had to do with Clea." She looked at Clea coolly. "You've got a really strange background, my dear—"

"It has never failed to fascinate me—like the woman," Bob said smoothly.

Ruel put his hands behind his head and leaned back,

grinning. "Remember in college when I fancied myself an actor and I swore I'd become a movie star? Some said I was good. Mom, you didn't like that choice at all and I soon changed my mind. Clea's background isn't so strange. I think it's interesting." He smiled warmly at Clea.

"Don't remind me," Reba said sourly. "You chose the right profession, law, and, practicing with your wife, you've become a major success. You're politically active and you'll be a judge one day, dear. Mark this well." She turned to Bob, grimacing.

"I—ah—put the arrowheads in the cupboard in the basement. I meant to call you, but I'm so busy as you know. I was going to throw them out."

"But you didn't," Bob said sharply, tensing.

"No. I want to keep everything of yours, even secondhand." Her eyes pleaded with her son to come back into her heart as he had once been. Bob's glance said those days were gone. He had a beloved wife and he was divinely happy with her.

"I'll go and get them. Be back in a jiffy," Eunice said and left the room.

Ruel tapped his foot, looked at Bob and Clea. "You two certainly look like you're in high clover. I'm happy for you."

"Thank you," Clea murmured, "we are happy." She and Bob looked at each other and the glance caught fire, shimmered between them.

Colette felt her heart constrict. She had always put up a good front, but she loved Bob Redding, had always loved him and she was heartsick when he turned from her to Clea. No, she thought ruefully now, he hadn't turned from her, because he'd never been serious about her. The romantic love had all been on her side.

Reba turned to Colette. "You look so beautiful tonight, my dear. Your skin is gorgeous and your hair . . ."

With narrowed eyes Bob looked at his wife's beautiful Afro that framed her silken-skinned dark face, making her look like an Ethiopian princess. Looking at her even features and sparkling dark eyes, he loved her more than he had ever loved anything or anyone. He smiled now at the compliment his mother paid Colette. Colette and he had always been friends, but with him it had gone no further. Clea was what he had always looked for, dreamed about. She had brought excitement and splendor and magic into his life. She still did. She always would.

"How's the clinic going?" Ruel asked.

"Everything's great," Bob said. "We've had a lot of summer flu and more emergencies than usual, but I'd say it's going really well."

Reba sighed with exasperation. "You're a trained heart surgeon, my love. Why on earth you'd waste yourself tending to a bunch of no-goods any fairly good doctor could serve I'll never know."

Bob exhaled sharply. "It's what I like doing, Mother. I never liked operating; it just isn't my calling. Dad once operated the clinic, loved it. You dissuaded him. I think he could have lived to be a very old man if he'd stayed with what he loved."

Reba's back came up. "Your father was building, had built, a reputation as one of the best heart surgeons in this country. He was smart enough to want fame and fortune."

"He loved you, wanted more than anything else to please you."

"He was happy. I made him happy."

"And I think he died too early because with all his fame and fortune, he wasn't happy."

"I never knew you felt this way."

"I stopped being close to you after he died. I had some bitterness."

"I thought so, but you drew away from me. I'd be glad if you returned at any time."

Eunice came back with the good-sized box of arrowheads. "Found them without any trouble," she said, putting the box on an end table. She began to collect the dishes, placing them on a tray.

Bob got up. "Let me help you with those."

Eunice laughed. "You're a prize, Doctor. I'm the housekeeper; let me be one. But thank you."

"You're more than any housekeeper. You're a jewel is what you are," Bob said gallantly as a flush rose in Eunice's face.

Bob took the tray from Eunice and took it out into the kitchen. When he came back, Ruel asked him, "What about the land you own outside of Crystal Lake? Developers are aching to put up a shopping mall on it."

"I'm saving it for my kids. It'll make a nice inheritance."

Reba's hand went to her face. "Oh dear. I hope you're not having children right away. It takes a while to know a marriage isn't a mistake."

Eunice shot Reba a keen look but said nothing as she watched a strange expression cross both Bob's and Clea's face. Had Clea been pregnant when they married? It would be sweet, if she was already carrying Bob's child.

"Don't concern yourself, Mother," Bob said easily. "Clea and I can handle our lives. You just get on with yours."

"I see," Reba said miserably. "Will you need me for your precious clinic picnic this year?" she asked Bob.

"Clea and I are both handling that."

"We'll need you," Clea said easily. "We need someone to coordinate activities for children."

"I can do that," Reba said as she looked at Clea. "If I hadn't asked you, would you have asked me?"

Clea thought a minute. "I don't know. I wasn't sure you'd want to be involved. It's not quite your cup of tea. There'll be a lot of drudge work, a whole lot of people there."

"Well, I volunteered and that's even better," Reba said. Her shoulders came up. "I intend to keep being a part of my son's life as long as I can. My heart's hurting me a lot these days so I don't know how much longer I'll be around, but I . . ."

Reba looked pale then and it seemed to Clea that her breath came heavily. Bob looked at his mother, too, with concern mirrored on his face. "You're not feeling well?" he asked.

"Pay it no mind. My doctor's sending me in to a specialist next week."

"Mom, why haven't you said something about this?" Bob demanded.

"I was never one to worry people unnecessarily. You both know that. Even when you haven't done what I would have chosen, I've stayed with you."

Bob got up, patted Reba's shoulder. "You let me know what your specialist has to say about you, will you?"

Reba caught his hand, pressed it to her cheek. "You know I will, dear." Her eyes on his face were full of love and an intention to control.

"We're going to have to go because we've both got a hard day tomorrow, but you call me and I'll call you."

Ruel stood up and the two brothers hugged. Bob touched the shoulders of Anne, Colette, and his mother and pulled Clea to him for a moment. Reba's eyes were bitter on her son and his wife, whom she hated above all others.

Chapter 16

"Steve Smith! Oh, it's so *good* to see you!"

Clea went into the arms of a stocky chocolate-skinned man with smooth black hair and brown eyes. He gave her a bear hug, then held her away from him. She looked lovely in a raspberry, sun-back, Egyptian cotton dress.

"Likewise," Dr. Smith said. "You're looking fabulous as usual. An old married woman, are you?" He hugged her again. "Well, marriage certainly agrees with you. Congratulations and all that. Where's my buddy?"

Clea couldn't stop smiling. Steve Smith had been Bob's best buddy since med school. "He went into town to pick up a few items we forgot. We weren't expecting you until next week."

Steve grinned. "Well, I changed a few priorities around and here I am." He took her left hand and looked at her rings, patted her hand. "Nice big rocks you're wearing, lady. Bob has always had good taste."

"Thank you. I certainly love them."

"I'm glad you changed your mind and married the poor slob. He was in hell after you checked out."

Clea was thoughtful then. "I couldn't let him go, Steve. He's my life and I was younger when I left."

Steve looked at her, appraised her carefully, his eyes narrowed. "You seem different somehow. More mature, and you look ethereal."

She hadn't meant to tell anybody for just a little while,

but she couldn't keep it from Steve. "We're pregnant," she said softly.

Steve laughed delightedly. "Well, I'll be damned. Triple congratulations. Do I get to be godfather?"

Clea laughed then deep in her belly and it was a joyous feeling. "We've had two young volunteers, but what the hell? Sure, why can't a lucky baby have *three* godfathers. You'll meet the other two here. Oh." She patted her abdomen. "This kid has it all going on already."

Artie Webb, shepherded by Cade and Marian, came to them. Clea made the introductions, telling them, "Two of my chosen godfathers are here. Has anybody seen Dunk? I think you three are gonna need to get your act together."

Artie grinned delightedly, saying to Steve, "I know you from way back."

Steve laughed, patted Artie's shoulder. "You were a smart little kid coming in for checkups when I left. You were only four then, but maybe you do remember. You were already good at drawing. How's that coming along?"

Artie's eyes went wide. "You remember that? I've gotten to be pretty good. I've been sick; now I'm so much better. Getting well."

Cade put his hands on the side of his son's shoulder as his mother beamed. "The kid's been through a lot, but he's getting on top of it now. Thank God for Dr. Redding and Artie's specialist."

Catching sight of Dunk, Clea waved and motioned him over. He loped toward them, his face wreathed in smiles.

"Dr. Smith, hey!" he said as Steve hugged his lanky frame.

Clea put her head to one side a little. "Now all three godfathers are here. All three of you still think you want to be our baby's second parents? No, third, because Mama Maxa and Papa Curtis will kill me if they don't come second."

"I'll take any level I can get," Dunk said. "And yes, I'm really straining at the bit to be next to this kid."

"And I'm gonna be right in there pitching." Artie chortled. "We'll grow up together. D'you know what you're gonna name him, Mrs. Clea?"

Clea thought a moment. "Probably junior, but my husband swears there will be others and you'll get your chance."

"I'll go for that," Steve said as he glanced warmly at the two younger people and the Webbs.

"Well, we got here and already the place is filling up," Mama Maxa said as she and Papa Curtis came up behind Clea. "It's a beautiful Saturday, perfect for a picnic." Papa Curtis carried a big woven Cherokee basket. They were staying with Bob and Clea, having a wonderful time.

"What's in the basket?" Clea asked as Steve hugged the older couple.

"Blueberry and strawberry jam tarts that Papa and I made," Mama Maxa answered. She pulled back the cover and offered them to the people standing there. Steve took one of the small blueberry tarts and bit into it, rolling his eyes at the delicious taste. Marian said Artie couldn't eat sweets, doctor's orders, so they wouldn't take one either. Dunk had nearly wolfed his down before he got started.

Bob came up, hugged Steve tightly, and kissed Clea. "You're beautiful babe," he told her. He turned to his buddy. "Is my wife the most gorgeous woman you've ever seen or is she the most gorgeous woman you've ever seen?"

Steve laughed. "I can never quite believe her; she sure is."

"You two flatter me," Clea said, flushing.

"Put me in there to flatter you," Artie spoke up. "That raspberry color looks great on you and the earrings make me want to paint you." He looked at his dad. "Can we run home after a while and get some of my painting gear?"

"No problem," Cade said, and Bob looked from the boy to his father, smiling, thinking about the changes a few weeks could bring. Artie was beginning to look robust and he was very, very happy. The leukemia had lessened greatly and his oncologist said in all probability he would heal completely. But Cade still prayed, had never stopped praying.

Bob looked at his wife, whispered to her, "You look good enough to eat. Be careful or I'll make you my picnic fare."

She swatted him playfully. "Act like the daddy you're going to be," she said as the group stood openmouthed at first, then surged around her with congratulations.

"What about me?" Bob demanded. "I'm very much an actor in this play."

Mama Maxa laughed. "But you don't have to lug it around for nine months."

"Ha, don't you forget, I'm the one who goes out to get the watermelon she craves in the snows of January."

They all laughed as others came to join them. Frank and Caroline Steele of the Singing Steeles would perform today. Nick Redmond was there with his combo and his beloved wife, Janet, who carried their year-old son. Caroline hugged Clea, who told her about the baby, and Caroline hugged her again.

Clea went closer to Janet and her heart turned over at the sight of the precious bundle she held. She had seen Nick and Janet many times when he performed at Wonderland.

Now she took the gurgling baby from Janet, who told her, "Hold him close because he won't be here long. He comes complete with nurse and she'll soon be taking him home."

The picnic was on the back twenty acres of Bob's estate, in front of a wooded section with clear streams in the hundred-and-ten-acre plot. It was a beautiful site, very well kept. A grove of widely spaced oaks gave them shade in the mild early September day. Cerulean skies stretched over them; only a few streamer clouds hovered.

Bob had gone to oversee the barbecue pit and Clea found herself alone. For a long moment she felt sad. Jack had loved these picnics, had been a major player. She felt her eyes fill with tears. Carlton came to her, touched her arm. "Surprised to see me?" he asked.

"I invited you, remember?"

"You didn't think I'd come. Of course, I'm devastated at your marriage, but I came up the hard way and I can handle it. Did you marry Redding because you were pregnant?"

She was bothered by the intensity of the question and shook her head. "I wasn't, but I am now."

He took her hand. "Congratulations," he said sincerely as his voice went rougher. "If you ever need anything at any time, I'm always there for you. I've said it before and I'll keep saying it. Clea, no matter who else comes into my life, you'll always come first."

Clea noted that he kept glancing at her abdomen hungrily and she knew he wished the child was between them. "You deserve much better than that," she told him. "You're a great guy, Carlton. Work on finding someone else."

"I've been married twice before. I've even thought I was in love until I met you. You've got it for me and I don't think that's ever going to be any different. Your song is getting kudos from the groups and they and single artists are begging to record it. Pregnant women work these days until they deliver. Say you'll stick with me; I want you to record this song." He smiled sadly then, living inside her song as he said, "I just can't let you go."

Bob heard Carlton's last words as he walked up behind Clea. "Hello, Kelly. How are you?"

"I've been better, hardly ever worse," Carlton said truthfully, and Clea's heart went out to him. Bob caught her hand.

"They've been barbecuing all night," Bob said, "and

the meat is fantastic." He turned to Carlton. "Did Clea tell you our news?"

"About her being pregnant? Yes. Congratulations," he said dryly, but his smile was deep at Clea.

"Thank you," she said softly. Bob didn't answer. Carlton was a hunk in gray Dockers and a gray polo shirt, but Bob had a brand of gorgeous manhood that few could reach. In navy trousers and a pale blue polo shirt, he was in his element. Tall and proud and godlike. Sensual, sexual, warm, and loving, he was everything she had ever wanted and she was never going to let him go.

"Listen, Redding," Carlton said tightly. "You need to know this. If you ever fail her, ever hurt her in any way, I'll be there. It's not the first time I've said it; it won't be the last. I want to make sure she keeps that uppermost in her mind. I love your woman and I've loved her for some time. I don't think it's ever going to change. Can you live with that?"

"Yeah," Bob told him. "I can live with it. Clea is my wife and the mother of my unborn child. I'll never hurt her and I'll never fail her and I think you'd better move your love in another direction. We're going to stay together—always."

Carlton came back fighting. "I didn't get where I am by giving up."

"Well, you had damned well better."

"Bob, Carlton," Clea said levelly, "let's stop this." She said to Carlton, "I told you, Bob is my life and I meant it. I hope we can go on being friends, working together, but Bob's right. We're having a baby and I want nothing and no one between us, not even you."

Carlton drew in a very deep breath. "Okay," he said, "Oka-a-ay. I'm going to back off, but I meant every word I said." He grinned wryly. "I think I'll go and sample the barbecue."

He walked away then and the sound of Nick Redmond's combo floated joyously. People crowded around the bandstand and Nick encouraged them to sing along with him. Clea reflected that everyone seemed to be having such a great time.

"Word gets around quickly," Detective Mitch Tree said as he came to them. "Congratulations!"

Bob and Clea thanked him and he explained, "I met Mama Maxa and Papa Curtis. They couldn't wait to spread the good news. You look right on top of it, Clea, and it couldn't happen to a nicer couple. Are you singing today?"

"I've got a new song. Yes. Is your family here?"

"Oh yes, my wife and four crumb crushers wouldn't miss it. They woke up and got on my case at four-thirty this morning." He got somber then. "Clea, I'm going to have to talk with you."

"I get left out?" Bob teased.

"Just for the moment. I really need to run something by Clea, but not until later. I'm still putting the pieces together and this picnic may help me do it."

The clinic picnic was a time for fun and games—and delicious food. Clea and Bob moved among the attendees, shaking hands, exchanging tidbits of information and thoroughly enjoying themselves. Bob was deluged with residents who were grateful and delighted to have him back. Mama Maxa and Papa Curtis knew many of the people since they visited Clea often. Their fruit tarts were a great success and people raved about them.

Although catered, the affair could not have been homier; so many people brought their favorite dishes. Long, red-checkered tablecloths covered the tables that groaned under the weight of slabs of juicy barbecued pork ribs, fat pork and beef sausages, barbecued chickens, roast beef, chicken and tuna salads, fried and baked fish, succulent baked hams, and platters of carved fresh vegetables. There were huge bowls of Alina's famous potato salad and Clea smiled thinking about her friend who would run Wonderland today. Going from table to table, she selected food and placed it into a large box to send over to Alina. Enough for her entire family.

Steve came to Clea, shaking his head. He sipped from a large paper cup of apple cider. "I think," he said, "I missed this most of all. No other apple cider is like what we make in Crystal Lake." He smacked his lips.

"And here I thought *we* were what mattered," Clea teased.

"Oh, people are a dime a dozen," Steve said drolly. "Really good apple cider is to be found in one place in a lifetime. Only thing that beats it is scuppernong wine."

Clea glanced at another long table that held desserts. "What's your sugar poison of choice?"

People moved around the table, eagerly selecting from the delectable chocolate and coconut cakes, eyes glazed at such plenitude. Apple and lemon and custard pies were beautifully laid out. There were huge containers of homemade fudge. The food looked as good as it tasted and there were big freezers of vanilla and fruit and chocolate ice cream, both homemade and commercial.

Steve licked his lips. "Lord, greed is going to be my undoing this day. Saint Peter will greet me at the pearly gates and tell me, 'Man, good food was your nemesis.' I don't like passing them by, but women and song I can be normal about. Show me food like this and I turn pure glutton. You're not eating much."

"I've sampled a lot and I'm singing in a few minutes. You don't gain a pound with all this eating."

"Good genes, I guess. My dad always teases me and says the fat's waiting around the corner for me when I get older. You're sure in great shape, girl."

Clea laughed. "Thank you." She ate chocolate fudge cake and licked the extra icing from her fingers. "Childish," she commented, "but oh so satisfying."

Nick Redmond loped over to them, greeted and hugged Steve, said to Clea, "We're going on, so we're ready for you. Are you ready for the crowd?"

"And me, a crowd of one." Steve chortled. "I worship at this woman's shrine. If Bob hadn't seen her first . . ."

"Flatterer," Clea said, smiling.

Nick rubbed his chin. "I'm not so sure he's just flattering you."

Clea sang at one o'clock, backed by Nick and his combo. Happiness hugged her like a second skin. She felt laid-back, at ease, yet excitement ran like a fever in her blood. Looking out from the bandstand, she saw that Bob was at the front of the audience, and he blew her a kiss, which she returned.

Nick stepped up to his microphone. "We've got another great song from a beautiful lady we all love—the former Clea Wilde, now Mrs. Robert F. Redding!"

The crowd roared its approval as Nick and his combo slid smoothly into Clea's newest creation. Only as she began to sing did she see Carlton standing a little apart near Mama Maxa and Papa Curtis. She smiled widely as she looked at the three; they knew how Carlton felt about her.

The new song was infectious, gay:

Last night we made love like heaven.
Your fire-hot kisses made me make a vow.
This I know and know for certain:
I'm NEVER GONNA LEAVE YOU NOW!

She breathed deeply and closed her eyes.

Lately we've been having trouble.
Last night has changed us and all that somehow.
Your sweet lovin's what I've just got to have.
I'm NEVER GONNA LEAVE YOU NOW!

Here she smiled directly into Bob's eyes as she sang the bridge section of her song.

I had made a firm decision.
I had said that we were through,
But when we got together last night,
You sure changed my old point of view.

Impishly she gyrated her body.

So we are right back on target,
With all the passion our love will allow.
You warm my deepest soul and I need you.
I'm NEVER GONNA LEAVE YOU NOW!

Clea's body moved rhythmically as she sang and purred the lyrics, and Nick came to her with his guitar moaning. There was an electricity in the air as Carlton stood thinking that this was one of the major frustrations of his life. This woman could be on top of the charts. She had it all, and what she wanted was what *any* woman could have, a husband and a baby. Damn it!

When she finished, the applause was deafening and everyone demanded that she sing the song again, then called for "Just Can't Let You Go" and older songs she had written. She was happy to oblige. Good feelings just seemed to come in waves, Clea thought, until she remembered Nightmare and sobered. He was out there somewhere waiting. Was he watching her now? A chill went the length of her body and her eyes met Bob's.

When the crowd let her go, Bob came onstage, hugged her tightly. The music died as he began to speak:

"I hope everybody's having a great time and I think you are. I know I am. Clea and I were married back in July, and that was the best news of my life—up to then. Now I've got another blessing. We're gonna have a baby!"

The crowd laughed and clapped. "Way to go!" Then "Clea! Bob!"

Bob grinned with happiness as he hugged Clea again and took the microphone.

"So you see," he said, "my wife had better be singing those songs to *me*." He kissed her then almost as deeply as if no one else was around and she trembled with wanting him. She had not felt well in the afternoons and evenings since she'd been pregnant and her doctor's medicine hadn't helped much. But she was coming out of it now and as her belly swelled a little, passion had returned and seemed to have a mind of its own.

Grinning wickedly, Bob held her close and whispered in her ear, "Tonight I'm gonna hit you with everything I have," and she blushed furiously.

He let her go and the smile died on her face as she saw Reba glaring at her—cold-eyed and hostile. She thought with a sickened feeling that Carlton had probably summed it up right: Reba Redding was going to be a world of trouble.

There was a footrace just after Clea sang. High school youngsters in the area competed for a silver cup donated by Steve, and ten youths with fleet feet gathered to strut their stuff. Young bodies gleaming, they lined up and Dunk came to her, his face alight.

"Remember when I ran that race and won it for three years straight?" he bragged. "I'm not sure I like getting old."

Clea and Bob laughed as they stood near the finish line. "Those were your glory days," Clea teased. "Now you're what—all of nineteen? I think you've got a few more good years left."

"You reckon?" Dunk's laughter shook his belly.

"I hear you're a business tycoon these days," Steve said to Dunk as he came up. "How's it going?"

"If things get any better, I'm gonna let my head swell" was Dunk's answer.

They quieted because the sound of a starter pistol

meant the race was beginning. Young bodies, young hearts on fire, the boys came down the track toward them with one youth ahead from the beginning. Then there were others in the lead temporarily. Suddenly, a slender youth of medium height was in the lead and sprinted to the finish line. He whooped for joy.

"Imagine," Bob said as they pressed forward with the crowd to greet the winner, "having a set of lungs that function like that after a run like that." One of the clinic workers handed Bob the silver cup to present to the youth whose face radiated joy at his success.

Things calmed then. It was a sign of the times, Clea thought, that they had three security guards there and one policeman on duty. She drank an old-fashioned, homemade root beer from a paper cup and Bob drank crystal water when Reba, Colette, Ruel, Anne, and their two little girls came up. One child was ten, the other twelve. Both were well-behaved children with an impish demeanor.

People came up to greet Reba as the widow of the picnic's founder and the mother of Dr. Bob. She introduced Colette to them, saying, "You all know her, of course. She's a banker and she handles many of your financial affairs. *I think of her as my daughter-in-law of choice.*"

Reba smiled widely as Bob's jaw dropped and Colette couldn't stifle a gasp.

"Mrs. Redding," Colette said softly, "please don't—"

"Mom!" Ruel admonished her, but Reba swept on as she looked at Bob.

"Oh, I roll with the punches. Clea Wilde is your choice, dear, but Colette is mine."

With his arm around her, Bob felt Clea stiffen. "Mother," he said sharply, "could we talk alone for a minute, just the three of us?"

With wide, innocent eyes, Reba acquiesced. "Well, certainly, love." He saw then that she'd had too much to drink and he thought on the few occasions he'd seen her since he'd been back, the same thing had been true.

Getting drunk, he thought now, *to speak her sober, public mind.*

They moved apart from the crowd and Carlton, who had stood nearby, watching with sad, angry eyes.

Near the empty bandstand, Bob stopped. It was shady there and a bright friendly sun gave the lie to Reba's hostility.

"I think you owe Clea an apology," Bob told his mother.

Reba shook her head. "No, I will *not* apologize," she told him. "*Colette* is my choice of a wife for you. Not this woman who does not fit into your lifestyle at all."

Bob's back came up. He took his wife's hand, squeezed it. "Clea and I belong together. We have from the beginning. You're fighting fate."

"Fate?" Reba scoffed. "You were raised to be a gentleman, you and your brother. That is your true fate. I have always loved you best, but he is the one who's never failed me. But then, neither did you, until *she* came along with her cheap wiles and—"

"Don't say any more, Mother. I won't stand for it."

Reba drew herself up. "You *will* stand for it. You're my son. That song she sang today is a perfect example that she's not for you." Her voice was scathing as she mocked Clea's song. "'Last Night we made love like heaven.' It's cheap, it's tawdry, and you more than anyone should know it doesn't fit what we're about."

"Clea writes many kinds of songs, some inspirational, and they're good too. And since when was lovemaking something to be ashamed of? Did you have Ruel and me from artificial insemination? Was there no bliss even on your honeymoon?"

Reba's face turned scarlet. "Don't you dare talk to me like that."

Bob's gaze was hard on the woman who had borne him. "The world has moved on and you're left in the dust trying to turn back the clock."

"You're wrong," Reba persisted angrily. "*She* will cause

you to be wrong many times. You didn't tell me you were getting married—"

"You would have done or said something ugly. I wasn't going to expose my wife to your hostility again."

"You admit that what I think bothers you. You said nothing to us about the baby. You made a public declaration and never told me or your brother."

Bob stared at his mother with deeper anger rising in him. "I have made my life my own as you forced me to do. Don't make me cut my ties to you altogether."

Reba put her hand to her heart. "You would do that?" she asked and then her hand seemed to clutch at her heart. "Oh my God," she cried. "I can't get my breath...."

Chapter 17

Others soon saw what was going on. Ruel and Steve came rushing over as Reba slumped onto the ground. Bob knelt beside Reba, barking to his brother and Steve, "Call an ambulance."

"Yeah," Steve said, "we've kept one on standby." He got on his cell phone and soon sirens sounded.

Reba was so pale as she lay there. Violet and Albert came rushing over. "Go and get me several blankets or some sort of padding," Bob instructed them. Bob eased his mother onto the grass as he and Steve knelt beside her. Quietly, Clea had gone to a nearby station and brought Bob's medical bag. Violet and Albert came swiftly back with blankets and spreads.

Bob checked Reba's pressure, her pulse and heartbeat. "Her heart's racing," he said, "but it could be a temporary thing."

Reba's skin was clammy; she suddenly looked worn, and Clea felt warm sympathy rise in her breast.

The medical team was there and they checked, then lifted Reba onto the stretcher and into the ambulance.

"I'll go with her to the hospital," Steve said to Bob, "with Ruel along for comfort. You're going to be needed here."

"It's probably just a false alarm," Bob told them. "She's had these *attacks* many times before."

Ruel nodded in agreement.

As the ambulance sped off, Bob took Clea's hand. "How are you holding up?" he asked.

"I'm okay. The question is, how are *you* holding up?"

Bob sighed deeply, looked thoughtful. "As I said, my mother has had these episodes all my life. It's the way she controls people. I'm afraid I've tuned her out."

He seemed tense to Clea.

"Should you though?"

Bob laughed shortly. "I'll reserve judgment on that. I do know that what has happened with you and me could have easily brought this on. Mother's major prisoner has escaped—me—and it leaves her less in control. Baby, she hurt you today and I cannot forgive her that."

"It's okay, sweetheart. We all love in different ways, and she *does* love you. I'm so grateful to have the fruits of that love."

Bob drew her close. "You're sweet."

"Am I? You're so bothered; I can tell."

"Hell yes, I'm bothered. She's my mother, and I guess no matter how furious I get with her, I remember all the good stuff. But I can't let her run my life, Wild Heart. I just won't do that."

Papa Curtis and Mama Maxa had hovered near; now they came to Bob and Clea.

"I heard you say you think she's going to be all right, and we're glad," Mama Maxa offered. "We were driving back tonight, but we can stay for support."

Bob hugged her. "You know you could *live* with us if you choose, but no, I think this is going to have a good ending. We'll be in close touch. My mother likes to give the impression that she's fragile, but she's steel all the way through. My dad spoiled her, I'm afraid."

Late that afternoon as Bob circulated, assured others that his mother would very probably be fine, that she'd had similar trouble from time to time, Mitch came to Clea.

They sat on a grassy knoll a little apart from the picnic crowd and he asked without preliminary, "How well do you know Dunk Hill?"

Clea's head came up in surprise. "His parents moved here when I was fifteen and I've known him since then. His father worked at Wonderland as a handyman until he died of cancer ten years ago."

Mitch expelled a harsh breath. "And his mother died last year; she was a schizophrenic."

"Yes, ever since I've known them. She had her good days, her bad days. I often marvel that he's the person he is with so much trauma in his life."

"You're fond of him."

"I think I love the kid like a younger brother. He's in my will, but he'll never need very much from me, from anybody. He's a hustler in the best sense of the word—and he's *really* smart."

"Then this is going to shock you. I said I'd get to the bottom of this and I'm on my way. The e-mails sent to you come from Dunk's computer."

Clea sat electrified, her mouth open. "How can you be sure?"

"Believe me, it wasn't easy. We're shorthanded, short-budgeted. I did much of this on my own time and you get limited cooperation because of concern about privacy. But law enforcement gets top priority, and I was just plain damned lucky. I have a friend high up at the Internet provider you and Dunk both use..."

"But *why?*" she breathed.

He shrugged. "Has he acted different in any way lately?"

She thought a long moment, then nodded. "Yes. He's been very anxious, hyper. A little while back he was supposed to clean my house and he took off because he said he had to talk with someone about his jewelry, someone who had a deal to offer him." She frowned. "There've been little things I can't quite put my finger on. He's seemed bothered. I told myself it was because he was setting up to forge ahead early. He's ambitious."

"Did you mention the e-mails to him?"

She shook her head. "No."

Mitch made pyramids of his fingers. "Everyone has friends. Maybe somebody else is using his computer, but he has to be my first line of investigation. It's *his* computer, *his* Internet account. Is he particularly *interested* in computers, do you know?"

"He could be called a computer nerd. Why do you ask?"

"Because he'd know something about how to cover his tracks, and even if those tracks aren't covered, it isn't easy to track things like this."

Clea couldn't seem to get her bearings. Mitch grinned narrowly then and told her, "I'm going to stop right here for a minute and congratulate you on your coming motherhood." He laughed delightedly. "No crumb crusher like a baby crumb crusher. Prepare to have your heart taken hostage, lady; it's going to happen."

"Thank you." Clea smiled and closed her eyes. "I think it's already happening."

That night in their bedroom, Bob walked around in his burgundy pajama bottoms and Clea admired his well-developed top body. She lay propped up on pillows on the bed in a lacy rose, very-low-cut gown that hugged her figure.

"Do you have any idea how much you turn me on?" she asked him, watching the flat black hair that grew on his chest, down his belly, and she knew onto his private parts.

Bob laughed. "You keep me so hot I don't have time to think about my effect on you."

"Are we always going to feel this way about each other?"

He shrugged, smiling. "I expect so. I've known people

where the romance has lasted into very old age. But with us, if it doesn't last, we'll have scorching memories."

She sobered then as he sat on the edge of the bed, took one of her feet in his hands, and kissed it lightly. "Hold off a bit," she said. "Let's talk about your mother, and there's something I haven't told you."

"Well, I talked to Mother's doctor and he's a bit concerned, but he's withholding judgment. Tomorrow, he tells me he's going to have her thoroughly tested. Her heart's racing, then slowing; arrhythmia, which means the rhythm isn't too good, but that can happen in cases of shock. I was frank in telling him how upset she is about us and he said that really could do it. I'm just going to wait this out, Wild Heart. I *have* to stand my ground with her."

"I know you do," she said slowly as she stroked his broad bare back. Then she told him about the conversation with Mitch and he looked shocked.

"What d'you make of it?" he asked.

"I don't know. I've always trusted Dunk."

"You love him like a younger brother."

"Yes. I asked Mitch if I could confront Dunk and he said it was okay, that it wouldn't interfere with his investigation. I'm going to talk with Dunk tomorrow. I'm going to his house early. He's got to answer some questions for me if I have my way."

"Maybe I should go with you. If he did this thing, then we don't know him. *You* don't know him. What if he proves dangerous?"

She shook her head. "I trust my gut feeling. He'll be shocked that I know, but Dunk could never be dangerous to me."

"He knows Jacy. And we don't really know what Dunk's ties are to him. You've said it often—Dunk's ambitious and Jacy is a thief, a con man. Who knows how successful Jacy's been, how much money he has access to?"

"Dunk knows Jacy, but he doesn't like him."

"With the right connections, he may have come to like him." His face was tender, concerned. "This is a scenario with questions we just don't have the answers to." He pushed her gown up until it was at the top of her thighs, bent, and ran his tongue over the silken flesh.

She moaned deep in her throat. The perfume of pink and deep red roses he had bought her the day before permeated the air. "Stand up," she told him.

He stood and she sat on the edge of the bed and slid his pajama bottoms off. He was smiling slightly, sensuality dominating his face. "Rose and burgundy," he said softly. "Your beautiful gown and my pajamas. We blend together, Wild Heart, in every way imaginable. But wait—"

He walked away from her and she caught her breath at the masculine beauty of his body, his face, his presence.

"Where're you going?" she asked.

"Checking out the music. I've set up a Barry White night for us. He's called the make-out artist and we're going to make out big time. I'm going to set your very soul on fire the way you've already done mine."

He stacked the CDs into the stereo and Barry White's enthralling baritone filled the room as she stood up, beginning to lift her gown. He quickly went to her side.

"Let me do that," he said, as he rubbed the soft tricot onto her body before he slowly and sensuously slid the straps off her shoulders and the gown down her body until it fell to the floor and pooled at her feet. She kicked the garment aside and went into his waiting arms.

For long moments they stood entwined, silent, breathing hard. The vivid sensuality of very warm skin on skin inflamed them both to a fever pitch. He walked her over to the chaise longue and gently pushed her down. On his knees, he stroked her, kissed her belly, then tongued her navel indentation.

As he moved down her body with hot kisses that scorched her, she went into a wild place when he reached her physical female triangle and loved her with a passion that thrilled her endlessly.

She grew torpid with wanting him inside her, but there was something she wanted to do.

On the bed, she moved over his body with joyous abandon, loving the salty taste of him, his muscular flesh and his erection that stood at attention—waiting for its reward.

He felt her tongue on his nipple and shuddered with passion as wild as her own. First one, then the other, and he caught his hand in her heavy hair and pulled her face to his. His kisses were ravenous as he told her, "Now, on the table!"

Chapter 18

Picking Clea up, Bob set her onto the exquisite piece of furniture she had purchased on Diamond Point. Fashioned of Kwiki wood, it was like golden oak, rounded like her voluptuous figure and polished to a satiny sheen like her lovely brown skin. He spread her legs and she wrapped them around his back, rubbing his back with her toes.

He stopped and traced a path across her belly with the outstretched fingers of one hand, asking, "What have we got in here?"

"A precious little baby," she murmured. "Yours. *Ours.*"

An even deeper passion gripped him then at her beatific face and the vision of the child they would know—from his sperm, from his loins. His powerful seed and her receptive womb; the thought thrilled him so he was trembling with excitement.

His big hands gripped her buns as he raised her a bit and pressed her farther onto him. She felt his shaft swelling as he filled her and she gloried in his touch. His hands roved her body, then pressed her, kneaded her. His tongue brushed her throat, went into the hollows and lightly licked her there, and she half fainted with ecstasy when his mouth found her breasts and suckled them. He felt so good inside her, throbbing mightily.

"How much do you want?" he asked her.

She smiled with naughty intent. "All you've got."

"I can't give it all to you in this position."

"I like it right here right now. A little later we'll change." She didn't want him away from her for even a second as her body thrilled to his thrusts, his honeyed endearments, and Barry White's honeyed, enchanting songs. Everything they had in this room created a world of magic that stroked her every nerve, her every cell.

His tongue danced with her own and left her gasping at the fervor of his kisses. Then ravening hunger unlike any she had ever known hit them as they moved in rhythmic wonder and she cried his name.

"Baby," he told her heatedly, "you're what I've got to have always."

She moaned softly beneath him as he patterned concentric circles over her face, her breasts, and her stomach. Passion caught her up in its glory as she moved her wide hips under him and he watched her hourglass figure, her beautiful face, and felt her wonderful spirit that was love itself to him.

She shuddered for a moment as he touched her womb and his swollen shaft lay still for a moment in silent homage. Now he pulled her legs over his shoulders and his eyes closed with the splendor of what they knew. The fever in him was building so swiftly and he didn't want it to end just now, so he lifted her hand, kissed the rings he had placed there, a symbol of the love they would know and share always. She moved heatedly, relentlessly, drawing him on. Her tight, hot sheath held him a willing prisoner. Her womb was a wondrous thing with a mind of its own as it ardently sought the touch of his shaft.

"I love you," he whispered. "I'll love you after a lifetime of making love to you, with you, and I don't think I'll ever get enough of you."

"That goes double for me," she responded. "I'm so glad I came back to you, married you."

"The way I always wanted us to do. We've got a lot of lost time to make up."

She laughed lightly. "We sure seem to be off to a good start."

He laughed as she made vivid, undulating, long movements with her hips and caught his breath. "Don't talk," he said huskily. "Move, baby, *move.* Keep it up and you're going to get all of what you're looking for."

And she did as he asked, clutching his rock-hard buns, forcing his shaft deeper until he shuddered and began to send his seed into her hotly receptive body. Tears stood in her eyes at the glory of this encounter. He breathed hard as he asked her, "Are you crying?"

"A few tears. Bobby, you rock my world. I really just can't let you go and I'm never gonna leave you now."

"You wrote those songs for me, even the first one when we weren't together as lovers. You knew then the way I've always known."

"Aren't you tired?" she asked him as they left the table.

"Not even a little bit. You've got your work cut out for you tonight."

"Okay. I'll go along with that. I feel so relaxed and energetic at the same time." She paused a moment to go back to the table, patted it. "You make good lovemaking support," she told it as Bob laughed.

Barry White's music for lovers wove them into his spell. She held out her arms. "Dance with me?"

"If I can stop myself from going into you long enough to dance."

But they danced in each other's arms and he held her tightly against his wide chest. She nestled there and they felt each other's heartbeats and stroked each other. "You're so precious," he told her. "We need to live forever to do all the things we want to do. Right now, I'm just getting started."

He took her hand and kissed the fingers, then the other hand. "I came for a long time," he said, "but I want more."

"You're greedy. *We're* greedy," she teased.

"When I get hold of something really good, I want a lot of it."

Bob stopped dancing. "There's a little something I need to do."

"What?"

"You'll see."

He pulled on his pajama bottoms and went out into the hall, then into the small sitting room next to their bedroom. In a few minutes he came back carrying two small glasses of crème de menthe. Setting the glasses of mint-green liquid on the night table, he picked up Clea and lowered her onto the bed. She lay looking at him with limpid, star-glazed eyes. "I can't handily drink my liqueur lying down," she said.

He chuckled. "That's not my primary purpose for bringing it in, but you can have a few sips."

"You're dominating me tonight."

"And you don't like being dominated?"

She licked her bottom lip. "I love it when *you* do it. What do you have in mind?"

He reached over and got the glasses of liqueur, handed her one, and she sipped it slowly, savoring the sweetness. He kissed her, sucking her bottom lip, desire building again in him like hot coals. Then he took the glass from her, set it on the night table but kept his own glass. Looking at her with a wicked smile, he poured a little of the liqueur into the palm of his hand and spread it over her breasts.

"What're you doing?" she asked shakily.

"You'll see," he answered as he set his glass on the nightstand. She held her breath as his ardent mouth found her breasts and slowly licked the liquid from them, pausing to suckle them, lave them as he worked.

"Oh Lord," she moaned, "this is so *good*."

Thrills shot the length of her body as he promised, "I'm going to make it even better."

With the crème de menthe licked and suckled from her breasts, she felt a wild thrumming all over her body and she wanted him again with a fierceness that surprised her. This time she sat astride him and slowly pressed herself down onto his shaft, feeling his massive power come up as she enveloped him.

He smiled at her. "Your honey-love slot is in great form tonight, but then when isn't it in fine form?"

"I like it when you call it that," she murmured. "Others say 'love box' or 'basket.' It's none of those things. 'Honey-love slot' perfectly describes what you're in."

"'Heaven' most closely describes what I'm moving in." He pulled her farther down and she gasped with pleasure. "Want it all?"

"Yes."

"Then you know what has to come next." Reluctantly, he released her and she ran her tongue over her lips at the size, the splendor of his shaft as he withdrew.

As they got onto the deep plush carpet, she stroked his erection. "You *grow*," she said. "I'm always astonished at how much your erection grows."

"*You* make it grow. It intends to make and keep you happy."

"It's succeeding." On her knees by the bed now, she felt him slide into her love slot from the back and she breathed long and deeply, savoring every second of his magnificent, measured thrusts.

He stroked her buns and squeezed them, stroked her silken back. When he was all the way in, she trembled with incredible thrills coursing through her as he moved with expert ease. This, she thought, was love and desire and passion. This, she thought, was life itself.

Poised behind her, thrusting with his heart and soul no less than his body, Bob knew they had reached a zenith of ecstasy.

After long, long moments, he asked her, "Are you nearly ready?"

"Yes," she murmured. "I'm on the edge."

He thrust deeply and evenly then, with rhythmic desire dancing in his brain. And again her womb beckoned him, craved him, and his seed seemed to him to come from his very heart and soul as he exploded in a storm of wondrous, ultimate activity and she felt herself swept up in raging swirls of a love-sea that carried her far, far out, then let her drift back to shore and the lover she still craved. Orgasms rocked her, scorched her, set up steamy delight through her whole being for long moments until she was shaken to the bone marrow.

They slept then and he dreamed the night's lovemaking all over again. Her sleep was dreamless, seamless. Both rested extremely well. She came awake early to find him with a rose-colored night lamp turned on low. He was on his elbow looking down at her, smiling.

"Good morning," she said sleepily.

He bent and kissed the corner of her mouth. "Good morning to *you*." Then his smile got wider. "It got good to you last night, didn't it, Wild Heart?"

She drew in a deep breath. "Don't tease me, Bobby. I love you and you're *always* good to me. You've got to be the world's best at just about everything, in and out of bed. With us, there's always been just two kinds of lovemaking: best and out-of-this-world."

"That's the way I feel about you, love. You—ah—get a little crazy when it gets *really* good to you."

"And you don't?"

He chuckled. "Okay, we both get a little crazy. I think about you when I'm not with you and I want you with me right then. I simply cannot get enough of you."

"I'm like that about you too. I think we're a well-matched pair. We're happy, sweetheart, made for each other, and I sure hope we stay that way."

"What're your plans for the day?"

"First thing, early, I'm going to talk with Dunk."

"Don't forget to charge and take your cell phone."

"I won't."

He drew her close and kissed her again. "A quickie to keep me from getting too hungry today?"

"I could use one too," she said as her slender fingers

stroked his face, then his biceps and his chest, and the waking dream began again.

She had checked her computer the night before and blessedly there was only a message from Alina telling her that everything had gone well in her absence and thanking her for all the food.

Now she checked for new messages and expected none, but sometime in the night, Nightmare had made his slimy presence known.

Subject: Promises to keep

So, Wild Heart, you looked happy today until your mother-in-law keeled over. Be happy while you can. The end comes soon enough.

YOU WILL NEVER GUESS WHAT HAPPENS NEXT!

Nightmare!

The thought of him watching her sickened Clea. She ran a couple of copies and deleted the e-mail. She would drop off a copy to Mitch when she left Dunk's and she would wait until tonight to show this to Bob. With Reba, he had more grief than he needed.

Chapter 19

The past night's splendor was very much on her mind as Clea parked down the lane from Dunk's brown-shingle, gray-and-dark-red-roofed bungalow and walked up to the house. Dunk was in the far side yard at his basketball board shooting baskets. He was so intent that he was unaware of anything save the shots he strove for and made every time. He dribbled the ball, made slam dunks, spun around in midair, and saw no one else.

But he came back to earth as Clea stood looking at him with solemn eyes. He let the ball roll and wiped his sweaty face with the back of his hand. He turned to her, grinning. "Hey, Clea, what brings you out so early?"

She walked toward him. "I wanted to catch you before you got away. I'm sorry if I interrupted you."

"It's okay. You look different, a bit sad, bothered, but still happy. You come by to talk about the godfather thing?"

He noted then that she hadn't smiled and he sobered. "Okay, Mama," he said gently. "What's up? What's going down?"

"I need to talk with you."

"Sure. You want to go inside? My porch furniture is comfortable. I'm enjoying it outdoors."

"The porch is fine."

Seated in the glider with its blue-and-white-patterned plastic cushion, she faced him and without further preliminaries began. "Detective Tree talked with you about your computer."

"Yeah, he did," he said dryly. "It seems he talked to you too."

"Are you sending me e-mails on your computer?"

Dunk shook his head and breathed harder. "No way! We talked about trust when you first asked me to help you. I've never done anything to hurt you or shake you up. I think too much of you."

He sounded sincere, earnest. She cared about Dunk, wanted to be his friend. "One day when you were supposed to help me and didn't come, you said you had to talk with someone. Was it about your jewelry?"

"You're right, it was."

To her surprise, sweat popped out on his face and he grabbed a towel from a nearby chair and wiped it off.

She grimaced. "This is like pulling teeth, Dunk. Tell me some more about this man you had to see. I'm assuming it *was* a man."

"Yeah, it was a man." His voice drifted off and he looked so uncomfortable. His body language was guarded, tense, as if he wanted to be anywhere but there.

He was making Clea tense. "You know I care about you a lot. You're the younger brother I didn't have. I hope you wouldn't betray me."

"Never!" he said fiercely. "I'd die before I'd betray you."

"Then tell me what this is all about. Who's using your computer?"

He sighed deeply then. "Oh hell, Clea, several people use my computer. I'm said to be good at computers. A nerd. And people want my help."

"Pantell?"

"Sometimes."

"Lately?"

"Uh-huh. He doesn't ask often, but he does ask a little more than he used to."

She drew a deep breath. "Have you seen Rip Jacy at any time lately?"

"Hell no, and I hope I don't. Jacy is the worst possible news."

Why didn't she believe him? He was talking too fast, protesting too much. Why did she get the strangest feeling that he wasn't telling the truth? His young male body seemed strained and he seemed to alternately barely breathe, then breathe too fast.

"Who else uses your computer?"

"A few others," he mumbled.

"Tell me who," she demanded.

"Clea," he said miserably, "believe me, it wouldn't help if I told you, and I can't. I'll take care of it."

"If you didn't send me the e-mails, then you know who did. You've got to tell Detective Tree and me. This is such a serious matter. This person is threatening to kill me. Did you know that?"

Horror was mirrored on his face. "No, I didn't know. Clea, I'm so sorry." His voice was hoarse and he reached over and touched her hand. "I need Detective Tree and I need you to give me a couple of days. That's not much. There're people I've got to talk to . . . get to the bottom of this."

Clea tried to assess his presence, feel his aura. He certainly exuded no aura like that in the god house the night Papa Curtis had talked with the gods and summoned up an evil spirit. But there was something dissonant about him, a division in him that she had never known to be there. His mother had been a lifelong schizophrenic. Had she passed this malady on to her son? And if she had, he would very likely deny the wrong he did.

"Will you give me time to do what I have to do?"

"What is it you plan?"

He didn't hesitate. "Play it cool. Try to get this person's confidence."

"Then there *is* a specific person you have in mind?"

"More or less..."

His voice drifted and she felt he was being evasive now and it irked her.

"Is the person you have in mind someone who can help you with the jewelry business? Rip Jacy may have access to money. God knows what he's mixed up in."

She could see his heart pounding as he said, "I don't want to go any deeper into this, because I can't say any more. You and Mitch Tree have got to give me time to find out what's going down. Just a couple of days could be enough."

"Why would that be enough when you say several people have access to your computer?"

Dunk's eyes didn't quite meet hers. "There's a certain dude I've wondered about..." he began, then stopped. He sounded breathless then, tripping over his words. "It drives me crazy when you say someone is threatening you, threatening to hurt you, kill you. Oh, I'm gonna cooperate all right, but I've go to do it *my* way."

Clea sat with her hands folded in her lap. Why didn't she believe him? His eyes on her were admiring with an edge of flirtation and it bothered her because it seemed inappropriate with what she had just told him. How much was real about him now and how much was false? She had the sick feeling that she no longer knew Dunk at all.

Getting up, she told him, "I have to go now. Please work fast and get back to us."

He stood up and kissed her cheek. "You're looking fabulous," he said softly and it unsettled her even more.

This was not a time for flirtation and business as usual. When had Dunk changed? When had she lost touch with him? She couldn't answer because she didn't know. What if *he* had sent the e-mails? He certainly knew her movements well enough. He was smart enough, savvy enough. The tone of the messages could easily be his. Yet she *had* to go along with his program. She touched his hand. "Bye now. I'm counting on you." What else could she say?

He seemed to her tense to the breaking point. "You do that and I won't let you down."

Mitch Tree was in early, eating an Egg McMuffin, when Clea was shown into his office. He looked at her face, said gently, "You saw Dunk. You look stunned."

She nodded. "What do you think?"

"Well, sit down and tell me what he told you."

"That several people use his computer. He told me they have his password. He seems to give it out freely, told me he just isn't very secretive."

"That's pretty much what he told me. I keep trying to figure out if he's sending you the e-mails. Believe me, he could be."

"He swore I could trust him."

Mitch looked at her with narrowed eyes. "All liars say the same. You get jaded in this business, Clea. People do things you'd never suspect them of. At least you're smart enough to know it *could* happen. He could have sent the e-mails to you. We're going to find out who he talks with. The only thing is, Dunk is savvy enough to know that. And if he is the perp, we'll get a bead on that too."

"Could he be cracking up with his mother's illness? He's always seemed so clear."

Mitch nodded. "He could be. He's a teenager and his hormones are just on the edge of settling down. If he has a buddy in this, we'll find out."

"He asked that we give him a couple of days. Did he tell you that?"

"No. Just that he'd cooperate in any way he could. I'm surprised he didn't say that to me. He kept saying vehemently that he had nothing to do with sending e-mails to you. He asked me what was on those messages and I didn't say."

"I didn't say specifically, but I told him I was being threatened with death."

"How did he take it?"

"Strangely. He seemed surprised, but then Dunk would know how to cover his feelings and his tracks. He seemed to want to help, but I couldn't get a bead on him. I don't feel I know him anymore. In the end he seemed a little distant and I'm frustrated. He could run, couldn't he? There's really nothing holding him here."

"He could and he might, but we'll be watching. Clea, stay safe and if anything happens please let me know immediately, if not sooner."

She forgot to mention Dunk's flirtatious behavior until she had begun driving off the parking lot.

Bob walked into his mother's room in Crystal Lake's excellent hospital. Reba was sleeping and he was shocked at how sad she looked. She came awake as he stood beside her bed.

"Bob," she murmured, "I'm so glad you came. I was afraid you wouldn't."

"I'm here," he told her, "and how are you feeling?"

"Not too well. I feel like I've taken a beating."

Was her voice really that weak, he wondered, or was she pretending again?

"Your brother and Anne have been here with me all night."

"I know. I kept in touch with him all night."

She looked at him directly. "Thank you for not bringing Clea. I'm not up to seeing her just now."

"She wanted to come."

"She would. I'm down now. That must be keen satisfaction for her to see me this way."

"Mother, don't. The hostility is all on your side."

"You *would* see it that way. Sit down, dear."

Bob sat, tense, in a chair beside Reba's bed. Even if she was ill, there were things he couldn't and wasn't going to back down on. "I'm sorry you're ill, but there are things you've got to face. Clea is my wife. She'll *stay* my wife."

Her voice got firmer with an edge of malice. "Unless she changes her mind. She's a flighty woman, Bob, from a flighty background."

"You mean she isn't Colette."

Her voice got a little stronger then. "Oh, if only you and Colette could have married."

"But we didn't."

"No, you didn't, and it will always break my heart." She paused a moment. "You're having a baby and you didn't tell me. You didn't tell me you were getting married."

"I wanted to spare Clea your wrath."

"You paint me as such a witch."

"No. I think you're a lovely woman, Mother, but you need to change. Accept Clea as my wife. In such a little while you'll be a grandmother again."

Reba smiled wanly then. "Ruel's two girls have been such a joy."

"Our baby will be such a joy. It would be nice to have you take his or her mother—Clea—to your bosom."

Reba shook her head. "I don't hide my feelings, dear. I'm incapable of pretense. When I don't like someone, I find there's always a reason."

"You didn't like Laura either."

"They're both the same kind of women, Laura and Clea, not nearly good enough for you. Don't you know your worth at all? Why do you throw yourself away on women like them?"

Bob felt his gorge begin to rise at this fresh attack on his wife. "Clea's the best, the best for me. I never knew what happiness was until she came into my life."

Reba stirred, sat up a bit, with the old fire in her eyes. "How can you say that? You and Ruel were the happiest of children."

"Okay, we were. But when I came to be a man, I felt something was always lacking in my life. I was searching and I wasn't finding what I was searching for. Then I met Clea and life has been so different for me."

"She left you and you suffered. My heart ached for you."

"And you know why she left, Mother? She couldn't take your hatred."

"I hate anybody who doesn't do you justice."

"Clea does me all the justice in the world. She's my life, Mother, and she's my wife. We're going to have a baby. I know you're ill and it hurts me to say it, but you can either come aboard or get left behind."

"You sound so cold, so harsh. I gave birth to you and you've always been my heart. Your father always teased me, saying you threatened *his* place. Yet only *you* have caused me pain."

"I'm sorry it had to be this way."

"She'll leave you one day. Her kind always does."

A shard of pure pain struck Bob's heart then. Clea *had* broken off with him. He told himself it wouldn't happen again. "No," he said. "We're together for keeps this time."

"She left you before."

"Mother, don't go there. Clea is my wife. I want you to accept that."

"Do you love me?"

"Of course I do. You're my mother."

She sighed. "This whole thing, your marriage, your baby, has left me so ill."

"You have heart trouble, Mother, or you feel you have. And you're subject to getting ill from time to time. Are you doing everything you're supposed to do?"

"Everything," she said flatly. "You can talk with my doctor. It's not just my heart, it's you and that woman."

"Please don't refer to Clea as 'that woman.' I told you she's the love of my life."

"And you would throw away all I've given you for her."

"The Bible tells us that a man or a woman holds to the

chosen mate, forsaking *all* others. That's the way I see my marriage."

Reba pulled herself up and onto the pillow, put the side of her hand over her mouth, then took it down. "I'm tired now," she said, "but please come back to see me again. I want us to be close even if I can't include your—Clea. And I'll love your baby because it's yours, but don't ask me to do what I cannot do."

Bob kissed his mother's cheek and walked out of the room. In the hallway he met Dr. Mark Willis, her cardiologist. The two men shook hands.

"How is she doing?" Bob asked.

Dr. Willis sighed and took a few moments to answer. "I wish I knew. Mrs. Redding has always been hale and hearty, complaining often about her heart, but before this I've found little evidence of anything wrong. Lately, she's had some edema and that bothers me. Her ankles have been swollen and when I've pressed them the tissues don't rebound immediately. She also may have a blood disease like polycythemia, but that remains to be determined. It would seem, Bob, that now there *is* something wrong with her heart after all."

Bob felt his own heart constrict as he asked, "How long has this been the case?"

"It's a recent occurrence. I'd say about a month. I've had tests run and I'm having more run. I've ordered treadmill, echo chamber tests. I'll have them all. This is the most puzzling case I've had in quite a while."

A month, Bob thought, developing after Clea and he had married.

For a few moments Bob felt as if he'd been blindsided. "At least she's in the best hands possible," he said.

"Thank you. You know I'll do everything possible and I will keep you well advised." And Dr. Willis said again, "I am puzzled. Basically she has always been so well."

Chapter 20

"I've got a gun. Just keep moving over to that dark green car. Don't yell a damned thing if you don't want to get hurt."

Clea fought to keep control as her heart nearly leaped from her breast. Her legs went weak, then stiffened as she tried to comply with the man's request.

"That's it," he said. "You're doing fine. Just keep it up."

They were on the outer edge of the huge parking lot of a shopping mall a short distance from her house. She had dashed out to get some thick bacon and fatback to make bean bread. Violet and Albert had not been around and the mall was well guarded. Nothing had ever happened there so she had felt safe.

"Where are you taking me?" she asked as the man walked beside her in the very cool afternoon. She shivered in her cardigan sweater.

"Ask me no questions, I'll tell you no lies," he chortled. "You always were the smart bitch. Let's see how long that lasts."

"If it's money you want, you can get it—"

"Shut up!" he hissed as they passed a security guard, with him on the guard's side. She tried to signal the guard with frantic eyes, but he was too occupied to do anything other than glance at them. Guards stationed inside the parking lots were the mall's attempt to provide added security.

As the man hustled her into his old Chevy from the driver's side, she made herself relax enough to get his decription. He was a heavy man around six feet tall, dressed in black coveralls with a black shirt and a black slouch hat pulled down over his odd-looking brown face. And his voice was strange, raspy, uneven, like no voice she had ever heard before.

With Clea in place, he got in and started the motor. "Now, if you doubt my ability to drive and kill you at the same time, think again," he said. She tried to place the strangeness of the voice. There was something *wrong* with that voice. It was as if he had undergone an operation that hadn't gone well.

At the gate with another security guard, she again tried to signal distress with her eyes, but the guard simply waved them on.

"Who are you?" she had to ask him.

"Someone who's going to be good to you, put you out of your misery." He turned to her. "Now I'm warning you. Don't talk again. *I'm* running this show. Talk again and I won't be responsible."

She thought it best then to do as he ordered. After a short ride, he turned off a side road and parked, opened a small bundle from the seat between them, and ordered her to put her hands behind her. With slender rope he bound her hands behind her back, bent, then tied her ankles together and gagged her with a white cloth. She desperately tried to think of something to fend him off. She remembered what Mitch Tree had taught her. "In any dangerous situation, *respect* your adversary." She could think of nothing save to go along with her abductor's program.

Lifting her, he got out and went to the trunk, which he'd left unlocked, opened it. Shoving her in, he locked it and got back into the car and drove away.

In the trunk of the car, she struggled to gain her balance and couldn't. It was so narrow in there. Every vestige of claustrophobia she had ever known closed in on her.

She had heard him lock the trunk and felt doomed. She thought then about Bob and his arms around her, thought about Mama Maxa and Papa Curtis, thought about her unborn child. Hot tears slid down her face and her body was turning to ice.

All at once she couldn't breathe. How long, dear God, was this going to last? She fought to scream, thrashed about as best she could in the narrow space, threw herself around as best she could. She was terrified of her own inner fear as much as of her kidnapper. *Focus on something outside of here,* she told herself and could focus on nothing because her mind was in such a jumble.

Then blessedly it came, blackness, as she slumped into oblivion. She was with God and the Cherokee gods then and nothing could hurt her anymore.

When she came to, she sat on an old, sloping dark wine-carpeted floor. A single lantern threw low light. She could not determine how long she'd been out, but her face was damp and the man in the lantern light loomed above her. "Coming around, are you?" he said, grinning. She focused on the greasy, stained carpet and stayed silent.

He was not someone she recognized, but then she wouldn't. Quickly, she saw that the face was a brown mask, a good one, but a mask nevertheless. He had thrown the black slouch hat aside and his black false curls sprang everywhere.

The man slowly pulled an open package of cigarettes from his coverall pocket and tapped one out, then he dug into his side pocket for a lighter. The lit cigarette sent acrid smoke into the air as he drew a deep drag, bent, and blew the smoke in her face. She jerked away. He stood looking down at her, grinning.

"You're just like the other bitch," he said. "All sass and brass. Only she didn't pass out."

"What other—woman?"

"You talk too damned much, ask too many questions. But your passing out gives me new ideas. Maybe I can fix it so you kill *yourself*."

She knew what was wrong with his voice then; it wasn't his. It was one of those fairly expensive false voice contraptions purchased from a mail order shop that specialized in devices one step ahead of the law. Devices to frighten, to hurt, to kill.

What did he plan to do? And she thought of the fact that the subject line of one of the e-mails she'd gotten had been *Plans for Wild Heart*.

"You smell good," he said as he came to her, sat down, and touched her breast and as she clenched her teeth, made her body rigid.

"A little later, maybe I'd pull off all this junk I'm wearing, but then you'd know, wouldn't you? And I can't have that. Not at first. But when I'm ready to take you out, I'll let you know then."

"Why would you kill me? I've never done anything to you."

"You've got a big, beautiful mouth and it's plain you're used to having your way, but you'll like what I'm going to give you before I take you out."

So he intended to kill her, she thought dully. Who *was* he? And why did he want to kill her? Rip Jacy was the likely one. Pantell? But the mask and the false voice device were like the things she had seen in the catalogs Dunk had shown her. The e-mails had come from *his* computer. He, Pantell, and Jacy were within a couple of inches of being the same height. God, if it was Dunk . . . Her heart broke at the evidence of his betrayal. He had asked for time to talk to someone. Was that, too, a lie? Dunk had looked at her lately with lustful eyes while he had not done so before. But he wanted to be her coming baby's godfather. Dunk was the product of a schizophrenic mother. Had this proved to be *his* fate?

"Wild Heart," the man whispered as he stood up, stretched his arms, and again sat down by her. He caught her close and held her as she began to struggle, realizing that the black coveralls and his black shirt were all padded. There was no way of telling his size. So much for alert descriptions.

His arms went around her. "I want to kiss you," he said, "thrill you, the way you thrill me. I've dreamed of this, but then I've dreamed of other plans for you." And the thoughts went racing down the corridors of her mind: *Plans for Wild Heart.*

"Don't struggle," he muttered. "Struggling turns me into a wild beast, I don't know my own strength when a woman struggles in my arms. *She* struggled."

Clea was certain he spoke of Laura and the thought made her blood begin to congeal. Icicles formed in her bloodstream, cold sweat poured down her back. He stroked her body, felt her with degrading, violating hands as she felt bitterness rise in her like gall.

Black tarpaulin covered the windows, the cracks around the doors. Had he done this while she was passed out or before? He had planned well and executed those plans. *Plans for Wild Heart.* When would Bob know she was gone, call the police? How could she have been such a fool to leave without telling anyone? But it had been light outside when she left and the mall she went to was the safest around.

"The other woman was like you. Lush. Inviting. The Bible tells us to beware of strange women. Evil women." He broke off then for a moment before he continued, "And you're going to have a baby."

"Yes."

"That makes you happy?"

"Yes. It makes me very happy."

He sounded furious then. "Enjoy it now because you won't be enjoying it much longer."

Her mind went numb at the thought. *Where* did he plan to kill her? she wondered.

She breathed a sigh of relief when he got up and went to a cupboard, poured liquid into two glasses and brought them back, then sat down on the dirty carpet beside her again.

"Drink this," he ordered and she took the glass of orange liquid from him. "It's bourbon and orange soda," he said softly. "This will add to your enjoyment. I've dreamed of this."

"I can't drink because of my baby," she told him.

He threw back his head, laughing, cold laughter. "Can't you get it through your head? You're going to die. I intend to get you really drunk, then you'll come to me as you go to Dr. Bob. Maybe you think I'm not good enough. Do you?"

"How can I think anything in a bind like this? I don't know what I'm thinking."

His grin became lecherous. "I know what *I'm* thinking and it's turning me on the way I've rarely been turned on." Then he muttered, "Evil women who turn men's lives upside down."

Clea remembered then that Dunk had cried when he was younger when he had told her about his mother's hatred of sex. His father had been so different, calm and loving and psychosexually mature. His mother had warned him about girls and women, calling them all, including herself, spawns of the devil. He had not let her know how much he helped Clea. Then she had died and he said he felt free. Had he felt guilty at wanting her to die so he could be free of her madness? He had no girlfriends she knew of; his jewelry consumed his time.

She wished she could see her abductor's eyes behind the mask. Dunk had often said he couldn't drink without losing it. *Was* this creature Dunk?

Clea felt the presence of the Cherokee gods, felt the spirit of her wolf guardians as the man moved closer, breathing hard. "I like a good time. Show me a good time. And I know you like a good time. I'm going to do all the things I've wanted to do to you. The things Dr. Bob does to you." His gloved hand stroked her body and her face.

She wanted to scream at him to stop using Bob's name; he wasn't fit to use her husband's name.

"Later," he said, "when the night is still young, I will put out the lights and my naked flesh will rub against your naked flesh. I will give you what you want, Clea. What you need. But for right now, padding and gloves must stay between us."

His leer was unmistakable in spite of the mask. "There *are* two points of nakedness available to us now, right now, and we will enjoy those to our heart's desire. I will blindfold you again." He pulled a long, narrow white cloth from his pocket and wrapped it tightly around her head, covering her eyes.

"Please don't do this."

"Don't order me around."

"I didn't—" she began.

"Shut up!" he roared as he tore the blouse from her body. The night air was cool against her skin and it helped to clear her head. She whimpered as his hands found her breasts and tried to reach around and undo her bra hooks and failed.

"Damn you," he raged. "I *will* have you, because this is what you want, and I'm your punishment and your savior."

With hot tears in her eyes she thought, *Oh, dear God, it was Dunk.* The biblical cadence of his speech, the terrible schism between desire and hatred of desire. Her heart hurt for him no less than it hurt for herself.

Was there nothing she could say to stop him? she wondered frantically as he caught her close and ran his lecherous hands over her rigid body. Thank God that with all the devices he wore, he couldn't put his filthy mouth on her. His fingers were bands of steel biting into her flesh. With rising horror she smelled a sickening stench from his body, his presence. It was the same stench they had smelled in the god house on her visit to her grandparents. And there was a mist behind her eyelids as the mist had appeared that night. This then was the presence the gods had brought forth for Papa Curtis. This was her nemesis and knowing it was nearly her undoing.

Then suddenly her wolf-god spirits were all around her, invisible to the fiend who threatened her, but slashing at his heels. She thought he began to let her go, but no, he held her even tighter and his hands moved down and farther down as he lifted her skirt. She struggled with all her might to stop him and he growled, "If I have to knock you out, I'll do it. My pleasure may be greater that way."

He laughed then, cold harsh laughter, and he raised her skirt, intent on what he did to her, and worse, what he meant to do. The wolf spirits came up in her then and she thought clearly. She had a baby to protect and she had to get back to her husband, undefiled, if possible. She forced herself to relax to make him think she was weakening. He growled deep in his chest. "Now you're cooking with gas. I'm gonna give you what you're hungry for."

Now her wolf spirits inhabited her body completely and she was one with them as she brought her knee up with sudden, incredibly powerful force into his groin, but she whimpered then because he didn't stop. She thought the padding had softened the blow. She heard him unzip his fly to better accommodate what he would do. He held her close to him, relaxed, breathing hard. She kneed him with all her might.

He screamed and clutched himself and she struck him a lucky furious blow under his nose with the edge of her hand, jabbed sharp fingernails into his eyes as he roared with pain and fell, doubling over, his gun under him.

Snatching the cloth from her eyes, she scrambled up and saw a slab of wood just to the right of him. She picked it up and struck him several hard blows across the head. He fell back moaning and she grabbed her blouse from the floor and sped to the door, unlocked it, and went out into the cool night air. The wolf spirits fled with her, surrounded her, gave her fierce courage and protection.

She could see plainly that the house where he had taken her was the old abandoned schoolhouse a mile back into the woods from the highway. This was a largely deserted area, with little hope of anyone coming along. Her breath was growing short and she wondered how long it would take the fiend to begin to recuperate and come after her.

Underbrush scratched her legs and arms; brambles tore at her. Tears helped her spirit, but they blinded her as she staggered along. She had to get to the highway. Then she knew she couldn't risk the highway. The fiend could recover quickly and he would look for her, his quarry. Sick with frustration, she wondered where to run to. It seemed she could hear the soft howls of the wolf spirits and she thanked them.

She had run and staggered what seemed an interminable time and she was near the highway running parallel to it when a light came close to where she ran and terrified, she crouched in a thorn bush and fought to keep from crying out with pain. Her body was cold with fear and hot with determination. Cold sweat wet her flesh and her heart felt as if it would stop beating.

Lord, she was tired, sick, *scared*. She spread her hands across her abdomen, shielding her child. The night was cool, but she was icy cold with fear and rage, the rage of hopelessness. But no, with the wolf gods running with her, there was no such thing as hopelessness. She *had* to go on.

"*Clea!*" That cry was loud and prolonged, clear on the night air. *Bob's voice,* then others. The night air resounded with her echoed name and she wept happy tears, but she had to get to them. *They* had to get to *her*. And how close was the fiend? Could he kill her before the ones who sought her could reach her?

She knew the voices came from the highway and she ran toward them. She had left the dirt path in fear of the fiend's tracking her too easily. She tried to call out, but no sound came from her paralyzed throat.

Then with a burst of speed, she saw the highway as voices continued to shout her name and she could cry out, send her voice onto the night air, saying "Over here! I'm over here!" The words were a mantra of life and hope as she ran to the highway, calling, "Bob! I'm over here!"

Bob's chest almost burst with joy as he vaulted the fence between him and his beloved, cutting his hands on the top barbed-wire strands. Then she was in his arms and he squeezed and rocked her as police and other cars lined the highway, lights shining, megahorns blaring. He pulled off his jacket and put it around her shoulders.

Hugging her to him tightly, he asked her, "What happened, love?"

Mitch and two other policemen came then and squatted beside her. Then Bob stood and pulled her up against him as he said quietly, "I'll need to get her home so I can see if she's hurt."

"You bet," Mitch said. "We'll come along for a few questions we need to ask, but we'll give you time."

As the policemen started back to their car, one stretched the barbed wire from the barrier with his hands for Bob and Clea to crawl through. On the other side, by the highway, she paused and took his hands and spread them across her abdomen. "I protected our baby," she said fiercely. "I always will."

He kissed her then, her body arched against his. "Yes," he said, then, "I love you, Wild Heart, with everything that's in me."

At home, Violet and Albert hovered over her. Violet drew her a hot bath with a whole big box of baking soda sprinkled in, then dribbled in melissa essential oil to relax her. Bob made the policemen welcome in his house as Albert and Violet made huge turkey and ham and roast beef sandwiches. Violet made Colombian coffee, tea, and chocolate. And the policemen waited to question a woman who had been a madman's quarry and was now free. They needed to know what had happened. Other policemen were canvassing the wooded area she had escaped from, seeking the perpetrator.

Soaking in the big, cream-colored tub, Clea lay back and looked at Bob, who squatted by her side. He lifted and kissed her wet fingers and she ran them over his face.

"Relax as best you can," he said. "Mitch and the others will wait. *I* will wait to hear what happened. Baby, I nearly went crazy when I found you were missing. I called police immediately, turned the place upside down when you didn't come back."

"We're lucky we live in a small city," she said. "In D.C. they couldn't file a missing persons report that fast."

"Yeah. The police chief gave the order. You've contributed so much money to them, worked so hard to help them. My wife and Wonder Woman."

Clea smiled and sighed. "I can talk now. Tell you everything. Then I'll talk with Mitch and the others."

Later that night Clea and Bob talked in their bedroom.

"So he got away after all," Clea said. A policeman had called Mitch at the house.

"Yeah, he escaped on foot, left the old car there, and they found nothing they think will help to track him. The car was very old with temporary tags, probably just picked up for your abduction."

They lay on the bed and he caught her close, kissed her gently. "I could kill the bastard," he said bitterly.

"I did him some damage, but apparently not enough since he got away."

"You saved yourself and our baby."

He softly kissed her fingers, wrists, arms, and she

wound her arms around his neck. He didn't want to crowd her after what she'd been through. She was glad then she had fought and won, because she felt more empowered than she ever had before.

"I love you so much," she said softly. "How did you find me so quickly?"

"Not quickly enough. It didn't take long to find your car still on the mall parking lot. When you weren't inside the grocery store or the other stores, we thought it had to be abduction. Fortunately, I came home early. I alerted Mitch immediately and the search began as a special favor. He thought the old abandoned schoolhouse was a good possibility and a helicopter went up, sighted the car outside, and things began to move."

"Know what I want?" she asked him.

"I'll get you anything your heart desires. Are you craving something yet?"

"Yes, you—inside me."

It thrilled him to his core when she said it. He was prepared to have her hating any man's touch for at least a while. Many rape and attempted rape victims caught hell from inside their heads and from lovers and husbands afterward.

"I'm glad you want me inside you, because that's where I want to be."

She was silent for long moments before she told him, "You spoke of healing when you're inside me. I heal with your touch too. Never so much as now." She took his hand, placed it between her legs. "See," she said, "I'm not crossing my legs. Remember the white peach caper?"

Bob chuckled, delighted at the memory. "You rebuffed me when I said I intended to get between your legs. You began and I finished saying that the road to hell is paved with good intentions."

She cupped his face in her hands, kissed him slowly before she told him, "My road to paradise has been paved with your good intentions."

But it wasn't over. It didn't end that fast. In the midst of all her passion for him, the padded, masked fiend stood, lay, sat between them. Was it Dunk who had done this? She wept inside as she wondered. Was he capable of the evil she had known this night?

Chapter 21

The next morning, Clea came awake around four o'clock. She lay close to Bob, who was snoring lightly. The night before, she had experienced a nightmare and there would be no forgetting it soon. Now she shuddered remembering. Who *was* the man? There had been that foul odor when he had tried to rape her, had intended to kill her.

Bob had taken her to the hospital where they had attended her scratches, bruises, and sore muscles. The intern had given her a sedative to take; she had needed nothing else.

She still felt the exhilaration of having fought the demon off. Animals mounted a savage fight to protect their young.

She leaned in and kissed Bob's face as he woke up.

"Hey, baby," he said softly. "You were sleeping hard when I dozed off." He caught her close and kissed her as tears trickled down her cheeks.

"I know," she said. "I expected to have hideous dreams but I only dreamed of fog and mist all night. It was like the mist in the god house when Papa Curtis talked with the gods. What do you think it means?"

"What do *you* think? You're the expert on this—the fledgling shaman."

She sighed. "I wish now I had trained to be a shaman. It would stand me in good stead. I'll tell my grandparents today what happened and they're going to be furious."

"I'm furious enough for all of us. I'd like to tear the bastard apart, limb by limb. I'm so glad you managed to get away."

"Bob?"

"Yes, love."

"Would you—would it have mattered if he'd been successful in raping me? Some men—you know, some men are turned off by their wives when they've been raped."

"Don't call them men; they're emotionally blighted fools. No, sweetheart, I'd never be turned off by you, no matter what happened, but you might have found *yourself* unable to respond."

"Last night I felt you so deeply. You came into my very soul, but then that's happened so often before. I love you so much it scares me sometimes."

"Scares me too, but it's also my glory. We forged a new bond last night, Wild Heart, one we'll keep forever."

"You were so tender with me. Thank you." She snuggled even closer, loving the feel of his hard, muscular body.

"Thank you for being my wife and my lover, my best friend, my everything."

They spoke of their courtship and their marriage, of the splendor they had known and the heartache they had endured. She got up and opened the window a little more, letting the cool breeze blow through. Getting back in bed, she lay quietly in his arms.

"I love your body," she told him. "You're so solid."

"And you're so soft. I'm going to fix and bring your breakfast in to you. I've got sourdough pancakes and blueberry syrup in mind. Have we got any blueberry syrup?"

"Uh-huh, a whole pint of it is in the back of the fridge."

"Scrambled eggs with extra-sharp cheese, scallions, and shrimp."

"You're going fancy, and I'm loving it all."

"And I'm loving *you*, the way you wouldn't believe."

He ran his tongue over her mouth and sucked her bottom lip as she clung to him.

"Don't ever leave me," she told him. "I couldn't take it now if you left."

"You're a strong woman and yes, you *could* take it," he said, tracing her jawline. "But I'll never leave, because I'll never *want* to leave you. You really are my soul mate, the best part of me."

"And that's what you are to me."

They got up and showered together and hugged in the sharp spray of the shower's three heads. She had taken a hard, long shower the night before, fiercely scrubbing off the touch of the monster who had attacked her.

"You seem calm now," he said. "*Are* you calm?"

"You do that to me. I think I could weather anything with you by my side."

"And that's where I'll be for the rest of my life."

Back in their bedroom, Bob dressed and went into the kitchen as Clea lay on the bed again. She placed a hand on her abdomen and thought of her coming child and she was happy in spite of the torment of the night before.

Yawning, she thought she really should check the computer, but she didn't. She didn't want to read anything the fiend might have to say. She was going in early to Wonderland; she would check for messages there. Bob's car was in the shop, so she would drive him to the clinic, pick him up this afternoon. She refused to avoid or escape what had happened, dragging out the terror into the full light of her mind. She felt you healed by facing whatever had happened, dealing with it.

She thought then of Dunk and felt very, very sad. Had he become schizophrenic like his mother? Did he no longer realize what he did? But his face had been honest the morning before when he'd begged her to wait, to give him a chance to talk with someone. Who was that someone? Rip Jacy? Pantell?

The computer in her study seemed to beckon her, but she ignored it. She didn't even intend to go into the room where it hunkered down, ready to pounce.

She picked up the phone on the first ring. "Clea." Mitch's warm, homespun voice came on the line. "I haven't got much time to talk, but I need to discuss a few things with you. Are you taking off today or a few days?"

She didn't hesitate. "No. I need to be busy."

"Can you come in before going to Wonderland?"

"I can. I can even come early. See you there."

At the police station, Mitch looked rumpled, irritated. He asked her to sit down and offered more coffee, which she accepted. She felt she needed bolstering.

"How're you holding up?" he queried. "You look fine."

"Thank you. I'm better than I would have expected."

"You look shaken and that's normal. Look, I hate a rapist almost as much as I hate a cold-blooded murderer, and this demon may be both. When someone is hurt, I become an avenging beast taking off after the perpetrator."

"He signs himself *Your Nightmare*, or simply *Nightmare*."

"I know. Rip Jacy's been sighted again in the vicinity of where you were taken."

"Sighted?" she asked because she could think of nothing else to say and Jacy's hateful face rose in her mind.

Mitch looked at her and shook his head. "I told you last night and I'm saying it again how happy I am you managed to get away. A hunter who knows Jacy saw him deep in the woods. They stared at each other and Jacy turned and ran. He will probably be leaving that area. The hunter came to us immediately. We found a pack of things under a huge oak that provided some shelter for Jacy. His stuff was covered by a small tarpaulin.

"There was a catalog there of objects of all kinds—books telling you how to steal, hurt, kill, and get away with it. Laser guns that cut through steel. A catalog displaying a devil's arsenal of devices to hurt and destroy. But we found no costume like the one you describe. He might have buried it, hidden it elsewhere."

Clea licked her suddenly dry lips as Mitch went on. "We searched the woods thoroughly with no sign of Jacy, but the hunter knows him well and was positive it was him. Then we talked with Pantell Hood..."

"And?" she said when Mitch was silent so long.

Mitch laughed ruefully. "Mr. Hood purported to be as clean as the proverbial whistle, but there were holes in his story. He said he spent the night with a new male friend and the friend would vouch for him. The friend tried to accommodate Pantell, but we leaned on him—*hard*. The friend is on probation for drugs and he doesn't want to go back in, so he told a straight story.

"It seems Pantell was spending the night with him, but he left and came back 'wired,' and said he might give up drinking because some things are better than liquor, more satisfying. The friend said Pantell was so excited he couldn't sleep and stayed up drinking and listening to party records the rest of the night."

"Then you think it's Pantell?"

"It could be. Then last, but definitely not least, is Dunk. This man was tall, you said. Dunk is tall, just under six feet, I'd say. Your tires were slashed a while back. Dunk works with knives and picks, hole-punching tools. We questioned him and he played out on top, seemed sincere, but you know, Clea, I'm discovering that people seem to be changing. More and more people can do their dirt and never seem to realize they've done it. Dunk's mother was schizo. He certainly may be. When I talked with him, he evidenced all the affection for you in the world, said he had asked to be your baby-to-be's godfather."

"He did and I had decided to take him up on it."

"As you probably know, we can never tell at what point a psychotic will change, do things with no rhyme or reason. Dunk may be the culprit and I'm checking it out twenty ways to Sunday. The messages came from his computer."

"He told me he needed time to talk with someone, to confront them."

"And he told me he knew who the culprit was, but he couldn't say. He didn't tell me that until late yesterday. This morning I requested he be put under surveillance, but we're so damned shorthanded."

"And you're running yourself ragged. Mitch, thank you. If it turns out to be Dunk, I'll suffer. He means so much to me."

"I know. How's Bob taking this?"

"He's being supportive, wonderful."

"You're lucky to have each other. Listen, no more messages from the creep?"

"I haven't looked. I've got to give myself a little time before I face that grief again."

Mitch shook his head. "You and we don't have that luxury. There may be no more messages if Dunk is the one sending them, and I have a hunch that another person may just be his alibi. Please call up your messages on that computer."

Clea got up and walked over to a computer hutch, sat down. She logged onto her Internet provider and put in her user name and password, struck for her mail. She scrolled down, hoping against hope that there would be no further message from him. Her hands trembled as Nightmare's name came up with his message:

This time you win, next time you lose—your life!

Nightmare

"Could Dunk do this?" she asked quietly as she printed copies and filed the messages in her folder.

"Psychotics sometimes need nothing except what their overheated, warped brains tell them."

"Jacy really hates me."

"I know. Be careful, Clea. We're closing in. I get the feeling it won't be long now."

At Wonderland, Alina came to her as soon as she walked in, hugged her tightly. "I was going to come over last night," she said. "I won't ask if you're okay. How could you be?"

"I'm better than I expected to be. I got away, Alina, with only scratches and bruises from bushes and a sore ankle where I fell. Bob has been beyond belief."

"You both are. You've got a visitor."

"Who?"

"Your sister-in-law. Does she know what happened?"

Clea shook her head. "No. Bob and his brother are cordial, but not really close. I didn't want Reba to know."

Clea went directly to her office and found Anne seated. She was solemn as she greeted the other woman, asked gently, "What brings you here?"

"A dinner invitation. You're off on Mondays. Could you and Bob come for seafood this coming Monday? I know you're both fond of seafood, and we'll have that unless you'd prefer something else."

"Seafood is something we both always enjoy."

She looked at Clea, said tentatively, "You're all scratched up. What happened?"

Clea thought of the lie quickly. "I was gathering wildflowers in the woods back of our house. I'm a klutz; I slipped and fell face down in a clump of blackberry bushes."

Anne laughed. "I'm clumsy, too. You seem so graceful to me. Clea, do you mind if Reba comes too?"

Clea wanted to say she minded. Why spoil a perfectly good seafood dinner. "I guess it's all right. Does Colette come as well?"

"No. I'm surprised, but she has other fish to fry." She put her head a little to one side. "For what it's worth to you, Reba approved of *our* marriage, but she was cold—until Keisha was born. Now you'd think she's my very own mother. Trust me. People change. Wait until your little munchkin is born, begins to grow up."

Clea shrugged. "I have no doubt she'll love the child because Bob fathered it. I accept it, Anne. Reba Redding will always hate me. She doesn't consider me good enough, *fair-skinned* enough."

"But you and I and Ruel all know you *are* good enough. Give Reba time and space. I predict she'll come around."

Clea thought a long moment, got up, consulted her calendar. "Looks like you've picked a winner," she told Anne. "I'll check with Bob but I'm pretty sure we'll be there."

Bob came to Wonderland late that afternoon. "I just wanted to be close to my love for a little extra time," he said as he kissed Clea. "How're you holding up?" he asked.

"Better than I expected."

Wonderland employees were always delighted to have Bob around and they greeted him warmly. Sid was especially happy because Bob mixed drinks he'd learned to mix on Diamond Point and the drinks were very popular with patrons.

"Hey, Doc," Sid heralded Bob. "I want one of your Rum Bunnies as soon as you can swing it."

Bob laughed and drew Clea to him. "I'll kiss my wife and get to it," he said, grinning.

As Clea stood with Bob, she found fear was an on-again, off-again thing. *This time you win, next time you lose—your life* swarmed her brain like hordes of attacking, angry wasps. A vivid shudder ran the length of her body.

"What is it, honey?" Bob asked.

She told him then about the message she had gotten

on Mitch's computer and he swore. "Why didn't you tell me about this?"

"You'd worry and we've got a life to live. I'm not going to run scared every second of every hour of every day."

He took her hand. "What did Mitch say?"

"What *could* he say? We know now the messages are coming from Dunk's computer. That's all we know. I told you Dunk asked me for time to confront someone, but he wouldn't say who. Mitch and I agreed there may not be another person. It may be only Dunk involved. If this is true, it's going to hurt worse than I can tell you. Dunk means a lot to me."

Bob drew her closer. "I know, baby. I know. I've been thinking about a bodyguard for you."

"I've been thinking about that too. Let's hold off for a couple of days."

Clea walked away and to her office, and Bob went behind the bar where he mixed pineapple juice, grated coconut juice, and a little pineapple syrup, poured a couple of ounces of rum, a dash of cinnamon, and put it in a blender. Putting a cherry on a straw, he handed the finished drink to Sid, who took it, sipped it.

"Man, this is the stuff," Sid chortled. "When you were gone, so many people asked for this we put it on the drink list. As you know, they're still asking, but you've got a magic touch I'm still trying to get."

"Throw in a bit of love; that does the trick," Bob advised him.

In her office, Clea looked at her computer. Did it beckon to her? Forcing herself to relax, she sat down and checked her messages. A lot of spam, which she deleted. Two messages from other nightclub owners in Boston and Baltimore. Both gave her information about their trials and triumphs; she talked to these two often. Clea realized then she had been holding her breath. No messages from The Nightmare.

She looked at a list of figures comparing this year's sales to last year's. Wonderland was expanding. If they continued to grow, she'd have to formulate a definite plan for that growth, and she sighed. Wonderland was big enough; how Jack would enjoy this new surge.

Her mind was as active as a grasshopper. She thought of Jacy's sighting and it scared her. Jacy was an accident waiting to happen. His mad eyes as he had threatened her after his sentencing sometimes filled her dreams. At first, Mitch had thought Jacy might be thousands of miles away, but he was here in the Crystal Lake area. Who had attacked her last night? Dunk? Jacy? Pantell?

Aline knocked, came in. "Mitch Tree wants to see you. I came up instead of calling because something's wrong. He looks so sad." She stroked Clea's shoulders. "How're you doing, babe?"

Clea shook her head. "I've been better; I've been worse. Don't worry about me, sweetie, I'll be all right. Please send Mitch right up."

In a few minutes Mitch sat down heavily in the chair beside her desk. "Brace yourself, Clea," he said. "This is going to hit you hard."

"What is it?"

"We found Dunk's body deep in the woods a little while ago. I wanted to come to tell you."

The room swam around her. "Dunk's body?" The pieces wouldn't fit.

"Yeah." He glanced at his watch. It was six P.M. "The coroner has to do a study, but he says Dunk probably died before noon yesterday—was killed around that time. So he didn't try to rape you. He said he was going to confront someone. Looks like that confrontation took a nasty turn."

Clea couldn't seem to get her breath. She hugged and rocked herself and hot tears came. "He had so much going for him and he was getting his life together."

"The Dunk we knew was always headed up," Mitch said slowly. "This murder was a work of rage, Clea. He wasn't just shot, he was badly beaten. He had made somebody very, very angry and he paid the price."

"You think he knew his killer then?"

"Almost certainly." Mitch sighed deeply. "We'll redouble our efforts now to find Jacy. I think he's our best suspect."

"What about Pantell?"

"Both, but Jacy's the most likely, the meanest, the most vindictive."

She had read that it was normal to feel aftershocks after any attack. Now she suddenly felt her attacker's hands on her body, his evil on her spirit, and she trembled. "I want you to stay close," Mitch said. "We'll have you under heavy guard. We're hot on Jacy's tail and we're bringing Pantell in for questioning. With enough evidence, we can hold him for suspicion of attempted rape for a few days. His friend is going to testify against him. He may be angrier with you than he seems."

"He seems angry enough to me."

"To rape, yes, but not to kill. Somehow Pantell doesn't fit the killer mode to me. I could be wrong."

"Pantell seems to me to be just the type to threaten. He's that kind of man."

"You're right. Maybe it is just threats, but we can't take any chances."

After a moment, Clea said thoughtfully, "I'll handle Dunk's funeral arrangements. As young as he was, he talked about dying, said no matter where he was he wanted to be buried with his mother and father. He said if he had a wife and family when he died, he wanted them all to be buried together; that way his wife and children would know one set of grandparents. . ."

She found it helped to talk about Dunk. Now she smiled sadly. "He also wondered when he'd find time to court a woman properly; he was so busy. He fretted about being a proper husband. 'I'm sure I'll be able to give my family every material thing,' he often said, 'but how much of me will be left for them?'"

Mitch nodded. "Dunk had a rough life emotionally."

"I loved him," Clea said simply. "Bob loved him. Jack loved him."

"His life was unfortunate—and lucky. He should have had the world, the way he fought for it. Now he's lost everything."

Chapter 22

Ruel and Anne's house was in the poshest section of Crystal Lake near billionaire Carter Pyne's luxurious mansion, and was an imposing buff brick.

Anne and Ruel greeted Bob and Clea effusively. "We're the poor kids on the block," Ruel said, laughing. "Old Carter sets the pace and I'm left in the dust."

"Your few millions count," Bob said. "You could have picked a section where you'd be among the leaders, if not *the* leader—if that's what you hunger for."

Ruel shrugged. "I like rubbing shoulders with the kingpins, the biggest boys. My few millions are a pittance."

"It's enough for me," Anne told them. "But Ruel has dreams of grandeur."

"He gets that from Mother," Bob said.

The doorbell rang. The maid went to answer and found Reba and Eunice there. Immediately upon coming in, Reba asked immediately, "What on earth has happened to your face, Clea? You look terrible."

Clea flushed. "An accident." She repeated the lie about falling in a blackberry patch after she stumbled, and Reba looked at her long and hard, then smirked. "If you say so. Please don't drive my son to beating you."

"I don't think there's any danger of that," Bob said shortly. He put a protective arm around Clea, kissed her cheek as Reba glared at them with hostile eyes. "The only thing I've got for my wife is hugs and kisses."

"I've never thought much of public displays of affection," Reba snorted. "That should be a private thing."

"To each his own, Mother," Bob told her. "To each his own."

Eunice moved to Clea's side, patted her shoulder. "I've heard about your blackberry cobbler and very soon I want to taste it, if you'll be so kind."

Clea laughed, pleased. "Is day after tomorrow soon enough?"

"A woman after my own heart," Eunice said.

"You don't look well at all, Clea," Reba said coolly. "Pregnancy doesn't seem to be agreeing with you. When I was pregnant, I glowed. So did Anne."

"Mother, knock it off. Clea looks fine to me," Bob defended. "She's as beautiful as they come."

"Of course you're blinded by what you think of as love when it's really infatuation."

They were seated in a semicircle in the luxurious living room and a big CD player sent out waves of soft classical music. Clea thought it was Reba who really didn't look well. Her skin was so pale, drawn, and her lovely dark auburn hair was losing its luster.

"That music," Reba finally said, "is so beautiful," and she looked slyly at Clea. "Quite unlike *your* choice of music."

"Oh, I like classical music very much," Clea said. "It's just that I have catholic tastes in music. There's not much I don't like."

Reba wouldn't let go. "The songs I've heard you sing have been almost gross, my dear. I haven't cared for them."

Bob's head came up. "Some of Clea's songs celebrate love and lovemaking. An honorable, delightful pastime." Bob grinned at his mother, who didn't respond.

"Colette played for me this afternoon," Reba said. "She could have been a concert pianist."

Bob shook his head. "Her teachers said she was competent, but not good enough for that. We talked about it."

"You two talked about so many things, dear. I remember. She would have made you the perfect wife."

Bob took Clea's hand, squeezed it. "I've got the perfect wife and I'm a happy man. In time we'll have the perfect child. I'm coming into paradise."

Sensing the tension in the room, Anne said, "Speaking of perfection, Tillie's prepared the perfect dinner for us. I selected favorites for everybody, even you, Eunice. Lobster, candied yams, vegetables enough to please any vegetarian, rice pilaf, and to top it off your choice of blueberry cobbler or French vanilla ice cream with whiskey pound cake. I'm drooling just thinking about it."

"It certainly sounds mouthwatering," Clea said. "How are your kids?"

"My two munchkins?.." Anne began.

"*Our* two munchkins," Ruel said easily. "You didn't bring them into this world alone."

Anne grinned at him affectionately. "I forget because you don't spend enough time with them, with *us*."

Ruel shook his head. "I'll have to do better."

"I don't see much of Bob, I'm sorry to say," Reba said.

Bob was silent for long moments before speaking, "You know what my job is like, Mother, and I have a new wife, a coming baby."

Reba looked woebegone. "I always loved you more than anyone, even your father, and God knows I loved him, then Ruel."

Ruel smiled. "Mom, you've always had plenty of love to go around. I've never felt cheated."

"You wouldn't. You married the right woman for you."

With exasperation, Bob remonstrated Reba. "Mother, show some respect for yourself, Clea, and me. We certainly can't always help who we do and don't like, but be civil, be kind."

Reba smiled wanly. "It's just that I mourn the fact you and Colette didn't marry, love."

Bob sighed. "As I told you, I have the perfect wife for me. I'm sure some lucky guy will find Colette and they'll be happy."

Reba shot Clea a look of pure hatred. "Thank you," she said to Bob, "for that vote of confidence in Colette."

Eunice sat apart, quiet and thoughtful. "How're you feeling?" she asked Reba from time to time.

Reba finally said with irritation, "Don't mother hen me, Eunice. I feel as well as can be expected. I'm hungry for the dinner we have coming up."

"Well, remember what your doctor said," Eunice persisted, "you're not to eat too much."

Reba didn't answer, turned away.

They sat down to dinner at eight. The table was lovely, the food superb, and they complimented Tillie profusely. "Cooking's my best suit," Tillie said. "Nothing makes me happier than pleasing people's stomachs."

"You set a fine table, my dear," Reba complimented Anne.

"*Tillie* sets a fine table," Anne corrected.

"Under your supervision. Dealing with servants is an art. Don't you find that to be true, Bob?" She seemed to ignore Clea's presence now.

Bob looked at his mother, said levelly, "I wouldn't know. Albert and Violet are like family to Clea and me and we treat them accordingly."

Reba pursed her lips. "Gauche, but understandable. I never raised you two like that. People are born with certain levels in society and I've always found that the ones who hold to that level are happiest."

"There are exceptions," Ruel said. He looked at Clea, smiled. Clea felt he was being especially nice to her to make up for his mother's hostility, and she was grateful.

When the conversation lagged a bit as they ate, Reba asked Clea, "Do those scratches hurt?"

"Very little," Clea answered.

"I notice you limp some." Reba was in hot pursuit now, pleased at Clea's apparent discomfort.

"I twisted my ankle a bit. It's not important."

"I imagine in season you gather blackberries in that patch for your blackberry cobblers that my son is so fond of."

"Yes, I do."

"Ah, you healthy country girls. So at home with the great outdoors."

"I was largely raised here in Crystal Lake, but I did spend a few years on my grandparents' farm—wonderful years."

"Then she came back here and lived with Jack," Bob said.

"And he was a gambler. How fascinating." Reba's eyes gloated. "As teenagers in finishing school, we used to talk about going across the tracks, finding disreputable men to run away with, shock our parents."

"Mother, Jack wasn't just a gambler. He ran one of the finest, most profitable nightclubs imaginable. And my wife still runs it well."

"You don't have to keep reminding us that she's your wife, dear. We're all too aware of it. As for the nightclub—I'm afraid it's just not my milieu."

"Wilde's Wonderland," Bob said, smiling. "Best of the best. Clea's been cited in business magazines so many times. I'm proud of her." His eyes met Clea's and they both melted.

Reba saw the look and stiffened.

Anne laughed a little, got merry as Tillie cleared the table.

"This has been a scrumptious meal," Reba told Tillie.

"Yes, ma'am," Tillie said. "Thank you for saying so. As I told you, it's my gift."

"Royalty could ask for no better," Reba said. "But then we *are* royalty."

Anne rubbed her hands together. "Now for the dessert, the pièce de résistance. We'll honor whiskey pound cake and French vanilla ice cream as only Tillie can make it."

"Only a small portion for Mrs. Redding," Eunice told Tillie.

"Oh nonsense," Reba scoffed. "Dr. Harrison says I can eat sweets from time to time and in moderate portions. I should think *he* knows."

"When did he tell you this?" Eunice stood her ground. "Certainly not in my hearing."

"You're forgetting your place, Eunice," Reba said sharply. "I'm your mistress. I think you'd best remember that."

"I know the roles and I know the rules," Eunice said coolly. "I'm here to protect you as well as wait on you, and I intend to do just that."

Ruel clapped his hands. "Brava, Eunice! Take care of Mom as only you can do."

Reba shot Ruel a furious glance.

Tillie brought in the dessert cart, rolled it around the table, putting a scrumptious dessert before each person.

Reba tasted hers, rolled her eyes, and let out a long, pleased purr of satisfaction. "This is pure elegance," she said.

"I'd say pure passion." Bob licked his lips. "Only my wife can do better. I get really passionate about truly good food."

Reba sat back in her chair, stopped eating for a minute. "Oh, my dear, it's all lust with you these days. How much you've changed."

Bob shrugged. "I'm a lusty, lustful soul. There's nothing wrong with that."

"And I don't suppose your *wife* has anything to do with that." The word was bitter in her mouth.

"She has *everything* to do with that. She's the linchpin of my life and she brings me joy beyond the telling. We're passionate people."

"You're not the way I raised you."

Bob meant to cut her. "Thank God for small favors.

We change, Mother, and to enjoy life we have to learn to accept change."

Clea looked from mother to son, then to Ruel, who watched silently. Reba turned to her dessert again and ate rapidly. Finishing, she asked, "May I have a wee bit more?"

Eunice spoke up quickly. "Mrs. Redding, I don't think so. We've got to be mindful of your health."

Grimly, Reba looked at her servant-companion. "Well, *I* think yes," she retorted.

Tillie stood poised to serve or not to serve.

"Let her have a bit more," Bob said. "If she hasn't eaten sugar for some time, it shouldn't hurt her."

Eunice mumbled something under her breath, and Reba's face shone with victory. You won what battles you could, Reba thought. She found this an unusually delicious dessert and she ate it as swiftly as she had downed the other.

After Tillie removed the dessert dishes, they drank thick black Turkish coffee and made desultory conversation. As they moved to a smaller sitting room, Eunice said, "We'll have to think of leaving soon. Dr. Harrison doesn't want Mrs. Redding up after eleven, and she has quite a ritual for getting to bed."

"Good lord, Eunice, you're getting more like my jailer every day instead of my servant, and stop telling my personal secrets. Everybody has a bedtime ritual. Don't *you*, Anne?"

Anne laughed. "Guilty. Ruel and I both have a hard, long day tomorrow, so we can't stay up late either. Oh, this has been such a delightful evening. We've got to do this more often."

"Next time, our place," Bob told them.

"Yes," Clea echoed, "next time our place."

"If we get your blackberry cobbler Bob has talked so much about, I'll dream of coming." Anne's face crinkled with laughter. "Do you use frozen berries in the off-season?"

Clea nodded yes and wondered if Reba would have to be there.

They were laughing at one of Bob's wry jokes when Reba suddenly clutched her chest and sat forward, a look of pure panic on her face.

"What is it, Mother?" Bob asked, springing to her side.

Tears ran down Reba's face; he found her skin clammy, her pulse slow. "I can't get my breath," she whimpered. "Dear God! I can't get my breath."

Even this small cry seemed too much and she tried to get up. "No, Mother, don't talk. Try to relax. Just nod when I ask you questions, or shake your head. Do you have pains in your chest?"

Reba nodded.

"Under your arms, on the underside of your arms?"

Again she nodded.

He felt her heart and found it racing. Her eyes were cloudy. He took his cell phone from his pocket and called emergency at Crystal Lake Hospital, thankful now that it was such a good hospital. Then he called Reba's doctor and asked him to meet him there. Getting his bag, he continued his examination.

"I'll go with you," Ruel offered.

"I'll come with you, too." Clea wanted to help.

But Reba was coherent enough to protest, "No. Don't. My two boys only—and Eunice."

"Okay, Mother," Bob promised her. "Don't talk any more. We'll do as you wish, but it would help if you could give up some of your hostility. Life's too short."

Chapter 23

At his mother's bedside, Bob felt his heart grow heavy when Dr. Harrison questioned Reba gently about her past day's activities as she lay mildly sedated and more relaxed.

"How much exertion did you undergo today?" he asked her.

"Very little," she said slowly. "I did my exercises this morning. I read a lot this afternoon. We had a wonderful dinner. I was happy."

No, Mother, Bob thought, *you were anything but happy. Your morbid dissatisfaction with my life is taking its toll on you.*

The slightly corpulent, older doctor nodded. "Did you have heavy food?"

Reba tried to smile. "I wouldn't say so."

"We had lobster and I'd say that's about as heavy as it comes," Bob said bluntly. "Mother had whiskey cake and ice cream and a small second helping. I thought it was okay."

"My," the doctor said dryly. "We really tied it on. That doesn't sound like enough to cause the trouble. You've eaten no other sweets lately?"

"No, none," Reba said tersely. "I'm getting sleepy. Could the rest of this wait until tomorrow?"

"It can. You'll get a heavier sedative later on." He patted Reba's hand. "They'll wake you up to put you back to sleep."

Reba smiled at his humor and settled down, but her

eyes fluttered open again. "Dear one, will you stay here with me tonight?" she asked Bob.

"You'll be asleep," Bob said. "I'll see you in the morning." He bent and kissed her brow as she smiled, but looked disappointed.

"Oh yes, of course, but you're a doctor and I just thought. . ." Her voice trailed off as a tear slid down her cheek. "You go home to be with Clea—where your heart is."

"Hey now," Dr. Harrison said. "Do I detect a note of self-pity here? You're too beautiful a woman to be wallowing in that. *I'm* at your beck and call. You don't need Bob."

"You're so kind," Reba said, "and I thank you." But her eyes lingered with longing on her eldest son. There was bitterness in her voice as she told Bob, "I've loved you best, but you've gone your own way since you met Clea."

"I went my own way even before Clea. I'm that kind of person."

"Yet I loved you best," she insisted.

"Rest, Mother, and get better. Be good to yourself."

In the waiting room Dr. Harrison turned to Bob. "Well, Doctor, would you like to go to the doctors' lounge?"

Bob shrugged. "Let's just sit here. It's empty and likely to stay that way for a little while. Do you need a cup of coffee? We could go to the cafeteria."

"No. I've had my quota for the day. Bob, I'm so puzzled about your mother."

"Why?"

"She's been my patient for many years and we've talked about it, you and I. Your father and I talked about it. We've felt Reba uses her heart to get her way."

"I've always called her Fred Sanford's twin sister, but never to her face."

"Yes, but Ruel once told me that we doctors don't know

it all, that we're wrong at least as often as we're right. And that's true. Something has happened to Reba in the past couple of months. She's sad, depressed, and she isn't cooperating with me. I hate to say it, but you need to know. She's operating like a woman with a death wish. Can you think of anything that's happened?"

Bob didn't bite his tongue. "I got married. She hates my wife."

Dr. Harrison drew a sharp breath. "I'm utterly charmed by your beautiful wife, Clea. My wife and I love Wonderland and go there fairly often. Great entertainment. I love her gorgeous voice. She does it all. I admired Jack Wilde. You know he was my patient."

"I *would* know. He was in love with my first wife, Laura. That was a tangle. He died of a broken heart after she was murdered, a murder never solved. Doctor, is my mother going to make it?"

Dr. Harrison thought a long moment. "I will, of course, order every possible test. I ordered many when she came into the hospital from the clinic picnic, but I wasn't worried then the way I am now. Her heart has some fat around it and that shouldn't be. She has the heart rhythm of a person who dotes on sweets. I asked if she ate sweets and she said seldom. You told me she ate none at the picnic."

"I certainly didn't *see* her eat any, but I was near her only part of the time. We'll just have to take her word for it. I can think of no reason she'd lie, but then I don't think she was going to tell you about eating the dessert tonight."

Dr. Harrison drew a deep breath. "I'm thinking about what you said about Reba hating your wife. How does your wife feel about her?"

Bob pondered the question. "Clea isn't a hater; there's too much that's good in her life. In spite of losing her mother at an early age, she came up mostly happy, close to her father and her grandparents. Why do you ask?"

"Because your mother weathered your father's death better than I would ever have expected. She's been well. As we've said, she was always healthier than she thought she was and your father knew that. I've never known anyone to do a hundred-and-eighty-degree turn like this. And I've suggested she see a mental health professional, or her minister, someone to talk it through, but she flatly refused."

Dr. Harrison's eyes on Bob were kind, sympathetic. "If this keeps up, we could lose her. The deterioration I've seen in Reba for the past month alarms me now. After the picnic, I thought it was just a fluke, but this tells me she's going downhill—fast."

"Mother has to have her way," Bob said doggedly. "She always has and she's gotten it, but this time we're talking about *my* life."

"And you're going to have a baby."

"Well put, because I feel as if I'm bearing this baby too. I don't have to tell you that I love my wife above all others."

The other doctor nodded, and sitting there, Bob couldn't remember a time when he'd felt more miserable.

Dr. Harrison leaned over, patted his shoulder. "Pray, son," he said gently, "Only God's love can help at a time like this."

At home, Clea and Bob talked into the night. She held him and they made very gentle love. He found some measure of peace inside her welcoming body as he grieved what might come to pass.

Finally she told him, "You're not saying what's really on your mind. I can feel it. Darling, what is it?"

After long hesitation, Bob forced himself to say it. "I think we could lose her."

"Is that Dr. Harrison's assessment?"

"It's a gut feeling, Wild Heart. Mother's won all her life; she doesn't know how to lose."

In the low light of the bedroom lamps, Clea looked at her husband, saw and felt him emotionally torn and bleeding, and her own heart hurt for him, for herself, and for the child yet to be born.

"I told you Anne thinks that once our child is here, it will be different."

"I've had a lifetime of experience with Reba; she doesn't seem to me to ever change. I don't know if she's capable of change."

"Yet change is life itself. I've been praying, sweetheart, for her, for us. That's all we can do."

"She's begun demanding a lot of me, of my time."

"Then give it to her. I can make that sacrifice. You've got Steve at the clinic to take up the slack."

He drew her close, nestled his face in her hair before he said, "I need you now, baby, the way I need air and food."

"Your mother needs you, too. Be with her. I understand."

"Mother believes in the Bible, yet she seems to pay no attention to the fact that book says a man or woman cleaves to the mate and forsakes all others. That's her blind spot." His thoughts shifted. "Did you get a computer threat today?"

"No, thank God, but I feel there will be others."

He held her close to his body, and their hearts beat measured beats in their sorrow.

"Spend more time with your mother," Clea said. "We can't help loving others too much."

"Or loving not wisely, but too well."

"She helped make you the person you are and I'm grateful beyond the telling."

"Thank you. I'll be on the run between my mother and the clinic, but I'll be with you too. Clea, I want you to promise me that you'll be very, very careful. Anything that happens to you happens to me. How can I make you know how much I love you?"

Clea smiled. "I will be very careful, take no chances, and I do know how much you love me because I love you that same way."

After Bob left that morning, Clea stood naked in front of the triple mirror. She was eight weeks' pregnant and she thought she saw an almost imperceptible thickening of her waistline. It was surely too early for her breasts to begin to swell. But the glow about her was unmistakable, even with Reba's illness and her demands on Bob. Then there was the hated Nightmare. A cloud came over her vision. She could never forget Rip Jacy's face etched in the acid of hatred as he swore vengeance.

And Dunk? The glow faded when she thought about her young friend. She was busy planning his funeral. His maternal uncle had called from Canada to say he was just recuperating from severe influenza, asking her to please delay Dunk's funeral for a week so he could be there. This was the only living relative she knew Dunk to have.

Clea wanted a special, gorgeous funeral for Dunk, with at least some of the pomp he would have known in his later life, a life she was sure would have been glorious. Who had taken him away? Her heart flattened with pain and regret. Whom had he gone to confront about the threatening messages sent from his computer? Her tires had been punctured and Dunk had appeared. Inside, she longed and searched for answers when she didn't even know what questions to ask.

In her favorite specialty shop later that morning, Clea looked through a set of naughty boxer shorts for Bob and chose a couple of pairs with varisized plump red hearts and another couple of pairs with languid costumed dancing girls. Smiling as she walked away from the counter with her gifts, she bumped into a masculine figure and looked up.

"Hello, Pantell," she said calmly.

"Yo, Clea," he mumbled and would have walked on without further conversation.

"How are you?" she asked, thinking she really didn't want to know.

"I'm fine." He didn't ask how she was and seemed wired, anxious to get away, but her presence stayed him. He couldn't seem to meet her eyes as she stood trying to fathom him, to decide if he had tried to rape her. His breath came hard.

"Too bad about Dunk," he said.

"Yes. Too bad about a lot of things." Did he cringe? Or did she imagine it?

For the first time since she'd fired him, he didn't ask about getting his job back. There was no doubt about it, he was very, very anxious to get away.

He shifted from foot to foot until he said, "Listen, I've got things to do, places to go. Be seein' ya."

She said nothing further as he went to the back of the shop.

When she walked into Wonderland that afternoon, Alina came to Clea, hugged her. "You look sad," Alina said. "What's up?"

Clea's heart felt heavy. "Very little. So much is going on. I saw Pantell downtown today."

"'Gimme another chance,'" Alina mocked him and rolled her eyes. "They broke the mold after they made Pantell Hood. He was by here earlier asking for you."

"He said almost nothing to me. Did he tell you what he wanted?"

"No. He was in a big hurry."

"That's so odd. He couldn't get away from me fast enough."

"Oh yes, he did say he'd likely be back."

"This is puzzling."

"Did he seem friendly? Unfriendly?" Alina asked.

"Neither. Just rushed."

"That's how he seemed here. Where were you shopping?"

"At the specialty shop that carries the great gifts for men."

"Hmm, giving hubby a treat?"

Clea laughed. "Dancing girls, no less, and big, fat red hearts. Bob's going to love his presents."

"He loves you."

"And I love him." She felt a strange chill go through her as Alina looked at her closely. She found herself wondering how much longer she and Bob could weather Reba's destructiveness.

"Is the creep still sending his messages?" Alina asked.

"Still." Clea told her the latest one from memory.

"My God. Maybe you need a bodyguard."

"We've talked about getting one, but I don't want my life to be like that. I've always lived free. Running with the wolves, and all that."

Alina shook her head. "That was then and this is now. Give it a try, Clea the bodyguard thing. I couldn't take it if I lost you."

Clea smiled wanly. "That's what Bob told me this morning."

Later, Clea sat at her curved desk when Alina came to say Pantell wanted to see her.

"What the hell?" Clea began, frowning. What game was Pantell playing?

"I came up rather than buzz you because I wanted to tell you he looks haunted. Do you want me to sit in with you?"

Clea shook her head. "No, just stay around and have one of the bouncers stay in the hallway up here. I've still got a good pair of lungs. He didn't seem dangerous this morning."

"People change, and sometimes they change fast. Good luck."

When Pantell knocked and she let him in, Clea saw the bouncer in the hall, pacing, and he flashed her the A-OK sign. She smiled at him.

Pantell shambled over to a seat and sat down heavily. "Look, I'm sorry I acted like a fool this morning. I just couldn't get it together."

"What's on your mind?" she asked, unsmiling.

"A whole lot. Like I said, I'm sorry about Dunk. I really liked that kid. He was a young master at computers. Taught me a lot."

He looked at her computer a long while and she frowned.

"Dunk once told me you were pretty good at computers," she said.

Pantell's face brightened. "He did? I value that kid's opinion. I just can't believe he's gone. He was teaching me so much."

She wasn't comfortable and he didn't seem to be either. "Did you talk with him recently?" she asked.

Pantell shifted in his seat. "Couple of days ago."

"Were you supposed to talk with him the day he died?"

"Yeah. He called me, said he wanted to ask me some questions. I went to his house and he was gone. Never came back. I told police everything I know. You think I killed him?"

She felt like Mitch Tree. "Did you?"

"Nah. He was my friend. Great kid."

"Sometimes friends are who kill you fastest. Pantell, why are you here?"

"Well, it ain't about coming back to work. I've got a job with the city, Clea. I'm in rehab and I'm intending to turn my life around. I've been bugging you long enough and I'm letting go. I applied for my job on the anniversary of the day Mr. Jack died of his heart attack. Lord, I miss that man."

"So do I. That's good news. I'm happy for you."

"Be starting next month. I'd be grateful if you'd let me work part-time if I get my act together."

He clapped a rough hand to his forehead. "Hey, I just said I was going to stop bugging you. That just slipped out." He shook his head. "You just don't know how I miss this place. I'm not drinking much anymore and I'm going to stop altogether."

Clea thought then of what Pantell's friend had quoted him as saying, that he'd found something else more satisfying to do. Was that something sending threatening computer messages? Killing? Because Mitch Tree had told her often enough that murderers were often a strange breed. They knew how to lie with a straight face and they often believed their own lies. Was Pantell Hood a psychopath? He certainly had many of a psychopath's failings, she thought. He didn't see himself as he was, but as he wanted to be.

Nothing in Pantell Hood told him that as a bouncer, he shouldn't break heads, that he should respect all others. No, he saw himself as judge, jury, executioner. That was his right. But sitting there with his hands between his knees, Pantell seemed the most humble man on earth. But Clea thought unless he had changed drastically in the past month or so, that was the biggest lie.

"I have to say congratulations on your new job, but I don't need anyone else just now. Our bouncers are working wonderfully well."

"I was the best." He was pleading again.

"Not always. You have a wicked temper. Are you doing anything about that?"

He snorted. "They call it anger management. I never hurt nobody real bad."

"There's always a first time. You hurt your girlfriend."

"That woman had it coming."

That was every psychopath's defense, Clea reflected. If Pantell had changed, he hadn't changed enough.

Pantell drew a very deep breath. "Clea, listen." He

swallowed hard. "I need to borrow five hundred dollars to tide me over to my first paycheck."

Clea's head jerked up. "How have you *been* making it?"

He shrugged. "Friends. I had some saved. I'm running out. Mr. Jack used to lend me money in a hot minute."

"My father is dead."

"Yeah, I know and it still hurts me. He was so good to me. I guess I started being mad all the time when he died."

Clea shook her head. "You were mad before he died. When will you repay this loan?"

His face lit up. "Out of my first and second paychecks. They pay well."

Clea buzzed Alina, told her to give Pantell the money. She could envision Alina asking why.

Pantell looked so relieved. "Thank you more'n I can say."

Clea only nodded and wondered about the man before her. Jack had liked him; she never had.

For the short while he stayed after that, Pantell said nothing further about coming back. Now she asked him, "When I saw you earlier, you seemed uncomfortable, not too friendly. What was on your mind?"

He sighed deeply. "First, I wasn't expecting to see you and I didn't have it together. I wanted to tell you about my new job, about my new life. I needed money. I was scared to ask you to let me come back part-time if I turn it around. I knew you'd be grieving Dunk the way I'm grieving him and I didn't want to bother you. It just all got messed up in my mind. That's why I came back by here."

Clea nodded, congratulated him again, then said, "Let's give this new job time to work out without thinking of Wonderland."

"Yeah." He sat only for a little while, then asked, "Will you talk with me from time to time? You're Mr. Jack's daughter and I get my head straight from talking to you, even if you don't want me back." He sounded so aggrieved.

"Sure, I'll talk with you," she said evenly, "if I have time."

He got up then and took his leave. And after he left she wondered if the room had a strange, dissonant smell bordering on the smell in the god house the night Papa Curtis had talked with the Gods. And the recent night when the fiend had tried to violate her body? Or was that malodorous scent fastened in her senses? And most of all she wondered if he'd done these dreadful things. She knew then why she'd lent him the money. She wanted to keep him in sight, find out where he fit in this vicious puzzle.

An hour later Clea was still in her office. She couldn't get Pantell out of her mind. She had felt deep anger in him. Because Jack had hired him, liked him, he obviously thought he had a right to his old job. Her buzzer sounded and she got on intercom. "Detective Tree is here to see you," Alina told her.

Clea's heart lifted. "Send him up."

Clea got up and stood at the door waiting as a beaming Mitch took the steps two at a time.

"Yo, Clea! Have I got some news for you!"

"Well, it's certainly making *you* happy enough."

"We apprehended Rip Jacy just a little while ago. The media is just getting it, so they haven't broadcast it yet. I raced here to let you know."

With a glad cry she went to Mitch, who hugged her tightly. Tears of relief streamed down Clea's face until she reflected that it didn't have to be Jacy who'd made her life hellacious.

"I can't stay long," Mitch said, "but I wanted you to know that everything ties in to Jacy. We've got two red-hot pieces of evidence. We found his nest further back in the woods with a couple of catalogs of *Power Mad* showing a lot of devices to hurt and kill and padded costumes. He's about the height you described this monster as being.

"And get this." He took an evidence bag from his jacket and displayed a gold bangle. "Examine it," he said.

She took the bangle and looked at it with trembling hands. Engraved inside were the names Laura and Jack.

"Recognize it?"

"Oh yes, I helped Jack pick it out. I had it engraved. He was so in love. It was a love present, my father said. He gave it to her the week before she was killed."

"This was in Jacy's pocket. He said he'd found it in the woods before he went to prison."

"You think he killed Laura?"

"Probably. Jacy looks like the devil from where I stand, and I think he's guilty as hell."

Clea looked thoughtful. "Jack always wondered what happened to the bracelet. We assumed the killer took it."

"There's other evidence. We think he met with Dunk the day he was killed. There was a note on Dunk's message board scheduling a meeting with Jacy, and Jacy admits he was to talk with Dunk. Dunk wrote that police would be after him because he was consorting with an escaped prisoner, but he *had* to see him. He didn't say why. We're going to push Jacy's butt to the wall, squeeze him. Clea, I think your computer messages will stop. I think your troubles are over."

Chapter 24

As Clea drove along on her way to Wonderland, she thought about what her life had become. Mama Maxa and Papa Curtis were coming up to be with her, bringing Cherokee-god blessings for her coming baby. She smiled just thinking about them.

She needed whatever she could find to smile about. Reba had left the hospital, at first a bit improved, but once home she was growing ill again, quarreling with Eunice, with everyone except Bob. She demanded his presence constantly, since Steve had taken over many of Bob's duties at the clinic.

Glancing at her face in the car mirror, Clea felt a bit of alarm. She looked worn, but grimly thought Bob was the one who was catching hell.

She pulled into the parking lot slowly and a little way in going back to her private space. Hearing a car horn tap, she looked in the direction from which the sound had come and saw Carlton's Humvee parked in a sea of empty spaces. She stopped and waved to him as he got out of his car and walked over to her, stood talking.

"Hello. Clea. I was waiting for you to come in. I'm dickering with a new group in D.C. I'm thinking about signing, and I just thought I'd stop by to talk with you."

"You're looking very well indeed," Clea told him, appraising the shades of gray apparel he wore. Sartorial splender was his long suit and he carried it off well without seeming foppish.

"And you're looking a bit frazzled, but beautiful as usual."

"You lie so well. I'm catching it these days."

"Let me in and I'll ride on with you. We need to talk."

He got in and she drove on slowly. They didn't talk at all. She parked and they went in to the greetings of her employees. Alina came to them, said to Clea, "You're early. Everything's quiet here. Are you okay?"

"I am," Clea answered.

"And, Carlton, how are you? I love the threads you're wearing. I always describe you to my husband. He's a walking ad for stylish men, too."

"Thank you," Carlton said, grinning. "I do my best. You're looking well."

"And feeling even better." Alina turned to Clea. "Sweetie, your ever-loving called, said he may be by later."

Clea nodded, wondering if something new had happened. Yesterday Reba had fallen and refused hospitalization, saying she wasn't badly hurt. Clea tensed just thinking about Reba and how long this would last.

In her office, with Carlton seated on the sofa, she stood at the inner windows looking down on her magnificent nightclub that her father had been so proud of.

Carlton patted the seat beside him. "Come and sit down."

She walked over slowly to him, sat down as his half-closed eyes lingered on her.

"I love your outfit," he said. "You have such great taste."

"You're the one who deserves *that* compliment."

Clea glanced down at her raspberry-colored silk sweater and matching silk slub-weave skirt. She wore wide, gold hoop earrings and backless tan leather sandals.

Carlton took her hand. "Sometimes I wonder if you know how beautiful you are. Do you?"

She shook her head. "If I am, it doesn't always help."

He sat forward toward her. "You're bothered and I want to know what I can do. You're married now and it makes you off-limits to me, but my heart doesn't recognize legal boundaries. I've said it before and I'll keep saying it. If your marriage doesn't work out, I'll always be waiting."

"I'm having a baby."

"How well I know that. I'd raise any child of yours as my own and be damned proud of the chance. Clea, please recognize my love for what it is. Will you?"

"I always have and I thank you, but you're too fine a man to waste your precious love on me."

"It's not wasted, I don't think. Look, I know your mother-in-law has been in the hospital. I have a cousin who's a nurse and has recently been added to the staff at the hospital. She mentioned that Mrs. Redding is giving them all fits."

Clea drew a deep breath. "She's difficult all right. I don't know how long Bob can hold up under the demands she's putting on him."

"What about Ruel?"

"He's ready, willing, and able to stand by her, but Bob is the one she wants."

Carlton nodded.

"The strange thing, Carlton, is that everybody's always believed that Reba's heart trouble was all in her mind; now it seems to be real. We were wrong and I'm sorry about that."

Carlton looked at her closely. "We all make mistakes, so don't feel bad. The doctors were wrong too, or was it something that's developed lately."

"That's it, it seems." Clea's teeth clenched before she said, "Reba's dying, I think, because her son married me and I'm bearing his child." She felt the start of tears.

Carlton drew her close. "Clea, you musn't blame yourself. The hostility of mothers-in-law isn't joked about for nothing. It's a frequent fact that many women hate the women their sons choose. You're not the first and you won't be the last. Go easy on yourself. Think about your baby."

"That's who I am thinking about. Carlton, I don't want my children to grow up in an atmosphere of hatred between their mother and their grandmother. I believe Reba will love my child, or my children, because they're Bob's too, but I know what this will do to them, to me. I was wise enough once to know that and let that knowledge rule my life. Why did I change?"

Her words were getting to him and he leaned farther forward, hugged her. "You're in love, honey, the way I wish you were with me. Love jerks you around sometimes. And it often seems synonymous with pain . . . If you need to get away, I've got places in Aruba, Spain, Mexico. They're yours at any time for as long as you want to stay. And I'd never bother you there."

She looked at him gratefully. "Thank you. I've thought about it a lot and it might be a good thing for me to go ahead and record 'Just Can't Let You Go.' Could it be done in Nick's studio out in Maryland? He's got one in Baltimore now too."

"You bet. Anywhere you choose. I get excited just thinking about your songs. A single release now, then an album later on this year. I even like 'Never Gonna Leave You Now,' although I know who both songs are written for. You'll be on the shortest possible tours with a luxury bus you wouldn't believe."

"I'm not sure this will work," she said thoughtfully. "If things get worse with Reba, I can't leave my husband to bear it alone. My plans are good only if Reba's situation gets better."

"Fair enough. I can have Nick go ahead and record with his vocalist, get the listeners accustomed to the tune, *then* you'll record. I may be able to get Quincy Jones to arrange for you. If not, I know another great arranger. Whenever you can do it, it's going over the top. I'll see to that."

"Thank you for understanding." She was vividly impressed by his choice of arrangers.

Carlton drew a deep breath. "You're going to hate me for saying this, but if this set-to with Reba continues, if she keeps on beating you with her meanness, maybe you need to get out of this marriage while you're still whole and while you still have hope."

Clea shook her head. "He's my husband. I love him so much."

"And your life is yours to keep and care for, Clea. You've got to save your life for your baby's sake."

His words, his caring touched her and she leaned closer in to him.

Then there was a brief knock and Bob came in, stood on the threshold, his face haggard. "I want to talk with my wife, Kelly," he said evenly, with no show of malice.

"Sure," Carlton said. He wanted to touch Clea again but thought it best not to. "I'll see you around." Reluctantly he got up and left the room as Bob came in and stood aside.

Clea continued to sit down as she looked up at him. "You were sleeping so hard when I left. You were exhausted."

"Yeah. Mother wanted to talk much of the night. You were pretty tired when I came in."

"You should have woken me up."

"No. I just undressed and slipped into bed. You didn't wake up. I knew by that you were worn out. When I leave here, I'm going by the clinic, then back to Mother. She's reliving her whole life." He looked grim then. "And getting sicker."

"Steve called," she said quietly. "He didn't want to call your cell phone number. He just wants you to know everything's going well and you're not to worry. He said to tell you Artie came in for his exam and he's in top form."

"Good." He still stood and his eyes went over her hungrily. "Mother's getting worse, Wild Heart. I have to fight to get away from her."

"And she criticizes me endlessly and that hurts you."

He nodded and hot tears stood in his eyes as she said, "Let me get up for a moment, set things straight."

Chapter 25

Clea locked the door, closed the vertical blinds, and called Alina. With her voice trembling, she told her, "Hold my calls, sweetie. I don't want to be disturbed for *anything.*"

"You've got it. Go for it, tiger."

Clea went over and drew the drapes at the big plate-glass window. No one could see in and she didn't want to see out, wanted nothing to interfere. Bob's haggard face said he wanted her, *needed* her in his arms, and her body was heavy with her responding need. She went back to him, took his hand, and pulled him down to her side. He went on his knees, put his hot face in her lap and put his arms around her waist. He was crying and his tears wet her skirt.

"What is Dr. Harrison's opinion about Reba?" she asked quietly.

"She's going to die if things don't change."

"And we both know why, don't we? Bob, I couldn't take it if Reba dies and you turn against me."

"I never would. I love you too much."

Her voice was choked with tears. "I should have stayed apart from you as I planned, but I—"

"Hush! We love each other too much to be apart. You're my wife, my lover, my woman, the only one I need and can't live without."

But she knew very well the torment in his soul, for Reba devotedly loved both her sons and both had thrived on her love. She stroked his hair, his shoulders as he hugged her tightly and she leaned across him, crying. Finally she murmured, "Make love with me, sweetheart. We need each other now."

He rose, pulled her up, and they slowly began to undress each other. They craved comfort, emotional sustenance they could find in no other.

For long moments he hugged her, then released her and got up. She threw the pillows from the sofa to the floor and he opened the sofa to the always-made-up bed. They finished undressing each other with trembling hands, and her dark and beautiful face and body had never seemed more alluring, more desirable to him.

As they stood naked, he held her, told her, "Know that I will always love you. You're my life and I cannot do without you."

She felt hot, fresh tears sting her eyelids then and she leaned into him, craving his warmth as he rose mightily against her.

"I do not want to ever be without you again," she whispered, and he wondered at her words, her emphasis on the word *want*.

"Then don't ever be without me," he said softly. "And I will never again be without you."

His shaft was so hard against her belly as she closed her eyes, let the delicious waves of sheer, steamy heat wash over her. Soft, soothing pop music played in the background. Barbra Streisand sang "Evergreen," and Clea thought that song best described their love. Rising on tiptoe, she took his face in her hands, grew delirious as she kissed him deeply, her tongue courting his. Then he combed the shallows of her mouth, seeking honey, getting its full, rich flavor, and he groaned. She was sweeter than honey, sweeter than anything he had ever known.

His big hands cupped her soft, firm buns, pulled her into him, and her slender hands cupped his rock hard buns so that they were closer than close, and both breathed hard, savoring every second.

He bent his head and suckled her breasts, very lightly at first, then harder so that she felt the ravening hunger in him no less than in herself. When he penetrated her, going into the syrupy, snug wetness, she moaned and her fingernails lightly raked his back. "You're so good to me," she whispered.

He played their old game as he wickedly whispered back, "How much of me do you want?"

She closed her eyes, smiling as she told him, "I want everything you've got to give me. I want to take it all."

Her saying it never failed to thrill him to his core. His tumescence grew as they spoke and she felt him inside her, raging to make love, to touch her wondrous womb, to know what they felt for each other, as high as the heavens and as deep as ocean beds.

Thrills shot wildly through her body as he lifted her a bit and slid farther in. "I'm going to faint if I don't lie down," she murmured.

He lightly licked the corners of her mouth and told her, "Faint if you must. I can hold you up." She gloried in his massive strength and power, felt it as her own.

Without withdrawing, he laid her on the sofa and she wrapped her legs across his back and felt him go even deeper. She gasped with pleasure as he took her legs and put them over his shoulders. Her womb always felt glorious with him inside her and yearned for his loving movements.

Thrill after thrill shot through them both as the love they felt for each other knew its fullest fruition. His movements were smooth, expert, and satisfying beyond the telling. Grasping her buns again, he wanted this time to go on forever, lessening his pain over Reba, sealing his world in with the woman who was his wife, his lover, his helpmate.

"Sweetheart?" she said softly.

"Yes, love."

"What makes us so good together?"

He never stopped his deep, rhythmic strokes. "I've thought about that a lot and I don't have an answer. I just know we *are* good together. I can't get enough of you; I don't think I ever will."

He kissed her savagely then, his tongue ravaging her mouth. They clung together like drowning swimmers who meant to save themselves at any cost. She moaned aloud at the sensations he had set free that fluttered wildly inside her brain and the rest of her body. They were intent on spending their wealth of passion.

After a while, they moved to lie cater-cornered, with arms and legs wonderfully entangled. She thought his shaft was one of the most beautiful instruments in the world. He thought her body with its secret treasures more precious than anything.

"I feel sorry for anyone who never knows passion like this," he told her.

"And I thank God for what we know," she responded, her words interrupted by her gasp as she felt him throbbing, throbbing like a giant heart. Her belly felt alive with gorgeous sensations of loving lust. She smiled with bliss filling her no less than his splendid shaft filled her.

"Why are you smiling so?" he asked.

"I'm thinking about our baby. I know now what I want to name him or her."

"Oh?"

"He will be a junior: Robert Frank Redding. She will be Roberta Francesca."

"Don't I get consulted on this?"

She hugged him. "Of course you do. What's your choice?"

He laughed and repeated the names she had just mentioned. "I love those names too." He raised himself up and splayed one hand across her abdomen. "You're going to be free, little one," he said to his coming child. "Your life will always be your own."

WILD HEART

Clea's heart hurt for the torment he knew with Reba. She stroked his big body.

"What're you trying to do?" he asked her.

"It's just an excuse to feel you up." Her long, slender fingers avidly stroked him, delighting in the smooth, muscular flesh. "You have the most wonderful body," she told him. "I get turned on just thinking about you."

"Yeah," he said slowly. "I look at you, and everything I own goes into high gear at turning on. I go inside you and I've got my paradise on earth. I can tell you in our long life, we're going to get a lot of loving done."

"When the baby comes, there won't be as much time to make love."

"We'll make up for lost time in quality. We're both high-octane sexually and sensually, baby. We'll find a way."

Clea felt her breath constrict then even as he throbbed with desire and passion inside her body. She could not help wondering by the time the baby was born, what would have become of Reba. She didn't want to think about it.

They were lazy then, moving slowly, enjoying each ravishing thrust to the maximum until he moved into a spot that thrilled her even more and she bit him lightly in the hollow of his neck as he shuddered, furiously turned on, and asked her, "Are you nearly ready?"

"Not just nearly," she gasped, "I'm *there*."

Waves of pure passion and hot desire shook her body like waves of a midsummer oceanic tide sweeping in, and he heard her very softly cry his name with the endearments she always showered on him. Her heart beat swiftly, loving what it knew, and for this moment only her world was what she wanted it to be.

Arched by her side, Bob rose and covered her, moving relentlessly, seeking in the depths of her body what he needed, what he had to have. And passion hit him with white-hot heat as he exploded like gorgeous Fourth of

July fireworks. He clutched her to him and she clung as if they wanted to meld and never be separate again.

For a few moments, it was as if he had passed into another world, then he became aware of the tears on her face.

"You're crying," he said. "Why?"

"Because I love you so much. It's hard to believe what we have together. I don't want it to ever end."

"Stop crying," he said, suddenly grim. "Our love is never going to end. Till death do us part was written with us in mind."

But the thought crept into Clea's mind and stayed there. Whose death? It didn't have to be Bob or her.

He kissed her tears away, tasting the salt and the sweetness of her.

Spent, they hugged and stroked each other, fluttered play kisses over each other. She lay back and he propped himself on one elbow above her. "You didn't really get all of me," he said. "We have to put you on your knees for that. Do you want more?"

Clea laughed delightedly. "I *always* want more with you."

"You keep coming as if you can't stop. Do *I* do that to you?"

"Silly question. Who else am I in bed with?"

He laughed merrily and half closed his eyes. "It had damned well be nobody else but me."

She stroked his face, looked into the light brown eyes with the large sea-green flecks. "You've got me tied up for good. Now what about you?"

He went sober then. "Wild Heart, when I was away from you, I . . . We've never talked about the time I was without you. It was pure hell."

"Tell me now. At first when you came back we couldn't breathe from wanting each other so badly. Since we did the sensible thing and got married, there's been my pregnancy, the clinic . . ." She paused.

"*And my mother.* We're not going to talk about her,

Wild Heart. Not now. This is *our* time. I'm only a few minutes out of you and already I need to be back inside you. I'm still aching."

Clea stroked his penis. "He's clamoring to go back in. He knows when he's wanted."

He laughed at her comment and kissed her throat. "When you left me, I did things you may not want to know about. I used to go crazy wanting you all the time. I did all the wrong things trying to cool the anger, soothe the pain. I felt like my heart had been ripped out and left hanging by threads to my body.

"Clea, the day I kissed you at the clinic, licked the peach juice from your face, I went home that night, like I've told you, and my dreams nearly drove me mad. I thought about leaving again, for good. I didn't see how I could stand being here and not having you. Then you came to me and my glory days began."

She lifted her arms, hugged him. "Just what did you do when you were away from Crystal Lake?"

He hesitated a long while before he told her, "I led a wild life of wine, women, and song, but I was numb to all of it. Your beautiful face came between me and anybody else. Any body I entered made me feel your body so sharply I nearly went under with pain. Your voice and your face haunted me until I thought I'd go insane. Your phantom filled my bed. I came back determined to win you again, to do whatever I had to do...."

"And I did it *for* you. I couldn't live without you either."

"I've never been one to run around before, and my running didn't last long. It was hopeless anyway. Now we're together with a baby in your womb and I'm happy."

Clea shook her head. "Not entirely, sweetheart. Your mother is in trouble and we've got to think about her."

"I am thinking about her, Wild Heart, but I have a right to live my *own* life. We have a baby on the way. We'll deal with it, honey—*together.*"

He kissed her long and hard then, pressing her deep into the sofa bed, and his shaft was rising, hardening, demanding entrance again.

He teased her. "How much do you want of me?"

"But you already *know*," she murmured. "All you've got."

When she was on her knees, he stroked her buns, kissed them, then her back, glorying in the feel of her dark, silken flesh. Dark cloves and honey, he always thought.

When he entered the wetness she offered him, he grinned and told her, "Your honeyed love-slot is grabbing me again, messing with my mind."

Clea laughed, turned her head a bit. "*Messing* with your mind usually means something's upsetting, bothering you."

"That's what I mean. Any thought of being without you bothers me, drives me crazy with anxiety. Don't make me talk, love. My whole soul is tied up with *feeling* right now."

"Umm, I'll go along with that." Her voice went slightly hoarse with emotion as he went deep into her welcoming body.

He bent and kissed her back, tonguing it lightly. "Like I said, don't make me talk. Along about here, I'm all action."

Clea felt heavy with mounting desire and multiple orgasms waiting to happen with this man who was her husband, friend, and incredible lover.

Bittersweet was the word that filled her mind, because in the midst of all this, Reba's harsh spirit glowed like hell's own coals in the background. Their emotional sky was full with a gorgeous moon and galaxies of stars. But on the ground Reba's malice glowed fire-hot and dangerous, posing endless threats to their marriage and their wonderful life.

Chapter 26

"Good morning, Clea. How *are* you?"

Clea picked up on the second ring. "I'm fine, Marian. And you?"

"Couldn't be better. Listen, I wonder if Artie and I might come by this morning. He's on his head to show you a drawing he's done of you and others. I would have called last night, but we weren't sure he could finish it."

"You sure can. I'm here all morning. What time's best for you?"

"Ten-thirty would be great. He's practically standing on one foot with anxiety, wanting to know how you'll like the drawing."

Clea laughed. "If Artie did it, I'll love it."

She glanced at the kitchen wall clock and wriggled her shoulders when she and Marian had finished talking. Eight o'clock. She got three eggs from the refrigerator, went to a counter, cracked the eggs, and put them in a small bowl. Getting a long-pronged fork, she beat the eggs lightly. Bob liked his eggs half blended. Smiling, she was lost in thoughts about Artie, when she felt a kiss on her neck and turned.

Bob pulled her robe back, kissed her shoulder. "How's my sweetheart this morning? Why didn't you wake me up?"

She nuzzled his face. "Never wake a sleeping lion."

"More like an old, exhausted tiger. How're you?"

"Me? I'm remembering our time in my office day before yesterday and loving your loving from my scalp to my toes. Do you feel better? You were pretty bushed last night."

He took the bowl from her and set it down, turned her to face him. "Was it only two days ago that we made love, Wild Heart? It seems like a couple of weeks, and I want you again as soon as I can keep my eyes open long enough to take you."

She patted his face. "You came in pretty late last night. I was hoping you'd sleep late. You look pretty good to me. How're you *feeling?*"

"I thought you'd never ask."

Her face was solemn now. "I was trying to see for myself. You hide it when you don't feel well. Couldn't you go in late, sleep awhile longer?"

He shook his head. "Steve needs me to check out some old charts. There's another battered kid coming in that he and Gloria want me to see, talk with his parents. Lord, Clea, I'm always shocked at what some people can do to their children."

"I hope you have the same results you had with Artie. He's coming by this morning."

"Oh? Anything special?"

"Yes, to bring me a drawing of me—and others, Marian said. I didn't ask who. I thought I'd leave it as a surprise. You sure turned that family around."

"With God's help and yours. You're looking fabulous in that blue robe. Sexy, yet maternal." He spread his hand over her abdomen in the nylon tricot robe. "How's my kid coming along? Kicking yet?"

Clea laughed merrily. "Don't push it. If it's your son, he'll be kicking soon enough. A daughter, well, maybe she'll be a little more sedate."

Bob hugged her. "She'll be a wolf-woman, like her mother." He shook his head. "You don't know how this makes me feel. Like I'm some god bestriding the earth in ten-league boots. A wizard's got nothing on me."

Clea drew a deep breath, felt her spirits dampen as she abruptly asked, "How is Reba?"

He was silent a very long moment. "I had a very long talk with Dr. Harrison and he's baffled as hell. He keeps having to hospitalize her against her will. After a couple of days she's a little better and wants to go home. *Insists* on going home. He lets her and she comes back at death's door again. He intends to hospitalize her for a long stretch, but she's trying to refuse. I read her the riot act last night and she cried.

"Her electrical impulses are flawed and the left atria and the left and right ventricles aren't functioning well. He's afraid of cardiac arrest at any time. Mother *needs* to be in the hospital." He clenched his fists. "She wants me with her a lot whether she's at home or in the hospital. Ruel's been great, but she keeps saying I'm a doctor and that's why she needs me. I don't know how much more of this I can take."

Her heart hurt with sympathetic pain.

He rubbed his chin thoughtfully. "I guess we're all feeling a little guilty at thinking it was just in her mind."

"Couldn't it once have been? Bob, you're not facing the fact that Reba has been getting sicker since we married. She first passed out at the picnic after you made the announcement about the baby. Emotions matter. You know that. Emotions can *kill*."

He lifted and kissed her hand, held it tightly. "Don't remind me. She's wrong to feel the way she does. How could anyone not love you?"

Clea smiled wanly. "At least two people don't. Your mother and Rip Jacy."

"Yeah, Jacy. I hope they send the bastard up for good. You've gotten no more e-mails. That's one blessing."

"In spades. Mitch says he's pretty sure Jacy's been my tormentor, so at least *that* nightmare is over. Listen, love, I've set Dunk's funeral for next Monday. His uncle will be able to make it now."

Bob's eyes were sad. "Poor Dunk," was all he said.

Bob helped her as she halved and put oranges in the juice extractor for juice she mixed with cranberry juice. The sourdough pancake mix was ready. He poured small pools of batter on the griddle and tended the cakes to crisp, golden brown. Canadian bacon and pork sausage sizzled on the other end of the grill. Eggs with sharp cheese and chopped green onions waited for cooking. Once finished, they took everything on big trays to the breakfast room where Rufus looked at them from his perch with fond, beady eyes.

"Say good morning," the parrot croaked.

"Why don't *you* say it first?" Bob told the bird. "Lord, I'm starved. Has this young reprobate had his breakfast?"

As if in answer, Rufus answered, "Gotta have a cracker—*now*."

Clea shook her head as she got a couple of graham crackers from a canister. "He's a heller. Richard trained him well. You've been taking him back to visit Richard for several weeks. What's that all about?"

"Advanced training."

"Advanced training for what?"

Bob grinned. "I'll never tell."

"You're both rascals. You deserve each other."

"Rufus is *yours*, sweetheart. I only had him on loan for a little while. You own him like you own me, body and soul."

Seated, enjoying the delicious food, they made desultory conversation. "I'm sorry I won't see Artie. Tell Marian to stop by the clinic if she has time. I still wish we could have the kid as ours, but God is good; we're having our own."

"When do you see Reba again?"

"She let me off the leash until this afternoon." He stared into space for a few moments before he said, "She looks bad, Clea. She's never been really sick before. I think we're going to lose her and I want to be able to live with myself, so I do what I can." He sounded bitter. Sad. Frustrated.

She placed her slender hand over his hand and pressed hard. "I understand, my darling, and you're right. If there's anything you want me to do, I will."

"Thank you."

They were so deep in communion with each other that they didn't hear it at first, then the joyous croak proclaimed, "Wild Heart's gonna have a baby!"

Clea looked up with amazement. "Oh, this is incredible."

Bob's wide grin lit his face, eased his tension. "He learned it fast too. Rufus is the *best*." He looked at the parrot. "Aren't you, boy?"

"Pretty girl!" Rufus squawked, and gave his lustful wolf whistle three times in a row.

"Hmm. I think I'm gonna see about chocolate-covered graham crackers for you." Clea chuckled with happiness. "Call Richard and see if the chocolate is all right."

Artie and Marian were prompt. Clea hugged them both, introduced them to Albert and Violet. The little boy was all manners. "You've got a beautiful house," he told Clea. "I'm gonna live in a house like this when I'm all grown up."

"Yes, your home is really something." Marian kept looking around her admiringly.

"Thank you. You have a nice home."

Marian smiled crookedly. "It doesn't compare with this, but it *is* nice and thanks to you and Bob, we're happy there now."

"We could do no less," Clea said gravely. "We both love Artie." She passed her hand over Artie's hair as he grinned up at her.

Clea looked down. "That package you're holding is almost as big as you are. What's in it?"

"A present for you. I hope you like it. Open it."

"Please open it, sweetie. You sound so dominating," Marian said.

Artie laughed. "You always say I'm just being a man."

Marian bent and kissed her son. "And so you are, but I want to see you keep the sweeter side of your nature too."

The package was held together with paper tape and was easily undone. Clea held it aloft, astonished at the sharp, clean lines of the drawing. It depicted her as she sat in a big chair with a baby in her arms and a halo over her head. Bob stood behind her chair, his arms half upraised in a protective embrace.

Clea drew in a sharp breath of pleased surprise. This was so far beyond anything she had seen of Artie's work. "This is bee-yoo-ti-ful, love!" she exclaimed. "It quite takes my breath away." She bent and hugged Artie's thin body.

"Do you like it then?" he asked anxiously.

"I *love* it. I guess I'd better start getting your autograph now while I can. A few years more and you're going to be swamped with autograph seekers. Artie, you're going to be able to afford ten houses like this if that's your heart's desire."

"You think so? Mom says I'm gonna be great and Dad's saying it too, but Dr. Bob told me to keep respect and love and trust in my life, and I'm gonna do that."

He sounded like an ancient sage, and Clea bent to hug him again, murmuring, "Precious, precious."

"You look pretty this morning," Artie told her, looking at her pale yellow silk sweater and knee-length skirt. "You've got great legs."

"Artie!" Marian laughed heartily. "Keep it up and by fifteen, you'll be a full-fledged ladies man."

"Mom. I'm an artist and we have to notice everything. You've got pretty legs, too."

Clea and Marian looked at each other, smiling. "Never mind, sweetie. You're already one of God's great gifts to our world," Clea complimented the boy. "Go ahead and love us females. Notice us to your heart's content."

At a loud set of whistles from the back of the house, Clea snapped her fingers. "I've got someone I want you two to meet," she said as she led them to the breakfast room. "And how about a giant chocolate doughnut. If you haven't had breakfast, I can whip you up something in a hurry."

"We ate early," Marian said, "and we're still pretty full."

"Mom, may I have one of the doughnuts?"

"Of course you may, honey."

By then they stood at the breakfast room door facing Rufus, who seemed to have immediate rapport with Marian and Artie.

"Say good morning," Rufus commanded, and all three people did as he told them.

"Hey, he's really neat!" Artie's face lit up.

Rufus shone then as he ruffled his feathers and said with gusto, "Wild Heart's gonna have a baby!"

Marian touched Clea's shoulder. "Dr. Bob made the announcement at the picnic and I'm so happy for you."

"Me too. You're gonna make a great mother." Artie's little face was so sincere as he looked up at her.

"Your drawing," she said, "is going to hang in my study. I want you to think about it and suggest a proper frame." She bent to hug him again. "Thanks to you, I already know what it feels like to be a mother."

Chapter 27

The next day Bob came home around one o'clock after spending a morning with Reba at her house. Clea met him in their bedroom, lifted her face for his kiss, which was long and ardent.

"Hey, how come you're out of jail?" she teased.

Bob sighed. "Hey yourself. Mother actually gave me time off on the promise that I'd come back late and spend more time with her. She talked about her life with Dad and us as kids. Talking seemed to make her feel better. She's in a bad way, Wild Heart. A *really* bad way. I'm going to snatch a few hours of sleep, meet Steve and Gloria at the clinic, then go back to her. I guess it's the least I can do."

He sounded resigned, sad, and her heart hurt for him. Going into the kitchen she fixed a tall glass of chocolate milk for him and put a huge chocolate chip lace cookie on a small salad plate. She had baked them that morning; they were his favorite cookie. Clea shook her head looking at the delectable goodie. *Killer cookies,* she called them. You were allowed only one.

Bob lay on the bed in a white T-shirt and boxer shorts emblazoned with a brown dancing girl. She felt a thrill shake her as she looked at him. Putting the milk and cookie on the night table, she stroked his shorts. "Shameless wretch," she teased again.

"Who bought them for me?"

"I was pandering to your wild libido."

She stopped stroking and squeezed his shaft a bit. He began to grow hard as he grinned wickedly. "Stop molesting me, woman. Let me rest." He pulled her down to him, cupped her breasts in his hands.

"Okay," she said. "Let's stop this. You need sleep and I'll let you get it, but I want to massage you a bit. Eat your cookie. Drink your chocolate milk."

"You're so good to me, in so many ways."

He sat up, swung his hairy legs over the side of the bed as she sat close to him. Reaching over, she fed him the cookie bit by bit and he drank the milk.

"You bake a mean chocolate chip lace cookie, ma'am. You ought to go commercial with them. We'd make a fortune."

"Oh, I like saving my best for loved ones. Besides, we have plenty of money. Let's just enjoy what we have."

"I like sharing the good things in life, and this cookie is definitely a good thing. Now, I'd never share much of you."

Clea smiled delightedly. "Hush. We're getting a wee one and she or he will sometimes take me away altogether."

"Well," he growled, "I'll stand still for a little of that, but you still belong to me and the wee one had better never forget that."

Clea nestled close to him, tucked her feet under her. "We're going to be fabulous parents; I can just feel it."

"Yeah," he agreed. Then, "I'm going to swing back by here before I go to Mother's. I'm tired now, but I've got unfinished business to take care of here." He tongued the hollows of her throat.

"You're insatiable," she told him dreamily.

"And you're my partner in crime. Let's never change."

"I'll go along with that."

He stretched back out on the bed, closed his eyes, and she massaged his neck and shoulders lightly while he sighed deeply and drifted off. He soon snored a bit and she stood up, picked up the plate and the glass, and went out. The telephone rang and she caught it in the kitchen, hurriedly putting the dishes on a nearby table.

"This will be a surprise, I'm sure," Reba said. She sounded weak, sick, fading.

"Yes, it is. I'll get Bob, but first how are you?"

Reba didn't waste time. "I need to talk with you. Of course Bob has told you I'm at home."

"He told me."

"Will you come? There are things we need to talk about." Reba's voice was stronger here.

"When do you want me to come?"

"You said Bob is there."

"Yes, he's asleep. I don't want to wake him, but I will. He's so tired."

"Then come now. This won't take long."

"All right, I will."

Reba hung up then and Clea stood looking at the ivory phone, thinking that the whole brief conversation was like a dream. Then she amended, more like a nightmare, because she was certain Reba would have nothing good to say.

Going back into the bedroom, she decided not to change from the stylish aquamarine sweater and slacks she wore. Going to the bed, she sat down and kissed Bob's face as he lay dead to the world. Poor guy, she thought. Reba was taking it out of him.

In the living room she called Alina and told her about Reba. Alina whistled. "What could she want?"

"I don't know, but I get bad vibes from her."

"Listen, sweetie, why don't you take the rest of the day off? Things will be slow today and I think you'll agree that I take over nicely from you. Be there to spend time with Bob before he goes back to Reba tonight. And, Clea?"

"Yes."

"You hang in there," Alina said fiercely. "You and Bob have everything to fight for. Reba's scenario is largely over; Bob's and yours is at its zenith. And good luck. I'll be praying for you."

"Thank you. I'm going to need your prayers, and I'm going to need a *lot* of luck."

Clea wrote a note telling Bob where she was going and asking him not to intercede. She left the imprint of her lips on the sheet of paper, touched his face, and placed the note on the pillow beside him.

Reba sat on her chaise longue in her bedroom, sick but resplendent in a turquoise silk dressing gown. She looked wan, but attractive, still the reigning queen as Eunice brought Clea in. Unsmiling, she told Clea, "Thank you for coming. I won't keep you long."

Placing long, red-lacquered and perfectly manicured fingertips on her face, she said, "Have a seat please. You look so uncomfortable."

Clea didn't respond, just eased herself into the needlepoint rocker.

Reba toyed with the expensive pearls around her neck. "You say you love my son," she began.

"I say that and I do."

"And he *thinks* he loves you. What *I* think is that he's defying the way *I* want him to love, the person I want him to love." Her voice grew rasping, harsh. "He changed after you came into his life, changed for the worse."

"I don't believe that."

"Your kind believes what they want to believe. I have truth in my corner." Reba was silent then, staring coolly at Clea, who stood her ground.

Anger seemed then to rise in Reba, a more virulent anger. "As I told you at your nightclub, you were wise the first time you let my son go. Then your conniving heart kicked in and you roped him into marrying you, getting you pregnant. He was over you completely."

Clea shook her head. "No, you're wrong. We were

never over each other. He was away so you couldn't know, but he'd told me. We love each other, Mrs. Redding, with a love few people ever know."

"More likely *lust*," Reba scoffed. "A woman like you would know all about lust." A malignant smile spread across her face. "I'll never forget your trashy lyrics at the picnic, Clea. What was the first line? 'Last night...'"

"Last night we made love like heaven," Clea finished for her. "It's a *lyric* line, harmless."

"Trashy, as *you* are trash, unfit for my son. You and your kind are ruining teenagers, leading them astray."

"No lyric ever raped, or hurt, or caused an out-of-wedlock pregnancy. I've told you before, teenagers are at a tenuous point in their lives. Hormones are going crazy; they need an outlet. Music has provided that for ages."

A crafty, cold expression came to lie on Reba's face. "You were having an affair with the record mogul when Bob came back. Are you sure your baby isn't his?"

Hot anger surged hot in Clea's breast and she longed to slap Reba's accusing face. "There was no affair," she declared tightly.

Reba half closed her eyes. "Yet you're angry at what I suggest. There is fire where there is smoke. We have only your word."

"I assure you I am totally trustworthy."

"Let my son go, Clea. For *his* sake, you *must* let him go."

"How can you ask that? We're going to have a baby."

"It probably isn't his. I don't want a little bastard carrying the honorable Redding name. We're a proud family. You would never understand such things. You have never known the glory the Reddings bear."

Clea sat thinking that Bob and she had known spiritual and soul, and physical glory beyond Reba's dreams.

Reba stroked her face, said sadly, "I am dying, Clea, and my blood is on your hands. In time my son will come to hate you as he grieves me. For, you see, he *does* love me as I love him. He is my firstborn and the bond between my two sons and me is stronger than any you will ever forge with him.

"I could rally, be well if you would let Bob go. You must know as he surely does that I am dying of a broken heart."

Clea looked at Reba levelly. "You don't have to die. You could accept the fact that Bob is living his life and making his own choices. We *love* each other." Clea's throat nearly closed.

Reba smiled narrowly. "I am beginning to be an old woman and I have seen lust in others. Thank God, it has never been a part of *my* life. I am an honorable woman and I raised honorable sons."

And Clea thought it depended on your definition of honorable. Was it honorable to die if you couldn't control another's life, build intolerable guilt in a son you said you loved? One thing she knew, Reba Redding was a cold woman, hell-bent on getting her way.

Suddenly Reba began to cough. Her face reddened and her eyes watered. Clea got up, bent over her. "What can I get you?"

With superhuman effort, Reba quieted down quickly. She didn't want Eunice to hear and come rushing in.

Reba fixed her with a steely look. "You can get me nothing. You can only do as I wish and save my life, or you can continue to imprison my son with your lust for him, and have me die. He is a pure soul who knows little of the world's evil. He calls you 'Wild Heart.' Doesn't that name tell you he doesn't respect you?"

Clea smiled a little then. "We've talked about it often. Respect, love, and trust are the foundation and cornerstone of our life together. Respect means to highly regard, Mrs. Redding, and we could not regard each other more highly."

Reba sat silent, fighting off the truth of this declaration, and said abruptly, "You may go now. I am finished with you. Use the wisdom you used once before and free my son from your lustful web. He deserves the best and you are not the best, but Colette *is* the best. Please leave now. The sight of you offends me. I am a decent woman and I do not like abominations."

Clea rose slowly, her anger barely in check. She felt sorry for Reba now because she knew Reba really would let herself die. And she knew, too, that guilt would mire Bob for the rest of his life, no matter what he said.

Standing, she told Reba, "I hope you will change your mind and see Bob's and my love for what it is: a precious, God-given thing. You are going to have a grandchild you could love if you let yourself, as I'm sure you will. I'll pray that you change your mind."

"Never!" Reba half shouted and called, "Eunice!" while ringing a buzzer by the chaise longue. Eunice came rushing in, looked from one to the other of the women.

"Yes?" Eunice said. "What is it?"

But Clea had something else to say. "I chose not to let it matter that you hate me."

Reba laughed scornfully. "*Despise,* not hate. I sometimes hate equals and you are certainly not my equal. Show her out, *now!*" Reba commanded. "I hate the sight of this wicked woman!"

With a heavy heart, Clea walked out of the room and to the front door with Eunice, who touched her shoulder. "I am so sorry," she said. "Mrs. Redding is in a bad way, I don't mind telling you. I think we can all expect the worst. She'll probably be hospitalized again this afternoon when Dr. Harrison comes. Good luck to you."

Eunice took her hand, pressed it. "I pray all the time for you and Bob. You both are precious to me. She is old now, set in her ways, and has never seen things clearly." Tears stood in her eyes as she opened the door for Clea.

Driving along, Clea reflected that talking to Reba had taken just long enough to destroy her life. Because Reba was right: in time, the poison of guilt would eat at Bob's heart until it ruined their life together, would eat at his life *and* hers.

She wanted to go home, but she needed time to think, so she turned and drove to the marina, chose an isolated spot, and parked. Getting out of the car she walked to the railing and stood looking out at the choppy bay water. The wind was high and the halcyon days of mid-September held full sway. Her heart was full of turmoil. She should have continued to let Bob go, yet how do you let your very life go away from you?

It was cool and growing cooler and her light leather jacket wasn't warm enough. Sighing, she got back into her car and started home.

When she entered their bedroom, Bob lay spread-eagled on the bed. His eyes were closed and he smiled as she came in softly. "Is that my gorgeous, sexy wife coming in on me?" Without waiting for an answer he kept on, "Come over here. Put your hot body in my arms and I'll show you what rapture means. I promise to thrill your very toes."

"Braggart," she managed to tease, her heart like lead. "If you open your eyes you'll *see* who it is."

"I don't need my eyes to see you. I see you all the time with my heart and my soul. Wild Heart, we've got to get you a sonogram, be sure you're okay."

"All right, but I don't want to know what gender the baby is." And as she thought of her baby, her heart broke and her voice trembled with tears. He opened his eyes, jumped up, and rushed from the bed, took her in his arms.

"Baby, what's wrong? I got up to get some water and Albert said you had gone out. What happened?" He was tense with alarm.

"Reba called and asked me to come over. She wanted, needed to talk."

He shook his head as he stroked her. "You shouldn't have gone without me."

"You were sleeping and you were so tired."

"And what did my mother say to you?" He stroked her hair, cupped the back of her head, and held her face close to his.

"She's dying, Bob. She's lost the will to live."

"What did she say to you?"

Clea hesitated a long moment, thinking. "She said you wouldn't be able to live with the guilt, that you would come to hate me. She may be right."

"No. I'd never hate you. How could I? I chose you. I will always choose you." He touched her belly. "I've put a baby in there and my first love and loyalty has to be to you both."

She pulled a little away from him. "She's your mother, love. You come from her womb. She gave you life. We cannot take hers. She loves you more than anybody and you love her."

"It's the biblical law," he said stubbornly, "that a man or woman cleaves to the mate. I've said that often enough."

"I could feel her slipping away and I could feel her hatred. I couldn't take it if you came to hate me one day. Guilt is like acid; it simply eats you up inside."

He held her fast against him. "Hush. We're going to fight this through somehow. I've got to get over there. I overslept so I can't go by the clinic. I've talked to Steve; he and Gloria can carry on without me."

The phone rang then. They stood near the nightstand and Clea picked up on the first ring. It was Eunice.

"Is Bob still there?" she asked.

"Yes, he is."

"Good. Dr. Harrison has hospitalized Mrs. Redding. He went with her to the hospital. I've got to talk to you both because there's something you should know. I've told Dr. Harrison. I'll be there as quickly as I can."

Once she was in their living room, Eunice trembled and paced the floor. Bob and Clea sat down. "I'm going to make this short," Eunice said, "then you've got to get to the hospital, Bob. She was calling for you when she left. You know Dr. Harrison has forbidden her to eat sweets. He found sugar greatly slows her circulation.

"I've felt ice cream in the fridge was disappearing too fast, but Ruel and his family come over often and I just thought they ate it. Mrs. Redding sends me out on frequent errands now and she's left alone to do what she wants.

"There was a new robe she wanted me to bring her in the hospital this afternoon, so I looked in her closet in one of her suitcases and found a suitcase full of chocolates. That case had a combination lock, but she had closed it without turning the combination. Five of the boxes were empty, two were unopened. Dr. Harrison was shocked when I called and told him a little while ago. He said that sugar could cost her her life."

"My God," Bob said, shocked and frowning. "Thank you for looking after her so well."

"You'd better get to the hospital. I'll see you there. She was upset after talking with Clea." Then she said fiercely, "You're both not to blame yourselves, do you hear? Mrs. Redding has taken a wrong turn on this from the beginning. I've told her her late husband wouldn't approve of her actions. And she told me, 'But then he's dead, isn't he? And I'm left with my boys. My husband always let me have my way.' I'm so sorry. You two have the best marriage I know."

Eunice left and Bob took Clea in his arms, held her. Pain was etched on his face as she stroked him, soothed him. "I'll be back as soon as I can."

After Bob and Eunice left, Clea moved about the big house, paced the floor as Eunice had done. In the bedroom, Bob's virile presence was palpable. She could feel him so strongly she thrilled, but she knew what she had to do. He loved her, but hatred was the other side of love, and she felt he could come to hate her as he struggled with his guilt.

He couldn't see it now, but guilt and hatred could set in if Reba died. She could never live with that.

Getting stationery and a pen, she wrote a short note for Bob.

My darling,

We will talk about this, but I will *not* change my mind. Reba gave you life. You must not take hers. Be kind to yourself and let me go.

Wild Heart

She put the note in an envelope and placed it on his pillow.

She was swift in pulling a few things together; she could move the rest later. Two medium-size suitcases, a dress bag, a cosmetics case were what she decided on. She needed the Burn storm-at-sea painting, the soul painting of the wolf-god, a table photo of Mama Maxa and Papa Curtis. Photos of Bob and her on Diamond Point the morning they were married.

With tears in her eyes she went into the breakfast room where Rufus snoozed. He muttered, "Wild Heart's gonna have a baby!"

"Yes," she murmured. "I'll come back for you. Take care of him until I do."

She found Albert in the backyard gathering some tools near the house. "I need you to help me put some things in my car," she told him.

"Sure thing. You going somewhere?"

She drew a deep breath. "I'm going back to my house—for a few days."

His eyes on her were concerned. Usually a reticent man, he spoke up. "Does Dr. Bob know about this?"

"Yes," she lied. "It's all right. Thank you for asking."

Albert looked at her carefully thinking something

wasn't right here. "I'll be right in. You'll need me to go with you, help you unload once you get there."

She shook her head quickly. "No. I can manage. I just need to carry in the smaller case for tonight."

"Okay," he said slowly, thinking he didn't like this one bit.

Inside, she dragged the suitcases to the back door, stacked the paintings and her tote bag. Albert soon came in, looked around him. "Whole lotta stuff for a few days." He was not a servant, but caretaker now, sensing her grief.

"You don't have to worry. It really *is* all right and Bob won't be angry with you."

Violet came into the kitchen from the basement and looked around. "What's going on?" she asked, looking at things by the door.

"I'm going back home for a few days," Clea told her.

"Does Dr. Bob—?" she began.

"He knows." Clea stepped forward, touched Violet's arm. "It really is all right."

"You need us to go with you."

"No. I explained that to Albert. I just need to unpack a small case tonight. Thank you for caring."

"I just don't want Dr. Bob taking our heads off. Then, we care all right, about both of you, the coming baby and all. You're sure now you can't wait until tomorrow?"

Clea nodded. "I'm sure," she said, and thought she had to go tonight. Bob would never let her go once he was back, and she had to protect him from his love for her.

It seemed to her that the couple dragged their feet helping her to load her car, but at last everything was ready. She got her purse, her tote bag, and got in.

"Now, you want to be careful," Albert cautioned her. "You got a precious package in the post office and Dr. Bob's loving it to death already." Clea smiled at his terminology for the baby.

They looked after her with grim faces as she drove

around the side and down the driveway. She keyed in her card at the gate and breathed a sigh of relief as the gate swung open.

Driving, she felt her heart was like lead as unshed tears burned her eyes. It was so much better this way, she thought. Bob would always have full access to his child and this way Reba had a chance to live. Aware that she drove slowly, she pictured her husband's face when he knew she was gone. He would be devastated for a while, but he would get over it. Guilt was a bed of jagged rocks no one should have to sleep on.

Driving up to the double gate of her house, she was thankful she had thought of everything. She got out her card and tried to key it in, but there was no answering buzz. Puzzled, she shook the gate, lifted the bar, and it swung open. She drove in to the side entrance. Exasperated, she knew then she hadn't planned this carefully enough. The security system was on the blink—or had been compromised. The lights seemed dimmer than she remembered. The gate stayed open where it usually closed. Well, she would walk back and close it.

The headlights of her car made a path ahead, but her shaman-oriented senses said something was wrong and she shuddered as her blood chilled. There was a very large japonica bush near the back of her car. Mitch had suggested that she cut it down for added security, but Jack had planted that bush and she couldn't bear to let it go. She got out, walked around to the car's unlocked trunk intent on unloading the painting and the photographs.

Her father's face rose before her, then Bob's face. She seemed to see Papa Curtis and Mama Maxa too. Together they all made a magic circle. Papa Curtis had warned her to stay close to Bob, but she hadn't told them about these new developments with Reba. He had spoken those words when Rip Jacy was in hot pursuit. Now that, at least, had ended.

She fervently wished she had made love with Bob before leaving, and the thought warmed her so that she was a mixture of cold and heat when the voice spoke behind her.

"Welcome back, Wild Heart. I've been following you, wondering when you'd come to me. This house is where you have always belonged."

Chapter 28

Nausea rose in sickening waves around Clea, and icy coldness seemed to well up from the very ground, threatening to smother her. Yet she willed herself to some degree of calmness, asking, "Who are you?"

His laugh was harsh but he was otherwise silent as he moved closer. In the deep shadows of the japonica bush, only their body outlines could be seen. "Who are you?" she repeated. One thing she knew, he was the one who had tried to rape her in the old schoolhouse. The horrible stench of him was the same, the altered voice was the same.

Then he spoke and his voice held the same malevolence. "You will know before I kill you . . ." He paused a long while before he finished, "As *you* are killing someone who means more to me than life itself."

Clea gasped and shivered. Even in her fear-crazed brain, she realized he spoke of Reba and she asked him, "Ruel?"

Coming closer, he held a silver pistol in his hand, pointed at her. He pulled the opaque nylon stocking from his head, and in the dim light his face was a study in evil and madness. Reaching behind his head, he disengaged the mouthpiece and it fell to the ground.

"Yes, Ruel. Like my mother always said, you were wise when you let Bob go. My mother was always right about your not being good enough for our family. We're black aristocracy, the best, and you are *nothing!*" His words were scathing.

Then his voice got softer, gloating. He came to stand behind her, ordered her to face the road. "Yes, you are nothing, as Laura was nothing."

"You killed her!" Horror filled Clea. She was so *cold*.

"I removed a piece of trash from our lives as I am now going to remove *you*. If my brother couldn't resist your beckoning body, *I* will simply send you from this earth. Bob is with Mom, as he should be, the way he *should* be with a wife like Colette. He can't help you now."

That hostile voice, the threat of the gun he held seared her brain, made it almost impossible to think. She prayed a silent, swift prayer and gained some measure of strength as he gave his orders. "Walk to the rear of the house, past the patio where I first threw your undergarments. They gave me pleasure as Laura's body gave me a few minutes of pleasure. Now you will give me a few more minutes of pleasure because I will finish what I began in the schoolhouse. A nobody like you could never escape my justice. Laura wanted me, you see, as you want me. You both want all men."

"No, I only want Bob." Her voice broke on her husband's name.

"Wild Heart." He drew out the name and licked his lips as the terrible stench of him assailed her nostrils more deeply. "Walk now!" he commanded.

So I am to die like this, Clea thought for a few terrible seconds, then she could only think of Bob and her unborn child.

"All right, I'll go with you," she said, "but if you're going to kill me, then I want to know what happened to Dunk. Did you kill him too?"

"Unfortunately. I liked the kid in spite of his black trash beginnings. But he guessed I was sending the e-mails to you after Tree questioned him. I was going to back him in his jewelry business with a large sum of what would become hush money. He was ambitious and I thought that would be enough to keep him quiet; it wasn't. He also guessed I killed Laura and asked me if I planned to kill you. Of course I vehemently denied it."

"I have never hurt you," she managed to say. "How can you do this? I thought you liked me."

He snickered. "I'm very good at lying and pretense. I was an actor in college and I was superb, but I despise the licentious life of the artistic class. Look at the show I performed for you. My hatred of you is deeper than my mother's ever was."

His gun hand shook with fury. "I won't let you kill my mother, Clea. My mother is pure gold and you and Laura and your kind are the scum of the earth." His voice went ragged, raging, and she felt the full fury of his viciousness.

"Bitch!" he thundered. "You have nearly destroyed my mother and I will never let you get away with this." He held the gun steady. "This drama ends. I will save my mother's life with your death . . . Walk! Now!"

For the briefest of seconds Clea closed her eyes. She wasn't going with him to her certain death. Her sudden screams rent the air as she flung herself onto him with movements like the ones she'd used when he tried to rape her. And remembering that night gave her superhuman strength. He was not padded now. She fought valiantly, gouging his eyes with her long nails, hitting his Adam's apple a powerful blow with the side of her hand. Kneeing his groin, she kicked like a madwoman as he howled and cursed. She was a woman possessed with protecting her unborn child and herself.

She heard a shout behind them that was Bob's beloved voice and he was there with them, facing his brother, wrestling him with his superior strength. Ruel had never let go of the gun throughout his assault on her. Now fire spurted from that gun and struck flesh. Her own flesh was numb.

"Damn you, Bob!" Ruel grated, still fighting doggedly, panting. "Mom needs you and you've left her again. I won't kill you; you're my brother, but Clea *dies*. I'm going to see to that."

Bob breathed fire, positioned himself for battle as Ruel barked, "Don't make me have to kill you. This bitch isn't good enough for our family. Laura wasn't good enough. Now they'll both rot in hell."

Ruel held the gun steady, aimed at Clea's heart as Bob rushed him again. With sudden clarity she saw that Bob was bleeding profusely and tears of anguish flooded her face, half blinding her. Bob's fierce grip held his brother's gun hand, but how long could he last? Clea came forward, fighting.

"Run!" Bob ordered her. "Get help!"

Frantically she dug into her jacket pocket and got her cell phone, dialed 911, told the operator where to send help.

Suddenly sirens screamed and several police cars roared through the open gate. Policepersons surrounded them as Mitch's voice shouted orders.

The two men still wrestled for the gun, but Ruel had the death grip on it. Somehow he pulled back, shot once again at Clea, and missed her. With a maddened scream, he pulled away from the police and turned to flee before a police bullet found its mark and he fell. They had aimed for his legs, but he ducked low and the bullets pierced his brain.

Bob collapsed at Clea's feet and a policewoman quickly examined him. "There's a shoulder wound for certain," one said. "We need to make sure his heart's not hit."

A policeman called an ambulance, and a policewoman came back from their pursuit of Ruel. "He's dead," she said. "No vital signs anywhere." And she crossed herself.

Bob was still conscious as Clea cradled him in her arms. "Wild Heart," he told her. "Papa Curtis told you to stick close to me. I could never let you go."

"Hush! Don't try to talk," she told him as her tears fell on his face.

He had to reassure her. "He would have killed you, and I won't let anybody hurt you, ever. Don't you know that?"

"Yes, I know that and I know I love you, *love* you."

She was frantic with worry. Why didn't the ambulance come? The fire department was not too far away.

"Ma'am," one officer said respectfully, "you have to move away a bit."

Reluctantly she let go of Bob's hand and squatted as close as they would let her get to him.

Then blessedly it was a very short while after when the ambulance pulled in and the crew rushed over. They were efficient, swift. "I'm going with him," she told them.

"By all means," an attendant said. As they put Bob on the stretcher, he smiled at her. "*Wild Heart, I love you so,*" he murmured and passed out.

It was the next morning before Bob roused from the sedatives doctors had given him. Clea had watched him through the night. He grinned weakly. "You look beat, baby. Go get some sleep."

She got up and kissed him, looking at the bandaged arm on the opposite side from her. "How do you feel? You have a serious shoulder wound, but you'll soon be good as new."

"I can hug you with one arm and you don't know how I'm looking forward to that."

"And I can hug you with two," she assured him as she put her arms around his neck. "What went down?" she asked him. "How did you get to me so quickly?"

He sighed. "Albert called me the minute you left, told me where you'd gone, and I set out. I didn't think of anyone else, just you. I had a bad feeling. I knew you were leaving me and I had to get you back, but I had a bad feeling beyond that. I guess these forebodings I get sometimes come from loving a woman who started out to be a shaman."

"You're so perceptive anyway. It's what makes you a great doctor."

"I take my title of being your great lover more seriously."

"You're all those things—and sweet besides. Keep telling me what happened."

"I saw the gate still open and your car in the driveway. You were standing stock-still and I could see you talk with someone. I thought Jacy might have escaped again. I got alarmed and I sneaked up behind the man. The outline of his body looked like Ruel, but this man was taller. I just new that you were threatened and I had to save you. Luckily his back was to me and I tackled him. My brother's stronger than I thought. What did he tell you?"

"That he killed Laura and Dunk."

"My God! Did he say *why* he wanted to kill you?"

"He felt I'm responsible for Reba's dying. He worships her, Bob."

"I know. I'd say 'poor wretch,' but he gets no pity from me when he tried to rape you and was going to kill you."

"He intended to make good on the rape threat tonight. He ordered me to walk to the back of the house. He was going to do it. That's why he didn't kill me there."

"Son of a bitch!"

"Yes."

Bob shook his head. "As I said, I was alarmed. I called Mitch at home and he got bad vibes too. He said even if it was a false alarm, he was going to check it out with plenty of manpower just in case. He thought Rip Jacy might be part of a gang who still threatened you. But Ruel? Dear God! I feel so sorry for Anne and Mother. She might have loved him a little less, but she loved him."

"Hey now!" Mitch's hearty voice boomed as he came into the room. "Nothing like love to make you recuperate fast." He came to the bed, looked down at Bob, grinned. "How're you doing, old buddy?"

"Right now I'm joyful," Bob teased. "The woman I love hanging on to my neck, feeding me love. Did I die and go to heaven?"

Mitch smiled broadly, then his face got serious. "I thought you both would want to know. We were thrown off by the description of the perpetrator, but we would never have guessed anyway. Ruel wore elevator shoes. We figure he wore them to change any description of him."

"He killed Laura *and* Dunk," Bob told him. "Dunk guessed that he was sending the e-mails, that he'd killed Laura. Also, that he planned to kill Clea. My brother and my mother are ultimate snobs. They're people who believe that some people deserve the earth, others don't. My father wasn't like that."

Mitch frowned, shook his head. "And you're certainly not like that."

"No. I have always believed we were *all* created in God's image and we all deserve the fairest shake life has to offer."

Only then did he ask Clea, "Do you know how Mother is? Does she know about Ruel?"

"Dr. Harrison came by while you were out," Clea said. "He told me your mother was sleeping and he wouldn't tell her until this morning. He wasn't satisfied with her condition, but he said he hoped for the best. He's going to keep her hospitalized for a while this time."

"I see," Bob said and looked sad.

Late that afternoon after Clea had changed to fresh clothes Alina had brought, she left Bob's side and walked down the corridor. Three doors down from Bob's room his mother rested. Dr. Harrison came out into the hall.

"How's Bob holding up?" Dr. Harrison asked.

"His doctor says he's doing very well, better than expected." For a moment she hesitated. "How is Mrs. Redding?"

"She's sleeping. Police have talked with me about her. As you know, I've talked with Bob and we both feel she should be told as soon as possible. She has, as usual, rallied a bit since I brought her in here. So, soon I'll tell her. I find I dread the outcome, but she *has* to know."

"I agree," Clea responded as Dr. Harrison walked with her to Bob's room and down the corridor.

Seeking exercise, Clea walked back to the end of the hall past Reba's door. The night's trauma had left her alternately numb, then shaking with disbelief, but she had Bob to see after. She had lived through a nightmare and almost lost her life, and Ruel was dead from a policeman's bullet after he had done his best to kill her. The whole scenario was surreal. The apparently good, self-sacrificing son had been a wolf in sheep's clothing. Deadly. It was warm in the corridor, but she felt the chill of near death deep in her body and her psyche, reliving the past night. The routine noises of the hospital brought her back to reality.

Back in Bob's room he ate a banana and a slice of late-season cantaloupe. She went to his bedside and sat down.

"Hi," he said, unsmiling. "You leave and the light goes out of my life. Where'd you go?"

"Just down the hall. And the light goes out of my life when you leave me. I talked a bit to Dr. Harrison. He's going to tell Reba when she wakes up."

He nodded. "I hate to think about how she'll take it. You're holding up very well, Wild Heart. How do you feel inside?"

She thought a moment. "I'm still in a state of shock. I'll be a long time getting over this. Do you want something else to eat?"

"Not right now. I'm waiting for dinner. I've still got an

appetite. Baby, we lived through this, but I still can't quite believe it."

"I can't either, but your shoulder is our proof."

"Come here."

She got up, bent over him, and sudden tears dropped onto his face as she kissed him. He held her with his good arm. "We'll make it through this. I'm never going to let anything bad happen to you."

"He was your brother."

"And you're my wife, the best part of me."

She put the banana peel and the dish holding the cantaloupe on the nightstand and nestled against him as a high, prolonged, keening wail rent the air and they both jumped slightly.

"Dr. Harrison has told her," Bob said grimly.

Two hours later Reba was wheeled into Bob's room by a nurse. Dr. Harrison followed them. "May I come in?" Reba asked in a strained, hoarse voice.

"Of course you may," Bob said without smiling. "How are you, Mother?"

The nurse pushed Reba to Bob's bed and Reba looked over at him as anguish clouded her features. She looked from Clea to Bob. "I want to touch you both," she said, "but I am so ashamed, and I am so sorry."

Reba had aged incredibly. She looked frail, heartbroken. When she spoke, it was in a very low voice as if she had to force herself to speak at all. "I had to come now before I lost my nerve. Can you both forgive me for what I've done to you?"

"Mother," Bob said gently. "You're very ill and we can talk about this later when you're up to it."

"No. I wanted to come now. I had to come now. Clea? Can you forgive me? Can you ever forgive me? If you can't, I understand. My God, how could I be so blind? You must hate me." Sobs shook her.

"No, I don't hate you and I forgive you," Clea said simply. "We all take wrong turns, make mistakes."

"You're kind." Reba sounded choked. "And you, my son, you didn't say you'd forgive me."

"I forgive you, Mother, but you almost cost Clea her life."

"Oh God, how I know that." She looked at Clea and her eyes reddened with anguished tears. "I know I almost cost you your life with my hatred and I killed my son as surely as if I held the gun, pulled the trigger. I fed him the poison that led to this. I don't deserve your forgiveness. Can even God forgive me? I've been killing myself with sugar, not taking my medicine. Perhaps I should kill myself."

"No!" Dr. Harrison said forcefully.

"That is not the way, Mother," Bob told her. "Make amends the way you know you should. It will be hard, but we can get past this somehow."

Reba slumped, still crying. "Thank you both," she said, her voice trembling. "I don't deserve your forgiveness."

"God feels we *all* deserve forgiveness, even for a mortal sin," Bob assured her. "Pray, Mother, as we will pray, and we can all heal from this terrible blow."

Dr. Harrison stepped forward. "Mrs. Redding, I must see that you get back. We can't have you overstressed."

Reba nodded. "Very well." She touched Clea's hand. Clea smiled at her through a haze of memories she was determined to deal with in a positive way. Reba pushed the chair closer to the bed and pressed Bob's hand.

"I will do everything" she said, "to make this up to you both. If it is God's will, we will heal and one day perhaps I can forgive myself."

After Reba had been wheeled out, Clea and Bob looked at each other. "My darling," Bob told her, "I think we have just witnessed a miracle."

"I think you're right," she said, getting up and sitting on the side of his bed.

He stroked her growing belly, flattened his hand against it. "We're going to forgive her, Wild Heart, because we've got too much going not to forgive her." His face was etched with pain and tears stood in his eyes.

"And we'll forgive Ruel too; we'll pray for his soul. He was sicker than any of us knew." He sighed. "Give me a kiss, my darling, and we'll take it one day at a time."

EPILOGUE

Nearly a year later, the weather was stunningly beautiful the day of the annual clinic picnic. There were pale blue cloudless skies. Quite a few more people happily moved about than there had been the previous year. Clea sat near the bandstand listening to a group of singers warm up for Nick Redmond. She held her nearly six-month-old son and cuddled him as he seemed enraptured by the music.

"Starting early, aren't you, love?" she murmured as she lifted his precious chubby body to snuggle against her and hugged him. Bob came to them, squatted by her chair.

"How're you two precious ones coming along?" he asked.

"I'm truly happy," she said thoughtfully. "What about you?" She signed deeply. "Oh, the memories still haunt us, but we're steadily getting there."

He nodded as Reba slowly walked into view. She looked older now, still full of grief over Ruel and the tragedy she and he had been so much a part of.

Reba came to them, hesitantly bent, and chucked the baby under his chin. "You're so beautiful," Reba said and tears filled her eyes. "I thank God I got the chance to be with you, hold you."

"I'm glad too," Clea said and touched Reba's hand.

"Mother," Bob said softly, "I'm glad you could make it. Let me get you a chair."

Reba smiled a little. "I promised I'd help set things up

for the potato sack race so I've got to be moving. One day I expect to even have fun here. I'll see you three later." She touched the baby's face and left.

"She's really suffering." Clea's eyes on her mother-in-law were kind, concerned. "And Lord, she's changed so much."

Bob nodded. Reba was quiet now, a thinner ghost of her old self. She volunteered at the clinic and was amazingly good with the children. She asked that they let her babysit little Bobby and they did. Embracing her church with a vengeance, she found comfort there, living proof of God's love and redemption.

"Let's circulate, love," Bob suggested as he stood up. "It's plain this picnic is going to be a success from the beginning."

Walking, they greeted picnickers and saw Anne with her two girls. Her face was still shadowed, but she made a valiant effort to go on with her girls. She and Clea had grown close. Clea couldn't help remembering that last year Ruel had been there, pretending friendship, plotting her death. She shivered just thinking about it.

"Dunk had such a good time here last summer," Clea said. "I'm never at a fun occasion that I don't remember him."

"Yeah," Bob said, "but it helps that we've set up the scholarship for him at Crystal Lake Community College. He'd love that because he had big plans for his life."

Clea felt sadness wash over her and thought, too, of Laura, whose body had been reburied beside Jack; he'd loved her so.

Anne broke away from the group she talked with and came to them with the two girls, who hugged and kissed Clea and Bob. Bob and Clea saw her often, did what they could to help her.

"The girls and I have volunteered to serve the beverages all afternoon," Anne said. "It helps us so much to be part of something like this. Thank you for letting us."

Bob hugged her gently. "Whatever we *can* do, we will," he said gruffly. "Always know that."

Anne's eyes were dry, but her voice was full of tears. "How will I ever be able to make it up to you?"

"There's no making up to do," Clea told her. "None of it was your fault. We can't always know the people we love and so often people know little about themselves."

As Anne and the girls moved away, a hearty voice boomed, "Well now, I've struck the mother lode. Yo, Clea, Bob, and great little baby." Pantell chucked the baby's chin and met his steady gaze. "What's going on in your world, Doc and Clea?"

Clea smiled, liking Pantell a lot more than she had. "A whole lot and what's going on in yours?"

Pantell popped imaginary suspenders and his chest swelled with pride.

"It seems the city's youth program really appreciates me. My boss thinks I'm going a long way there. I never knew what helping others was. I'm really turning my life around. Thank you, Clea, for coming after me like a mother hen. I was headed straight for trouble, the way I was going."

Neither of them mentioned that Pantell had been a suspect in her stalking.

Clea touched his arm. "Jack would be proud of you. *We're* proud of you."

A wide grin spread across Pantell's face. "Next thing is to make my old girlfriend see how much I've changed." He looked at the baby wistfully. "Maybe one day I can get myself a little crumb crusher like this one."

"Good luck," Clea said, to comfort him. "You can do it if you try."

Alina waved at her from the dessert table. It was Monday and Wonderland was closed, so Alina and her family were all here. Alina handled more of the club business now, giving Clea more time to be with her baby. She had finished recording her songs before Bob Jr. was born and they were blossoming into hits.

Clea looked up and couldn't help laughing as little Artie Webb came running to them. Pantell spoke, grinned at him, and moved away.

"Hey, Clea, Doc." Artie reached up for the baby and patted his cheek, laughing. "Mom told me not to feel the baby too much, but he's so cute. *My godson.* Boy, am I gonna be good to you! Mom's paying me to keep the yard up and I'm saving my money to buy him things."

"You're sweet," Clea told him, patting his soft brown cheeks, "but don't spoil your godson now."

"Oh, I won't. I'll just love him to pieces."

Clea sighed thinking Dunk would have made a great godfather too.

Artie walked with them a short distance to where Carlton and Colette stood talking under a willow-oak tree. Carlton hugged Clea. "I'm going to need to talk with you, lady, about what we're going to do with your success."

Bob looked at him, smiling. "Wild Heart's gonna be my wife and our son's mother before she's anything else. When he's two, we might decide she can get back into the fray. God knows she's good enough." Bob put his arms around Clea's shoulders. "I'm very proud of her."

Colette smiled. Her eyes on Bob were warm, friendly—nothing more. "I've listened to your songs and I love them. And you know something, Mother Redding now listens to you too. The other day she told me she likes some of them. 'I've been blind and cold and wrong most of my life,' she told me. 'I'm going to ask Clea to forgive me, but there's so much to forgive.'"

Touched, Clea said, "Thank you for liking my songs and thank you for telling me about Reba. She did ask long ago that we forgive her and we did. Life is too short for grudges and holding hatred in our hearts."

"Yes," Colette said. She and Carlton were a new couple; they'd only been dating a month or so, but they seemed comfortable, at ease with each other. Colette laughed a little then, patted the baby. "Life hands you some wicked curves and some unexpected gifts," she said. "Who knows? With Carlton *I* may even learn to sing."

Carlton threw back his head, laughing. He seemed happy as he told Colette, "I'll take you just the way you are." To Clea and Bob he said, "That's one hell of a kid. He gives me ideas."

Bob and Clea walked on, smiling. She cuddled the baby. "He can't stay out too long. Violet gave me orders to bring him back in a reasonable time."

She and Bob stood close to each other as he took his baby's tiny fist in his. "We're a circle of three, Wild Heart," he said. "This weekend we're going down to Hampton to see Papa Curtis and Mama Maxa. Know what I'd like?"

To her questioning glance, he told her, "I want to go to the god house and give second thanks for what they told us, as I give thanks to God all day and night. We're together, the way we're always going to be together. With love like ours, we're going to give and get the best life has to offer."

He leaned across the baby then and kissed her as her lips parted and his tongue teased hers. "Fresh," she murmured, smiling.

Artie came up behind them. "Kiss her again, Doc. I got that picture in my mind and later today I'm gonna draw you kissing her. That was neat. One day I'll get me a wife to kiss."

Clea and Bob laughed with delight, and Clea told him, "One day, Artie, you're going to have everything life has to offer, the way we've got it now."

ABOUT THE AUTHOR

Francine Craft is the pen name of a writer based in Washington, D.C., who has enjoyed writing for many years. A native Mississippian, she has also lived in New Orleans and found it one of the most fascinating places on earth. To visit there is to fall in love.

She has been a research assistant for a large nonprofit organization, an elementary school teacher, a business school instructor, and a federal government legal secretary. Her books have gotten accolades from readers and reviewers.

Francine's hobbies are prodigious reading, photography, and songwriting. She currently grieves for her late soul mate and finds some solace in writing, her wonderfully caring readers, and friends.

Dear Readers,

Another year passes as I finish *Wild Heart* and I give thanks for many things, very much among them your constant, gracious support. Your helpful and pointed comments are all any author could want.

I am now planning *Dreams of Ecstasy*, in which an art gallery owner, Caitlin Costner, lives on with the memory of her late artist husband Sylvan Costner whom she still adores. Then into her lonely life comes another artist, Marty Steele, who had been friends with both. Embittered by a nasty divorce from an Italian beauty, he has always cared for Caitlin and quickly comes to love her. But she fights tooth and nail against loving him, against loving anyone save the dead husband she adores. The book is a May 2005 release.

I always fall in love with my characters and they stay with me for all time.

I thought you'd like to know that subrights for translation of *Star Crossed* were sold to Bulgaria last summer.

You know I love hearing from you. You may reach me at Francine Craft, P.O. Box 44204, Washington, D.C., 20026, my Web site, www.francinecraft.com, or e-mail me at francinecraft@yahoo.com.

My best,
Francine Craft

Put a Little Romance in Your Life With
Louré Bussey

__**Dangerous Passions** $5.99US/$7.99CAN
  1-58314-129-4

__**Images of Ecstasy** $5.99US/$7.99CAN
  1-58314-115-4

__**Just the Thought of You** $5.99US/$7.99CAN
  1-58314-367-X

__**Love So True** $4.99US/$6.50CAN
  0-7860-0608-0

__**Most of All** $4.99US/$6.50CAN
  0-7860-0456-8

__**Nightfall** $4.99US/$6.50CAN
  0-7860-0332-4

__**Twist of Fate** $4.99US/$6.50CAN
  0-7860-0513-0

__**A Taste of Love** $5.99US/$7.99CAN
  1-58314-315-7

__**If Loving You Is Wrong** $6.99US/$9.99CAN
  1-58314-346-7

Available Wherever Books Are Sold!

Visit our website at **www.BET.com**.